# The SILVER BLONDE

# Books by Elizabeth Ross

*Belle Epoque*

*The Silver Blonde*

ELIZABETH ROSS

# The SILVER BLONDE

DELACORTE PRESS

Text copyright © 2021 by Elizabeth Ross
Jacket photographs: woman copyright © 2021 by Richard Jenkins; city used under license from Shutterstock.com
Interior art used under license from Shutterstock.com

All rights reserved. Published in the United States by Delacorte Press, an imprint of Random House Children's Books, a division of Penguin Random House LLC, New York.

Delacorte Press is a registered trademark and the colophon is a trademark of Penguin Random House LLC.

Visit us on the Web! GetUnderlined.com

Educators and librarians, for a variety of teaching tools, visit us at RHTeachersLibrarians.com

Library of Congress Cataloging-in-Publication Data
Names: Ross, Elizabeth (Elizabeth Anne), author.
Title: The silver blonde / Elizabeth Ross.
Description: First edition. | New York : Delacorte Press, [2021] | Audience: Ages 14 and up. | Audience: Grades 10–12. | Summary: In 1946 Hollywood, eighteen-year-old Clara Berg dreams of becoming a film editor and going on a real date with handsome yet unpredictable screenwriter Gil, until she stumbles upon a murder mystery.
Identifiers: LCCN 2020048976 (print) | LCCN 2020048977 (ebook) | ISBN 978-0-385-74148-4 (hardcover) | ISBN 978-0-375-98528-7 (ebook) |
Subjects: CYAC: Motion picture industry—Fiction. | Mystery and detective stories. | Dating (Social customs)—Fiction. | Hollywood (Los Angeles, Calif.)—History— 20th century—Fiction.
Classification: LCC PZ7.R719648 Si 2021 (print) | LCC PZ7.R719648 (ebook) | DDC [Fic]—dc23

The text of this book is set in 11-point Warnock Pro.
Interior design by Cathy Bobak

Printed in the United States of America
10 9 8 7 6 5 4 3 2 1
First Edition

For Shane and Callum

"It's only shadows on the wall."

—Sam O'Steen, film editor

# Matinee

STEP INTO A PICTURE house on a sunny afternoon, and you can suspend time. Popcorn-scattered carpet under rows of tired velvet—the movie theater is the same the world over. Berlin or Los Angeles, it doesn't matter.

Cigarette smoke unfurls into the projector light. The usherette leans against the wall and gazes up at the screen, a rerun of *Casablanca*. Ingrid Bergman is luminous; Bogart cuts a dash. This girl must have seen the movie a dozen times, but each time, she's swept away—she slips into another life, shrugs off her own like an old coat.

In *Casablanca*, Victor Laszlo wants Rick to join the fight, and Ilsa is torn between her two lovers. The nitrate print is gorgeous: the highlights sparkle, the dark tones are deep and rich, all the detail in the textures. Up on-screen the characters are evading Nazis, still trapped in Vichy-controlled Morocco. Outside the theater, people are dancing in the streets.

May 8, 1945. Victory in Europe. The war is over.

## Chapter One

# Girl Friday

CLARA RACED UPSTAIRS AS though pursued, taking the steps two at a time, grabbing the handrail without needing to look, one final leap to the landing—she could have been flying.

The corridor was lined with cutting rooms on either side. She could hear the whir and babble of competing film soundtracks—glorious—like an orchestra tuning up. Her heart hammered in her throat as she reached Sam's door. Right before knocking, she caught herself—there's nothing more exquisite than wanting something when you're so close to getting it.

The editor was not alone in his cutting room. The head of postproduction, Mr. Thaler, and the screenwriter, Mr. Brackett, flanked him; dialogue crackled from the speaker. Clara paused in the doorway, ready to back out.

Sam turned. "Clara, come in. With you in a moment."

Clara perched on a stool by the film bench, folding her long limbs over one another. She heard Gil's teasing in her head: *Tall and not worried about it.* Clara pressed her lips together to keep from smiling. He had told her she was a shoo-in, he had told her she'd nothing to worry about. She straightened, rolled her shoulders back, head up—confident, or feigning it at least. Had she made enough of an effort? She'd chosen her smartest skirt and decent shoes, the peach suede pumps. She should have worn lipstick, but makeup made her feel like a clown, and jewelry was discouraged. It could get caught on the film equipment—she'd read that in the postproduction manual.

The men parted slightly, and Clara peered past Sam's shoulder to the Moviola, a metal contraption for viewing film footage, like an industrial sewing machine operated with a foot treadle. There was a close-up of Barbara Bannon frozen on the small screen. Glamorous Miss Bannon was the star of *Letter from Argentan*—famous for her side-sweep of ash-blond hair and husky voice.

"If I'm going to sell it, we need more pieces, some close-ups," said Sam. "Her hands pushing him off, her feet scrambling, she reaches for the letter opener—that kind of thing. Right now the struggle is too quick. We need to draw out the suspense."

Clara's ears pricked up. Nothing studio people said when it came to filmmaking was irrelevant to her. She hoarded information like this.

"I hear she's difficult," said Thaler. "Hates her co-star. Gives Howard a hard time too. Changing lines, storming off set."

Mr. Brackett smoothed his mustache. "She wants the widow

4

character to be stronger. Less of a limp noodle." Impeccably dressed, he brushed a fleck off his dark navy suit. "I believe that is the expression she used."

Thaler shook his head. "She's playing a war widow, not a femme fatale. We're not making *Gilda*."

Clara had read about these rumors in Hedda Hopper's gossip column.

Director Howard Hawks and leading lady Barbara Bannon reunite for *Letter from Argentan,* Bannon's first role since the death of her husband and costar, Gregory Quinn. Hawks is also producing the picture for Silver Pacific, with principal photography under way. Sources tell me that the production is off to a bumpy start, with thesps clashing on set. Rumor has it that Bannon's new costar, erstwhile matinee idol Randall Ford, resents being cast as the villain in the suspense drama. The stakes are high all around. In this test of her star power, will audiences respond to Babe Bannon without her leading man (and box-office draw), Gregory Quinn, by her side?

Sam sighed. "I'll talk to Howard about the inserts. The studio won't be happy; we're already behind."

Clara cleared her throat. "Couldn't you use the stand-in?" The men turned. Mr. Thaler blinked at her as if the furniture had started talking. A flush spread up her neck. "I mean for the close-ups of her hands and feet," she said.

"This is Clara Berg from the film archive," said Sam apologetically, pushing up his shirtsleeves. "I think I mentioned her."

"Ah," Mr. Thaler barked. "So she's the one." He stood astride, feet planted, hands on his hips, like a sheriff in a Western. "Sam tells me you applied for the apprentice editor position?"

Clara stood up; this was her moment. "That's right." She raised her chin and maintained eye contact even though her legs felt like jelly.

"Quite the career move for a young lady—a union position with the promise of promotion." His voice boomed unnecessarily. She was only a few feet from him.

"That's the plan, sir," said Clara. Her breath was shallow, and her pulse ticked up. *Please say yes, please say yes*, she silently implored.

"And our boys back from the war"—Thaler frowned, a pause of disapproval—"with families to support."

"Thaler, it's 1946," said Mr. Brackett. "War's been over for a year." He winked at Clara.

Mr. Thaler ignored him. "How old are you?" he asked. His eyes ran over her, and she folded her arms, wishing she were wearing a cardigan over her thin blouse. Miss Simkin, the film librarian, had warned Clara about Thaler—he didn't promote women.

"Eighteen. Nineteen in the fall," she added.

"And once we've trained you up, who's to say you won't take off and get married—that's my concern."

A jungle cat began to pace inside Clara. She took a step

toward him. In her pumps they were the same height. "I'm not getting married anytime soon, Mr. Thaler," she said firmly. "I'll be too busy working my tail off in the cutting room."

Mr. Brackett chuckled and slapped Mr. Thaler on the back. "Never heard of the modern woman?" He nodded toward Clara, and his oiled hair gleamed under the light. "We've got a 'Girl Friday' on our hands."

She bit down on a smirk, grateful to the screenwriter for taking her side. She wondered if it was because she was friends with Gil. He and Brackett were partners, after all.

"Clara is well versed in postproduction," said Sam, chiming in. "She has a sharp eye and is quick to learn. Already helped us out on the bigger days when we were drowning in footage." He nodded a smile, reassuring her. "She's very keen." His eyes darted back to his boss, and he pushed his glasses up, a nervous tick she'd noticed before.

"Go on, Thaler. Give the gal a chance." Roger Brackett was enjoying this.

Mr. Thaler shrugged. "Well, Sam," he said reluctantly. "If you're happy with it." He relaxed his cowboy stance. "Okay, Miss Berg." He smiled like the Big Bad Wolf pretending to be Grandma. "We'll give you a shot."

Clara beamed. "I won't let you down." She knew there would be no second chances.

\* \* \*

Clara floated downstairs to the film archive a new person—older, more sophisticated. It was the same way she felt on her birthday, like something had invisibly changed, as though she'd been reinvented. *Apprentice editor.*

"Well done, Clara." Lloyd, the other vault runner, pumped her hand, his mop of strawberry-blond hair grazing his eyelashes in a way that made Clara blink and sweep her own hair away from her face.

"Thanks," she said. His surprise at her promotion made her feel a tinge of regret—she hadn't told him she was applying for the job. And truthfully Lloyd was no competition. He had little interest in film editing; his sights were set on casting or publicity. He reminded her of a golden retriever, too exuberant, sometimes annoying but generally harmless.

Not even Miss Simkin could dampen her mood. "Congratulations, Clara," she said, rearranging her mouth to form a tight smile. "I suppose we'll need to make the most of you while we still have you—there's no shortage of work to be done." Her eyes traveled to Clara's feet, and she noticed the peach pumps. "What are you wearing?" said Miss Simkin. "Appropriate footwear, please." She marched back to her office, her bobbed hair as rigid as a helmet.

From under her desk Clara retrieved the regulation saddle shoes and contemplated the ugly lace-up flats. With a glance at Simkin's office, she tossed the work shoes back out of sight. Today she would flaunt the rules.

For the rest of the day the colors of Silver Pacific studios were sharper and brighter, and everyone she passed was smiling. Clara could have leapt into song like in an MGM musical. It was Thursday, which meant just one more day under Simkin, one more day running reels of film back and forth from the cutting rooms to the vaults. And by Monday everything would be different. The world had given her what she wanted, as smooth as oiled gears sliding her future into place.

Well, almost everything.

Clara chewed her lip and glanced at the clock. It was nine p.m., and she was alone in the film archive waiting for Gil to call. To kill time she had a stack of *Argentan* dailies to watch. She had helped herself to the Moviola in Miss Simkin's office—it was used to check prints for flaws or to identify unlabeled reels. Clara's plan was to be familiar with as much footage as possible before Monday. *Apprentice editor.* She rolled the syllables over her tongue. It was still a thrill.

It was getting late for after-work drinks. But she wasn't about to let her triumphant day fizzle. She would give him another twenty minutes. How long could it take to fix a few script pages, anyway? All that white space, it was hardly any words at all.


The first time she'd met Gil, a rainstorm had drenched the Southland. The lot was deserted; everyone else at the studio was indoors staying dry. Clara had taken shelter under the awning of the Writers' Block (pun intended), not minding that her shoes and the edge of her skirt were getting wet. As the rain hammered the asphalt, she craned her neck and tilted her cheek to feel the raindrops, unaware that she wasn't alone.

"Watching the show?" When he spoke, she spun around like a skittish horse, and he apologized.

She laughed at herself, then nodded to the rain. "I like the change. A reprieve from endless sun."

"I like it too," he said, and stood next to her at the edge of the awning, hands in pockets. "Makes the city more honest somehow." A gust of wind took down a husk from a palm tree. He pulled up the collar on his suit jacket. A side glance, and Clara caught a flash of his dark hair, his jawline.

Normally she would have resented small talk with a stranger at a moment like this. But she could tell he was sharp, and she liked his wry turn of phrase. They stood there together for a while, just—as Gil said—watching the show.

Clara loaded the last reel of *Letter from Argentan* into the Moviola. It was a suspense melodrama, a woman's picture. A rich young widow (played by Barbara Bannon) is preyed on by a handsome stranger (Randall Ford) claiming to have served as a sergeant with her husband's unit in France. The sergeant brings her a letter, supposedly written by her husband after the battle of Argentan. The sergeant is, of course, a grifter, an AWOL coward, trying to swindle the rich widow. He charms her and takes advantage of her grief. When she finally figures out what he's up to, her life is in danger.

Clara had the script open in front of her. *INT. Drawing room—Night. The widow reads the letter.* Clara pressed the foot treadle on the Moviola and watched the footage. The widow—in a black sheer cocktail dress—is seated by the enormous fireplace, dying embers glowing in the hearth, shards of moonlight behind her. Opposite sits an empty armchair, her husband's chair. A few wide shots, and then the close-ups.

Clara consumed every frame, cutting the scene in her head, imagining which takes she would use if she were the editor. In the close shots Bannon was backlit, just the edge of her blond hair catching the light, her eyes glittering out of the darkness. Clara decided she would linger on that last shot of Bannon staring at the empty armchair. There was no dialogue—the scene didn't need any. All the emotion played on Bannon's face.

By the time Clara checked the clock, it was nearly nine-thirty. One last chance: she picked up Miss Simkin's phone and asked the operator to connect her to Gil's extension in the writer's building. She cradled the receiver under her chin, hearing the buzzes and clicks, listening for Gil's voice.

"No answer, miss," said the switchboard operator without sympathy. "Can I connect you to someone else?"

"No, thanks." Clara hung up and rolled her chair back abruptly, trying to shrug off her disappointment. So Gil had gone home. Their plans hadn't been set in stone. And he could be like that sometimes—distant and hard to pin down.

It was time to call it a night. Clara returned the *Argentan* reel to its canister and turned off the Moviola. She didn't relish a trip to the film vault in the dark, but Miss Simkin would kill her if she didn't return the reels. The evenings were cool, so she put on her cardigan, slung her purse over her shoulder. With the *Argentan* reels balanced on her hip, she locked the office.


The film vaults were housed in a concrete building a short walk from postproduction. Clara's footsteps rang out on the asphalt; the studio was dead quiet at this time of night. A waft of jasmine—the scent stronger at night—tasted like honey in the back of her throat.

She reached the vaults, a long corridor open on both ends, with a series of doors at short intervals. Sprinkler pipes snaked overhead. The nitrate film stock was flammable and unstable—the smallest spark could ignite an inferno. The vaults were designed to contain a fire and prevent it from spreading. She passed a large NO SMOKING sign plastered on the wall, as if anyone would be stupid enough to light up in the vaults.

Clara's footsteps were muffled now, insulated by inches of concrete. She reached the correct door—vault four—and spun the combination on the lock. (She had the combinations memorized, unlike Lloyd, who needed a cheat sheet.) The door opened outward to reveal a second door, which she pushed inward, and then stepped inside. The storage vault had a narrow aisle, just wide enough for one person, with floor-to-ceiling film racks on either side.

A memory—a flash of Gil in the vaults. He had come with her once, a few weeks after they met. She'd been asking him something about story structure—they talked film all the time—and he had offered to walk with her. Other than the rainstorm, it was the first time they'd been alone together.

"It's so quiet," he marveled, and moved to the back of the vault to check out the air shaft. When he brushed past her in the tight space, her stomach flipped. "Look at those cobwebs."

She came up behind him, explaining automatically about the fire risks and the purpose of the vent. He wasn't wearing a suit jacket, and she could feel the heat of him through his shirt. His dark hair was cropped short, and she could see his scar, a neat swooping curve from behind his left ear to the nape of his neck. Her eyes traveled along the line of his shoulders and down his back. She squeezed her fists to resist reaching out and touching him. She wanted him to turn around. She wanted him to kiss her, right there against the film racks.

Standing there alone, Clara flushed at the memory. He hadn't kissed her in the vault that day. Or any day after that. They were work friends, and that suited her fine.

Clara found the empty slots for the *Argentan* reels and slid them back roughly, banging her elbow against the metal upright.

"Damn it." She rubbed her throbbing arm and blamed Gil for no reason.

Clara closed both doors and spun the dial to lock the vault. She hit the switch on the wall, and the bar of light on the floor disappeared. Up the corridor something glinting caught her eye. It was poking out from under the door of the next vault. She took a couple of steps closer. It was silvery white—a piece of trash? Miss Simkin would not approve. *Who's been littering in the vaults?* Clara bent down to pick it up. As soon as she touched it—soft and silky—she recoiled, cutting off a breath. It wasn't trash. It was a tuft of pale blond hair.

## Chapter Two

# Vault Five

WITH TREMBLING FINGERS CLARA spun the dial of the combination lock, her insides whirling along with it. After she reached the last number, she froze—hand hovering above the door handle. She squeezed her eyes shut, and ignoring the flash of terror at what was inside, she sliced down on the handle.

The door sprang outward.

On the floor of the vault, wedged between the film racks and the inner door, lay Barbara Bannon. Dead.

Clara exhaled a noise that was immediately swallowed by the thick concrete walls. Then silence. Just the sound of blood rushing to her head, ringing in her ears. The dress from the dailies footage—black silk, sweetheart neckline. That's what she recognized—that and the blond hair. There was no need to check for a pulse. It was the stillness—a body, a heap, no longer a person. Clara edged closer. Bannon's neck was covered in swollen bruises and raw red marks. Clara could feel the pulse on her own neck twitch beneath the skin. A lock of blond hair maintained its perfect glossy wave. The rest was matted with blood from a gash on the side of her face—strands of hair stuck to her cheek. A glimpse of an eye, partly open. As empty as a blank screen. The actress's hands were grubby or bruised, the dark red fingernails chipped—one nail ripped off, hanging by a thread. She must have fought back. Instinctively Clara balled her fists.

A noise from outside, and a streak of fear seized Clara. She backed away from vault five as she would a cliff's edge. She braced herself against the corridor wall. Adrenaline kicked in and she was moving, retracing her steps, hand on the wall for support, as though she were in a rocking train carriage.

Outside, the scent of jasmine sent her reeling—its cloying sweetness masking something rotten. She was running, stumbling in her suede pumps toward the postproduction building. Like an earthquake, the ground seemed to roll beneath her, asphalt turned to ocean.

Fumbling with the key, she burst into the office and lunged for the phone, scattering Miss Simkin's paperwork. She heard her voice ask for security, and the switchboard connected her to the front gate. He picked up right away. "Joe, it's Clara in the archive." Her voice was unfamiliar; she could hear the hint of her old accent. "There's a woman in the vault." Her mind was still trying to reconcile what she had seen. "Barbara Bannon, she—she's dead."

## Chapter Three

# Vault Girl

IT WAS LATE, AND Clara was sitting on the patio of the studio café, where the uniformed police had told her to wait. Out of the darkness she could see the water tower looming over the executive building. From this angle the scrolling *S* of the Silver Pacific logo wrapped itself around the tower like a snake. Overhead a string of patio lights twinkled merrily—out of place. The day had come crashing down. The studio, *her* studio, had collapsed on itself, like some kind of Buster Keaton stunt where everything falls off the car and he's left standing in the wreckage holding the steering wheel. She had seen an ambulance arrive, and then—more sinister—the coroner's van.

Someone had given her a Coke, and she watched the tiny bubbles rise to the surface, without taking a sip.

"Clara Berg?" She looked up to find a burly man in a brown suit, eyes skimming a notepad. "I'm Detective Ireland. Mind if I sit down?" He didn't wait for her to answer. He sat down heavily, eyes still on the notepad. "You work in the film archive?"

"I'm a vault girl," Clara said.

He met her gaze. "Vault girl?" he repeated.

Clara nodded mechanically. "I run reels of film back and forth from the vaults to the editors. Usually it's 'vault boy,' but during the war, with the men away fighting . . ."

"I get it. Rosie the Riveter. It's no picnic, though." He checked his watch. "After ten. That's a long day." The detective had the shoulders of a boxer, thinning sandy hair, a face that had lost a fight or two.

"I got a promotion today." This fact was suddenly meaningless. "I was waiting for my friend to call. We were going to go to the Formosa after he finished work."

"He works here at the studio?"

Clara nodded.

"Was he with you when you went to the vault?"

She shivered. "No." Her cotton cardigan was flimsy, and her calves felt bare in thin nylons. "He had to work." Privately she knew that Gil must have forgotten about their date and gone home. He couldn't still be on the lot, working through all this. The growler sirens on the cop cars had drawn all the night owls from their burrows and set off a chorus of neighborhood dogs. The few employees working late were congregated behind the police cordon. She caught them staring at her. *She's the one who found her,* she could almost hear them murmur.

"And you're sure you didn't see anyone, either on your way to the vault or after, when you called for help?"

Clara shook her head. "No."

Detective Ireland frowned at his notebook. His brown suit was rumpled, and Clara noticed there was a stain on his tie, looked like mustard or gravy.

A uniformed officer approached. "Excuse me, Detective." He darted a glance at Clara. "We found Miss Bannon's dressing room unlocked; lights were on. Nothing seems to have been disturbed."

Ireland nodded. "Anything else?"

"Studio brass are on their way, sir," said the uniformed officer.

"Right. Let me know when they show up."

"Clara!" She looked up to see Gil darting past the perimeter cordon.

She sprang to her feet. Pins and needles immediately seized her calves; she winced and sat down again. Her eyes welled up at the sight of a familiar face—*his* face. She bit the inside of her cheek. She wasn't about to blub in front of the detective.

"Clara," he said again, a hint of panic in his voice. He approached the café, his eyes scanning the scene with her and the detective.

Ireland stood up. "Back up, buddy." The detective held a solid hand in the air, meaty fingers splayed and pushing against an invisible wall. Gil stopped and glowered at Ireland. Then he nodded to Clara, his face ashen. "You okay?"

She saw the detective's eyes flit between them. "Who are you, the boyfriend?"

"We're friends," said Clara quickly. She saw his copper's brain making a mental note.

Gil took a step toward her. "When I heard—a woman in the vault, I immediately thought"—his eyes locked on hers and his breath dropped to a whisper—"vault girl." He made a move as though he was about to reach out to her—but stopped himself. "What happened?"

She was about to answer, but Ireland stepped on her line.

"I'll ask the questions," Ireland barked. "Take a seat." Ireland pointed his notebook to the free chair at their table. Gil glared at him, then scraped back the chair and sat down next to Clara. As Ireland flipped through his notepad, Gil gave her a private smile.

"All right, what's your name, son?" said the detective.

"Francis Gilbert—I go by Gil."

He scribbled it down. "And what do you do, Mr. Gilbert?"

"Screenwriter."

The detective nodded. "And you were on the lot this evening?"

"Yeah, I was working. Rewriting a scene for tomorrow." Gil's voice was flat.

"Where?" said Ireland.

"My office in the writer's building."

"You work alone?"

Gil sighed. "Tonight I do. My partner, Roger Brackett, left early—busy social life."

"You were there all evening?" said Ireland. "Didn't leave for any reason, take a breath of air?"

"No, I was there the whole time—until I heard the sirens."

Clara remembered the switchboard trying him—no answer. She flicked a glance at him. Maybe the girl had tried the wrong extension. Or had he been so absorbed in his work that he hadn't heard the phone? Clara blinked her doubts away.

"What's the movie you're writing?" asked the detective.

"*Letter from Argentan.*"

"That the Babe Bannon picture?" He didn't wait for an answer. "You know Miss Bannon pretty well?"

Gil gave a noncommittal shrug. "She's the star of the movie. My partner deals with actors. He chitchats; I type—what's that got to do with anything?"

Clara tensed up. She knew what the detective was building to.

"There's no official ID yet," he said, his gaze steady on Gil. "But it looks like Barbara Bannon was murdered."

Gil's shoulders dropped, and he leaned back in his chair like he'd been pushed. "She's dead?" he breathed, incredulous.

"I went to the vault to return a reel," said Clara, inhaling a shaky breath. "I found her—on the floor of the vault, dumped there, like a piece of trash."

Gil flinched. His mouth tightened, and the shadow behind his eyes descended.

"Miss Berg's had quite a shock," said Detective Ireland.

A beam of headlights swept over the patio, and they all watched as a huge black Cadillac pulled up. Mr. Pearce, the head of Silver Pacific studios, got out and was immediately rushed by his executives. The uniformed officer signaled Detective Ireland. He got up with a sigh, rubbing his red stubble with a huge hand. "Here we go," Clara heard him mumble.

Gil pulled his chair closer. "How long have you been sitting here?" he said, pressing his warm hand on hers. "You're freezing."

"I'm okay."

"Hold on." Gil stood up. "Detective!" he called after Ireland. "Can you cut her loose?"

The detective stopped. "Gimme a second. Rivetti." He summoned another detective, thin and wiry. Clara watched them confer for a moment. Then Ireland turned back to Gil. "Okay, Miss Berg, you can go. Thanks for your help." Detective Ireland pointed at Gil. "Make sure she gets home safe."

Clara got to her feet. Her limbs felt stiff and clumsy. Gil took her by the hand. "Come on." They left the patio and ducked under the police cordon. He guided her past the small crowd of studio employees, who parted to let them through. Clara could see their eyes burning with hungry questions. It was strange and darkly thrilling, striding past a crowd of spectators, hand in hand with Gil. She was that tall girl from postproduction— a vault girl, a nobody—and now she was the object of the gaze, like some notorious movie star, a beacon for gossip columnists and flashbulbs.

They had made it past the water tower and were closing in on the parking lot when they heard a voice.

*"Klara!"* Clara turned to see Max, the projectionist, instantly recognizable by his thick shock of gray hair. He was trotting toward them, out of breath. "Klara," he said again. Max peered at them over his spectacles with an anxious expression. *"Was ist passiert?"*

Without thinking, Clara answered in German. *"Barbara Bannon ist tot."* The image of Bannon's lifeless body flooded her mind's eye in close-up.

Max gasped. *"Schrecklich!"* He raked a hand through his wiry hair. *"Im Studio?"*

*"Ja, ich habe sie gefunden."* Clara could feel her face pucker. *"Sie wurde ermordet."*

Gil stepped forward. "Maybe the questions can wait, pops." He said it like Max was a bum on the street asking for change.

Max bristled. "I'll ride the streetcar with you, Klara." He patted his pockets and pulled out a chain of keys. "I just need to lock the projection room." Clara looked between them—she felt torn. She'd known Max for years. He was friends with her parents; he'd gotten her the job at the studio.

"Come on," said Gil, pulling her arm gently. "Car's just over there."

Max glared at the interloper.

"Gil said he'd give me a ride," Clara explained. She smiled an apology. "It's okay, Max. I know him."

They left Max forlorn on the edge of the parking lot. Gil steered Clara swiftly across the nearly empty lot toward a pale convertible. The top was down and the chrome finishes glinted in the lamplight. He held the passenger door for her, and she got in, collapsing onto the seat. She was rigid, shivering. Gil darted around to the driver's side. "Soft top's ripped, I'm afraid," he said, reaching behind the seat and grabbing a blanket. "You can put this on your legs if you get cold."

Clara took the bunched-up blanket and hugged it against her chest like a stuffed animal. Gil tried the ignition. It made a high-pitched grinding sound. Eventually the engine revved to life, sounding too big for the car—a small dog with a big dog's bark. He executed a swift arc in reverse and then shifted gears and gunned it for the studio gates. He slowed to a crawl past the security booth and saluted the guard, who nodded, and the barrier rose, letting them pass. Outside the gates a squad car was idling, its solid red light a reminder of the scene in the vault—as if she could forget.

Gil made a right turn onto Gower. "Los Feliz, right?" he asked.

"Yes, off the boulevard." It was a relief to answer a normal question. "Near the Brown Derby." She'd never ridden in his car before. If they'd gone to the Formosa, they would have been sitting in one of the red booths, sipping a cocktail, and after, maybe he would have driven her home. They had made the plan at lunchtime; it felt like years ago.

Going east on Sunset, she let her head fall back against the seat. Ragged palms flew by, a shade darker than the sky; a fire truck screamed; frenetic neon signs danced above nightclubs; cars swerved and honked to avoid a drunk stepping into traffic—Hollywood at night.

After a few blocks Gil offered her a cigarette at a stoplight. Clara shook her head, Miss Simkin's voice like a parrot inside her head: *No smokers around my film stock.* He lit one for himself, shielding the flame with cupped hands. The light distorted his features. The Plymouth rumbled a low growl as they waited.

"Who could have done this—who would have wanted to hurt her?" Clara said, breaking the silence. "Do you think it was a crazed fan, or a stalker?"

Gil shook his head. "Not any schmuck off the street can waltz onto a studio lot. My money's on someone she knew." He took a long inhale on his smoke, then blew it out. "A movie star is an industry in themselves. Think of all the hangers-on who rely on her for their living—the ten-percent crowd: agent, lawyer, manager . . . they all want their pound of flesh. Then there's the studio." His cigarette smoldered. "If the movie bombs, there are careers on the line. Plenty of folks with an axe to grind."

The light turned green. He stepped on the accelerator.

"But someone at Silver Pacific?" Clara turned to him. "Someone we *know*?"

Gil shrugged. "Sure, why not? The studio never wanted her for the part, Hawks had to fight tooth and nail to have her.

Pearce wanted Joan Fontaine—a 'real' actress." Gil rolled his eyes. "Didn't think Bannon's blond bombshell could act her way out of a paper bag."

Clara thought it over. "Could her murder have something to do with all the drama on set? I read in the scandal sheets about Randall Ford. They say he resented Bannon from day one because she got top billing. He didn't want to be sidelined playing a villain."

"Could be. Brackett would know," said Gil. "He's always hanging about the actors, sniffing out gossip. He told me that Randall hated Gregory Quinn. Some age-old feud."

"Wait," said Clara, shaking her head. "Casting squabbles and grudges are one thing, but *murder*?"

"In this town nothing would surprise me."

They cut up Western and onto Los Feliz Boulevard. It was darker here—pine trees replaced the palms of Sunset and blocked out the streetlights. Griffith Park was a hulking shadow on their left. They passed the Brown Derby and turned off Los Feliz Boulevard into side streets. The car tires swished through a puddle; someone had turned on their sprinklers, and it brought out the papery citrus of eucalyptus.

Clara pointed at the approaching block. "Just up here on the right, after Ben Lomond." A few of the streets in her neighborhood sounded like they should be in the Scottish Highlands and not sunny California. Gil pulled over and put the Plymouth in park. He killed the engine. They sat for a moment. Clara's exhaustion felt like an invisible weight pinning her to the seat. They didn't speak; their silence was filled with Bannon's murder.

There was a distant hiss of sprinklers, and the air shifted the trees overhead. Gil lit another cigarette. "I met her once, years ago—back when she was Ruby Kaminsky," he said. His voice was different, as if being on the quiet residential street had given him permission to talk. A memory lit, then faded behind his eyes.

"How did you meet?" said Clara, curious to hear something of Gil's past—for someone who wrote dialogue all day, he was tight-lipped about himself.

He blew out a cone of smoke. "I'd signed up for an acting class. Advice from a director: 'It'll teach you how to be a better writer.'" He chewed it over. "Suppose that's true." He rolled the cigarette between his fingers, watching it burn. "Ruby was in the class."

"It's strange," said Clara. "I never think of her by that name— Ruby—like it doesn't suit her. What was she like?"

Gil grunted a laugh. "She was a regular Joe. Mouth like a trucker." He ashed his cigarette over the side of the car. His other hand was resting on the steering wheel like it had been sculpted—long fingers, the ridge of tendons, smooth tan skin.

"Could you tell she'd become a star?" asked Clara.

He gave a shake of his head. "I never finished the class. It was during the war. I was called up." Gil was a veteran, but he never spoke about the war. The topic was off-limits. Just like Clara's past. "Next time I saw her, she was up on the big screen," he went on. "*Nightshade,* summer of '44. A month after D-Day. I was in France."

Clara remembered that summer before senior year: she'd gone to the movies with friends. Barbara Bannon and Gregory Quinn, the Hollywood golden couple on-screen and—as the gossip columns quickly revealed—off-screen as well. They married and did two more movies together in quick succession. Quinn was killed a year later, in 1945, entertaining the troops. His plane crashed on his way home to Los Angeles. Bannon retreated from public life until *Argentan.*

Gil leaned over and crushed his cigarette in the ashtray. "Didn't know you could speak Kraut."

Clara turned sharply; his gaze sliced her open.

He blinked. "Sorry. I mean German."

Of course: he'd heard her with Max. She tried to read Gil's face. She could pretend, make up a story: Swedes spoke German. She was good at languages. But no, she was done with the cover-up, with being careful. Since the murder, something had given way. She took a breath. "I'm German—a Kraut, as you say. We moved here from Berlin before the war."

"Why didn't you say?" said Gil. She was pretty sure he meant *Why did you lie?* "Lots of Germans came to the States after Mr. Hitler showed up," Gil went on. "What's the big deal?"

"I don't know." She looked down. "I suppose"—she fiddled with the blanket on her lap—"I knew you'd fought in the war. And I didn't want you to hate me." *I wanted you to like me* hung in the air, unsaid. She flushed a deep red, sitting there in his passenger seat, wishing she'd kept quiet.

A distant siren wailed. Gil pried her hand from the blanket and held it in both of his; they were warm. "I like you just fine— American, German, whatever."

She met his gaze. He leaned closer. Clara's heart began to punch against her ribs. Her lips tingled; she knew what was coming. She closed her eyes, thinking *this* was how she had wanted the day to end. But instead his lips brushed her forehead—a brief peck, and he pulled away. Before she knew it, she had gotten out of the car and Gil had turned on the engine, like the film had skipped ahead several feet. They had already said goodbye and he had executed a perfect three-point turn, and now she stood watching as his taillights disappeared into the throng of cars on Los Feliz Boulevard.

## Chapter Four

# Émigrés

CLARA ENTERED THE HOUSE to the sound of a shot ringing out and a woman's shriek. All thoughts of Gil vanished as she froze for a moment, pulse racing. The sound was quickly followed by a cheer and the clink of glasses. Champagne. A party—tonight of all nights.

She hung up her cardigan on the crowded rack and stood there for a moment, adrift, leaning into the coats, burying her face in their soft layers—the smell of streetcar, tobacco, and cologne. In the sitting room someone had started on the piano, and a heated discussion competed with the notes. Her mind returned to Gil, and she replayed the scene in his car. How it had ended with that chaste kiss on the forehead. A woman's laugh pierced through the muffle of coats. Clara straightened; she smoothed her hair and headed into the party.

When her parents entertained, it always felt as though half of Europe were squeezed into their small sitting room. She navigated her way through them, a hubbub of different languages, mostly German. After the cool air of Gil's convertible, the room was stifling. Frau Dreyer squeezed her arm, and Otto pinched her chin as though she were six years old.

"Klara! Finally." Her mother was by the piano. She was wearing one of the evening dresses that had lasted her through the war. Still attractive in her forties, she had deep-set blue eyes, and chestnut hair (with no gray) swept into an old-fashioned style. Her bone structure was strong; it made her seem polished, more finished than Clara, who thought of her own face as too malleable—still under construction—a question mark as to whether she would be beautiful.

"You're home so late," said her mother in German.

"I know, I know," said Clara, giving her a quick hug.

"*Wie ist das* show business?" said Otto, grinning. Clearly everyone had had a few drinks.

Clara smiled on cue. "Fine, thanks." The moment she'd seen her mother, Clara had decided that she wouldn't tell her parents about the murder—not tonight. Since the war, they'd been well practiced in receiving bad news. She would spare them for an evening, let them enjoy their party. A movie star murdered; it would be splashed across the papers soon enough.

Her father, topping up glasses, raised the bottle of champagne in welcome. He came over, wiping the neck of the bottle with a dishtowel, a splash of champagne on his shirt. "They wouldn't hire you at the Ritz, Papa," she said in German, giving him a peck on the cheek.

"A glass for Klara," said her father to no one in particular. It was strange how her name in German always sounded like it belonged to someone else.

Clara shook her head. "I'm fine. Save it for the others." Champagne was the last thing she could stomach.

"I insist," he said, and a glass was produced. Her father filled it up, the frothy fizz shooting to the rim. His eyes were bright and smiling. Seeing him happy and unaware made her want to burst into tears. There was a time when she would have kept nothing from her parents, when a hug from her mother or a soothing word from her father had been able to put the world to rights. Those days were long gone.

She took the glass, her head swimming. Babe Bannon was dead. Just holding a champagne flute felt wrong. Clara shook off the thought and forced a smile. "What's the occasion?"

Her father regarded her fondly, then turned to his guests. "The last time Klara saw Europe, she was a girl of eleven." He shook his head slightly. "Now she is a young woman." The piano music had stopped. There was the usual thread of sadness and nostalgia tugging on his words; all refugees had that tendency because of the war. They'd lost so much, and yet they were the lucky ones. Clara scanned the room. Her parents' friends looked back at her with jolly faces and glistening eyes: expectant. She felt as though she were playing a part but hadn't learned her lines. Then it clicked—the champagne, the party in the middle of the week. Clara's breath quickened; her eyes raced across her father's face. "No!" she breathed. "A new job—already?"

Her father nodded. "University of Bonn."

Germany. The news stung Clara like a slap. She froze, holding her breath, the eager faces beaming at her. "Wonderful!" she blurted out. What else could she say, with all eyes upon her and her parents looking happy for once. "Congratulations, Papa." She felt the floor disappear from under her.

Everyone raised their glasses once more. Clara followed suit, swept along in a performance of dutiful daughter. She took a sip of champagne, and the sour fizz of celebration—*their* celebration—caught in her throat. Her mother drew next to them. "We sail in summer. End of June if we're lucky."

Just over a month. So soon. The room was spinning. Clara had thought she'd have more time—time to set up her own life, get the promotion, save for the deposit on an apartment, and time to figure out how to break the news that she wasn't going back with them to Europe. "But, *Mutti*, I—"

"You'll have to start going through your things, throw out all those magazines," her mother prattled on. "And any clothes that don't fit. We'll need to get you a decent winter coat. German winters." She shuddered. "Mrs. Shuler wants to find a new tenant immediately. She said she'll start showing the place next week. I don't know how we're supposed to pack *and* keep the place tidy."

Both Clara and her father started to protest. Clara's "I don't want to go back" was overlapped by her father.

"Inge, all that can wait," he said kindly.

"You're right, of course." She didn't mind being told off. "Tonight we celebrate." She patted Clara's cheek. "Finally we're going home."

Clara was grateful when her parents were pulled away by their guests. She watched them over the rim of her glass. Did they even know what awaited them back in Germany? It wasn't the same country they'd left eight years before. Everyone had seen the newsreels of bomb-damaged cities, piles of rubble, civilians in long queues for food—nothing more than dehydrated potatoes and milk powder. Not to mention the other newsreels, the liberated camps, the piles of bodies, survivors like skeletons. *Stop.* How could they want to go back?

"Schönberg is at the Bowl tonight. Have we missed it?" Frau Dreyer said, motioning to the wireless, her face flushed from alcohol. "Someone turn it on. I'm sure it's tonight."

Clara choked on a sip of champagne. Her mind raced to the possibility of a breaking news report: *We interrupt this concert with tragic news from Hollywood.* Thinking quickly, she turned to Otto, taking his arm. "Why bother with the radio when we have a maestro right here?" The guests nodded their approval. Otto bowed to the room and took a seat at the piano. He'd been famous in Berlin *before the war*—that ubiquitous phrase that all her parents' friends used when referring to their former lives.

Otto began playing, and Clara retreated from the others. As piano music filled the sitting room, she stared vacantly at the floor, letting the music wash over her, relieved for the pause in her charade. Her gaze landed on her shoes. There was a mark

on the toe of her right foot. She peered at the peach suede—
a streak of dried blood. Her stomach lurched, and her heart
began to race. The body in the vault flashed across her mind's
eye like the lurid cover of a pulp magazine. She tried to concentrate on Otto's music, forcing herself to breathe deeply—in and
out—in time to the sonata. But thoughts of Bannon's dead body
kept surfacing. Squeezing her eyes shut, she pushed them away.

"Klara?" She opened her eyes to find her mother watching
her. "Are you all right?"

"Just a bit of a headache," Clara said, holding up the champagne flute.

"Have something to eat. There's leftover schnitzel in the icebox. Heat it up first."

"*Mutti*," said Clara before her mother turned away. She had
a sudden notion to come clean and blurt out everything—about
the promotion, about the murder, how everything about the
day had turned on its head and she didn't know what to think.
But another guest swept her mother away to settle an argument
about composers. Clara set her glass down, and with everyone
else applauding Otto's playing, she slipped away.


In her bedroom Clara discovered that her old trunk had magi-
cally appeared—her parents must have pulled it from storage.
Clara glared at it, annoyed that they had already begun packing.
On top was a small box with a note from her mother: *Found this
inside.* Clara took the box, kicked off her shoes, and plumped

down on her bed. It was a pale blond cigar box with Spanish writing, vaguely familiar. She opened it, and the smell of tobacco brought her back to her grandfather's house. She must have been ten years old when he let her keep the box once the cigars had been smoked.

Clara leafed through papers and knickknacks. She remembered now; she'd used the box to store keepsakes around the time of their trip to America. There was a deck plan of the ocean liner, the SS *Europa.* November 1938. She could still remember their cramped second-class cabin. Her parents had waited until they were safely on the Atlantic to break the news: it wasn't a vacation; they weren't returning to Berlin. They were fleeing Germany. *Political refugees.* The ship was a dividing line, the boundary between childhood and adolescence, between Germany and America, and between her two selves: Klara and Clara. After a year in America, Klara with a *K* had decided that the German spelling of her name didn't match her new life—it was too foreign, spindly and knock-kneed, like the schoolgirl who had arrived in the United States. She rechristened herself Clara—the American *C* was curvaceous and mature, a C-cup she planned to grow into.

Clara traced the deck plan with her finger. The upper decks were for first class. She had a vague recollection of exploring where she didn't belong. Memories spliced together like frames of film: chandeliers in the ballroom, wood paneling and thick carpets, stained glass with the ship's motif, the covered promenade deck lined with deck chairs.

Under the map of the *Europa*, there were train tickets from the *Super Chief*, New York to Los Angeles; and a receipt from a New York diner—*amerikanisches Frühstück*. She recalled her eleven-year-old self gobbling up her first American breakfast. Tucked away at the bottom she found a dried daisy chain, paper-thin petals and brittle stems. Freya—a sharp twist in her heart as the summer of '38 bloomed for a moment. The daisy chain was nestled on a handkerchief. She unfolded it carefully. It was edged in lace, and in the corner were the embroidered initials *LR*. Who was *LR*? A school friend, a relative, a neighbor? Clara scanned through a roll call of faces from the past, but she came up empty. By now her head was throbbing. It was all too much; she didn't want to confront the ghosts of Berlin days. It only reminded her of her father's new job. She closed the lid on the past and slid the box under the bed.

At her bedroom window Clara gazed at the city lights and the inky sky free of cloud. The same city as this morning, when the studio and everything she wanted had been within reach. Nearby in Griffith Park a coyote yipped and a more distant call answered. She heard the switchboard operator in her head. *No answer, miss. Can I connect you to someone else?* Since her discovery in the vault, something had shifted. There was before and after. Clara lived in the after now; Los Angeles had admitted her to its dark side.

## Chapter Five

# June Gloom

A MOB OF PRESS greeted employees of Silver Pacific at the pedestrian gate the next morning. They were kept at bay by a couple of uniformed officers, but it didn't stop the reporters from yelling out to people arriving for work: "When will the studio release a statement?" "Do the police have any leads?" "Hey, honey, how does it feel, coming to work with a murderer on the loose?"

Clara kept her head down and followed the train of other employees. The line at the gate was slow. She watched as extra security guards examined ID. It made her think of immigration officers scrutinizing passports and faces, as though she were about to enter another country. Berlin was split up into zones now, cut up like a cake, the allied countries each taking a piece.

After the crush of the gate, the studio lay bare—flat and uninteresting. A marine haze had descended and blocked out the sun, turning the world dull and grubby: June gloom in May. This was the first time walking through the gates that Clara hadn't felt something singular and pure and completely hers.

When she entered the archive, Lloyd was on the phone and Simkin was in her office, behind her typewriter—neither of them looked up. Clara went to her desk, put her purse in a drawer, and shrugged off her jacket. The office smelled stale and familiar, and she couldn't help but feel resentful. Today, Friday, was supposed to be her last day in the archive—it was supposed to feel triumphant like graduation or the last day of term. But now the production of *Argentan* had been upended, along with Clara's new job.

Lloyd slammed down the phone. "Dammit," he said, and stormed out of the archive. The door rattled in its frame. Clara had never seen him lose his temper. It was most unlike him.

Simkin poked her head out of her office and regarded the closed door. "Unacceptable." She folded her arms. "A tragedy has struck, but we don't need to sink to melodrama."

"I suppose everyone is on edge," Clara offered. She wanted to talk about the murder, about Babe Bannon. Miss Simkin had worked at the studio since the dawn of time. She knew all the goings-on. "Do you think," said Clara, fishing, "the cops already have a suspect? Maybe someone who worked on the movie? Seems like Bannon created as much drama off-screen as on. I heard that—"

"Enough gossip," Miss Simkin said, shutting Clara down.

She removed her glasses and regarded Clara. "Miss Berg, I don't know why you were in the archive after hours last night."

"I was watching *Argentan* footage. I wanted to be prepared—"

Simkin cut her off. "I've been lenient with you. Overly so. You're keen and a hard worker, but this isn't your office in which to do as you please. Given the shock you've had—yes, I heard that you made the discovery—I shall say no more about it."

"So is the movie shut down?" Clara watched Simkin's pinched face and wanted more than ever to be out of her clutches.

Simkin raised an eyebrow. "No film star, no film," she said, confirming Clara's worst fears. "I can float you for a while in the archive, but your replacement starts Monday." She let out a disgruntled sigh. "At least you'll be around to train the new lad." Miss Simkin gestured to Lloyd's empty chair. "Your colleague is no shining example." And with that, she returned to her desk. As usual Miss Simkin was all business and no emotions. What would it take, Clara wondered, for her to be human?

"There's still work to be done," Simkin called out from behind her typewriter. "Of course with the vaults out of bounds, we'll have to wait for the all clear from the police." She put her glasses on and peered at the page she was typing. "For now, Clara, why don't you go help Sam. He's been here since six a.m."

The second floor of the postproduction building was a negative image of the day before. Clara dragged her feet along the corridor. Today the squawk of Moviolas was bothersome—the shrieking notes of competing dialogue sounded like a murder of crows warding her off.

Sam was hunched over his editing bench. "Hi," said Clara. He hadn't heard her knock, and startled when she spoke.

"Clara, come in." He pushed his glasses up and blinked at her, bleary-eyed. "I still can't believe the news." He shook his head. "Babe Bannon murdered." His reaction was the complete opposite of Miss Simkin's.

"I know," said Clara, and sank into the chair by the Moviola. "Why are you here so early? Isn't the movie shut down?"

Sam let out a long sigh. She could smell the sour reek of stale coffee breath. He pushed his glasses back onto his nose and gestured to his editing bench. "Mr. Pearce has demanded that we try to salvage the film with only three-quarters of the scenes shot." She noted the two crusted coffee cups, the slew of continuity reports and script pages across his desk in the corner. He looked like he hadn't slept.

"And my assistant called." Sam pointed at the phone accusingly. "He already found himself a new job over at Warner, an editing position." Clara had never liked the first assistant editor. Where Sam was open to showing Clara the ropes, his assistant had resented her frequent visits. Sam shrugged. "Can't blame him, I guess."

"And the movie—can you finish it? Is that even possible?" she asked, hoping she still had a shot at the apprentice job.

"Writers are working on some ideas: voice-over, reworking scenes, additional dialogue recorded with a soundalike." Sam shook his head, rolled his chair back, and stretched his legs. "We'll spend a week chasing our tails, and the movie will be scrapped anyway."

It was the same cutting room as the day before—no different, except now it shrank from her. The light had shifted; colors were dull, objects turned flat and mundane. The murder had changed everything.

He leaned back in his chair and gazed at the ceiling. "I never met her, you know. Barbara Bannon."

"Really? How come?" said Clara.

Sam shook his head absently. "I try not to let the actor intrude on the character they're playing. It breaks the spell for me." He sighed. "I shake hands with them at the premiere, and they don't have a clue who I am. Whereas I know every inch of their face, every expression, every inflection in their voice." He gave a sad smile. "I wish I had relaxed my rule this time."

Clara rolled her chair closer. "Do you think it was someone on the crew? The murderer?"

Sam met her eye. "There was tension, yes." He started to say something, then thought better of it.

"What is it?" said Clara, her eyes fixed on the editor.

"Her co-star, for one. Randall Ford gave Babe a hard time on set." He nodded to the film footage on the bench. "Downright nasty sometimes—I've seen the outtakes." He turned back to Clara, his gaze steady. "And Howard did nothing to stop it."

The phone rang and Clara jumped.

"Editorial." Sam frowned into the receiver. He listened for a beat, then glanced at his watch. "Any idea what it's about?" He nodded to whoever was on the other end of the line. "Thanks." Sam hung up. "There's a production meeting on stage eleven in half an hour—the whole crew's been asked to attend." He pushed up his sleeves and turned back to his film bench. "I don't have time for this," he muttered.

Clara picked up some continuity pages that had fallen on the floor and started to put them in the right order. She felt a little flash of daring. "I can go to the meeting if you like," she said, trying not to sound too eager. "I'll report back, tell you what happens."

"Would you?" Sam said gratefully. "It's probably just the official announcement." He held a strip of film up to the light. "Hopefully Pearce has come to his senses and decided to shut it down. I can't work miracles."


When Clara crossed the lot, she didn't recognize the feel of the place—it was a new and strange country to which she had no allegiance. Silver Pacific studios had shrunk, all the magic wrung out of it. It was just a collection of office buildings and some tatty stages in peeling white paint, graying like old socks; grimy corners under drainpipes; patches of dead grass where employees had trampled a shortcut. Bougainvillea, brassy and cheap, threw itself over the studio walls, like a bit player trying to get noticed.

Outside the commissary she passed two secretaries bickering, and for a split second she was sure they were speaking German. She spun around quickly. Of course she had imagined it; the women were as American as Betty Grable. They were talking about the cops commandeering parking spaces. Somehow these commonplace things rattled her.

She took the long way to the stage—out of her way—past the Writers' Block, and automatically scanned the vicinity for Gil. The building was two stories and it had an outdoor staircase, like a motel, which led to the offices on the second floor. Gil and Mr. Brackett's office was upstairs. Clara was hoping she would run into him; then they could walk over together. She wanted to talk to him. It had been nagging her: Why didn't he pick up when she called last night? She squinted up at the second floor, but there was no sign of Gil or Mr. Brackett. Maybe they had already left for the meeting. She quickened her pace toward the stages.

With the production suspended, stage eleven—the set for the mansion house—was silent and lackluster. There was no sign of Gil yet. The rest of the crew milled around a craft table, helping themselves to coffee and tea, talking in hushed tones as though they were at a wake. Clara wouldn't have minded a coffee, but she was curious to check out the set. Working in postproduction, she usually didn't get the opportunity to visit the soundstages.

She wandered into the widow's mansion house—a life-size dollhouse opened up at the hinges. There was a huge entryway with a grand staircase (leading to a second floor whose set was on another stage), a library, a drawing room, and a dining room.

Compared to the version on-screen that Clara was used to, the set looked disappointing and unremarkable. Natural light flooded the house and exposed the cheap plywood flats, which looked as though they could be knocked down in a breeze. The stonework of the fireplace was obviously made of plaster, and the "marble" staircase was painted wood. Through the back windows there was an unconvincing painted backdrop of formal gardens—crude and two-dimensional. Why did she want movies so badly? It was all an illusion, a cheap trick—an expensive game of pretend.

Her parents had balked at her desire to work at the studio. They had reacted as though she had announced she was running away to join the circus. It had taken Max to help convince them, and even then it was supposed to be temporary. Her parents assumed that movie studios were sordid places, not appropriate for a young woman. She still hadn't told them about the murder. She had scooped up the newspaper from the doorstep—with its screaming headline—and taken it with her. She'd tell them tonight.

On the side wall of the library set, Clara could see the craft table and the crew, perfectly framed through the leaded glass window. Howard Hawks, raking a hand through his silver hair, was in a tense conversation with Randall Ford. In person, the former matinee idol appeared older and paunchier than he did on-screen—his hair was thinning, and he wasn't wearing his toupee. The man with the beard and the cravat she pegged as the set designer or the cinematographer. He was talking to the costume designer. Dressed in a vivid green suit, she was dabbing her eyes. Clara stared at them like suspects in a drawing-room mystery. Was one of them a killer? Someone pouring cream into his coffee, helping himself to the sugar, someone feigning shock and disbelief like everyone else and yet he—or perhaps even she—was a cold-blooded killer? A murderer. Observing them through the set window, she was the detective in an Agatha Christie novel, except this wasn't a stately English home. It wasn't a drawing-room mystery. This was Los Angeles; there were no manners here. Clara recalled Gil's description of the crew, everyone wanting their pound of flesh. Babe Bannon's murder had to be mixed up in the dark side of Hollywood—something from the pulps or the scandal sheets.

Clara caught sight of Gil and Mr. Brackett walking through the wide stage doors. She moved to the edge of the set. Gil clocked her and headed over. As he got closer, his eyes pinned her in place. He smiled, in a contained way in front of his colleagues. "How are you doing?" He jerked his head toward the doors. "It's nuts out there. I nearly ran over a reporter."

Clara nodded. "It took me ages to get in as well."

Roger Brackett was addressing a handful of the crew. "We live our lives not in years—we measure time in movies. It's the film's title you remember, not the date."

Gil rolled his eyes and whispered to Clara, "He'll start quoting Keats any minute—it's the only bit of poetry he's learned by heart." He touched her arm. "Come on."

They moved away from the group and found themselves in the vast entrance hall of the set.

"Any idea what the meeting is about?" asked Clara.

Gil shrugged. "Pearce will have some trite words of sympathy and warn the crew not to blab to the press. No love lost between him and Bannon."

The prop telephone gleamed on the hall table, prompting Clara to remember her question.

"Last night," she said, watching him carefully. "Where were you? You didn't call."

Gil stopped and looked at her, confused.

"The Formosa," said Clara. She hoped she didn't sound desperate or disappointed. She knew Gil and how he could be; she wasn't a swooning bobby-soxer pining for a date.

He smacked his forehead. "I completely forgot. I was wrestling with that scene."

"I called you," said Clara quickly. "There was no answer."

Gil froze for a moment. "I was probably in Roger's office—his couch is comfier than my chair." He shrugged. "I guess I didn't hear the phone."

Just then a murmur rippled across the crew, and they turned to see that the head of the studio, Mr. Pearce, had entered the stage at a brisk clip, flanked by Ireland and his partner, Detective Rivetti. The three of them looked grim. Mr. Pearce commandeered an apple box from a grip and stepped onto it like a politician making a stump speech. Clara, Gil, and the rest of the crew gathered around him. He was dressed in a three-piece suit and his hair was oiled and shone under the lights—he was elegant in that way rich people always are. The vast stage fell silent.

"Sorry to have kept you waiting." Pearce adjusted his tie, and his cuff links gleamed. "You've all seen the headlines, and you know why production has been suspended." His manner was clipped, controlled. He cleared his throat. "However, the situation is rapidly changing. The police have just informed me—" He tried a deeper register. "There's been a development. The short of it is . . ." He swallowed, and Clara detected a hint of panic crossing his face. "Barbara Bannon is alive."

## Chapter Six

# Miss Bannon

A COLLECTIVE GASP ROSE from the crew, and Clara felt the color drain from her face. *Alive?* Untethered, she was suddenly hot and light-headed. It was a floating feeling, out of body, a crane shot pulling back, high above her. *She's not dead. She's alive.* Clara had made a mistake, a terrible blunder. They should have called an ambulance, not the cops. But an ambulance *had* come—and gone. Then the coroner's van had showed up. Again, tight close-ups flashed across her mind: the one eye open, the gash on her face, blond hair matted with blood. Bannon *alive?* It couldn't be true.

"Let me finish!" Mr. Pearce held up his hands to silence the crew. "Last night at the studio, a young woman was killed—but it *wasn't* Barbara Bannon." The volume on the stage rose again as the news sank in.

Gil shook his head. "What's he talking about?"

*Someone else?*

"It's impossible." Clara turned to Gil. "I *saw* her—it was Bannon. She was wearing her costume, same blond hair—it was *her.* I'm positive."

"Mr. Pearce." The script supervisor stepped forward. "Mr. Pearce," she repeated, fighting to be heard.

"Quiet, everyone," said Pearce sharply. He turned to the script supervisor. "Go ahead."

"Who was it? Who was in the vault?" It was the question on everyone's lips.

Pearce shook his head. "I am unable to say at this point. We're waiting for the official word." His voice—trying for calm and commanding—was thin and reedy across the vast soundstage.

"What about Babe?" asked Bannon's dresser.

"Yeah, where is she?" said a gruff voice. It came from a middle-aged man wearing a tool belt.

Pearce exchanged a look with the detectives, and Ireland stepped forward to address the crew. "Her cabin in Big Bear. She woke this morning, went to town for coffee, saw the headlines in the paper, and called her agent, who alerted us. A police escort is taking her back to the city as we speak."

Clara was still in disbelief. It was that same recoiling confusion as when you mistake a stranger for a friend, that momentary limbo when your mind has to play catch-up.

"Why'd they say it was Bannon?" said a camera guy, a combative air about him. Voices from the crew:

"It's in all the papers."

"Who told them?"

Clara's heart was hammering. She felt the heat of humiliation. It was worse than any mistake she could make at work—worse than leaving the vault unlocked or a reel in the office overnight or forgetting to turn in the time sheets—and she didn't make mistakes. She wasn't Lloyd. And yet somehow this was *her* fault: she had misidentified the body.

Pearce cleared his throat. "Several people on the scene assumed it was Bannon. A similarity of appearance." Bannon's dresser threw a glance in Clara's direction. Did she know it was Clara who'd found the body? Was Pearce going to point the finger of blame at her in front of everyone? Clara could imagine other heads turning, other pairs of accusing eyes. She felt a wave of nausea rise from her gut, and for a moment she wished she could disappear behind the set, but she remained straight-backed and staring at Pearce.

The other detective, Rivetti, stepped in. He was dark with a thin mustache, and a garish tie—more like a gangster in a B movie than a cop. "The studio never released Bannon's name. They hadn't made an official statement. The press got a jump on the story," he said in a nasal whine. "'Movie star murdered.' It spread like wildfire."

"On that note," Pearce interjected, "we're asking that none of you talk to reporters about the case. We have to think of the victim's family, still to be informed. There's been a great deal of upset already."

"Whose fault's that?" Clara recognized the voice of Randall Ford but couldn't place him in the crowd.

The sun had managed to burn through the marine layer, and now it poured through the open stage doors. It was at that moment Clara noticed someone standing there: a woman in silhouette. Something about her stance was deliberate.

"When will we resume shooting?" she heard the script supervisor ask.

"Too early to say," Pearce said quickly.

Now the grip next to Clara noticed the woman at the stage doors. *"Miss Bannon?"* he muttered. A ripple of incredulity, and like a wave building, heads began to turn.

"The detectives have set up—" Pearce stopped short.

On cue, Barbara Bannon made her entrance, striding across the stage. An apparition, she was backlit by the brash sun. It could only have been sixty feet from the open stage doors to where the crew was assembled, but for Clara time slowed and she saw Bannon walking toward them in an endless tracking shot. Her gait immediately recognizable—staccato steps, hips swinging. She was holding something—a bat, a stick? As she got closer, Clara realized it was a rolled-up newspaper. The crew parted to let her through, almost wary of this phantom.

Barbara Bannon was very much alive. And she was furious. "Conrad Pearce." She spat his name. "What the hell's going on?" Her voice—low and gutsy—filled the whole stage.

Pearce stepped off his apple box and moved toward her.

Bannon was wielding her paper, and for a moment Clara believed she would strike him with it. Instead she threw it to the ground by his feet. It hit the floor with a slap, unfurling the familiar headline in block capitals. BABE BANNON MURDERED. "Care to explain?"

Some movie stars are disappointing in the flesh. Not Barbara Bannon. Petite, dressed in a white shirt, wide-legged pants cinched with a man's belt, wedge heels, a silk scarf tied around her ash-blond hair, and no makeup. She was stunning. Clara had never seen her up close before (the gruesome discovery in the vault no longer valid). There was something arresting and forceful about her; she was electrifying. Clara caught the trace of her perfume and could discern a smattering of freckles on her cheekbones. Howard Hawks made a move toward her, but something about her stance pulled him up short. Even the detectives looked in awe of her, their professional guise slipping, their mouths hanging open.

She stood under the crew's gaze as though illuminated by a spotlight. Everyone on the stage was mesmerized. It was like the effect of the most powerful theater. Clara recalled a review of the actress's breakout role: *Bannon sizzles on-screen, her chemistry with Gregory Quinn red-hot. Audiences won't be able to take their eyes off her.*

"Let's talk in my office." Pearce tried to guide her away from the assembled crew, but she stayed put, feet planted.

"This some kind of stunt?" She shot a dagger glance at

Hawks, then back at Pearce. "Your publicity boys getting creative? We're shooting a suspense movie, after all." Her accent in real life departed from the mid-Atlantic polish of her movie roles. *She was a real Joe. Mouth like a trucker.* Gil's words echoed in her head.

"We're trying to piece it together," said Pearce. His eyes flicked nervously at the crew. "A young woman was murdered at the studio last night."

*"Who?"* Bannon fired back without taking a breath. Her eyes flashed, and she looked like she would bite him.

Rivetti and Ireland stood, as dumb as chess pieces waiting for someone to move them. Pearce managed a taut grimace. He shifted his weight from one foot to the other. "The victim hasn't been officially identified."

Bannon could sense his waffling. "Spit it out, Conrad." *That snappy dialogue.*

The crew, hackles raised, murmured their assent. The head of the studio looked as though he might wring Bannon's slender neck himself.

"Who was it?" Clara heard a voice and realized it was her own. She had stepped forward. Her heart was thumping, and her cheeks flamed at her own daring. "Who was in the vault?" Pearce flicked a glance at Clara. She could feel the entire stage silently side with her—they all wanted answers. Pearce was on the spot. He looked warm in that nice suit. His eyes darted to Ireland for permission. The detective gave a small nod.

"We're waiting on confirmation," Pearce said to Bannon, "but it's likely the victim was your stand-in, Connie Milligan."

A murmur of surprise swept across the crew. Bannon took a step back, like a stumble, reeling as the name sank in. She nodded slowly, absorbing the news, blinking her emotions away. The stand-in. It was now blindingly obvious. Who else could be mistaken for Bannon? Who else would be wearing her costume—same height, same build and color of hair? And with the blood obscuring her face. Clara wobbled. She felt Gil's hand on her back, and she leaned into him. A hive of bees was swarming in her head, the buzzing ringing in her ears.

Bannon turned to the crew. "I could use a drink." She scanned the faces. "My house, any time after seven. You're all invited." Her jaw was set, and Clara noticed how she threw her head back, jutting out her chin, the way she did before delivering a killer line. "We'll raise a glass to Connie."

At that, she turned and strode off, Mr. Pearce and Howard Hawks following her at a safe distance.

Gil let out a shaky breath. "Jesus."

Frozen to the spot, Clara's eyes followed Barbara Bannon as she disappeared. What had they just witnessed? It felt something close to supernatural. She blinked at the open stage doors, and the white rectangles of sunlight burned into her eyes.

The chatter on the stage swelled, the crew clamoring with questions.

"Okay, everyone, pipe down," Detective Rivetti snarled. "We

still have a murder to solve. The more we can find out about Connie Milligan, the closer we'll be to finding her killer."

"What if it was random—some crazy nut with a thing for blondes?" asked the young grip who had first noticed Bannon.

"Unlikely," said Rivetti. "A random killer wouldn't have access to the lot."

Ireland nodded. "Most murders are committed by someone the victim knows—often, in the case of a female victim, by someone she was romantically involved with." Clara shuddered at these words.

"We need your help filling in the blanks in Connie's life. She only began at the studio a few weeks ago," said Rivetti. "Before that she worked as an extra and as an usherette at the Vista Theater. Anyone with information, please come forward."

"We'll be conducting interviews this afternoon," said Ireland. "No one is to leave the studio until cleared by one of us. We have an office set up in the costume shop."

The meeting was finally over. The stage felt oppressive, the air stale. The crew, as mindless as sleepwalkers, stumbled toward the open stage doors and into the dazzling sunshine.

## Chapter Seven

# Melrose Gate

GIL WAS IMMEDIATELY PULLED away by Mr. Brackett and a flurry of studio people—with their starring actress alive and well, would the movie resume filming? That could mean Clara's coveted promotion would be reinstated. She should have felt relieved. And yet she felt strangely numb, as if the thing she had wanted so badly had lost its significance—her dream was now a stranger to her.

By the Melrose Gate Clara caught sight of Lloyd watching the tributes pile up for the wrong victim. She drew next to him, and they stood contemplating the sea of flowers, cards, and headshots of Bannon.

Lloyd, hands sunk in his pockets, half-heartedly kicked the railing. "No flowers for Connie Milligan."

Clara's head whipped around. "You knew her, the stand-in?"

He gave a long sigh. "I knew it must have been her in the vaults." He nodded in the direction of the stage. "Even before I clapped eyes on Babe Bannon marching across the lot. I mean, I didn't know for sure—I just had a bad feeling since this morning. I couldn't get a hold of Connie."

"Lloyd—I'm sorry," said Clara, her mind racing.

He gave a sharp jerk of his shoulders, shrugging off her sympathy. They were both silent for a beat. "When she auditioned to be Bannon's stand-in," Lloyd went on, "she said it was like auditioning to play the right-size vase." He gave an empty laugh. "They looked through her, she said, like she wasn't a person. She just had to be the right dimensions, to match Bannon." His mind drifted off somewhere for a moment. Clara was holding her breath, waiting for him to continue. He remained quiet.

"If you were friends with Connie," Clara prompted, "you might know something that can help the detectives. They want anyone with information to come forward."

"And tell them what?" he snapped. "She was friends with a vault boy and she ended up dead in the vaults?" There was a look of anger or fear in his eyes.

"But you didn't do anything . . ." Clara trailed off. She didn't know whether she was stating a fact or asking him a question.

The energy of Lloyd's outburst drained away, his shoulders dropped, and he looked a little lost. Clara wanted him to assure her that he wasn't mixed up in this. "Lloyd?" Clara asked. But his gaze had drifted back to the tributes on the other side of the fence. "What a mess, all those flowers," he said. "Security's going to have to clean it up."

## Chapter Eight

# Beachwood Canyon

GIL HAILED THE NEWSBOY at a stoplight and gave him a coin. "Evening edition?" he asked.

The boy nodded. "Yes, sir." He gave them a copy of the *Los Angeles Times* and jogged to the car behind.

Gil handed Clara the paper. There in black and white was a photograph of Connie Milligan staring at them from above the fold—bright and sunny, her blond wave darker in newsprint. Finally—face to face with the girl in the vault. She looked different from what Clara had expected—unsophisticated, softer edges, cheekbones like apples, finer brows. Clara felt an empty pit in her stomach, and the feeling grew as she stared at the face. This girl wasn't a movie star. Like Clara, she was just another girl on the lot, one of the many invisible young women who toiled behind the scenes, whose names wouldn't appear up in lights.

"You okay?" asked Gil.

Clara nodded, shrugging off her emotions. "You think she looks like Bannon?"

Gil studied the picture. "Not really. Maybe it's an old photo."

A car behind them beeped; the light had turned green. Gil stepped on the gas. As they passed Hollywood Boulevard, Clara took in the bars and restaurants and theater marquees, and all the people hustling, dreaming, striving for a piece of this town. As the car flew north on Vine, Clara turned back to the paper. She consumed the face in newsprint until the ink danced before her eyes. *Who are you? What happened to you?* The world felt unjust and random. Clara Berg was on her way to a movie star's house in the Hollywood Hills; Connie Milligan lay dead in the morgue. She folded the newspaper tenderly and slid it under her seat.

"They're already talking about the schedule," said Gil. "I'm guessing the shoot will start after the publicity has died down." He looked across at her. "That means your apprentice editor job will be back on."

Clara sighed. "I suppose you're right." She couldn't muster any enthusiasm because at that moment the whole thing felt impossible. Her parents would never agree to it. Even before the murder, the idea of them allowing her to get her own apartment, to remain behind in Los Angeles without them, had been a stretch. Now, with a murderer on the loose, it was unthinkable.

\* \* \*

Bannon's home was a Spanish villa in Beachwood Canyon—white stucco and arched windows draped with frills of bougainvillea. Her famous powder-blue coupe was parked in the drive. As they walked up tiled steps and approached the front door, Clara could feel herself seize up.

"We don't have to go in," said Gil, assuming her hesitation was nerves.

"No, I want to—for Connie's sake."

It was more than simply raising a glass out of respect for an apple-cheeked stranger. Clara felt something deeper. She felt a sense of duty, responsibility. She tried to excavate her feelings further. She wanted an answer; she wanted the truth. Someone on the crew must know something.

The front door was ajar, and Clara caught the scent of lilies. Once she and Gil stepped inside, they were consumed by the smell. She had to clap a hand over her nose and mouth to keep from gagging. As they crossed the terra-cotta tiled foyer, she could see that the long table in the hall was laden with masses of flowers. As they got closer, Clara saw handwritten notes addressed to "Babe" or "Miss Bannon," and more than one teddy bear.

Horrified, Clara whispered to Gil, "The tributes from the gate."

"It's like a wake," said Gil under his breath. They waded through the smell of ripe bouquets to the living room.

Despite its modest appearance from the street, the villa was expansive—it dropped down another floor and spread out, with incredible views from the living room over Hollywood and east to downtown. A knot of people stood by the lacquered bar, and others hovered near jewel-colored couches, but no one was brave enough to sit down. Clara felt out of her depth. She didn't know anyone apart from Gil—perhaps Roger Brackett to say hi to, and of course Sam (if he showed up after his morning of fruitless cutting). The crew hung about, slightly uncertain, like extras waiting for the assistant director to cue them: "Background action!" and they would mime having a good time at a party.

Through an archway there was a dining room with a buffet of food laid out, and beyond the living room, patio doors led to a tiled terrace, a swimming pool, and landscaped grounds. There was a Moroccan theme to the furnishings: brightly colored pillows and throws, patterned tile, ornate mirrors. It took no time to locate their hostess. Babe Bannon was outside on the patio. Her voice—unmistakable—floated inside every so often. It kept Clara on her toes, reminding her that she was in the presence of Hollywood royalty.

At the bar the costume designer handed Clara a champagne cocktail, and Gil fixed himself a scotch and soda. Clara sipped from the shallow cocktail glass, trying not to spill. She could hear half-hearted attempts to recount anecdotes of Connie.

"First time she saw the craft table, she asked me where to pay for her coffee." Followed by a forced laugh.

"On the 'martini shot' she asked for a twist!" Everything on the craft table was free, and the "martini shot" was movie speak for the last setup of the day.

The stories trailed off. The intimacy was threadbare and gave the crew away. They hadn't really known Connie. Many of the crew had worked at the studio for years, on movie after movie. Certain departments were literally a family affair. The studio was tight-knit, and Connie had only gotten the job a few weeks prior, at the start of filming. Before that, as an extra, she would have been herded around like cattle, a step down from the rest of the crew. According to Gil, she hadn't worked as Bannon's stand-in—or anyone's stand-in—before.

Drinks in hand, Clara and Gil were crossing the room to find a seat when they came face to face with Barbara Bannon herself. She wore an ivory crepe evening gown, with capped sleeves, and drapery that clung to her curves. Her hair was down and she had minimal jewelry, just a huge ruby ring. The gem was the size of a raspberry. (Clara had read about it in a magazine. It was a gift from Quinn.)

"Gil," Babe said, leaning forward, tilting her cheek so he could kiss it. "Haven't seen you since the read-through. I figured you'd taken another movie." She was smooth, unhurried. It was still unreal to see her smiling, living, breathing.

"I'm around," said Gil. "Endless rewrites."

"I suppose you blame me for that—don't deny it." Her eyes drifted to Clara. "And who's this? Your secretary?" Babe's long lashes blinked, and Clara felt like she'd undergone an X-ray.

"This is Clara Berg," said Gil. "She works in editing."

Bannon's eyes flashed. "Tell me, before my resurrection, were you cutters trying to piece together a movie without me?"

Flustered, Clara groped for a response, but Bannon didn't care to listen. She nodded to their cocktails. "I see you found the bar. There's food in the dining room." She glided past them to other guests. "You'll have to serve yourselves," she said over her shoulder. "My housekeeper practically dropped dead when she laid eyes on me. I sent her home for the day."

Gil was pulled away by a group of guys who looked like teamsters—salt of the earth, burly guys, who were drinking beer instead of highballs—and Clara found herself on the velvet couches, where Mr. Brackett was holding court.

"So there we were carrying the Ping-Pong table into the swimming pool. The Racquet Club staff couldn't tell off Clark Gable—who, by the way, is a sore loser at table tennis." Everyone laughed, including Clara, but her eyes darted back to locate Bannon. Being around a famous person was like being near a lighthouse, her very presence a sweeping beam of light at once attracting your attention and warding you off. Clara watched Bannon cross the room, cocktail in hand. She paused to let one of the teamsters light her cigarette, and the rowdy conversation came to an abrupt halt as the men watched her. But Bannon didn't linger. She sailed away, just out of reach.

After making tragic noises about the murder—the shock, the injustice, and some blaming studio security—the crew settled into their drinks and their anecdotes. Clara observed them.

Their initial awkwardness had worn off. They could have been at any party. Had they forgotten why they were here? She supposed it was natural. Life was for living. But as the chatter and laughter grew, an acute sense of loneliness flooded over her.

She overheard Randall Holden chatting with the director of photography. "Billy Wilder told me once," he said, leaning in conspiratorially, "that he never dates his leading lady. But the stand-in . . ." He changed his voice to mimic Billy Wilder's German accent. "'Just as pretty but a lot less trouble.'" Both men burst out laughing, and Clara felt rage bubble up on Connie's behalf. The stand-in. She's no trouble. Treat her however you want. A below-the-line girl, a nobody, someone replaceable. No one cared. Clara summoned Connie's face from the newsprint. She felt a stinging prickle behind her eyes, a sharpness in the back of her throat. Her breath was hot. Fighting tears, she got up and left the room.

In the powder room next to the entryway, Clara splashed water on her face. On the wall there was a framed snapshot of Bannon and Quinn by the pool. Staring at them looking happy together, Clara had a vague recollection of a photo spread in *House Beautiful*, back when Quinn was alive. *Gregory Quinn and Barbara Bannon open the doors to their hacienda in the Hollywood Hills.* Clara had been sitting at the hairdresser's, poring over the color photos—the same Moroccan tile, the same pool and stone patio. The article was fawning, of course. Quinn and Bannon played the part easily because they were truly in love. There had been a dog in those pictures—up on the lounger next to Bannon, floppy ears, lolling tongue. What was his name? Arthur, Augustus—something amusing and dignified that didn't suit. There was no dog now.

Clara left the powder room and strolled around the main floor, voices and laughter drifting in and out from the living room. She could hear Babe entertaining the crew by reading her own obituaries. Peals of laughter and boos would rise and fall. "'This column was not always a fan of her personal life.' You don't say," Bannon quipped, and someone snickered. "'But she had talent and beauty to burn.'"

Clara recognized the column: Hedda Hopper's Hollywood. She had read the same obituary on the way to work on the streetcar. Hedda Hopper had always been critical of Barbara Bannon and hadn't approved of her romance with Quinn, given that he'd technically still been married when they met. And over the years Bannon had been a target of Hopper's barbs lamenting Hollywood morals.

Clara found herself in a long arched hallway off the dining room. The floor was covered with shiny terra-cotta tile, and the walls were lined with framed posters of Bannon's films, as well as Quinn's earlier movies. Clara stopped in front of the poster for *Nightshade*—Babe Bannon's breakout role. In the illustration, Babe was painted in high-gloss Technicolor, and was cheek to cheek with Gregory Quinn. The golden couple. They looked perfect together—any age difference melted away.

As Clara reached the end of the hallway and the last framed movie poster, she heard voices, hushed but arguing. She froze in place and listened. The voices were coming from a little room off the side patio. It wasn't lit, but she'd assumed it was a small office or a sunroom.

"Jesus, relax, will you?" She recognized the voice of Howard Hawks, the director, because she'd heard it dozens of times on the dailies footage, snapping at the crew and barking at Bannon. "No one will find out. Besides, she's alive and well. Don't worry about it." Clara held her breath as she strained to listen, but the other voice was indistinct. She heard the snap of a lighter. A door opened and the voices faded. She could smell cigar smoke drifting inside from the patio.

Clara waited in the hallway for a few minutes to make sure the coast was clear. She repeated the words in her head. What was that about? Feeling like a trespasser, she thought it wise to return to the living room. As she walked back along the hallway, she heard a footstep on the tile. She spun around, her heart pounding.

"Escaping the crowd?" Gil smiled at her, and she felt instantly relieved, and grateful that he'd come to find her.

"Something like that."

He drew alongside her, and she caught a hint of cigar smoke. Was *he* the other party in the conversation she had just overheard? "Did you come from outside?" she asked.

"Yeah, I was looking for you." His eyes flickered over the poster of *Nightshade.* "Hollywood parties aren't really my scene. Wanna get out of here?"

Clara nodded. "You read my mind."

To get to the front door they had to cross the living room, where they found a dramatic performance underway: Babe Bannon, script in hand, voicing an unflattering impersonation of her co-star, while the gaffer (pitching his voice higher) did Bannon's dialogue. The crew were in stitches—Randall Ford being the exception. He stewed near the patio doors. Bannon had the entire room captivated. It was at that moment, at the climax of her dramatic performance, with everyone in stitches and the booze still flowing, that the cops showed up.

The room hushed as Detectives Ireland and Rivetti strode across the rug, removing their hats. Just behind them was Conrad Pearce, the studio head. His arrival had more of an effect than that of the detectives, and the gaffer instantly sat up from his comically seductive pose on the couch.

"The door was open," Ireland said, jerking his thumb toward the entryway.

"The grown-ups have arrived," Bannon drawled. "Here to break up the party?"

"Sorry, folks." Ireland gave an unconvincing smile.

Pearce folded his arms and gave the detectives a terse nod. Ireland stood in the center of the rug and addressed the crew. "Connie Milligan has been officially identified by the next of kin. Cause of death was strangulation." The crew shifted uneasily; they looked guilty for having a good time.

"Poor kid," said Bannon. She hugged the script to her chest.

The cops' arrival had dampened everyone's mood; the reality of the murder had set in again, and people began to leave. Clara was used to this change in tone. It was the same at her parents' refugee parties. There would come a certain point in the evening when the past would rush in—a shadow cast at a moment of merriment. Someone would start crying, the music would stop, and Clara would be asked to make a pot of coffee.

As the party quickly thinned, the detectives approached Babe. "A word, Miss Bannon. In private." Babe showed them outside to the patio, still clutching her script. The detectives closed the patio doors behind them.

"Let's go," said Gil, with a light touch on her back.

But just then Brackett summoned him to a huddle with Mr. Pearce and Howard Hawks. "Could use your input on this schedule, old sport."

Gil gave Clara a resigned smile. "Back in a minute."

Clara could hear car doors slam and tires on gravel as people left. Waiting for Gil and not wanting to hover, she gravitated to Bannon's kitchen, which partially overlooked the patio and pool. Maybe a window was open so that she could hear something. The kitchen was a mess of glasses and picked-over plates of cold salmon and roast chicken—the crew hadn't had much of an appetite. Clara got the coffee percolating and found some cups. She lingered by the window. The detectives were shadows on the patio. Bannon was pacing; the edge of her gown would catch the pool lights every so often. Unable to resist the prickle in her fingertips, Clara unfastened the catch and gently pushed open the window.

"Did she have a date that night?" It was Ireland's voice. Clara waited for the answer.

"That's what I assumed," said Bannon, a little edge to her voice.

"Who with?" asked Rivetti.

"I don't know, Detective." She sounded impatient. "She was my stand-in, not my best friend. I told her sure, she could use my dressing room. I didn't hang around and give her the third degree."

Clara's heart thumped with this new piece of knowledge. Connie had had a date the night she was killed—with Lloyd? And she never showed. Is that why he'd suspected something was wrong this morning? Clara leaned closer to the window to catch what they were saying next.

"What time did you leave the lot?" Ireland again.

"I don't know, exactly," said Bannon.

"Big Bear—that's quite a drive, late at night." Clara couldn't tell if it was Ireland or Rivetti. Their voices were fainter.

Bannon must have turned away, because Clara couldn't discern more than a mumble now, the voices tuning in and out like a radio frequency. Clara stood there frozen, straining for intelligible words. But all she could hear was her pulse thumping in her ears.

The coffeepot hissed and sputtered, and Clara started. She

attended to the coffee and went to the icebox to get the cream. There was no cream; there was no real food at all. Instead she found bottles of champagne, exotic fruit, small jars of expensive-looking pâté, smoked oysters, and olives.

"That coffee ready?"

Clara spun around, as though she'd been caught stealing. It was Detective Rivetti. "Get a cup for Miss Bannon." He jerked his head in the direction of the patio. "She should go easy on those highballs."

Clara poured a cup of black coffee. She felt the uptick of her pulse as she realized that an audience with Bannon awaited. She walked through the living room toward the patio doors and cast a glance at Gil—stuck in a huddle of studio people and now joined by the detectives. Quietly she let herself out the patio door, heart thumping against her rib cage, the cup rattling in its saucer.

She found Bannon lying in the dark on a sun lounger, gripping her highball, staring at the pool. The underwater lights cast an eerie glow across her face.

Clara needed both hands to still the cup and saucer as she drew next to the movie star. She cleared her throat to announce herself, feeling silly, like a butler in an old movie. She put the cup on a side table next to the lounger.

Bannon glanced at the coffee. "Thanks, honey." An invisible string pulled a smile like a reflex, then slackened. The script sat on her lap covered in ring marks from her glass.

"Are you all right, Miss Bannon?" Clara nearly bit her lip at the sound of her schoolgirl voice.

"Sit with me," Bannon said. Her voice was low and rich. It was an appeal rather than an order. Who wouldn't oblige this woman?

Clara sank down onto the other lounger. The seat was too low to sit comfortably. She hunched over, her knees almost brushing her chin. She was the opposite of Bannon's relaxed grace, legs stretched out as though posing for a photo shoot.

Bannon looked down at the script on her lap. "Connie left this in my dressing room." A long beat. "The cops said she fought back." Her words had a rough edge.

Clara shifted in her seat, unsure what to say. "I was the one who found her." Bannon's head snapped up. Clara went on, "The left side of her face was badly beaten. With the costume and the blond hair, I assumed . . ."

Bannon swirled the remains of her drink around, the ice cubes long since melted. "I hope they fry the bastard."

Clara recalled Connie's photo in the paper, her sunny smile. "Me too."

They sat in silence, save for the whirring of a cricket. Clara couldn't resist the itch of curiosity. "What was she like? Connie?"

Bannon shook her head. "I didn't really know her." The actress tossed the dregs of her cocktail into a planter and set the glass down hard on the tile patio. "I mean, sure, we talked on set a few times, between setups, if I didn't go back to my dressing room. She was new; I didn't take the time."

Clara leaned forward. "Do the cops have any leads?"

Bannon rolled her eyes. "They're going to put a squad car out in front of the house. Keep an eye on me."

"Why? They think . . . ?"

"That it was supposed to be me in the vault—it's a theory." She gave a hard little laugh. "Between me and the stand-in—who do you think has more enemies in this town?" Clara watched her closely, and wondered if the movie star seemed a bit reckless. There was a fire in her eye, something simmering beneath the surface.

Clara glanced back to the house. She should get going.

"You're Gil's girl?" Bannon asked, out of nowhere.

"We're friends," said Clara, a hint defensive. She folded her arms across her chest.

"Ah." Babe smirked and let her eyes rest on Clara. "I used to be friends with him too." Her voice was feather light.

"I know," said Clara, not wanting her to think Gil kept things from her. "The acting class."

Babe barked a laugh. "I thought he tried to blot out that memory." Her gaze drifted past Clara. "August '42," she said, reminiscing. She shook her head softly and sighed. "The end of something—of Ruby, I suppose, and the start of a new life."

It was the same feeling as the projector coming to life on the big screen, like a movie playing as she spoke. Barbara Bannon—back when she'd been Ruby Kaminsky, back before Gil had been called up. Together in acting class. *Together.*

"He liked me better back then," Babe said, her voice harder. "I was someone else, someone nicer."

Clara flushed crimson in the darkness. The realization illuminated like a neon sign on Sunset: *Love.* Bright pink letters pulsing in the sky over the pool—flashing at her, mocking her. Gil and Babe Bannon.

Of course. He had been in love with her.

Clara replayed their conversation, the night of the murder when he drove her home. He had said nothing to imply a relationship, but from the way Bannon spoke, there was no denying it. Clara had been caught up with her own confession that night, and she hadn't pressed him on his history with Ruby.

Bannon picked up the script on her lap. *"Letter from Argentan.* Christ—who wants to see a war picture these days?" Without warning, she flung the script into the pool. They watched it bob for a moment before it settled into a teetering glide. The underwater lights illuminated its progress as it reached the other side of the pool, water soaking through the pages marked *Property of Silver Pacific Studios.*

Abruptly Bannon pulled herself out of the sun lounger and disappeared inside. Clara glanced at the untouched cup of coffee and shivered. She should find Gil, get a ride home. But her gaze was drawn back to the pool. Before she could second-guess herself, she had darted around to the far side. She knelt down. It was a stretch, but she fished the sodden script out of the water and laid it on the tile in a puddle of water.

Connie's copy of the script. Why had Bannon hung on to it? Clara squinted at it. There was handwriting on the cover page. The ink had run, but it looked like a phone number. She angled it to the light. Maybe *Spring 3191* or something close to it. Impetuously Clara tore off the page and folded it up into a neat square.

"Clara?"

She started at the sound of a male voice and saw Gil standing at the open patio door, shards of light from the house slicing across his face.

"Come on. Let's go."

They drove along the canyon ridge, and Clara gripped the soft leather of her seat. She could feel the growl of the engine vibrating underneath her, the conversation with Bannon turning over in her mind. Clara had gone to the party to find out something about Connie Milligan. Instead, she had learned more than she bargained for about Babe Bannon. She replayed the moment after they'd arrived, when the movie star had leaned forward and Gil had kissed her cheek.

*Is he still in love with her?*

A breeze whispered through the canyon and snaked across Clara's neck. With the breath of air, she felt a presence, as though Babe Bannon herself was perched on the rumble seat behind them, enjoying the drama she had caused.

Around a bend, the city came into view; the city lights glittered for miles.

"I wonder what the cops wanted?" said Gil, downshifting. "They didn't drive up the canyon for nothing."

"I overheard them talking to Babe." Saying her name aloud gave Clara a small charge of electricity. "She had let Connie use her dressing room that night."

Gil shook his head. "Poor kid." It was the same thing Bannon had said. "They're looking at Tuesday," he went on, "to start filming again—they're not missing a beat."

"Right," said Clara. "The stand-in can easily be replaced, but not Barbara Bannon." She watched him to see if this sparked something.

Clara decided she wouldn't divulge that she knew about Gil's past with Ruby. Instinctively she felt that it was something to hold close, something she shouldn't give away. They drove down the canyon into the beating heart of the city.

## Chapter Nine

# Home

BY THE TIME CLARA crept into her parents' house, it was after midnight. She hung up her jacket and silently slipped off her shoes. Her stealth was unnecessary. As she tiptoed past the sitting room, a light snapped on and her mother leapt off the couch like a coiled spring. "Where have you been?" Her distraught face loomed toward Clara in the dim light.

"I should have called," Clara said. "I didn't mean for you to wait up." Without warning her mother embraced her right there in the hall, with a force that took Clara by surprise. "*Klara*," she whispered. When she finally let go, her eyes were moist with tears. Clara knew instantly: they had found out about the murder. She had been so caught up with Barbara Bannon and the party with the crew that she had totally forgotten about her parents.

"*Mutti*, I'm all right." She tried a reassuring smile. Clara hated seeing her mother cry. It was like watching a treasured vase or ornament slip from your grasp and smash to pieces.

"Come and talk to us." Her mother led her to the living room, where her father was dozing in his armchair, a book open on his lap. The floorboards creaked, and he stirred.

"Klara," he said in a croaky voice, coming to. "There you are. We've been worried about you." He removed his glasses and pinched the bridge of his nose. He gestured to the newspaper on the coffee table. "We read about what happened at the studio."

"It's horrendous," said her mother.

Clara reluctantly took a seat next to her on the couch. She recognized her mother's familiar "wartime" expression. It brought back memories of all the evenings they'd spent huddled around the radio, listening to endless BBC World Service reports of bad news: the fall of Holland and France; troops stranded at Dunkirk; the shock of Pearl Harbor.

"A young woman was really murdered?" her mother asked.

Clara nodded. "I'm sorry. I should have told you myself. . . ." She trailed off.

"Max gave us the details." Her father looked grave. "He says you found her?"

"That's right," Clara whispered.

"Why didn't you say something last night?" her mother added in a rush, her face a mixture of exasperation and concern.

"Your celebration," said Clara. "I couldn't ruin it."

Her mother's hands were tightly clasped. "Of course you should have come to us—celebration or not. And what about this morning? When we were sitting at breakfast?" She let out an exasperated sigh. "But no—you dashed out of the house and went back there," she hissed, "to that studio." She shook her head. "I blame Max, getting you the job in the first place."

"Inge," her father pleaded. "That's not helpful right now." He turned to Clara. "Tell us what happened. She was an actress—is that right?"

Her mother gave a theatrical shudder. The more excitable she got, the calmer Clara tried to appear. "She wasn't an actress; she was the stand-in."

"Stand-in?" Her mother looked to Clara's father. "*Was ist ein 'stand-in'?*"

In spite of feeling guilty for not telling her parents about the murder, she felt irritated by her mother, who could be willfully obtuse when it came to the English language. It brought back scenes of deep embarrassment: with shop assistants and bank clerks, even passersby on the street—someone innocently asking directions—and her mother's ensuing panic. Clara always had to translate. She was the buffer between her mother and the American public, blushing, apologizing for her mother's halting English and cringing at her German consonants.

"Similar to an understudy in the theater?" her father said.

"No," said Clara, losing her patience. "She can't replace the movie star. She never appears on film. She *stands in* for the actress when they're setting up—lighting, blocking. You know, so the actress doesn't have to wait around for ages on set. Never mind—it's not important."

"Where were you tonight?" asked her father gently.

"We were worried sick when you didn't come home," said

her mother. "We called Max. He said you must be with your boyfriend."

Clara cringed.

"'Klara has no boyfriend,' I assured him. Joke's on me, apparently." She pressed her lips together in indignation.

"Inge." Her father tried to signal his wife that she was getting off topic, that she wasn't helping.

But her mother couldn't resist. "Max says he's older than you and drives a convertible."

"We're just friends," Clara snapped, then instantly wished she hadn't. Her parents and Max were worried about her, that's all. "I was out with the crew," she said in a softer tone. "They wanted to take a moment to remember Connie."

"Is that the poor young woman?" her father asked. Clara nodded. "We're glad you're home safe."

His kindness made Clara feel worse. She plucked at a thread on the couch cushion. "I'm sorry. You should have heard about the murder from me—not from Max or the newspaper. I suppose I thought you'd had enough bad news."

"Have they arrested anyone? Do they have any idea who would do such a thing?" he asked.

Clara shook her head. "I don't know. I don't think so."

"To think it could have been *you*, Klara." Her mother shook her head, her lips trembling. "What if it was minutes later and you crossed paths with this murderer?"

"She's home now." Her father tried to soothe her mother's agitation. "Klara, I'm sure your employer will understand, given the circumstances, if you hand in your notice now. You'll be leaving in a month anyway. What's a few weeks earlier? Surely they can't expect you to return to work after what happened. Obviously it's not a safe place."

Clara stiffened. Her parents had firm expectations that she would finally enroll at university—*a proper European institution.* Probably the same one her father was going to be teaching at. For them, life in America had been a hiatus, and now it was time to go home. Home was Germany. How could Clara tell them she was already home, that she felt more American than German? How could they understand her absolute dread of being, once again, considered an outsider, her fear that Germans would surely detect something "off" in her accent, and in her limited eleven-year-old's vocabulary? Clara had come to recognize her mother's sharp look of betrayal when Clara spoke in English—perfect American English. It conjured her Italian teacher, tapping on the blackboard and saying, "*Traduttore, traditore.* 'Translator, traitor.'"

There was no "good time" to come clean. She had to stop keeping secrets. Clara sat forward on the couch; her mouth felt dry. "About the studio, that's the thing, Papa." She swallowed and forced herself to keep going. "You weren't the only one who was offered a new job. I've been promoted to apprentice editor. It's a union position and the pay is better. If I work hard, I can become an assistant editor and it's possible—one day—a film editor."

Her mother regarded her with a baffled expression, as

though she were speaking a foreign language. "Klara, what are you saying?"

"I want to become a film editor." Clara's gaze darted between her parents—they both looked bewildered.

"What?" said her mother, peering at her.

"I don't want to go back to Europe," she blurted out. "I want to stay here in Los Angeles." The admission was a jolt of electricity that had finally completed a circuit—the words felt charged and dangerous.

"How can you—you don't mean that, Klara, surely?" said her father, puzzled.

"Stay here by yourself? Nonsense!" said her mother. "You're too young. You belong with your family, not alone in Los Angeles. And as for that *studio*—a woman was murdered. No one should be working there until they find the culprit."

Clara's shoulders sank. Their reaction was just as she had expected—they still thought of her as a child. And the murder only made it worse. They all sat for a while saying nothing, just the chill of Clara's admission between them. She surveyed the room, all the books, their spines as familiar as wallpaper, the clock on the mantel, the piano. Soon the set dressing of their time in Los Angeles would be dismantled, a film set struck. A part of their lives over and done with. She should have felt relief at having finally told her parents the truth, but she felt unsure. What if the job didn't pan out? Bannon was alive, but production hadn't yet resumed. What if Clara messed up at work and

Sam fired her? What if she couldn't afford to live on her own? What if she was lonely? After the murder, LA felt more dangerous. These doubts began to churn, but it was too late to take it back. The thing had been said.

Her mother got up. "I think I'll go to bed. It's been a long day." She plumped the sofa cushions vigorously, fighting tears. Clara felt responsible, and she couldn't think of a reassuring thing to say. Everything had changed.

Her father got to his feet and put his book on the coffee table. "Yes, it's late." He patted Clara's hand. "We can talk more tomorrow," he said. "Get some sleep."

That night Clara dreamed she was back in the vaults, returning the *Argentan* reels. In the dream she knew what to expect—she was braced for the discovery—but when she checked the floor, there was no sign of blond hair poking out from under the door. Heart racing, she opened vault five, and to her astonishment there was no body—just neat racks of film canisters. A huge wave of relief washed over her; she almost laughed with the lightness of that feeling in her dream. But as she turned, a shadow lunged for her. Before she could react, there was a cord snug around her neck, squeezing tighter and tighter. She woke up in a sweat, fighting her tangle of sheets.

After her heart had stopped hammering and her familiar bedroom had replaced the feeling of being in the vaults, Clara lay awake thinking about Connie. *What happened to her?* Who had she been meeting that night, looking like a movie star?

Clara couldn't get back to sleep. She lay awake thinking of all the secrets she had been hoarding: her promotion, her editing ambitions, her plan to stay on in Los Angeles. And then there was Gil and his past with Barbara Bannon. Out of nowhere a memory surfaced. Over lunch in the commissary, Gil had been complaining about Roger Brackett's long-winded phone calls catching up with theater friends, and trading gossip. Gil had been bemoaning the thinness of the office walls—he had had to plug his ears with cotton to drown Roger out. That meant he *must* have heard the phone ring the night of the murder. Had he been avoiding her call? Had he been blowing her off? Maybe Gil had lied to the cops and he wasn't in his office that night. Or Mr. Brackett's. But then, where was he?

She heard Detective Ireland's voice addressing the crew: *Most murders are committed by someone the victim knows— often, in the case of a female victim, by someone she was romantically involved with.*

No, that was absurd. She wrestled with the stew of uneasy thoughts until she finally fell asleep.

"Sort through those magazines, Klara," her mother called out from the next room. "I expect you'll need to get rid of most of them." It was Sunday, and their small house was turned upside down. Her mother was a whirling dervish of spring cleaning and organization: cupboards and drawers were emptied and cleaned. Items were sorted into three piles—one to keep, one to sell, and a third for donation. A further collection—to give to friends—accumulated on the sideboard. It was the first step in the dismantling of their American lives. In response to Clara's confession that she wanted to stay in Los Angeles, her mother simply pretended it hadn't happened. She'd cheerfully gone about her work on Saturday and into Sunday as if nothing had changed. Clara understood her tactic; she had been wounded, and her knee-jerk response was denial. Her parents probably assumed that her desire to stay on and work at the studio wasn't serious, that she would inevitably cave. It was an uneasy truce.

Clara lay sprawled on her bed, poring over the classifieds, circling apartments for rent. Her approach was to not rock the boat. She agreed to go through her bedroom closet (which, if she moved to an apartment in Hollywood, she reasoned, she'd have to sort through anyway). Clara could hear her mother in the hallway talking to her father. "You're just as bad, Heinrich. You can't keep every newspaper since coming to America."

It was true, her father had piles of newspapers from their first weeks in America, and after that he had continued to archive the momentous war headlines: GERMAN ARMY INVADES POLAND; ALLIED LANDINGS BEGUN IN FRANCE; FULL VICTORY IN EUROPE. His tiny study was still home to yellowed piles of newsprint and drafts of his academic papers strewn about the floor. His typewriter and its familiar tapping, a soundtrack to her childhood. A sharp pang when she remembered all of that familiarity would be gone with her parents. If only she could keep some things under glass like a snow globe.

Clara rubbed her eyes. They smarted from staring at the small print in the paper. She noticed the box of keepsakes poking out from under her bed. She picked it up and emptied the contents onto the bed. From among the papers, ticket stubs, and receipts, she retrieved the fragile daisy chain and placed it carefully on her head. She got up, went to the mirror, and stared at herself, imagining her childhood friend Freya behind her, a blond twin, the same plaits and rosy cheeks. *Deutsche Mädels.* It was Matthias's voice in her head—"German maidens."

The end of summer, 1938. Matthias was Freya's elder brother. How could a fourteen-year-old boy have seemed worldly to her? But Klara had been only eleven at the time. He had returned from a camping trip full of stories of adventure. They had pitched the tent on the lawn. She could still conjure the smell of canvas and grass clippings; the taste of Frau Thome's *Baumkuchen.* They had sung camp songs in the dying light. A wave of longing swept over her.

"Klara, come now. You're playing dress-up?" Clara's mother entered the room without knocking. She marched across the rug, still buzzing with energy from all the activity in the house. "Did you sort your clothes?"

"Yes," said Clara, removing the flower crown, shedding dried petals onto the floor.

Her mother prodded the pile on the bed. "These for donation?" She flipped through them, a quick inventory. She retrieved a raspberry-colored skirt from the pile. "Oh, I remember this color on you."

Clara laid the daisy chain on the bed and once more caught sight of the mysterious handkerchief.

"It really doesn't fit anymore?" Her mother held up the skirt next to Clara. "That's a pity."

"*Mutti,* have you seen this before?" Clara unfolded the handkerchief. "Do you recognize it?"

Her mother took it and examined the embroidered initials. *LR.* Her forehead wrinkled. "Who is LR?" she asked.

"That's it—I don't know. Did someone give it to me before we left Berlin? A friend or neighbor?"

"No idea." Her mother shrugged and returned it. "But it looks expensive; that lace is hand-stitched."

Her mother's gaze landed on the newspaper classifieds. There was an awkward silence. Clara could see her mother steel herself. Then she abruptly scooped up the pile of clothes for donation, and bustled away.

## Chapter Ten

# The Silver Blonde

WHEN CLARA WALKED INTO the accounting department on Monday morning, the chatter stopped. Doris, who usually didn't look up from her typewriter, sprang to her feet. "Clara."

"Hi," said Clara cautiously. She was about to put her paperwork in the correct cubby when Doris rushed over, hand outstretched, coral nails flashing. "I'll take that," she said with an eager smile.

Normally Clara would have deposited whatever paperwork she had—time cards, purchase orders, petty cash envelopes—then leave without saying a word. A little bemused, she handed her papers to Doris across the wooden counter. "It's the start papers for my new position."

"Congratulations. What's the job?" asked Doris, her eyes wide, corkscrew curls trembling. Clara noticed that the other accounting clerks, Rita and Marianne, were watching in pin-drop silence.

"Apprentice editor. I'm working with Sam."

Doris nodded sympathetically. "I guess they didn't want you going back to the vaults again." A knowing look. "You must be so relieved."

Clara wasn't about to explain that her apprentice job had nothing to do with the murder, that it wasn't some consolation prize handed out because the studio felt bad—that, in actual fact, she had earned the new job.

She forced a smile through her irritation. "Sure, I'm glad of the promotion." But was she? It was her first day as apprentice editor—she'd gotten what she wanted—but it felt anticlimactic. The filming of *Argentan* wouldn't resume until tomorrow, and editorial wouldn't have new footage until Wednesday. Sam hadn't even shown up to work yet. Clara had spent the first hour of her morning trying out different combinations of the telephone number on Connie's script. SP 3191, which was short for the telephone exchange Spring 3191, or perhaps Spruce 3191. Unless the nine was a seven—and had that three originally been an eight? She'd gotten nowhere—a beauty salon, a grumpy old man, an accounting firm, and a couple of hang-ups. She had spent the next twenty minutes spinning her wheels, before deciding that a trip to accounting would give her *something* to do.

Marianne, the quiet one with the pale blue eyes and lashes so fair they were invisible, rolled her chair closer. "Are you okay, you know, after what you saw?"

Rita drifted over and dropped an envelope into the outgoing-mail tray. "It's awful," she said. "That poor girl." She sounded full of awe rather than pity.

Clara surveyed the three of them over the counter. She wasn't fooled by their sudden interest in her. It wasn't friendliness, or concern—it was curiosity. Their ears were pricked, their eyes hungry, and they were almost salivating. What they really wanted was gossip; they wanted gory details; they wanted the murder.

"I'm surprised you came back to work," Rita said, waggling her pen back and forth, majorette style, between her fingers. She had hair like the Dreyers' spaniel, dark and wavy. "I wouldn't blame you if you quit." Her head was cocked to one side, her eyes bright.

"I'm fine. Thanks for asking."

Normally when Clara entered accounting, the girls would be gossiping and blatantly ignore her. She knew that they thought she was stuck up. Clara was a loner who didn't belong to a group, which made her hard to classify. She would survey them coolly, stuck behind their typewriters, while she was armed with her cans of film. It put a zip in her step to think of them trapped at their desks, sullen and bored, typing contracts, punching numbers, licking stamps. What did they know about filmmaking? A brush with stardom, a celebrity sighting, or a secondhand anecdote was as close as they would come to film. They might work at the studio, but they would never conquer it like Clara was planning to.

"I mean," Marianne stage-whispered, "are any of us even safe at the studio?" They were all relishing the crime, like passersby rubbernecking at a car crash. Doris darted to her desk and grabbed the newspaper. She snapped it open and held it up. THE SILVER BLONDE MURDER was splashed across the front page.

Clara had seen the headlines. On the streetcar that morning the man seated next to her had been poring over the same article. The reference was a nod to the studio's heyday when the contract starlet du jour—always a blonde—would be the face of the Silver Pacific logo, the figure in Grecian robes at the start of every movie. The newspaper hacks had needed a moniker for Connie Milligan. She hadn't been a movie star or a celebrity—she wouldn't be selling papers with her own name. Connie was a below-the-line girl no one had heard of, just like Clara and the accounting girls. It could just as easily have been one of them.

"Did you know her?" Rita asked Clara.

Clara shook her head. "No."

"I loaned her a bobby pin once," said Marianne. "We were in the ladies by the commissary."

"You don't know it was her," said Doris, rolling her eyes.

"I have an excellent memory for faces," replied Marianne, indignant.

"Did the cops tell you anything?" asked Rita.

"Do they have any leads, or a suspect?" Doris chimed in. "What have you heard?"

To be in the center of a gaggle of girls, that rush of energy, the intensity, it had been a long time since Clara had felt part of a group like that. "They didn't tell me anything," she admitted. Technically this was true. It was Babe Bannon who revealed the cops' theory that the killer might have gotten the wrong girl. The accounting girls would eat this up, of course, but Clara didn't feel like sharing. She was guarded about the details of the case.

Rita leaned on the counter. "I saw Connie Milligan and that fellow you work with—the redhead." Her eyes were steady on Clara.

"You mean Lloyd? Yes, they were friends."

"You should keep your eye on him," said Rita darkly.

"Lloyd?" Clara let out a laugh.

"I'm serious." Rita cast a furtive glance at the others.

Clara's mind was whirring. They knew something, and they might be persuaded to share, but she would have to give something to get something. Clara leaned her elbows on the counter that separated them. "I did overhear something." She took her time, and the accounting girls held their breath. "The cops said Connie borrowed Babe Bannon's dressing room the night she was murdered. They think she was getting ready for a date."

Doris jumped in. "With the vault boy?"

"Maybe," said Clara, wanting to tease out more information. "What do you have against Lloyd?"

Marianne and Doris looked to Rita, who pretended to struggle with whether to share her story. She tossed her hair back. "When I started at the studio, back in the fall, I was at a diner on

Melrose. I was sitting up at the counter having a soda, and Lloyd was in a booth with his uncle—the casting executive Trace Lester, as I later found out. Lloyd came up to me, asked if I'd ever considered being "in movies," layering on the compliments. I wasn't about to tell him I was only an accounting clerk. He gave me his uncle's Silver Pacific business card, wrote his own name on the back, and said to call the office and mention 'Lloyd,' and that would get me past the secretary."

"Did you call?" asked Clara.

"What do you think? Of course I did—I was curious. 'Actress' sounds more exciting than 'accountant.' Like Lloyd said, I got straight through to Mr. Lester, who told me to come in for an audition at seven-thirty p.m."

Clara's stomach tightened; she saw where this was leading. "And the audition?"

Rita composed herself. "Compliments one second, hands everywhere the next. When I told him to back off, he followed up with threats: 'You'll never make it as an actress without some help; you don't want to be blacklisted.' I pushed him off and told him where to stick his threats. I told him that acting was a lark but I wasn't serious. I already had a decent job in accounting at this very studio, and the head accountant wouldn't be amused if I told him what Mr. Lester was proposing. After I said that, he changed his tune and apologized." She shuddered. "I hightailed it out of there."

"And did you tell your boss?"

"What would I say? It's my own fault—audition after hours." Rita shook her head. "I blame Lloyd, of course. He acts the innocent, he's the seemingly harmless lure teeing up Red Riding Hood for auditions with the Wolf."

"I had no idea," said Clara, horrified. She wondered how much Lloyd knew about his uncle's "casting" methods.

"What if Connie met Lloyd the same way Rita did?" Doris said. "But *she* played along?"

Clara nodded, considering it. "The detectives said she worked at the Vista as an usherette and did some background work. To go from that to—"

"Stand-in for a big movie star," Marianne said, finishing her sentence. "It's a plum job."

Rita folded her arms with a *Told you so* expression. "Somebody pulled strings for her."

Doris's phone rang, and at the same time the payroll accountant came out of his office, asking Rita to find a contract. Their chitchat was over and the girls filed back to their desks.

After accounting, Clara headed straight for the film archive. She mulled it over. She'd heard stories about the film industry and the casting couch—but that was nothing to do with *her* world in postproduction, and it always struck her as an exaggeration or not the kind of thing that could possibly go on at Silver Pacific. Now she felt foolish and naive. The thought of Lloyd being mixed up in this turned her stomach. He always bragged about his uncle, which irked Miss Simkin, who knew it would only be a matter of time before Lloyd was promoted to some executive office and given four times her salary.

When she entered the film archive, there was a new boy at her desk—her replacement. "Is Lloyd around?" asked Clara, not bothering to introduce herself. The new kid—skinny with acne scars—appeared petrified by Clara's question. He didn't have a chance to answer.

"Lloyd's not in this morning." Miss Simkin materialized in the doorway of her office.

"Is he sick?" said Clara innocently, probing for more information.

"He'll be in tomorrow." By her tone of voice and pinched face, Clara knew that Simkin wouldn't reveal more. Clara's mind started spinning with possible scenarios.

"Did you meet Walter, your replacement?" said Simkin, changing the subject. "He's just finding his feet." Simkin gave him a decisive nod, as close to a smile as she knew how, and Walter shifted in his seat. Miss Simkin pointed to the stack of reels on Clara's old desk. "Given that we're a bit shorthanded, Clara, would you mind giving these reels to Max?" Clara opened her mouth to make an excuse, but Simkin was ready for it. "Sam's not going to have much for you to do this morning; there's no new footage." Before Clara could push back, Miss Simkin was handing over the film canisters.

\*   \*   \*

Clara's first official day as apprentice editor, and here she was running reels to the screening room. She could have kicked herself for setting foot in the archive. Would she ever be free of Miss Simkin's marching orders? Clara skirted the fountain outside the grand art deco entrance of the executive building. Balancing the film canisters under one arm, she opened the door and crossed the marble lobby, which was lined with photographs of the studio's early days as well as its biggest contract stars.

In the executive building she usually felt a heightened awareness of other people, the prickle of static, the pulse of possibility. Film stars could often be glimpsed crossing the lobby, going to meetings with Mr. Pearce, or chatting with one of his flock of executives. But today she didn't even slow her pace by the awards cabinet. The Oscar statues couldn't distract her. As she descended the stairwell leading to the basement level and Mr. Pearce's screening room, all she could think about was Connie's murder.

She had several unanswered questions: Connie and Lloyd. What was their backstory, how had she landed the stand-in job, and had it involved Lloyd's uncle? Whose phone number did Connie write on her script, and did it have something to do with her date the night she was killed? And then there was Babe Bannon. *Could* she have been the intended victim, or were the cops just paying lip service to a film star? And the night of the party, who was Hawks telling not to worry? *No one will find out— besides, she's alive and well.* All these questions hung like the selects of footage in Sam's trim bin, not yet cut together. If Clara could find some answers, the pieces would fit together and tell a story—the truth of what had happened to Connie.

Along the basement corridor, Clara passed the framed photographs of behind-the-scenes shots—they were all candid pictures taken on various film sets, and not the posed glamor shots on display in the lobby. She must have passed them dozens of times without noticing. But today one photograph caught her eye. Clara stopped and stared. It was a shot of Bette Davis and her stand-in. The caption was titled *Seeing Double.*

*Bette Davis (left) and her stand-in, Sally Sage, pictured together on the set and in costume. They resemble each other considerably and are the same size, even to shoes and gloves. They bring their knitting on set to help pass any idle moments.*

Clara moved closer. The women were similar, but they weren't twins. Bette Davis—instantly recognizable—was obviously the star. Her costume was more detailed and refined. The movie star and her shadow. How much had Connie truly resembled Babe Bannon? Clara had mistaken her in the vaults, but her headshot in the paper looked nothing like Bannon. Clara read the caption once more. The photographer's name was credited. And then it hit her: *still photography.* There would surely be behind-the-scenes photos like this from the *Argentan* set. If she could get her hands on those photos, what would they reveal?

## Chapter Eleven

# Stage Fourteen

AT THE END OF the day, when Clara stepped out of the post-production building, she spotted Gil leaning against a wall. The sun was low in the west, and it bathed the white stages and office buildings in golden light. Gil stubbed out his cigarette and sauntered toward her. "Wanna stroll for a minute?" he asked.

His question was casual, but knowing he had been waiting for her made Clara swell inside. "Sure."

"How was your first day?" Gil asked. "We missed you at lunch."

Clara smiled, feeling proud but not wanting to show it. "It was pretty good."

"No more slumming it with the writers," he teased.

After Sam had shown up, the day had moved into gear. Clara was shown the routine for dailies, organizing the paperwork—camera and sound reports, the script supervisor notes, and codebook logs. Sam had explained that the assistant editors on the Western next door would do the heavy lifting of syncing dailies and conforming reels. Eventually she would be trained to do these tasks as well. She had eaten lunch with Sam and the assistant editors. From time to time her eyes would flit to the writers' table, scanning for Gil. The afternoon sped past, and thoughts of Connie and her murder were pushed to the back of Clara's mind as she was happily distracted by her new job. All the chaos and upset of the past few days faded, and her film dreams came into sharper focus once more.

Gil gave Clara a friendly nudge. "Hey, I'm sorry about the other night—drinks at the Formosa. With everything that happened . . ." He trailed off. "How about tonight? You got plans?"

Clara was tempted. "I shouldn't," she sighed. "My folks are bent out of shape about me working at the studio. I promised them I'd be home for dinner tonight." It wasn't an excuse—it was the truth. But the minute she'd said it, she regretted refusing his offer.

Gil nodded. "No sweat."

Clara was glad he was trying to make it up to her, but she was still bothered. Where was he that night? She had to broach it somehow—there was something he wasn't telling her.

As if he could read her mind, he asked, "What's wrong? I saw you drift away for a second."

She shook her head. "It's nothing, really. It's just, on Thursday night I called your extension, and even if you were next door on Roger's couch, you would have heard the phone. Remember, you complained that the office walls were like paper?"

Gil stopped walking and turned to her. His blue eyes were like cut glass in the low sun. "You got a few minutes? I want to show you something." He sounded serious.

"Okay." A little unnerved, Clara strode with him along the alleyways between the vast stages, avoiding golf carts and trucks full of equipment. "Where are we going?" she asked.

His face was grave. "Not far." Finally they stopped in front of stage fourteen. "In here." He gestured to the side door, and they stepped out of Los Angeles and into the summer of 1944 and the Allied invasion of France. "The battle set," said Gil. His voice was a little thick. Clara had never seen this set before. It was the bombed-out town of Argentan in Normandy during the deadly eight-day skirmish. American troops had fought the Nazis for control of the town.

"God, it looks so real," said Clara. The designer had done an excellent job with the ruins of the French village: walls riddled with bullets, burned-out buildings, shell damage, everyday items—a child's pram, a lady's shoe—in piles of rubble.

"Watch your step." He took her hand and helped her over a pile of fake bricks.

There were a couple of art department guys—a plasterer and a matte painter—finishing some work. "Over here," said Gil, and they approached the matte painter. Gil nodded to him. "Mind if we take a look?"

The matte painter, in paint-speckled overalls, stepped off his apple box to let them look at his work. "Go ahead. Watch out— some of the brushwork isn't dry." He walked away, wiping his brushes on his overalls.

Clara climbed onto the apple box. It was a painting on a plate of glass that extended the bounds of the set to make it look as though there were a whole town in the background. When the camera was placed at the right position in front of the glass, the set would meld seamlessly with the painted extension.

"It's really neat," said Clara as the real set blended with the painted one. "It's like a magic trick."

"On film it will look even more convincing," said Gil, switching places with her to have a look.

"I don't get it," said Clara. "Why did you want to show me this?"

Gil got down off the apple box and they moved away from the matte painting. He stopped and surveyed the battle-scarred set. "You asked where I was the other night," said Gil, nudging a piece of masonry with his foot. "I wasn't at my desk. I was here."

Clara turned to him, puzzled. "Why?"

"On Friday we were supposed to shoot the flashback battle scenes. Brackett wanted me on set—normally he likes me chained to the typewriter, but on that day, because of my combat experience, Brackett thought it would be useful to have me around: 'Authenticity, old sport. Make sure they get it right,'" said Gil, impersonating Brackett.

"Oh," said Clara. "I see."

"I was preparing myself, I guess. Brackett never thought to ask whether I wanted to be back in a war zone." Gil rubbed a hand across his stubble.

Clara surveyed the set. "And all of this, it's too real," she said.

He nodded. The war loomed, that unspoken destroyer they chose not to talk about, the event that had shaped both their lives.

Gil bit his lip. "Sometimes I get these"—he blinked quickly—"these episodes, I guess you'd call it. Something will trigger it—a car backfiring, a clap of thunder, the smell and sound of fireworks. And when it hits, it's more than a memory." He took a sharp breath. "It's like my body thinks I'm back there. Adrenaline, fear, it shoots through me." He made a sweeping motion down his arm. "I break out in a sweat, I need to find cover—get my back against a wall, I'm reaching for my sidearm." His hand grasped to his right side where an imaginary pistol might be holstered. "You get the picture." He shook his head, suddenly self-conscious, and let out a long breath, the relief that comes after a confession.

"It's nothing to be ashamed of," said Clara.

"I'm like a dog on the Fourth of July, I guess—it's pathetic."

"Not at all; it makes sense." She put a hand on his arm and felt how tense he was. "Brackett's an idiot for not considering how it would affect you."

Gil sighed. "It's just pretend." He gestured to the set. "It's make-believe. Smoke and mirrors." He looked down, his expression pained.

"How long did you stay here, on the set?" she asked.

He gave a half shrug. "I don't know exactly. It brought back some memories, and I just sat with them for a bit." He ground a loose piece of plaster to dust.

As a rule, they never talked about the war, which suited Clara—skirting her German past was second nature. But she was curious about Gil's experience, so different from hers.

Clara turned back to look at the matte painting, but seen from the wrong angle, the effect vanished. "From over here, the painting looks unfinished—that big void in the middle," she commented.

Gil gave a hollow laugh. "Reminds me of how I felt when peace was declared—we'd won; I'd never felt so lost."

"I know what you mean," said Clara quietly. "I spent years wanting the war to end, and when it finally happened I realized that nothing would return to the way it was."

He shook his head softly. "It's too late, I guess." There was a crack in his voice. When their eyes met, Clara wanted to take him in her arms. She wanted to know all of his pain and take it away.

The matte painter approached them. "We're wrapping up for the day. Stage manager will lock up if you're done here."

Gil nodded. "Sure, we're done."

"Thanks," Clara added.

They headed for the stage door. "Hey, Clara." Gil scratched his head. "Look, you mind not saying anything about this to anyone?" He gave a throwaway shrug. "I don't, usually, you know, share that stuff."

"Of course I won't." She was flattered he had opened up to her—for once. She felt singled out. Worthy of his trust. He held the door open for her and she brushed past him—aftershave, cigarettes, body heat.

After they left the stage, they were bathed in warm light again and the memories of war shriveled and vanished. "Maybe tomorrow or Wednesday," Clara said casually. "Drinks after work."

Gil smiled into a slant of golden light, eyes twinkling. "It's a date."

## Chapter Twelve

# Rear Projection

THE NEXT MORNING CLARA was on a coffee run for the assistant editors when she finally caught sight of Lloyd. She hadn't seen him since the tributes at the gate, when he'd told her about knowing Connie. She felt herself tense up; she knew she had to confront him. Instead of heading for the café, she followed him from a distance. He was heading to the process stage, carrying a canister of film, and she watched as he disappeared through a side door.

Stage eight was painted with the words "Process Stage" in fading blue letters. Clara tugged hard on the heavy door until it admitted her into that blanket of cool darkness marked by a musty, faintly chemical smell. Her eyes adjusted to the dim light. All sorts of scenes used rear projection—whether it was a location that would be expensive or complicated to film, like the middle of the ocean or Paris, or everyday scenes, like a driving scene, or a busy street. The actors would be filmed in front of a screen projecting the right background. Today it was a train carriage, and the screen behind would project scenery rolling past.

Clara made her way across the studio, around lights and over a dolly track, and eventually behind the large screen. Lloyd was at the projector, struggling to load the reel of film.

"Want some help?"

When he saw it was Clara, he gave a warm smile. "Thank God you're here. I'm supposed to test the reel before this afternoon's shoot. Projectionist's call time isn't until noon."

Clara helped him load the reel and turn on the projector. Images of the English countryside rolled by—thatched cottages and fields dotted with sheep. They moved to the other side of the screen to see the effect of the landscape sweeping past the train windows, giving the impression that the train was moving.

"Where were you yesterday?" asked Clara. "Out sick?"

"At the cop shop." Lloyd rolled his eyes. "Helping them with 'inquiries.'"

"Really?" Clara's coolness hadn't registered with him yet. "Did they give you a hard time?"

He gave a half-hearted laugh. "You could say that."

Instinctively they wandered toward the train interior, and Lloyd sat down wearily in the first-class carriage. Clara sat opposite him, and it must have looked as though they were off on a day trip.

"You were gone all day. What happened?" she said.

Lloyd leaned forward and put his head in his hands. "They

grilled me for hours because I knew Connie, because she was found in the vaults." Lloyd rubbed his face, then leaned back against the upholstered seat. "Detective Rivetti is a real cretin," he muttered. He looked at Clara through his long fringe of sandy hair. He seemed suddenly much younger, like a schoolboy who'd been separated from the group.

"What did they want to know? If you had a date with her that night?"

His eyes narrowed. "How did you know?"

Clara shrugged. "Just a guess."

"I didn't have a date with Connie. And that's what I told the cops for hours on end." He turned and looked out the window as the countryside whipped by, craggier hills, rivers, and glens. Maybe it was Scotland, not England. Clara waited for him to go on.

"I was at a deli on Fairfax," said Lloyd finally. "Chatting up a waitress, or trying to—she has a boyfriend. Took long enough to track her down yesterday. Detective Rivetti was ready to throw away the key. But she finally confirmed my story, that I was at the counter all evening."

"Were you and Connie ever an item?" Clara didn't take her eyes off him.

"No, just friends—when I was useful to her, I guess." He gave a resigned smile. "She ran hot and cold like that."

"What do you mean 'useful'—did you help her get the job on *Argentan*?"

Lloyd shook his head. "No."

Clara cocked her head. "It's quite a leap from the usherette to a movie star's stand-in. Seems like she would need to know someone?"

Lloyd didn't answer.

Clara brushed her hand across the plaid upholstery. "What about your uncle in casting? I've heard stories . . ." She watched Lloyd's face darken. "Is that how Connie got on the lot—a late-night audition?"

He winced like she'd poked him. "No, she never met my uncle. Look, we were friends. We met at the Vista. We chatted about movies; she'd let me into the double features for free. Connie needed a lucky break, something better than working at the movie theater." He was getting hot under the collar. "And no, I didn't send her to my uncle," he said indignantly. "I know his reputation." He raked a hand through his hair. "Well, I do now," he added sheepishly.

"So how did you help her, exactly?" asked Clara. She was getting impatient.

Lloyd traced the studded leather of the armrest. "I got her some extra work on the lot, crowd stuff. My uncle doesn't bother with low-level things like that. The extras casting woman is really nice." He lifted his shoulders. "It was easy."

Clara raised an eyebrow. "That doesn't explain how she got to be Bannon's stand-in."

He vaguely shook his head. "She figured that out herself. But it wasn't anything to do with me. She was pretty giddy about it. I mean, it was a union gig, decent pay, and she got her own dressing room."

"Huh." Clara chewed it over. "Last Thursday, do you know who she was meeting that night? She used Bannon's dressing room, and the cops think she was going on a date."

"No idea." He shook his head thoughtfully. "But something changed in her when she started on that movie."

Clara frowned. "Changed in what way?"

"She was moody. Some days she was okay, happy even, but other times she was serious, kinda sad. I saw less and less of her. I guess she worked long hours. The last time I saw her, I teased her about it—told her they lightened her hair and her mood got darker."

"They changed her hair?" said Clara.

"Yeah. I guess the director wanted her the spit of Bannon. Her natural hair color was a couple shades darker."

This detail struck Clara for some reason. She leaned back in her seat and gazed out the window at the fake view, mulling it over. "Why 'the spit' of Bannon?"

Lloyd shrugged. "Isn't that the stand-in's job? To resemble the actress?"

"But Connie wasn't a body double—she never appeared on camera. Why did Howard Hawks need her to be that exact shade of blond?"

"They use the stand-in to set the lights, do the blocking.

Maybe her hair color affected the lighting? Maybe the director of photography requested it?"

"But it's a black-and-white movie—doesn't that seem like overkill to you? Besides, you just said it was the director."

"I don't know who it was." He let out a long sigh, annoyed by all the questions.

"Well, someone on the movie wanted her a dead ringer for Bannon." Clara stopped short when she realized what she'd said. The words crackled in the air, a live wire between them: *a dead ringer.*

Through the train windows the screen flickered to white. The reel had run out of film. In that instant Clara recalled the photo of Bette Davis and her stand-in. "Lloyd," she said, leaning forward, "you have friends in the publicity department, right?" She didn't wait for him to answer. "Could you get ahold of some stills—behind the scenes on the *Argentan* set? It might tell us something."

Lloyd nodded. "Sure, I can try."

"Good. Anything else you can remember about Connie? Any small detail, like the hair thing, something she said or did recently that sticks out in your memory?"

He thought for a moment. "She always said she was fated to work here."

Clara turned sharply. "What does that mean?"

Lloyd swept the hair from his eyes. "I don't know. I guess I thought she meant Hollywood. Like she'd always dreamed of it, and it came true. But now, I'm not so sure what she meant." His eyes met Clara's. "That movie, *Letter from Argentan*—she was mixed up in something. I know it."

Clara waited while Lloyd rewound the reel and turned off the projector. They were walking out of the process stage when Clara remembered the phone number on Connie's script. "Lloyd, do you recognize this number?" She scribbled it onto the back of her paper with the coffee orders—she had memorized it by now. "SPRING three-one-nine-one, or something close to it?"

Lloyd squinted at it. "Doesn't ring a bell."

"Look at it. You're sure? It was on the cover of Connie's script."

He shook his head. "No clue."

She watched him closely. Affable Lloyd, the friendly retriever: that was how she'd always thought of him. But since the murder, Clara couldn't be sure about him—about anyone. It was strange to think that there were hidden layers to Lloyd that she'd not seen before. But then, no one is just one thing.

## Chapter Thirteen

# Letter from Argentan

LLOYD'S SINISTER FEELING ABOUT the *Argentan* set stayed with Clara, but what could she do about it? Despite being a member of the crew, she worked in the postproduction building. She didn't have access to the set and the action of the film shoot.

However, the opportunity to get onto the set came unexpectedly the following afternoon when Sam asked her to deliver a list of pickup shots—inserts and missing pieces he needed for scenes they'd already shot. "Give it to the script supervisor," he said. "She'll know when to broach it with Howard and the assistant director." Clara took the list. "And avoid any studio executives," he called after her. "Pearce will put his foot down about adding shots to the schedule."

Clara stood outside the stage, waiting for the red wigwag to stop flashing. When the camera had stopped rolling, the light went off, and a production assistant opened the door to let her in. Finally, she had been admitted to the action and buzz of the set, and not as a lowly vault girl but as a member of the crew, someone with a purpose. It was the *real* business of moviemaking, the actors and cameras and stage lights, and so many people. Stage eleven, the mansion house set, had transformed since Friday's announcement. Today under the stage lights it seemed as grand and believable as the real thing: parquet floors, stone fireplaces, and lavish furnishings. Clara held the pickup shot list like a VIP ticket. It was her permission to be there.

As she picked her way over cables and dolly tracks, she surveyed the crew, scanning for the script supervisor. The camera was on a huge crane, and there were a myriad of lights and flags set up in the entrance hall of the mansion. What had Connie made of all this? It was a far cry from taking tickets in a dark cinema. The reminder caught her like a pinched nerve.

The script supervisor was easy to spot, there being so few women on set. Clara's surface mission accomplished, she turned to the *real* task at hand: information. What kind of drama or intrigue might Connie have been caught up in on the film set? Clara also wanted to get more background on the actors' feud. And what about Hawks? She still had no explanation for that conversation she'd overheard: *No one will find out.* Find out what?

Clara lingered by the craft table and helped herself to coffee. She was working up the gumption to talk to someone when she saw a familiar face. "Mr. Brackett!"

He was stirring sugar into his iced tea. "Girl Friday, how's the new job? You here to have a little look-see?" He took a sip. "Follow me." He took her by the elbow. "Front-row seat."

Chaperoned by Mr. Brackett, Clara was guided nearer the set and the throng of actors and hair and makeup people at the side of the stage. There were temporary dressing tables set up and canvas chairs with important people's names on the back.

"How's the shoot going?" asked Clara.

"Fortunately, all the drama is on-screen, for a change. Everyone seems to be on their best behavior." He nodded toward the mansion set, where Babe Bannon and Randall Ford were walking through a rehearsal with Howard Hawks.

"What was it usually like?"

Mr. Brackett raised an eyebrow. "Randall could be quite vindictive. You know what I heard?" He had a wicked glint in his eye, and he leaned closer. "In the scene where the widow looks at the framed photographs on the piano—you remember, she picks up that one of her beloved in uniform—well, Randall had the props man replace it with a picture of Gregory Quinn. Can you believe it?" Mr. Brackett shook his head. "What a swine."

"Nasty," said Clara, genuinely horrified.

"The wonderful world of moviemaking. And Howard is still changing lines on us, last-minute. He pretends to the studio that it's all Bannon's fault—says she refuses to say the scripted dialogue—but it's his little ruse. He never liked the character as written—"

"The wet noodle?"

"Exactly. Hawksian women are strong, independent. Whereas Mr. Pearce's tastes run more traditional and rather boring." He nudged her. "Don't tell anyone I said that."

Clara thought back to what she had overheard at Bannon's party. "Do they get along, Hawks and Bannon? I heard he fought to have her on the film."

"Barbara Bannon was his discovery—he knew he could make her a star. When he cast her as an unknown nineteen-year-old on *Nightshade,* it was a risk. But he understood the chemistry between her and Quinn. Underestimated how *much* chemistry. I'm sure he was grooming her to be his next conquest. But then Gregory Quinn swooped in and stole her. Silver lining was that Hawks had a hit on his hands with *Nightshade.* And he sold Bannon's contract to Silver Pacific, likely for a pretty penny."

"Do you think Hawks was in love with her?" Clara lowered her voice. "With Barbara Bannon?"

Mr. Brackett gave a lazy shrug. "If he was, he got over it—swallowed any sour grapes. He made two more movies with Quinn and Bannon."

"What about Randall Ford? Why did he have a feud with Gregory Quinn?" asked Clara, relishing the gossip.

"He lost a role to him; or a girl or a card game." Brackett gave a small laugh. "Who knows? Once you dislike a man, it no longer matters why."

The rehearsal was over, and the actors were returning to their chairs.

A production assistant approached. "Mr. Brackett, the assistant director would like a word about some dialogue changes." Brackett theatrically rolled his eyes and handed his empty glass to the PA as though he were a waiter.

After Mr. Brackett was pulled away by the assistant director, Clara was left hanging.

"Coming through." A burly man with sandbags under each arm was barreling toward her. She leapt out of his way and accidentally collided with the makeup man, who shot her a withering glance. She stepped away, mortified.

"You want a seat, go ahead." Clara recognized the voice.

She turned to see Barbara Bannon pointing to the free chair next to her. Clara hesitated, glancing at the name stitched across the canvas back: *Mr. Ford.* "Don't worry, it's someone's idea of a joke," said Bannon. "Randall keeps his distance. Go on, sit down. I don't bite."

"Thanks." Clara settled into Randall Ford's chair, not entirely relaxed—Goldilocks before the bears got home. It wasn't her place, to be lounging with the talent. In her eyes, actors had their own red wigwag lights that prevented ordinary people from getting too close. Babe Bannon in costume—a pale evening gown—was flicking through her sides, the script pages for the scenes that day. Clara noticed her heavier makeup; she was camera ready.

A minor flap of activity, and Clara looked up to see that Mr. Pearce had arrived. Bannon's face tightened as she watched the head of the studio cross the set to talk with Howard Hawks.

"Our fearless leader," said Bannon. There was a glimmer of something behind her eyes. Clara caught it, and then it was gone. "He'll be glad to know we're ahead of schedule. I've been doing my own stand-in work—to make a point, I guess." Her voice hardened. "It makes them quicker at setting the lights, that's for sure."

"Who's the director of photography?" asked Clara, thinking back to Lloyd's suggestion that it had been the DP who had made Connie dye her hair.

"Michelangelo over there." Bannon pointed to a bearded man wearing a cravat and holding up a light meter.

"Is he a real perfectionist?" said Clara.

"He says he paints with light." Bannon sighed. "More like watching paint dry, the time it takes him to light the set."

Now that they were chatting, Clara pushed herself to ask a more direct question. "Have the police got any new leads?" she said carefully.

Bannon gave her a sideways glance. "Those cops are useless. They don't have a snowball's chance of solving a crossword puzzle, let alone a murder. They keep asking if I have any enemies, harping on about someone holding a grudge." She rolled her eyes. "I asked Detective Ireland: 'How long do you have?'"

"Aren't you worried, though?" said Clara, leaning closer. She caught the scent of perfume. "If the killer was after you—what if he tries again?"

Bannon jutted her chin out. "I can take care of myself." That defiance again. She was a Hawksian woman, all right.

There was a loud squawk, and Clara looked up to see that the assistant director was addressing the crew through a bullhorn. "Picture up. Last touch-ups, please."

The clock was ticking. Clara had to find out *something* before Bannon went on set.

Bannon's makeup artist appeared and dusted some powder onto her nose. She waved him away. Then the hairstylist smoothed a few stray hairs back into place. "That's enough, Frank."

Thinking back to the "dead ringer" theory, Clara pulled on a strand of her own mousey blond hair. "I wish my hair was a nicer color." Her tone was confiding, and like an adoring fan, she threw a furtive glance at Bannon's blond tresses. It was a long shot, but it might spark something.

"I'll let you in on a secret," Babe whispered. "This ain't natural." She tossed her hair back and barked a laugh.

"Your hairstylist, Frank, is it? He does a great job." Clara cringed at her own fawning.

"Frank?" Bannon looked incredulous. "You think I'd trust the studio hair department with my color? Never." She raised an eyebrow. "I always go to my girl Rosa on Beverly—she's been doing my color for years. It's never brassy." Clara filed away this piece of information. "If it were up to the hair department," Bannon went on, "I'd be looking like Barbara Stanwyk in *Double Indemnity*. Did you see that wig? My God, it was appalling!" She laughed again and got out of her chair.

The assistant director approached. "Ready for you on the set, Miss Bannon."

"Take care, kid." She swept away.

## Chapter Fourteen

# Ash-Blonde

CLARA WAS SITTING ON a mint-green barber's chair, facing a large oval mirror; copies of *Life* magazine and the *Saturday Evening Post* spilled from a rack on the wall; shelves of hair products and brushes were on display near the cash register. Babe Bannon's hairdresser was still with a customer. Clara had called three salons on Beverly, asking for Rosa, before she'd found the right one. After she'd given Sam the vague excuse of "an appointment," he'd let her go early. She'd promised she would make up the time.

It's a fact universally acknowledged that women talk to their hairdressers. Since her first haircut in Los Angeles, Clara had overheard a fair number of secrets spilled at beauty salons, and if Connie had indeed gotten her hair done here—as was Clara's hunch—this was her angle to find out who insisted she dye her hair and why. The doppelgänger idea was still niggling her.

A few more minutes dragged past. Clara got up and helped

herself to the nearest magazine. As she sat back down, she caught her reflection in the mirror, and a memory surfaced.

"Don't wiggle, sweetie." Klara's first American haircut at a salon in Los Feliz. Rain pummeled the awning, the windows were fogged, and she could hear car tires rhythmically swishing through puddles. "That's right, keep still." The hairdresser steadied the blunt edge of her scissors against Klara's forehead as she trimmed the girl's bangs. Klara was hot underneath the synthetic cape, and she was itching to shift her legs, which were stuck to the vinyl seat. "Wiggle." Klara didn't recognize the verb (it sounded comical), and yet she knew she wasn't supposed to move. Then it struck her—like dialing the tuner on a radio, the static had cleared—Klara understood English.

The hairdresser combed her bangs, checking the length. "Almost finished." Klara gazed up at her in awe. The forty-something redhead with sun-speckled arms was a messenger from another realm. She had broken through, made contact, and for a brief moment the veil of confusion between Klara and the English language had fallen away.

The woman put down her scissors and appraised Klara in the mirror. "All done. Cute as a button." She dusted a soft brush over Klara's nose, neck, and caped shoulders. Then she worked the pedal on the barber chair, and Klara watched her own reflection slide jerkily down the mirror. Like a royal attendant, the hairdresser removed the cape in one swift motion. The ceremony was over. Klara studied her own reflection. It wasn't just the new bangs. She was a different person now—she was American.

The hairdresser turned to Klara's mother, who was flicking through a magazine. "She's all finished, Mom. You can pay Suzy at the cash register."

Inge looked up from her *House Beautiful* as though caught in headlights. How was it possible that even her mother's facial expressions were awkward. Klara abruptly peeled herself off the seat. The skin on the backs of her thighs smarted, which underscored her annoyance.

Her mother ran a hand over her daughter's new haircut. *"Sehr schön, Klara."* Klara shrank from her mother's touch, noticing the foreign words register on the faces of the other customers.

The light bulb moment of comprehension at the hairdresser's didn't last. Klara finally started school in February, a couple of grades lower than in Berlin. Learning English was a constant back-and-forth between clarity and confusion. Life in a foreign language was like bumbling around an unfamiliar house, grasping for a nonexistent light switch; bashing knees on ill-placed table legs; trying to force a key into a sticking lock. She was embarrassed at the artifice of it all, forcing her mouth to work itself around the new sounds. At the end of the day, Klara was left feeling bruised and frustrated. Speaking German at home came as a relief.

On these bad days she resented English. As a language it was straightforward, direct—logical to the point of being dull. But it didn't truly translate. There was no narrative, no history to the words. Where her native tongue conjured images, American English sanitized; it lacked contour, shape, and texture. It simply was. English words were as tasteless and meaningless as American bread—uniform cotton wool, pre-sliced, no bite. *"Brot"* couldn't possibly translate to "bread." The term "bread" was merely an approximation, a stand-in for the real thing.

With her parents' imminent return to Germany, this wasn't the first time Clara's memories of her first weeks in America were surfacing. Her eleven-year-old self was ever-present.

"Clara?"

She turned, and Babe Bannon's hairdresser was sweeping up locks of hair at the next chair. She was petite with olive skin, black hair streaked with gray, and eyes as dark as cherries.

"Hi." Clara put down her magazine. "Miss Bannon recommended you. I work with her at the studio." The "with her" was a stretch, but Clara managed to get the words out without blinking. "She said you're the only one she trusts to do her color."

Rosa handed the broom to an underling and came over. "Miss Bannon's been coming to me for years." Rosa smiled and stood behind Clara, addressing her reflection. "The studio hair department." Rosa made a face. "A bunch of old men."

Clara laughed. "What shade is she?"

"Miss Bannon is a light ash-blond—it's a cool tone." She fingered the ends of Clara's hair. "You're a darker blond. We could lighten it up, bring out the tones in your natural high-lights."

Clara took a breath. "What about her stand-in? What color was Connie's hair?"

Rosa rested her hands on Clara's shoulders. "That poor girl." She shuddered. "I couldn't believe it when I saw her face in the papers. It wasn't even a month ago when she came here, maybe a few weeks." Clara's hunch was right.

Rosa went to a drawer and took out a card with color pictures of different shades. "Connie had a warmer tone than Miss Bannon—honey." She pointed to a natural shade of blond. "Something closer to this."

Clara took the card and studied it—a catalogue of blonds. "Did the new color suit her?"

"I thought she looked real good. It was very close to Miss Bannon's shade, which is what she asked for, but"—Rosa shook her head—"she didn't seem excited about it."

"Oh?" said Clara.

"The color was right, so I asked her if it was the cut. I mean, I only took an inch off to even it out. It wasn't drastic."

Clara watched her carefully in the mirror. "What did Connie say?"

Rosa shrugged. "She said it was fine. Kept repeating that. But she got real quiet, closed up." The hairdresser folded her arms and thought about it. "It was strange. I felt terrible, but I only did what she asked."

"Did she say why she was getting her hair done? Was it for the movie?"

"I assumed so." Rosa thought for a second. "It was Miss Bannon who called and made the appointment."

This didn't sound quite right to Clara—Barbara Bannon making Connie's hair appointment? Wasn't that beneath her?

The hairdresser put a hand on her hip. "Why all the questions? I thought you wanted your hair colored?"

Clara thought on her feet. "Actually, Connie Milligan was a friend," she said, looking down. The lie was easy because Clara almost believed it. It came as easily as breathing. This tricky habit had started as a form of self-protection back in high school, to avoid her inconvenient German past. But it had soon become second nature—in certain situations—like the time when Mr. Brackett had assumed her surname was Swedish and Clara had never corrected him.

Rosa squeezed her arm. "I'm so sorry, *pobre chica.*"

"Did Connie say where she was going after—another appointment, a date, perhaps? With her hair done, I just wondered." Clara was pushing a little, her tone a bit desperate, but it sounded right if Connie was a friend.

Rosa swept a strand of hair from Clara's cheek. She smiled apologetically and shook her head. "Sorry, honey. She never said."

After Clara left the salon—her hair set with a new wave— she walked a few blocks to mull over what Rosa had said. She tried to play devil's advocate. So Connie hadn't loved her new hair color. Was it as simple as that? Had it just been a standard request for the film shoot—or had Connie done it for someone else? Why had *Bannon* made the appointment? She hardly knew Connie. That could be innocent enough, and yet Babe didn't strike Clara as someone who would go out of her way for someone else. She was a movie star, not a PA.

Clara tried to imagine Connie's reaction at the salon—staring at her reflection, looking more like the movie star with her hair done. And yet, something had been troubling her—but *what*?

## Chapter Fifteen

# The Formosa Café

IT WAS BEFORE SIX p.m., and the neon lights of the Formosa Café weren't switched on yet. Clara could have powered them herself, from all the electric energy buzzing inside her. All the unanswered questions about Connie were on a loop in her brain. Gil was leaning on the bar when she walked in, his hand loosely wrapped around a beer. He looked up, and Clara felt her insides do a somersault, which was daft. It was just the same old Gil, a different setting was all. The place was quiet; it was midweek and still early. Clara ordered the cocktail special of the day, a whiskey sour. It came overdressed, with frothy egg white, a twist of orange, and a maraschino cherry skewered by an umbrella. She sipped through the straw—aware of how silly it looked for a casual Wednesday evening, next to Gil's beer.

After they moved from the bar to a table, Clara caught Gil scrutinizing her. "You do something to your hair?"

Clara cringed inwardly. It probably looked like she'd had it done especially. "Research," she said, trying to play it down. And after Gil's quizzical reaction, she gave him the rundown of what she had discovered at the salon on Beverly Boulevard.

Gil's brow was furrowed. "You're following up on leads, you're doing police work?" He shook his head and gave a small laugh.

It wasn't the reaction she had expected. She couldn't tell if he was teasing or disapproving—she had hoped he might be more impressed. "It was just a hunch," said Clara, trying to dismiss it.

"But isn't that the deal, for the stand-in to resemble the actress?" said Gil. "Why the red flag?"

"It's probably nothing. But there are all these small things that don't add up. It's a black-and-white movie. Does a shade of blond really matter for setting the lights? And Barbara Bannon making the appointment—I don't buy it. And then Connie's lackluster reaction. Something is definitely off."

Gil worked a fingernail under the edge of his beer label, mulling it over. "Roger and I have to hash out this kind of logic all the time. If I'm thinking of it like a scene in a script, I might come up with something like this: Connie gets her hair done to match the movie star, takes a look in the mirror and realizes she's still the bridesmaid, never the bride, that she'll never be in the big leagues." Clara liked it when Gil was in his writer mode. His eyes twinkled when he was on a roll. "She's never going to get a speaking part or even be seen in so much as a frame of film. She's the stand-in. Even with Bannon's beauty salon making her up like the star, she'll never have Bannon's career."

"Maybe," Clara conceded with a smile. "That doesn't explain Bannon making the appointment."

He batted his hand like that was no big deal. "Come on, what else you got?"

"What, so you can knock down all my theories?" she said playfully. "Fine, so forget the hair—even though something is still off about it." Clara sat up taller in her chair. "I have three questions," she said, listing them on her fingers. "Number one: How did Connie get the stand-in gig? Everyone who gets a job on the lot knows someone—that's how it works. Max got me in. What about you?"

Gil nodded vaguely. "Yeah, an army buddy."

"Two," said Clara. The cocktail had loosened her tongue, and she was enjoying herself. "Was there some weird or sinister vibe on the *Argentan* set?" Gil gave her a puzzled look. Clara explained the backstory of Connie's friendship with Lloyd. "He said that something changed in her once she started working on the movie. He chalked it up to something bad on set. And three: How did the killer get the vault combination? Which brings me full circle back to Lloyd because he's the only one I know who carries a cheat sheet with the codes. I think we can rule out Miss Simkin as a suspect."

Gil raised his eyebrows, faintly amused. "You done?" He

laughed softly and shook his head. "Go easy on this stuff, Clara. There's not much you can do." His eyes drifted to another table.

Clara thought she was being clever. She didn't want him laughing at her. Suddenly annoyed at herself, she wished she could switch off her brain, but the case was prodding at her. And now she was ruining their date by talking nonstop about the murder.

She leaned her elbows on the table. "How was your day?" she said brightly. Maybe they could start over and talk about something else.

He gave a noncommittal grunt. "Saw the cops—had to sign my written statement." He took a sip of beer. "Everyone on the lot that night had to do the same thing. The detectives have an office in the costume shop. Otherwise, just rewrites." He sighed. "Hawks came up with dialogue changes last minute. The usual."

"Wait—with the cops, did you tell them where you were, on the battle set?"

He threw her an incredulous smile. "No. Are you kidding?"

"But what if—"

He shook his head. "It's irrelevant."

"But what if you saw something or someone?" said Clara. "You don't know where the investigation is going, what might be important."

He gave a small shrug. "Look, I didn't see anyone. Besides, you don't admit that you lied to the cops. They'll hound you for it." She must have looked unconvinced. He went on, "I had a CO like that Ireland guy. Loved to throw his weight around. Best thing you could do was keep out of his way. I'm not looking for trouble."

"Gil, it's unwise—lying to the cops."

"This isn't Nancy Drew. Everyone with a badge isn't a good guy." He laughed. "Come on, it's no big deal. I told them I was in my office, and I'm sticking to it." He leaned back in his chair.

Clara stirred her drink vigorously. She felt annoyed—obviously he was implying that *she* was Nancy Drew, a kid detective. Well, she didn't want to drop it. "What if someone saw *you*?" she blurted out. "How bad would it look then?"

"I'll take the risk." He looked out the window, and she knew he didn't want to talk about it anymore. Outside, the sky had turned a grubby shade of lilac; the sun had sunk without ceremony. The neon lights blinked on.

Clara removed the umbrella from her drink. The cherry had fallen to the bottom of her glass, oozing a blood-red trail. "I talked to Babe Bannon on set this morning." She took a slow sip of her drink and watched Gil carefully over the rim of the glass. "The cops have been asking who might have a grudge against her."

"Why?" said Gil sharply.

Clara shrugged like it was obvious. "They think she's in danger, I guess. It's possible she was the intended victim." It was the opposite of sugarcoating—she had deliberately added a dash of vinegar. It came from a mistrusting place, the part of her that wanted to provoke a reaction, gauge if he still cared about Bannon, and how much.

Gil drained his beer. Did his face darken? It was hard to tell in the low light.

The waitress stopped at their table. "Anything else, folks?" She removed the empty beer bottle.

"Just the check," said Gil.

## Chapter Sixteen

# Rushes

THURSDAY MORNING, A WEEK since Connie's death, and the screening room was deserted. Clara was waiting for the detectives to show up. They had requested to screen rushes from the day of the murder, and Clara had been asked to attend in case they had any questions about the footage. She wandered down the aisle and watched the dust motes spiral under the house lights. There were three rows of large velvet seats. Mr. Pearce always sat up front with his secretary—producers and executives relegated to the rows behind. Next to his seat there was a narrow table, room for a telephone, the intercom to talk to Max, a notepad, and a cup of sharpened pencils. She glanced up at the white screen, imagining his perspective at dailies: *Next setup, Max. Next reel. That's enough.* Normally if Clara had contrived to stay for dailies, she would have been in the projection booth, her nose pressed against the small window, devouring the images until Max remembered she was there and chased her out.

She debated whether to try one of the velvet chairs, but chickened out, hovering in the aisle like an usherette. *Usherette*—she thought instantly of Connie. Clara imagined her leaning under the portrait lights at the Vista. The theater was in Los Feliz, where Hollywood and Sunset Boulevards met. Clara had been there dozens of times. She wondered, was it possible they'd run into each other? Perhaps Connie had taken her ticket or waved her flashlight to guide Clara to her seat?

Clara returned to the projection booth to wait for Max. On his chair was a copy of today's *Los Angeles Times.* She picked up the paper. SILVER BLONDE MURDER STUMPS LAPD. The moniker still bothered her in a way that felt personal, reducing Connie to the color of her hair and the place where she'd worked.

The door banged, and Clara expected Max to walk into the projection booth. Instead she heard voices in the theater. She peered through the projection window. Detectives Ireland and Rivetti. They were arguing. Clara shrank back from the window and listened by the projection room door. She opened it a crack wider.

"My money's still on Connie Milligan." It was Ireland's voice. "Gut feeling."

"But we have nothing—not one hint of a motive," said Rivetti. "Nobody gains anything from her death, so far as we can tell. She wasn't dating anyone—we cleared the vault boy. All in all, she didn't have much of a social life."

Ireland exhaled a laugh. "A girl like that—an attractive young blonde—you really believe she lived like a nun? Her mother said the past couple weekends she spent at the library—gimme a break. She seem like the bookish type to you? It doesn't add up. The mother must be holding something back."

"Why would she hide anything that could help us find her daughter's killer?" There was a moment of quiet. "It's been a week since the murder," said Rivetti, his tone less antagonistic. "The Milligan girl is a dead end."

A beat before Ireland answered. "Maybe." Clara heard a chair creak, followed by a frustrated sigh. "There must be something we're missing."

Clara dared to peek through the projection window again. Rivetti was pacing in front of Ireland, who was lounging in Mr. Pearce's chair in the front row. "On the one hand we have a murdered stand-in and no motive—not one suspect," said Rivetti. "On the other hand we have an actress she resembled who happens to have a laundry list of people with a grudge against her. It's a who's who of Hollywood." He counted them on his fingers. "An agent she recently fired, a studio contract she's threatened to break, a beef with a costar, a testy relationship with the director. Her dead lover's ex-wife is no fan. *Mrs.* Quinn—she kept his name—had some colorful things to say about Miss Bannon. Who knows what other skeletons are in the closet next to the fancy gowns."

Clara was riveted to the spot, her mind racing. If the cops knew about Gil's past with Babe, wouldn't that make him another suspect on Rivetti's list? *The lowly screenwriter hung up on a summer fling with Ruby Kaminsky.* She pushed the thought to the back of her mind.

"Come on. It's all gossip for the scandal sheets." Ireland wasn't buying it.

"We have to follow up on the Bannon leads," Rivetti went on. "If we don't, the killer could try again—this time get the right girl. Then we'll have two murders on our hands."

Ireland stretched and clasped his hands behind his head, legs splayed out. "Two different women; two different cases." He sighed. "It's messy. I don't like it."

Clara turned back to the newspaper and stared at the unfeeling headline. She felt truly sorry for Connie—her own murder eclipsed by Babe Bannon. *The Silver Blonde.* It wasn't just the treatment that Connie got in the press. Her no-name status had even affected the police investigation. They were giving up on her and turning their attention to the movie star instead. Connie Milligan was barely playing a supporting role in her own murder.

The screening room door banged. Clara's heart leapt. Footsteps, and Max joined her in the booth. A few moments later Detective Ireland appeared in the doorway. It probably appeared as though Clara and Max had arrived together.

"Sorry to keep you waiting, Detective," said Max, turning on the projector. "Just a few moments and we'll be ready."

"Miss Berg, you going to talk us through this stuff?" said Ireland. "Come and sit up front."

Clara caught Max's surprised look. She had never been allowed to sit in the theater before. "Sure, let me grab the notes." She scooped up the script supervisor's notes and followed Detective Ireland down the aisle.

Settling into the plush velvet of a front-row seat felt like riding the streetcar without paying. Rivetti sat on one side of Detective Ireland, and Clara sat on the other, Mr. Pearce's table between them. The screen flickered to life. Max cued up the reel and paused it on the head leader.

A knock, and a uniformed officer entered the screening room. "Excuse me, Detectives." He strode down the aisle and handed Detective Ireland a brown paper grocery bag. "The victim's belongings from her dressing room. The forensic examination is complete. This can be returned to the next of kin."

Detective Ireland nodded. "Thanks, son. I'll handle it." He took the bag and dismissed the young cop. Clara watched Ireland rustle open the paper bag and poke through the items. She sat up tall in her seat and tried to get a peek inside—but Ireland's large hands blocked her view.

Ireland rolled up the paper bag clumsily and placed it on the narrow table between them. Clara stared at it out of the corner of her eye. Despite its mundane appearance, she couldn't ignore it. She desperately wanted to know what was inside.

"Right, let's watch this stuff," said Ireland. Nothing happened.

With a small charge of adrenaline, Clara pressed the button on the intercom. "Roll it, Max." She felt like a studio mogul.

Max turned down the house lights, and the screening began.

The head leader counted down, and the sound of the sync-pop was a switch that flicked in Clara's brain. It completed a circuit, and she sat transfixed as the silver images came to life—it was night and day from the small screen on Sam's Moviola.

"What's this?" said Detective Ireland.

"Scene twenty-six," said Clara, angling the notes to catch the light of the screen. "This is the part where the widow starts to doubt the sergeant. She tries to catch him in a lie. But he's too clever and smooth. She begins to think she's going crazy."

It was a wide shot of the characters on the mansion set, in the library. It was followed by medium shots of the same scene. The cops watched with serious faces.

"Why'd they film the same stuff over and over?" asked Rivetti.

What did he expect, a finished movie? "It's so they have options on the performance. And the different angles they need to cut the scene together, so it feels real, not like a stage play."

Ireland shifted in his seat. "I don't know about this flick. My wife likes comedies and musicals, a bit of escape. This is kinda grim."

Clara turned to him. "It's a suspense film, Detective—not a musical. It's supposed to be dark. Haven't you seen *Double Indemnity* or *Laura*?"

"The black and white—it's depressing."

"It's stylized," said Clara. "The lighting is important. It expresses what the character is feeling. It adds to the suspense."

"Everyone's a critic, huh?" said Rivetti.

Max changed the reel. The screen flickered to life again. The new setup was a close-up favoring Babe Bannon. Clara fancied there must have been a shift in the room, a small electric current pulsing across the detectives' seat backs. They leaned forward slightly.

"She looks good," said Ireland. An understatement. In the close-up Babe Bannon was a vision: her face was luminous, her cheekbones sculpted by the key light—that famous arched brow, and of course the ash-blond hair framing her face like a halo. Confronted with her beauty, Clara realized she would never graduate to this kind of womanhood. But watching Babe Bannon on-screen, somehow you got to be her.

Clara saw from the notes that the next take was a series: Bannon would do the line several times without the camera cutting between takes. The slate was held up to the camera in front of Bannon's face. The clapper loader gave the scene, setup, and take number, "Twenty-six, Charlie, take five." He snapped the arms of the slate together and disappeared from frame. Bannon pursed her lips, blinked a couple of times, and then focused. She waited, a runner before the pistol fires.

From off-screen the voice of Hawks said, "Action!"

Bannon took a beat, then threw her head up and tossed out the line of dialogue. "It's been a long time for me too, Sergeant." And she held her gaze past the camera, still in character.

"And again; keep rolling." Hawks's voice was impatient. She

repeated the move, uttered the line again. "Put some emotion into it, girl," Hawks barked, off-screen. "Again." Bannon said the line again. Hawks boomed, "I don't care, honey. Convince me." He was wearing her down. She glared at a point past the camera—where Clara assumed the director was standing—and quietly refused to say the line.

"Almost out of film," the camera assistant shouted.

"Cut it," Hawks said, his tone defeated. Bannon vanished from the frame before the camera stopped rolling.

"Nice guy," said Ireland.

"This must have been when she stormed off set," said Rivetti.

Clara told the detectives which were circle takes and what was NG—no good. These were the takes that normally wouldn't make it to the dailies screening. Max changed reels again, and a different scene came on-screen. It was a night exterior.

"Now what are we looking at?" said Ireland.

Clara skimmed the script supervisor notes. "The last scene they shot was the downtown alley—filmed on the back lot." The set was dressed to look like an unsavory part of town, with over-turned trash cans and tramps. Bannon, wrapped in a huge fur coat, stood with her back to camera in lashing rain (a rain machine in the foreground, not on the actor). After the assistant director called action, they watched the widow walk away from camera, up the alley, casting a dramatic shadow behind her. The sergeant character, dressed as a tramp, enters the frame and follows her down the alley.

Clara said, "This is his first attempt to steal her purse to get the address book with the safe combination. He's foiled, of course."

Ireland tutted. "This guy's a scoundrel. We should lock him up," he said, suddenly absorbed in the story. "That's a US soldier preying on a fallen comrade's wife." He shook his head with disgust. "What's the world coming to?" Clara smirked and looked down at the notes.

The last setup was the alley establishing shot, a crane shot. The clapper loader held the slate up in frame—it read "MOS"— and then the camera mounted on the crane moved up to its starting position.

"What happened to the sound?" asked Rivetti.

"'MOS' means no sound was recorded. They'll add sound effects later in the sound mix."

"What time was this shot?" said Ireland.

Clara looked at the notes. "It was seven-thirty p.m."

He frowned. "Looks later than that."

"They exposed the film to make it look darker than it was," said Clara.

Detective Ireland turned to Rivetti. "We should get a list of the extras on set that night. See if anyone has a criminal record."

They watched as the widow wrapped in her huge fur walks away from camera down the alley. This time the camera rises slowly above her, making her small and vulnerable, the sergeant lurking in the shadows behind her. Several more takes played out.

"Here's my point," said Rivetti. "Seeing this broad from

behind—it's dark, she's wearing the right duds, blond hair—can you swear on your mother that it's Barbara Bannon and not Connie Milligan?"

He was right. Clara sensed Ireland knew it too.

Rivetti leaned in close. "The killer got the wrong girl—I'd put money on it."

Ireland mulled it over. "We should talk to Bannon again."

Clara waited in the projection booth for Max to give her back the reels. She heard Rivetti barking into Mr. Pearce's phone. He was calling the precinct. The screening room door banged. Ireland must have just left. Grabbing the reels, Clara hurried after him. He was already up the stairs, and she lagged behind. It was hard to run with a stack of film reels in her arms. Quickly she checked behind her to make sure Rivetti wasn't following. She wanted to speak to Ireland alone—he was on Connie's side. Upstairs, he crossed the art deco foyer of the executive building, then walked through the main doors and into the sunshine. She rushed after him. "Detective!"

Her eyes were honed in on the brown paper bag of Connie's belongings. Clara caught up with him by the fountain—the female figure holding a globe aloft.

"Detective!" Clara called again. He turned around. Clara caught her breath. "Detective, I wanted to ask you—" She was breathless. What should she say? She hadn't planned this. "You're not giving up on Connie Milligan, are you?"

He flinched. "No, of course not."

"Connie is dead, and everyone is still acting like it's all about the movie star."

Detective Ireland sized her up. "Look, I understand—you found her. That's no small thing. You have some complicated feelings about this." He leaned toward her. "Don't worry. We'll find her killer. It's possible Babe Bannon was the intended victim, but either way, we'll solve the case."

"I want to help." Clara shifted the film canisters to perch on her other hip. She nodded at the paper bag. "What if I were to return Connie's belongings?"

"You?" He looked at her quizzically. "Why?"

She couldn't tell him the truth—that she felt a connection, a link to this girl. Somehow they were the same, even though they hadn't met. "I couldn't help overhear what you said about Mrs. Milligan, that there might be more to learn from her. Maybe she would talk to a young woman, someone closer in age to her daughter? Someone who's working on the movie."

Detective Ireland chewed it over. "You knew Connie?"

Clara shook her head. "But I don't have to lie. I work on the movie. She might assume . . ."

Detective Rivetti caught up with them and glanced at Clara out of the corner of his eye like she shouldn't be there.

Ireland removed his hat and fanned his face with it. "Rivetti, hear me out on this." He squinted in the sunlight. "We both suspect that the victim's mother is holding something back. That, or she just doesn't like cops." He winked at Clara. "Detective

Rivetti doesn't have the best bedside manner." Rivetti narrowed his eyes. Ireland continued, "Seems to me like she might open up to a woman—a young woman closer to her daughter's age." He was parroting Clara's words and pretending they were his own. Clara didn't mind as long as he could convince his partner.

Rivetti shifted his position. "Yeah, like who?"

By four-thirty p.m. Clara had been given permission by Sam to leave work early—again. She stood in front of the post-production building while the detectives gave her instructions for meeting Connie's mother.

Ireland paced back and forth in front of her, and Rivetti leaned against the Chrysler, glaring at her like a suspect.

"This is not a license to concoct any stories," said Detective Ireland. "Definitely don't cop to her that you found the body. You worked with Connie—that's all. We're looking for a bit more background on the victim. Keep your ears open for anyone the mother might mention: a friend, boyfriend, neighbor, a beef with a work colleague—any kind of grudge or disagreement. That's it. Listen to the mother and report back."

"Sure." Clara nodded and took the sad brown grocery bag. Her heart thumped, a thread of intrigue tugging at her.

"I still don't like it," said Rivetti. "She'll be in over her head."

Clara eyed him, clutching the bag.

"She's smart, not pushy," said Ireland, gesturing to Clara.

"She looks well brought up. That girl's mother will give her a lemonade, and I bet she'll have something to say."

Rivetti ran his tongue over his teeth. "You think so?"

"The mother isn't going to spill her guts to us," Ireland went on. "The girl can't do any harm. It's worth a shot."

"I can do it." Clara held Rivetti's gaze, defiant.

He looked away first. "Knock yourself out."

Ireland opened the back door of the Chrysler, and Clara got in. Then the detectives got into the front. As they swept toward the main gates, they passed the Writers' Block. On cue there was Gil walking toward the building with Roger Brackett. They had to step aside to let the detectives' huge car pass, and Clara watched Gil's face cloud over when he saw her in the backseat.

## Chapter Seventeen

# Gramercy Place

THE COPS DROPPED CLARA off in front of a tatty apartment building on Gramercy Place, south of Beverly. A zigzagging fire escape slashed down the stucco, and in the strip of yard, dusty rosebushes cried out for a drink. Up the street, a few girls were playing jump rope. They called out a chant, and two girls, braids flying, expertly ducked under the rope. As Clara approached the front door, she felt the swoop and thwack of the jump rope beat in her own chest.

Clara entered Connie's building inconspicuously, as if she lived there. Behind her the main door closed with a bang; the world outside was reduced to rectangles of white through the frosted glass. Her eyes adjusted to the feeble light. The hallway was coated in the smell of fried onions and old carpet—her stomach twisted. In someone's apartment a phone was ringing and a door slammed; a small dog was yapping, and she could hear children's laughter punctuated by quick footsteps. The building hummed on a different frequency from the drone of traffic on the street. She inhaled a long breath of stale air and set off down the hall.

There were two sets of stairs, one at either end of the long narrow building, and as Clara moved past apartment 1A, then 1B, the noises shifted around her, impossible to pinpoint. A shriek made her spin around suddenly, but it was followed by a fainter echo, from a higher floor. She continued undeterred. She refused to be thrown by the unfamiliar building and its knack for trickery.

She replayed Detective Ireland's instructions: Get invited in, get Mrs. Milligan talking. It seemed simple enough. She felt alert and clear-eyed. If she was honest about the butterflies, it wasn't nerves. It was anticipation. She was hungry for knowledge and confident she could find out something from Connie's mother.

She shifted the brown grocery bag to her other hand. Of course, the moment the detectives had driven away, she had peeked inside, and found a cream sweater, pilled under the arms; a garnet-red lipstick, nearly finished; a blunt kohl pencil; two pay stubs; and a packet of gum. The sum of Connie's belongings.

Apartment 1C was at the far end of the first floor. She rang the bell and waited, gripping the bag tightly, her hands crushing the paper. From inside she heard a clatter of dishes and a child's whining—that threw her. Had she gotten the wrong apartment?

Finally the door opened to reveal a middle-aged woman—

fine lines on her freckled face, hair hastily clipped back—wiping her hands on an apron. A drumroll of quick footfalls, and a little girl, about three years old, thrust herself past the woman and scrutinized Clara for a moment. Cheeks flushed, she held up a cookie, shrieked an utterance, and thudded away again.

"Mrs. Milligan? I'm Clara. I work at the studio." Her voice was more halting than she had practiced. The woman studied her for a cold moment, and Clara responded with a confused smile. "I'm sorry. I must have the wrong address."

"What do you people want now?" said the woman, her face set, her lips a thin line. "I don't have time for this." She went to close the door.

"I brought you Connie's things," said Clara quickly. Grateful for the bag, she held it up like an offering.

The woman stopped short, a shadow of suspicion behind her eyes.

Clara continued softly, "May I come in?" She watched the woman weaken and steel herself at once.

"Just for a minute." Mrs. Milligan took the bag from Clara. "But I have to get the little one an early supper." She disappeared into the apartment, leaving the door open for Clara to follow.


Clara sat on a lumpy couch in the living room, one half of it draped with linen waiting to be ironed. Wooden blocks and toy cars lay scattered across the hardwood floor; the little girl was lining up an army of dolls and stuffed animals on the rug.

"Excuse the mess. She's a hurricane, this one." Connie's mother gave a weak smile. She would have been pretty once, but she looked dog-tired.

Clara nodded vaguely, still wondering who the little girl belonged to.

"I'll get you an iced tea," said Mrs. Milligan. She was cradling the bag Clara had given her.

"That would be great." The apartment was stuffy and sour with the reek of damp laundry and turned milk. Clara's eyes wandered to the mantelpiece and the collection of family photographs. Hungrily, she scanned them, homing in on a wedding photo: Connie and a young man in air force dress. He was terrifically handsome, with a dimpled chin and an excellent smile. The cops hadn't mentioned that Connie had been married. Next to the wedding photo there was a framed certificate from Miss Webster's typing school, awarding C. Milligan "distinction."

Mrs. Milligan took a shabby armchair near the little girl, no attempt to fetch the iced tea, as though the offer of refreshment had already been forgotten. She placed the bag of Connie's belongings carefully on a side table, and Clara understood that she wasn't going to open it in her presence.

Clara tucked her hair behind her ear, rehearsing avenues of conversation in her head, assessing the best approach. A fan blew a stale breeze across the room in a sweeping arc. It did little to refresh. It just managed to ruffle the little girl's curls with each pass.

"What's her name?" Clara asked. Mrs. Milligan stiffened, and Clara realized she had somehow blundered.

"Mae," she said with a snap in her voice. The little girl looked up for a moment at the sound of her name. Mrs. Milligan folded her arms. "Connie didn't tell you about her?"

She was *Connie's* daughter. "No," said Clara, simply. She had learned from her years in high school—when her German background had proved a liability—not to elaborate unnecessarily. Clara calmly waited for Mrs. Milligan to go on.

"It figures," she said, in a softer tone. "Connie didn't like to tell movie people about the little one." Her eyes rested on Mae. She shook her head. "Said it didn't fit with her image. She even went back to using her maiden name. Jim's name was Polish—Connie said it didn't sound right for an actress."

"Is that Jim?" asked Clara, nodding to the photo on the mantel. "He's very handsome."

"He was good-looking, right enough. Killed in Normandy—the D-Day landings."

"I'm sorry." Clara shifted her position on the couch. Something sharp was poking into her thigh. She retrieved a doll from under the cushion. "Mae, is this yours?" Clara asked.

Responding to the upbeat tone, the girl perked up, snatched the doll from Clara, and added it to her brood of stuffed animals on the rug.

"You worked on the movie with Connie?" Mrs. Milligan said.

"Yes," said Clara brightly. "She did pretty well, going from extra to stand-in so quickly." Clara was pushing a little, hoping Mrs. Milligan would offer something.

Mrs. Milligan shrugged. "She had the look, I expect, of that Bannon woman. Not to mention sheer will." She exhaled a sigh. "I thought secretary work was a decent paycheck." She shook her head. "Connie was adamant we leave San Bernardino. So off we went—a few months after Jim was killed—the three of us to Los Angeles."

Clara glanced up at the wedding photo on the mantel, trying to form a picture. Connie Milligan: small-town secretary, newly widowed with Hollywood dreams.

"Did she always want to work in movies?" Clara asked.

"I suppose so. She always loved the pictures." Connie's mom nodded to the little girl. "Why do you think she named her after Mae West? She was always enamored with movie people—ever since she worked as a secretary in Palm Springs, rubbing shoulders with Hollywood types. They 'winter' in the desert, apparently." Her face hardened. "She should have stuck to typing." The words stung.

God, it was warm in the apartment. They sat watching the little girl as if she were the sole reason for Clara's visit.

"I've called her Connie more than once," said Mrs. Milligan.

Clara forced herself to say something. "It's awful—I can't imagine." The words were thin and meaningless. She had no business trespassing on the Milligans' grief. The ripples of Connie's murder were tidal waves to the people left behind. "Mrs. Milligan, I should probably leave—you have your hands full. Thank you for taking the time." Clara went to get up.

But it was as though Mrs. Milligan hadn't heard. "Apartment living," she said, and continued to stare at her charge. "The little one needs space to roam. In San Bernardino, when Connie was little, we had a yard, and a park down the block. . . ." She trailed off. The fan swept the air across them. Neither of them spoke.

Clara studied Mrs. Milligan. She looked exhausted, the joy of this child smothered by the loss of her own. Her wide, freckled brow, no makeup; her roots were needing done, and her wave was limp. What was she thinking? That if they hadn't left San Bernardino, Connie would still be alive?

From the hallway there were raised voices, a baby screaming, and a door slam. It set Clara on edge. Her eyes returned to the photographs. Connie Milligan: pretty enough to be a stand-in but not a star. Done up to look like someone else, she had been in the wrong place at the wrong time. Had she just been unlucky?

"Why are you here?" Mrs. Milligan's gaze landed on Clara like the beam of a searchlight. "You going to dish the dirt for one of those gossip rags?" Her voice had a rough edge to it. "They've been pestering me for days."

Clara's heartbeat pounded from her throat to her diaphragm. Connie's mother had seen through her.

Mrs. Milligan narrowed her eyes. " 'The Silver Blonde.' " She turned away, disgusted. "She had a name."

Clara clasped her hands together to keep them from shaking. "I work at the studio, on the same movie as Connie, but I'm

152

sorry, I didn't know your daughter very well." Her throat felt as dry as sand. "I didn't mean to give you that impression." She swallowed hard. She felt like some kind of swindler, wanting to nose around the victim's home, playing detective, assuming Mrs. Milligan would somehow open up to her, where Ireland and Rivetti had failed. "Mrs. Milligan, I would never go to the papers."

The older woman studied Clara for a moment, and her shoulders dropped. Clara's face must have convinced her of something. She dusted some lint from her apron. "Would you like to see her room?"

Connie's bedroom was neat and fresh, and full of life. It looked more like it belonged to a teenager, not a widow or a mother. There was a vanity littered with makeup and perfume bottles, an open closet stuffed with shoeboxes and cocktail dresses. The walls were papered with images of her idols torn from the pages of *Photoplay* or *Modern Screen.* Clara recognized the shiny dreams, the hungry pursuit; it was the same desire for a piece of Hollywood that Clara felt.

Mrs. Milligan sat on the edge of the bed, a hand absently smoothing the flowered bedspread. There were framed photographs on the night table: Mae as a baby in Connie's arms, and a candid of Jim and Connie on the beach. There was an openness to her face, a softness. She'd probably had one of those easy, infectious laughs. In the biggest photo frame there was a professional shot of Connie—the same one the newspaper had printed. It pulsed like a beacon, and Clara reached for it.

"May I?"

Mrs. Milligan nodded.

Clara held the cold metal frame and stared at Connie's picture. The original color photo was much clearer than the one in newsprint. It was a high-angle shot. She was wearing an off-the-shoulder dress, her head turned up to the camera as if someone had just called her name. Clara took a seat on the bed next to Mrs. Milligan. "She's pretty," said Clara.

Mrs. Milligan nodded. "She turned heads, all right. Two years since Jim passed, but she wasn't interested in dating. He was her big love. 'Lightning doesn't strike twice,' she would say." Connie's mom tutted. "Always thought she had an advantage with her looks." There was a brittle edge to her voice. "Instead, that's what got her killed."

"Is that what the police said?" Clara turned to Mrs. Milligan. "Because she looked like Babe Bannon?"

"I don't know." She shook her head like it hurt. "Connie didn't have *enemies*. She got along with people; she wasn't in with a bad crowd. Her life was just her job, and me and Mae." Mrs. Milligan peered over Clara's shoulder at the framed picture. "I always liked her natural color, dark blond with highlights from the sun." Her voice cracked a little. She turned to Clara. "Much like yours." Mrs. Milligan's eyes were glassy, her high round forehead crinkled. "I suppose the hairdresser did a nice job on the new color." She chuckled. "But you wouldn't have thought so.

The day Connie came back from the salon, she was in a foul mood—I mean she hardly remarked on her hair. Normally she'd be preening at herself in every reflective surface, wanting to take her new hairdo out for a spin." Mrs. Milligan caught herself on the sunny memories. "But she wasn't herself at all that day."

This confirmed what Rosa the hairdresser had told Clara. "Did you find out what was bothering her?"

Mrs. Milligan frowned. "No, she wouldn't say. It was around the anniversary of V-E Day. I don't think it was anything to do with a hairdo. She would have been thinking about Jim."

"Did you mention any of this to the detectives?"

Mrs. Milligan made a face. "Those two nitwits? Yes, I told them she was out of sorts, but they kept asking me if Connie was dating someone, as though anything that happened to her didn't make sense without a man in the picture." She rolled her eyes. "That Rivetti is about as perceptive as a brick. I'm sure he thinks all women are moody and hysterical."

"Was she out of sorts for a while?" asked Clara, trying for concern, not curiosity.

"A few days, I think. Eventually she came around—she went out a couple of times with Miss Bannon, which cheered her up. They even went dancing."

*Connie and Babe Bannon out on the town?* This didn't sound right.

Mrs. Milligan sighed. "They got on well. I expect they spent a bit of time together on the film set."

Clara forced a smile. "Yes, of course." She recalled Bannon by the pool, swirling her drink around, shrugging and saying that she'd hardly known Connie. Bannon was *lying,* but why?

There was a sudden crash from the living room and a beat of quiet before a sharp cry rang out. It soon escalated to a wail. Connie's mom sprang off the bed and dashed off. "Mae, what's happened? Nana's coming." Clara put the photo frame back on the night table and cast her gaze around the room. Everything about it was rooted in the present. It was a strange feeling, as though Connie had just stepped out to get something from the kitchen, and any second Clara would hear the click of her heels on the hardwood floor.

As Clara crossed the room to leave, the open window caught the lift of a breeze. It wafted through the curtains and hit her with the sweetness of a meadow. Clara stopped and inhaled. She was standing in front of the vanity, and her eyes ran over the makeup and perfume bottles, the curling iron and hair rollers. There was a little dish with matchbooks from Hollywood hotspots. Clara recognized the names from the gossip columns: Romanoffs, the Cocoanut Grove, the Mocambo. Were they mementoes, like Clara's cigar box of keepsakes?

Connie had collected magazines too. On the floor next to the vanity, piles of them were stacked by publication: *Vogue, Harper's Bazaar, Photoplay, Variety.* There was an odd one out: on top of the stack of *Vogue* magazines was a copy of the *Saturday Evening Post.* It looked out of place—a news magazine among all the fashion and Hollywood gossip. The cover was a

Norman Rockwell–style illustration of two little boys staring at airplanes. Clara picked it up. The date was March 30 of this year, and the address on the label wasn't Gramercy Place—it was for a beauty salon on Beverly Boulevard. Her heart thumped. It was where Connie had gotten her hair done—she must have taken the magazine from Rosa's salon. Curious, Clara began to flip through the pages.

There was an article about wounded vets, titled "We Will Walk." She scanned it quickly. *Today's veterans are taking a new lease on life and learning to be independent.* There were photographs of men in hospital beds, with crutches, another of a man in a wheelchair. Clara studied the faces in the photographs. *Staff Sgt. Howard Ogden learns to walk on inert legs, aided by handrails and a leather brace. Pfc. Louis Tepper works out at volleyball with a physical instructor. With the help of a physiotherapist, Lt. Harold Ritchey performs some basic exercises.*

Could Connie have known any of these boys? Perhaps they'd been with her husband's regiment, or they were friends from back home in San Bernardino. Mrs. Milligan had said it was around the anniversary of V-E Day when Connie was low. Could that be it, these boys reminded her of Jim? In the background she could hear that Mae's wailing had tapered off. She quickly skimmed through a handful of pages and then stopped. Her eyes landed on the title of an article: "NAZI PIN-UP GIRL continued from page 11." She flicked back to the beginning of the article.

On page 11, Clara was blindsided. A flood of recognition, a face from the past. This had nothing to do with Connie Milligan. Clara was back on board the SS *Europa*, at a table laden with *Kaffee und Kuchen*, beaming at a glamorous German passenger. A streak of adrenaline shot down her arms to her fingertips, and the thin newsprint trembled in her hands. Above the photograph, the shock of the name: *Nazi Pin-up Girl, Hitler's No. 1 movie actress, Leni Riefenstahl*. It was the answer to her *own* riddle—the owner of the handkerchief.

## Chapter Eighteen

# Easy Does It

SMALL FOOTSTEPS DRUMMED DOWN the hall, and Clara could hear Mrs. Milligan's voice cooing after Mae to have some milk. In a flash, Clara had shrugged off her cardigan and draped it over the magazine in her arms.

She left the bedroom and walked down the narrow hall. It was only a news magazine, but because she'd taken it from Connie's room, it felt like it was burning a hole in the pale cotton knit. Little Mae was charging toward her at full tilt, screaming some protestation. Clara managed to dodge her. "I should be going now, Mrs. Milligan," she said, pausing at the kitchen door, where Connie's mom was grabbing a pint of milk from the icebox.

The cardigan hung stiffly and unnaturally over her arm. "Thank you for taking the time," she said, moving a step to the side, trying to conceal her arm behind the doorframe.

Mrs. Milligan poured the milk into a small cup. "She's a terror when she's hungry." She tried a smile but didn't quite manage.

Clara scanned the chaotic kitchen. "Perhaps I can drop off some groceries sometime?" Behind her, Mae's yammering was getting louder. Clara had to raise her voice. "You've got your hands full here."

"Yes, that would be— Mae, I've got your milk. Here it is."

"I'll see myself out," said Clara. Holding her breath, she swiftly darted out of the apartment, and then closed the door firmly behind her with a surge of relief. The corridor was dark and still smelled of fried onions.

Outside, the girls playing jump rope were gone and the sky was draining light. Clara peeled her cardigan off the magazine and walked briskly up the street. She stopped abruptly, realizing she had another problem. The detectives were waiting for her a couple of blocks away on Beverly. Would they ask her where she'd gotten the magazine? No, it was just a magazine and it didn't have the Milligans' address on it. Still, when they'd dropped her off, she hadn't been carrying it. She had to improvise.

On the corner of Gramercy she darted into the bodega, bought a bag of licorice. Now it looked like she'd gotten the magazine with the candy. When she reached the corner of Gramercy and Beverly, she turned right toward Western. She could see the cops' Chrysler kitty-corner, idling by the curb. She crossed the street at a relaxed pace. At the next crosswalk she popped some licorice into her mouth and chewed nervously.

As she approached the car, they must have seen her in the rearview mirror, because the window rolled down. "Jump in," said Rivetti.

She slid along the backseat, which was as big as a boat. On the back of the magazine there was an advertisement for Coca-Cola, a couple of sunny teenagers doing chores. *Easy does it. . . . Have a Coke.*

The cops turned around. "So? What have you got?" asked Rivetti.

"The mother, what did she say?" said Ireland.

Clara took a breath and launched into an account of what she had learned. Connie was a war widow who had been in love with her husband; she wasn't dating anyone new; she'd been down or out of sorts around the anniversary of V-E Day—probably missing Jim. She'd gone out dancing with Miss Bannon, which had cheered her up. Clara added that this was around the same time that she'd gotten her hair lightened to match the movie star's. Connie had reacted strangely to the new look.

Rivetti rolled his eyes. "Her bangs too short?" he muttered.

Clara glared at him. She also pointed out that Bannon had claimed she didn't really know her stand-in, but that didn't match Mrs. Milligan's story. (Clara didn't want to come right out and call Babe Bannon a liar.)

Rivetti batted his hand in the air, dismissing this detail. "A regular guy spends five minutes with a movie star, he's gonna dine out on that story the rest of his life. Doesn't mean anything." He turned to Ireland. "Come on. We're running a murder case, not a Girl Scout troop. We're wasting time with this." He threw a nod to his partner. "And there's that other lead to check out."

From his low tone of voice, Clara knew this was something

161

they didn't intend to share. She felt a little shiver down her back and her mind leapt to Gil—his whereabouts the night of the murder and his secret past with Bannon.

The detectives offered her a ride home, but Clara, keen to be alone, said she'd take the streetcar. She supposed she had failed to find out anything helpful for the Connie Milligan case. Her observations had shriveled to nothing under the scrutinizing gaze of the detectives. Maybe Rivetti was right—Connie Milligan was a dead end.

## Chapter Nineteen

# *Europa*

THE BEVERLY STREETCAR LURCHED forward and ground to a halt almost immediately. The magazine lay on Clara's lap, her hands clasped on its innocuous cover, the two boys watching airplanes.

Clara turned and stared out the window. For once she was grateful for the rush hour traffic and the slow progression of the eastbound streetcar. Having debriefed the detectives, she now had time to think—not about the murder, but about her own riddle. Looking out the grimy window at the bodegas and markets and liquor stores of Beverly Boulevard, her mind drifted to the past. It was no longer a warm spring evening in Los Angeles. It was a bitter afternoon on the Atlantic Ocean.

The sundeck in November was miserable and deserted. Klara gripped the rail of the ship, heart hammering. A smattering of cold rain hit her face. Something huge was happening to her for once, something that would change the course of her life—a sharp pivot from the straight line of continuity and routine.

She had been excited about the ship—the *Europa*—Germany's fastest ocean liner. But now, all she wished was to be back home in Charlottenburg. She grappled with the realization that her parents had duped *her* and not the other way round. She had assumed it was her pleading and badgering that had finally convinced them to bring her on her father's lecture tour—two months and no school. Excused from sitting the end-of-term exams, a triumph! And yet all along, their show of reluctance had been masking something more serious. The Bergs were never returning to Berlin. They were *fleeing* to America. *Political refugees.* Only now, in the middle of the Atlantic Ocean, did they reveal the truth. She felt a wing-flap of panic when she contemplated the fate of her beloved possessions. Her mother had explained that Frau Krupke next door was to pack up the contents of the apartment, and her son would put the boxes in storage. But Frau Krupke had granddaughters. Wouldn't they be tempted by her collection of dolls, her porcelain horse figurines? How could they pass up the illustrated Grimm's fairy tales? She imagined them picking over her things like a rummage sale. If only Klara had known the truth, she would have packed differently—"forever" changed everything.

Blinking away her angry tears, she ducked back inside and down a stairwell, which led to first class. It was warm inside.

There were brightly lit shops in one direction and the grand dining room in the other. Her wool sweater was damp, her hair windswept. She noticed a ship's steward craning his neck, watching her. He began to move toward her. Klara darted the other way—down a carpeted hallway, through a door, and onto the promenade deck.

It was a long enclosed walkway with large windows that ran the length of the ship. Lined with cushioned deck chairs, it was sheltered from the wind and rain. She stared through the glass at the slate-gray ocean, the same color as the sky. America waited for them. In just three days she would be there—incredible. Germany left behind. For Klara, politics had been background noise, the dull hum of adult conversation, annoying radio static. She had tuned it out—they weren't Jewish; it hadn't affected her. Until now. She shivered, chilled to the bone.

There were voices behind her. She turned and watched a couple hurry along the deck. As they passed, the man gave a momentous sneeze. Klara didn't pay him much attention, for it was his glamorous companion who had caught her eye. The woman appeared to have stepped out of a magazine: fox fur, auburn hair, bright eyes. She strode along the deck ahead of her companion. The man, fumbling in his coat for a handkerchief, paused to catch another sneeze. At the decisive moment it erupted with such force that something fell out of his coat pocket—a wallet. An overripe fruit, it landed silently on the floor of the promenade deck, with Klara the only witness.

The woman had reached the bow end of the deck. "Ernst!" she called to him, and disappeared through a door. The man hurried after her, blowing his nose, as loud as the ship's horn. It drowned out Klara's feeble *"Entschuldigung!"* She needed to chase after him—*Excuse me! You dropped something*—yet she held back. Klara was trespassing. The first-class promenade deck was off-limits to lower-class passengers, and the last thing she wanted was to draw attention to herself. The wallet remained on the floor next to a row of empty deck chairs. Fat, juicy, unclaimed.

Another passenger might come along and hand it in. Klara looked both ways along the deck, but it remained deserted. She could find the steward, perhaps. But wouldn't that get her into trouble? The crew might suspect her of having pinched it. They probably wouldn't trust the word of a lower-class passenger. Was that what it was to be a refugee—always having a sneaking suspicion that you'd done something wrong? The Bergs were not typical second-class people; they used to travel first class. They were respectable (her mother's favorite word). And now they were something else altogether: *Enemies of the Third Reich.*

She moved off the rail by the windows and stood over the wallet. A fringe of bills winked at her. With the row of deck chairs watching, Klara, heart racing, snatched up the wallet and peeked inside—German marks and American dollars. A flash of daring, which instantly fizzled. She was no thief. With less confidence than the woman had shown moments earlier, Klara scurried toward the bow end of the deck.

There was a sign for the Winter Garden, and through the porthole she could see passengers on wicker chairs enjoying an elaborate afternoon tea. There were potted palms and curved windows that wrapped around the bow of the ship. The opulence made her hesitate. She thought she should drop the wallet where she'd found it and run, but there wasn't time. Someone approached: it was the man, Ernst, patting his pockets, eyes cast to the floor.

Klara wrenched open the heavy cabin door, holding the wallet like a prize. *"Entschuldigung."* Her voice disappointed her; it always sounded younger than she felt.

His face lit up. *"Ach so! Vielen Dank, vielen Dank."* The man gestured for her to come inside. "This deserves a reward."

The table was laid like in a luxury hotel: *Kirschtorte, Baumkuchen, Käsekuchen,* and English scones, served on fine bone china with gleaming silverware bearing the ship's insignia. This was nothing like the crowded second-class dining room.

"Your parents let you wander the ship alone?" asked the glamorous woman as she stirred her coffee. She had been introduced to Klara as Fräulein Richter.

"My mother has a touch of seasickness," said Klara. "She's resting in the cabin." Somewhat true. The lower-class cabins were situated in the bowels of the vessel, where the motion of the ship was stronger.

"I never get sick on a boat," Fräulein Richter said without sympathy. "Tell her to get out on deck and look at the horizon." She said it as though it were Klara's mother's choice to be seasick.

Ernst flagged down the waiter. "*Bitte.* An extra place setting for the young lady." He had a round, jovial face, and a familiar manner. Of her two hosts he was the more sympathetic but less interesting. Fräulein Richter was attractive, bright, and animated. Klara guessed she was in her early thirties. She had perfectly coiffed auburn hair, expensive clothes, and a quick laugh. Alert, her eyes scanned each newcomer to the restaurant. There was a restlessness to her movements, her hands always in motion when she talked.

"Where are you visiting in America?" Fräulein Richter asked.

"New York and then Los Angeles." Then, remembering that her family was fleeing the motherland, she elaborated nervously. "My father is a professor. He has a lecture tour for two months. After, we return to Berlin."

The woman didn't seem to care about Klara's answer. "I'm also going to California, to Hollywood."

Klara smiled. She was both intimidated and bewitched by the fashionable fräulein and studied her like the cover of a magazine. This woman was attractive in a more modern way than Klara's mother, or indeed any of the other mothers she knew.

The waiter produced an extra plate, and Ernst helped Klara to a slice of *Kirschtorte.* "A fitting reward," he said, with a deft execution of the cake slice. Klara smiled, delighted to be feted as a Good Samaritan. She couldn't remember the last time cake had been served in her own house. When Anna had still worked for them, perhaps. Months ago. She took a bite and felt a swell of pride at her single-handed invasion of first class—her mother would appreciate the surroundings. A flicker of guilt when she remembered how she'd stormed out of the cabin.

It had only been in recent months that life had unraveled for the Bergs. Her father had taken an unpaid sabbatical from the university to write a book. (Now she wondered if that were true.) Economies had been made, Anna, the housekeeper, let go. Instead of buying a new skirt for school, the hem of last year's uniform had been let down. In the evenings, when she'd been in her room, she'd heard tense arguments between her parents, fighting and shushing each other like hissing snakes in the drawing room.

Sitting in the Winter Garden with strangers somehow felt familiar, like a return to how life used to be. It was civilized and reassuring. She took another bite of cake, icing sugar cascading down her chin. As the waiter had neglected to bring a napkin for the extra guest, Fräulein Richter gave Klara a handkerchief. Klara dabbed her mouth elegantly, mimicking her hostess. For a giddy moment she let herself imagine that these were her parents and that this was how she was traveling to America—in first class, with good-humored adults.

"Ernst." A tall German man approached their table. He

slapped Ernst on the back and whispered something to Fräulein Richter with a meaningful look. He was introduced as Herr Klingeberg. He ignored Klara and beckoned over an older American couple who had entered the Winter Garden at the same time he had. The Americans were polished, bursting with confidence and toothy smiles. They made no effort to speak German. Herr Klingeberg's English was excellent, because when he spoke, it sounded like he had marbles in his mouth like the Americans. He aided Fräulein Richter, whose English was halting and peppered with German. But she made up for it with gestures and laughter. The others seemed to be in no doubt as to what she meant.

As an only child of a professor, Klara was all too used to the company of adults and was accustomed to being overlooked when grown-up conversation took over. As the adults talked, she looked around the Winter Garden, studying the other passengers. Even though she didn't understand the conversation floating above her head, Klara could decipher that their table—and this woman in particular—was a source of intrigue and importance. She caught surreptitious glances from the other passengers, and other than the forgotten napkin for Klara, the waitstaff were very attentive.

"Fräulein Richter," said the American man, tapping his nose. Klara didn't know what it meant, but they were all laughing. Eventually the Americans moved off and Herr Klingeberg pulled up an extra chair next to Fräulein Richter, who seemed to be glowing from the brief exchange.

"You see, you're quite the celebrity," said Herr Klingeberg. Then he signaled the waiter.

*"Nom de voyage,"* Ernst said, chuckling. "Even the ship's cat must know you're on board."

Herr Klingeberg shrugged off his scarf and tossed it onto the back of his chair. Klara froze midbite, a large piece of *Kirschtorte* lodged in her cheek. The pin on his lapel—an eagle clutching a swastika—was the *Reichsadler.* Swastikas were everywhere in Berlin, but only government officials wore this pin. She swallowed; the cake scraped down her throat like a stone. A voice in her head was echoing the words her father had uttered only an hour before: *Enemies of the Third Reich.*

After her father's revelations—he was on some list; he could be arrested—Klara was unsure what side she was on. Up until the *Europa,* she had believed like Freya and Matthias in the greatness of Germany, that Hitler was strengthening the country, bringing the German *Volk* together. She knew her parents didn't agree with Hitler, but she had chosen to emulate her peers and her teachers—and everyone else she knew. Admiring the Führer was the popular opinion, and who wouldn't want to be on the cheering side?

Klara fidgeted with the handkerchief on her lap. Retreat felt like the safest option. But how? She felt paralyzed in the face of grown-up civility. She was a well-brought-up girl. Wouldn't it be rude to suddenly get up and leave the table?

Ernst topped up his cup and smiled at her. Klara's stomach churned. He offered her another slice of cake, which she accepted but had no appetite for. She tried to silence the thoughts in her head, frantic that she was transparent.

Finally she set down her fork deliberately, wiped her mouth, and stood up abruptly as though she had been called on in class. "My parents will be wondering where I am. Thank you, Fräulein Richter." Keeping her eyes averted from the *Reichsadler*, she nodded to Herr Klingeberg and smiled mechanically at Ernst, who half rose, his napkin falling from his lap.

His face was not unkind. "Everything all right, Klara?"

She felt faint, the cake sitting like a paving stone in her gut.

"The child looks ill," said Herr Klingeberg.

"Perhaps a touch of seasickness," said Ernst helpfully.

"Ernst, take her to her parents' cabin," said Fräulein Richter.

Klara shook her head vehemently. "Just some air—I'll be fine. Lovely to meet you. Thank you again."

"It is *I* who thank you, Klara," Ernst called after her. She concentrated on walking as steadily as possible to the door.

"Poor lamb," she heard Ernst say. "Sick on a boat—it's the worst."

"Too much cake," quipped Herr Klingeberg.

Her hosts' conversation faded into the general babble of well-to-do Germans at *Kaffe und Kuchen*. Klara reached the door and clutched the handle like her life depended on it. She flung the door open and made her escape. She tore off down the promenade deck, ducked into a door at the far end, and ran down a flight of steps and back to the rabbit warren of lower decks. Two levels down, she was forced to stop and catch her breath. She panted, her throat dry, her belly full and lurching. Her hip throbbed where she'd caught it on the metal railing of the stairwell. She looked down at her hand. Balled up in her fist was the woman's handkerchief.

## Chapter Twenty

# Nazi Pin-Up Girl

BY THE TIME CLARA got home, it was nearly dinnertime. She poked her head into the living room and noticed that the piano was gone. Her parents must be in the kitchen. She could smell beef Stroganoff and hear the wireless and her mother's laugh.

As she passed the hall table she saw an envelope addressed to Klara Berg. She picked it up. There was a German postmark, and the sender's stamp said University of Bonn. A familiar feeling of dread resurfaced. This would be the acceptance letter. Her father had said that the offer of a place to study Modern Languages was all but guaranteed. She tossed the letter back onto the table, unopened.

The moment she stepped into the kitchen, her mother raised an eyebrow at the *Saturday Evening Post* under her arm. "You're buying *more* magazines, Klara?" Her mother shook her head. "Honestly, we're trying to prune things down." But she was smiling and her cheeks were pink. There was a glass of wine next to the stove. Her father was peeling potatoes at the sink. Clara felt suddenly bathed in the warm light and the familiar routine of a home-cooked meal.

She tossed the magazine onto the table and opened the fridge, looking for something to eat.

"There's a letter for you," her father said. "Did you open it?"

"Not yet." She could imagine them exchanging an exasperated look behind her back.

"Don't snack before dinner," said her mother. "It will be ready in a half hour, if my sous-chef finishes peeling potatoes."

Clara closed the fridge and noticed the stack of newspapers at the back door, probably to be tossed in the incinerator. An idea popped into her head. "Papa, do you still have the first newspaper you bought in New York? After we got off the ship, remember. You haven't thrown it out, have you?"

"That one I'm keeping," he said, pointing the potato peeler at her mother. "This woman can't throw everything out from under us." Her parents exchanged a smile; they were happy. He returned to peeling potatoes. "It's in my study. There's a box of newspapers behind the door. What are you looking for?"

Clara scooped up Connie's magazine. "Just curious about something," she said, already out of the room.

Her father's office was a small room at the front of the house. He had hung on to several of the newspapers he'd bought in New York and Los Angeles during their first weeks in America. She rifled through the box and found the copy of the *New York*

*Times* from November 5, 1938. Clara flipped through it, scanning every page until she found what she was looking for:

## HERE WITH REICH FILM
### Leni Riefenstahl here on visit only

**Leni Riefenstahl, German film star and director, who is said to be one of the few close friends of Chancellor Adolf Hitler, arrived yesterday on the North German Lloyd liner *Europa*.**

There it was in black and white. The air around Clara shifted. How curious. All these years, and she had never known who it was until today. Why hadn't she recognized the famous director?

Clara sat down at her father's desk and opened the *Saturday Evening Post* once more. *Leni Riefenstahl, Hitler's No. 1 movie actress, explains away—with a theatrical smile—her former status in Nazi Germany,* said the lede.

She wasn't just an actress. She was a film director—Hitler's film director—whose propaganda film *Triumph of the Will* was infamous the world over. The article dubbed the film *a kind of cinematic bogeyman to frighten little nations.* Before making propaganda documentaries for Hitler, the article described Riefenstahl as a *German pin-up girl of the early thirties, famous all over Europe for her adventures in the Alps, in Iceland, and in various boudoirs, and for her ability to combine these interests in the successful productions of such films as* The White Hell of Pitz Palu, S.O.S. Iceberg, *and* The Blue Light.

After Hitler came to power, she embraced his philosophies and agreed to make films exclusively for him (and it was rumored that she became his mistress). *Leni slid down from her profitable glaciers, wrapped her trim figure in the swastika flag, and energetically went to work on a series of films dedicated to a man with a lock of hair over his forehead and a cloud of hate over his mind.*

Klara had never been permitted to watch *Triumph of the Will* in its entirety—only snippets on newsreels. It had been shown once in her elementary school at the end of term. She must have been eight or nine. Her mother called the school that day and said her daughter had come down with the flu. Ruth Hoffman—her Jewish friend—was also kept home. Klara overheard her mother on the phone talking to Ruth's mother. The women weren't close, but Klara gleaned that this film screening had broken through some barrier of polite acquaintance.

But the following month Klara managed to sneak away to a matinee screening. She was desperate to see what the fuss was about. The ban on Riefenstahl in the Berg household extended to her next film of the '36 Olympics. Klara took issue with this because *Olympia* wasn't political. It was about sports, and hadn't the Bergs watched a fencing match at the Olympics? So why couldn't they see a film of the other sports? This was her child's logic, at any rate. Miss Riefenstahl won a prize for *Olympia*, Klara heard it on the radio, presented by Dr. Goebbels. The film was nonetheless forbidden.

Perhaps that was why Klara hadn't recognized the woman

on the *Europa*—Leni Riefenstahl had been a name and an idea, not a distinctive face. Besides, the woman she had met had been introduced by quite a different name: Fräulein Richter. And why would Klara question the word of well-dressed grown-ups in first class? They had no reason to lie.

Now, all these years later, Clara stared at the face in the magazine. It wasn't obvious in the photograph, but her hair, from memory, was light auburn. She had tanned skin, and in the picture she was smiling, relaxed, leaning on a deck chair in a white shirt and leather jacket. She was older in this picture than Clara remembered, but it was definitely her.

A car engine revved on the street outside. At the same time her mother called from the kitchen. *"Klara, set the table!"*

Clara ignored her, still lost in thought. It had been a strange afternoon. From visiting the Milligans' depressing apartment—snooping in Connie's room—to revisiting the past and her conflicted feelings about coming to America. And of course the irony was that now she didn't want to leave.

As Clara stood up she glanced out the window. It was getting dark, but under the streetlamp she could see a pale convertible idling in front of their house—Gil. Her pulse quickened. He cut the engine, the headlights went dark, and she watched as he opened the driver's-side door and got out.

Clara darted to the hallway and lunged for the front door to intercept him. She stood on the front step and pulled the door closed behind her. Gil strode up the path. He gave her a casual nod, as if it were the most normal thing, his showing up at her house unannounced around dinnertime.

"What are you doing here?" Clara said, realizing she sounded out of breath.

He paused to light a smoke. "Wanted to check you were okay. I saw you drive off with the detectives this afternoon."

After grabbing her purse and shouting a garbled excuse to her parents about having plans, Clara slammed the front door and hopped into Gil's car. Her mother would be furious—she'd have to deal with that later.

They drove to the Brown Derby around the corner. There was an energy to Los Feliz Boulevard; Clara always felt that the city came alive at night.

Neon light splashed over the car as they pulled into a drive-in spot.

"You went to her apartment?" Gil cranked the hand brake roughly. "But why? You didn't even know her." On the short drive over she had told Gil of her errand to return Connie's belongings.

"Like I said, I was helping the detectives." Clara shifted in her seat. "They asked me to go." She couldn't meet his eye.

"Does her mother know you found the body?" He sounded appalled.

Clara's head whipped round. "No, of course not."

Gil raised his eyebrows. "I dunno, Clara. Talking to a hair-dresser is one thing, but bothering her mother—barging in on that family's grief. It's not a game. You should be careful."

"I wasn't bothering her. Mrs. Milligan was glad of the company." Another fib. She pressed her lips together.

"Was it worth it?" He gave a little jerk of his head. "What did you find out?"

Clara fidgeted with the strap of her purse. "Nothing important, nothing useful." Gil had hit a raw nerve. What had she achieved other than upsetting Mrs. Milligan and delaying Mae's dinner? "The cops think that the Connie angle is a washout. They're only interested in who had a motive to kill Babe Bannon." Her eyes snagged on Gil. "All they can see is the movie star."

Bannon's real name was lodged in the back of her throat— Ruby Kaminsky. She desperately wanted to blurt it out, to ask him everything about her. Her heart beat faster as she anticipated how it would feel to bring up the past.

The waitress came to the driver's side and handed them a menu. Clara would have preferred to go inside the restaurant; she could see couples seated at tables through the window, their heads bent toward one another—intimate.

Gil ordered a coffee—nothing to eat—and Clara did the same, even though her stomach twisted with hunger at the smell of fries from the next car. A couple entered the restaurant holding hands. She watched the hostess greet them warmly and show them to a table.

Clara couldn't hold back any longer. "You know, you should be careful, Gil." The roar of a motorcycle nearly drowned her out as it tore down Hillhurst.

"Wait—what?" His eyebrows knit together. "What do you mean?"

"You and Ruby—your history." Her words felt like weapons, a grenade tossed carelessly into conversation. But he didn't flinch—he barely reacted.

Gil blinked slowly. "Years ago, when we were kids. Ancient history."

The confirmation—from his lips—felt like a gut punch. Suddenly all of Clara's feelings about Gil and Babe Bannon lay exposed under the neons—her burning curiosity, her sense of inferiority compared to the movie star, her fascination with their love affair. Clara wanted him to confide in her, as he had done on the battle set. She wanted him to tell her everything.

"Well, why do you keep it a secret?" she asked. "Are you on bad terms or something?" The words came tumbling out, thin and petty.

Gil adjusted the rearview mirror. "It's not a secret, it's just not that interesting." He didn't answer her second question.

The waitress brought their coffees. Gil appeared relieved at the interruption. He carefully handed Clara a piping hot Dixie cup, then gave the waitress a few coins.

Clara wasn't ready to let the subject drop. "Why do you avoid Bannon?" she asked. "You're never on set."

"I don't avoid her. It's the same reason I'd rather sit in the car than go inside the Brown Derby—I don't do well in crowds anymore." A flash of reproach. "If I have to be somewhere—like the other night at the Formosa—I go when it's quiet, and I sit with

181

my back to the wall and my eye on the door." The cold light cast shadows like bruises under his eyes. It had been a year since the war ended, but Gil was still fighting.

Clara held her coffee cup lightly, her fingertips prickling with the heat. "The cops are looking for motives, any connections to Bannon. They would pounce on something like this." His face betrayed nothing. "You don't have an alibi, Gil. It doesn't look good."

He sipped his coffee, then winced like it had burned his lips. He wiped his mouth with the back of his hand. "Clara, what are you trying to say? You think I had something to do with Connie's death?" He glowered at her like a junkyard dog

"Of course not. But I'm worried. Shouldn't you try and get ahead of this?" she said. "Think how it would look to the cops if they find out."

The night air felt charged with danger. The glare from the neon was unrelenting. Gil's face had changed; his stubble was darker, aging him.

"I have nothing to hide." He spoke slowly, deliberately. He barely moved, as though he was welded to the seat. Taciturn: how Brackett had described his partner. He would tease Gil about never smiling.

Clara felt reprimanded by his silence. She took a sip of the scalding coffee, a nauseous pit in her stomach. What was she trying to achieve by confronting him? Was she truly concerned about what the police might think—or was she just satisfying her own curiosity by churning up his past? Or was there a third possibility? Did she have her own doubts about Gil?

They sat drinking their coffee, listening to the traffic. Maybe there was a show at the Greek. Vermont would be snarled going into the park.

Gil slugged back his coffee. "I have to be someplace," he said, out of nowhere.

Clara went to toss the cups of coffee in the trash. When she returned to the car, she retrieved her purse from the front seat and rested a hand on the open door. "I think I'll walk home, I could do with the air."

Gil went to turn on the ignition. "Come on, I can drive you." There was an edge to his voice. He didn't look at her.

"No, I'd prefer to walk. It's not even ten minutes." Clara slammed the passenger door shut. "See you at work." She walked down the line of cars at the drive-in spots, past the brightly lit restaurant, and onto the street to join the restless city at night.

## Chapter Twenty-One

# Mismatch

"DID YOU CATCH IT?" said Sam.

Clara looked at him quizzically. "Catch what?"

Sam rewound the scene. "Watch again."

Friday morning, and Sam was playing a scene of cut footage on the Moviola. It was one of the film's opening scenes, when the sergeant gives Babe Bannon's widow character the letter from her dead husband. Clara's mind was somewhere else— replaying the visit to Mrs. Milligan's and then pivoting back to her argument with Gil.

"Ready?" said Sam. "Now pay close attention."

Clara watched the scene play again: the widow takes the envelope, turns her back to the sergeant, and reads the letter. Nothing unusual jumped out at Clara. She shook her head. "I don't notice anything, Sam. It plays."

The editor wore a knowing smile. "Watch the sergeant's hat." He rewound the scene once more, and paused on the tight shot where the sergeant handed over the envelope. Sam stepped through it in slow motion to the next shot. Clara finally noticed the discrepancy. Randall held his hat in his left hand, but it jumped to his right hand in the wider shot. In plain sight but completely invisible.

"I see it," said Clara. "The continuity doesn't match, but your eye is on Bannon's face reading the letter. You don't notice the hat." She gazed at Sam like he'd performed a magic trick. "Play it again." They watched the scene once more at regular speed. "I keep missing it. I'm with Bannon and the letter."

"Exactly." Sam smiled. "It's one of my tricks—cutting with a mismatch. I can get away with it because I know the audience is looking at another part of the frame—they're distracted."

Clara rolled her chair back to her desk where she was organizing the camera and sound reports. One of his "tricks." Distract from a mismatch, fudge an eye line, steal a line from another take, cheat dialogue on a character's back, lose a scene, kill a character—the very language of film editing was criminal. A film editor was really a con artist trying to sell a story with sleight of hand. Sound effects sold a punch that never landed; swelling strings cued the heartache or the romance that the actors failed to convey. The edit was the lie.

There was a knock on the door, and Lloyd stepped into the cutting room. He handed Clara an interoffice envelope with a knowing look, then slipped away. She flicked a glance at Sam—he was still hunched over the Moviola, tinkering with the scene. All the same, Clara casually swiveled her chair so he couldn't see what she was looking at. Holding the envelope as if it might self-ignite, she unwound the string and gently teased out the contents: a handful of contact sheets—photos from the *Argentan* set. Lloyd's buddy in the publicity department had come through for them. She slid them back into the envelope and silently left the cutting room.

In the detectives' eyes Clara might not have discovered any concrete evidence that was useful to the case, but in her own unofficial investigation, Clara had a question she intended to answer: Had Connie Milligan and Barbara Bannon been close? Detective Rivetti might have dismissed this, but Clara thought it was important. If Bannon had lied, there must be a reason.

Moments later Clara and Lloyd had ducked into an empty cutting room up the corridor, and they pored over the thumbnail pictures. In lieu of a light box Clara held the contact sheet against the window.

"I brought a loupe," said Lloyd, and handed her the small glass magnifier.

"Good thinking." Clara held it over the postage-stamp-size photos.

The contact sheet was a set of photographs from a roll of film, but printed small, and organized in rows. Clara could get an idea of what was happening on set and behind the scenes; as the photographer kept snapping, a sort of photo story emerged. Grease pencil marks crossed out the frames that weren't usable: someone blinked, someone was out of focus, a hand blocked part of the shot, or the actress had deemed the shot unflattering. These were marked "kills."

"Hand me the next one," said Clara.

Lloyd obediently gave her another contact sheet. "What are you looking for?" he asked, trying to keep his voice low.

Clara studied the images. "I'm trying to figure out if Bannon and Connie spent time together on set."

To Clara's eye the photographs confirmed what Connie's mom had implied—the women looked like friends. There were shots of them laughing together, playing cards on an apple box, drinking coffee at the craft table. In another shot, they had switched places. The name stitched on Connie's canvas chair was "Miss Bannon," and Bannon sat on Connie's chair, which fittingly had no name. The women's faces were turned toward the camera, laughing.

"Were they close?" Clara peered at the faces. "Or was it just playacting for the stills photographer?" She turned to Lloyd. "Did Connie ever mention Babe Bannon? Did you get the impression they got along?"

Lloyd shrugged. "By the time she was working as a stand-in, I didn't see much of her. Can I have a look?"

"Hang on," said Clara. There were other photos, without Connie. Some showed Howard Hawks directing the actors, setting up a scene, going over lines. Bannon and Randall Ford stood next to each other looking at Howard, who was gesticulating dramatically. In these pictures, no one was smiling.

Eventually Clara handed the loupe to Lloyd, and they switched places. "What's the big deal if they were friends or not?" said Lloyd.

"Because it means Bannon lied. She made a point of saying she hardly knew her stand-in." Clara pondered this for a minute, an idea forming. "Hey, Lloyd, take a look at Connie's costume. Is it different from Bannon's? They're not identical, right?"

Lloyd squinted at the pictures. "Yeah, I guess you're right. It's not as fancy."

"Because it's the stand-in's wardrobe." Her pulse ticked up, and she snatched the loupe from Lloyd.

"Hey," he said. "I wasn't finished."

Clara ignored him and peered at the outfits herself. Bannon's black dress had been made to measure, no expense spared. The silk bodice was molded to her curves; the delicate sheer layer grazed her collarbones. Connie's was the right color and a similar cut but had no details and definitely looked like a cheaper fabric.

They heard a noise from the hallway. "We should go," said Lloyd.

Clara peeled the contact sheet from the window and handed it back to him. They slipped out of the empty office and stood in the corridor.

"The night I found her, Connie wasn't wearing the stand-in garb," said Clara, fidgeting with the loupe. "I'm pretty certain she was wearing the real deal."

"What does that mean?" said Lloyd. "That she borrowed Bannon's costume?"

Clara nodded slowly. "Yes, but why?" She was about to say something else but stopped herself.

"What?" said Lloyd. "Spit it out."

Clara bit her lip. "I'm trying to remember." She cast her mind back to when she'd been waiting at the car wash for her father's car to be detailed. The magazines and papers in the waiting room had been of the pulp, lurid variety. Of course she'd read them; there had been nothing else to do. Clara shifted her weight. "Okay, hear me out. I read this story in the scandal sheets, about a prostitution ring that was busted by the cops, where the girls were all dressed like movie stars, look-alikes, I guess." This was awkward. Clara met Lloyd's eye. "You don't think—"

Lloyd shook his head firmly. "No way. No way Connie was mixed up in something like that."

Down the hall, the cutting room door opened and Sam peered into the corridor. "Clara! Mr. Pearce wants to see you."

## Chapter Twenty-Two

# Spotlight

FOR THE FIRST TIME in her short career at Silver Pacific studios, Clara took the elevator up to the hallowed third floor of the executive building.

Clara didn't care to meet with the head of the studio. Until last week on stage eleven, he'd been a man she'd known vaguely by sight; by the back of his head in the front row at dailies; by the sound of his voice barking into the intercom in the projection room; and by his reputation, from the stories Lloyd or Miss Simkin had recounted about the man in charge. Conrad Pearce had been born into money; he had purchased the failing Silver Pacific studios for a song in the early 1930s after old Manny Silver had bet big on expensive pictures that had later tanked.

The elevator dinged, and Clara hung back as the doors gaped open. When they started to close again, she darted between them, feeling foolish. So he was the head of the studio.

What was there to be nervous about? She hadn't done anything wrong.

The plush carpeted hallway was cool and quiet, like a hotel corridor. She entered the large outer office, and the stillness of the corridor fell away. There was a buzz of energy, the hum and crackle of a wireless on low, the murmur of voices from behind the closed doors, and somewhere the bleating ring of an unanswered phone. There were two secretaries side by side, separated by a potted plant. In front of them was a waiting area with a love seat and a coffee table scattered with issues of *Variety* and the *Los Angeles Times*. The secretary closest to Clara—the more senior of the two—was on the phone. The younger one was typing furiously, her fingers attacking the keys like Otto at the crescendo of a performance.

The closer secretary noticed her. "Hold on," she said into the phone, and looked at Clara. "Yes, dear?"

"I'm supposed to see Mr. Pearce," said Clara.

"Your name?"

Clara rolled her shoulders back. "Clara Berg, editorial."

A beat while the woman scanned her calendar.

"I work on *Letter from Argentan*," Clara added.

The light bulb went on. "Right, here you are," said the secretary, finding a note on her calendar. "Take a seat, please. Mr. Pearce will be free in a minute." She gestured to the small couch and returned to her phone call.

Clara hesitated. "Do you know what it's about?"

The secretary interrupted her call a second time. She covered the mouthpiece. "No, I don't," she said with less patience. "Have a seat, honey." Another line buzzed. She pressed a button. "Mr. Pearce's office. Hold, please."

Clara sat down as instructed, her hands tightly clasped, pressing into her lap. The ominous closed door of Mr. Pearce's office conjured a feeling of dread, like being summoned to see the principal. It must be something to do with Connie's murder—why else would she be requested by the head of the studio?

She eavesdropped on the secretary; her phone didn't stop ringing.

"Mr. Pearce will be giving an update this afternoon."

"I'm not in a position to say. Thank you for calling."

"Yes. Hold, please."

"He's in a meeting right now. Care to leave word?"

"It's New York. Transferring."

She was brisk, efficient, and handsome—isn't that how her father would describe an attractive woman his age? She was made up, her lips a neat red cupid's bow, not gaudy but tasteful, and her hair was set in a smooth wave and pinned at the back. She wore a cream silk blouse and a fine gold chain. Clara noticed she held the phone receiver a fraction away from her, to keep her earring from scraping the receiver. Occasionally, when she was on two calls at once, the younger woman would interrupt her stern typing and answer the phone. It was a fluid ballet of answering questions, deflecting requests, and fending people off. Listening to her made Clara's little corner of the studio quite insignificant in the grand scheme of moviemaking.

Eventually the door to Mr. Pearce's office burst open and a knot of suited men strode out, among them Roger Brackett in conversation with a bald man she recognized as the head of the story department. Trailing the group—his face buried in a notebook—was Gil.

Clara's throat seemed to squeeze shut. "Gil," she said, a little raspy. He looked up, and his expression loosened. He tucked the notebook into his suit jacket; then, as if he remembered their fight, he hesitated. Clara got to her feet. Gil approached her slowly and they stood like opponents sizing each other up.

The group of men congregated in the hallway talking over each other. Gil jerked his head in the direction of Mr. Pearce's office. "You got a meeting with the big cheese?"

Clara gave an exaggerated shrug. "Not sure why." She eyed him, a little wary. "It could be about the case." She pursed her lips, regretting bringing it up.

"He'll ask you how you're holding up and remind you the studio is a great place to work. Don't worry about it; you're low priority." He gave a forced smile. Clara noticed his tie wasn't centered and she wanted to reach out and straighten it. She kept her arms clamped by her sides.

"What about you? What did Mr. Pearce want?"

"Script meeting. Can we rewrite the attempted murder

scene?" He rubbed a hand over his chin—she noticed he was clean-shaven. "We'll have to reshoot the whole thing. This movie is never going to end."

The studio small talk was stilted and painful. Clara couldn't bear the tension any longer. She took a step closer. "Look, Gil, about last night—"

"Skip it," he said sharply.

"Mr. Gilbert." It was Brackett's mellifluous voice bellowing from the hallway. "Care to join us?"

"Be right there," Gil called over his shoulder and then turned back to Clara. "We should talk." He lowered his voice. "Not here. Away from the studio. I'll pick you up after work." He gave her a meaningful look.

"Sure," said Clara, matching his serious tone.

A buzz sounded on the secretary's desk. "You can go in now, Miss Berg."

"Good luck," said Gil.


Mr. Pearce was sitting behind a vast white desk, with the phone receiver (also white) clamped to his ear. He gestured for Clara to come in and pointed to the guest chairs.

The office was huge. Besides the desk there were couches, a bookcase, and a bar. Every surface in the office was white or chrome and reflected the light. Immaculate. It was the opposite of the utilitarian cutting rooms or film archive; it was more like a hotel suite or a Park Avenue apartment. Clara had the impression that she had stepped onto a film set, one of those fast-talking romantic comedies from the thirties with witty banter, no stopping for breath. She half expected Katharine Hepburn and Cary Grant to be lounging on one of the white couches. *Martini or gimlet?*

Clara sat down and surveyed his desk. Two telephones, a neat stack of screenplays, and framed photos of girls on ponies and young men on boats.

"Forgive me." Pearce hung up the phone. "One of those days." He leaned back in his chair and contemplated her from across the vast white ocean of desk. Conrad Pearce was as immaculate and cold as his office. "This murder business . . ." He frowned. "Damn awful thing. How are you coping?" Gil had called it as if he'd written the script himself.

Clara fought a smile, imagining relating the anecdote to Gil after work. "I'm doing okay, thanks."

"It's a terrible business. A nice girl like you." He gave a grave shake of his head. Clara felt she should point out that nothing awful had happened to her. She had merely seen something horrible. He leaned toward her. "I don't mind saying it, but I'd rather it had been one of the vault boys who had come across it." "It" being Connie's body. "Even Miss Simkin—she's as tough as old boots, am I right?" He gave her a well-practiced smile void of any feeling. "But a nice girl like you." Again that rueful shake of the head.

Clara squirmed in her seat at the patronizing tone. Across the courtyard the sun reflected off an open window and dazzled into the office, blinding her like a follow spot, forcing her to lean to the side at an awkward angle.

"Well, Miss Berg, we got you out of the vaults. You happy working with Sam?" He didn't wait for her to answer. "Daft that we ever hired a girl in the first place to be a vault boy. What did they have you do, lug cans of film all day?"

Clara nodded. "That's the job. I did it as well as the boys."

"I'm sure," he said insincerely. "Now, I wanted to run something by you. Our publicity fellow came up with the idea of doing a piece for the studio paper, the spotlight column—'Women Behind the Scenes.' We're keen to shift the recent bad press and show that Silver Pacific is a wonderful place for a young woman to work—a morale booster, so to speak. It's going to be a series, and we'd like to start with you."

"Me?" Clara shifted in her seat. "What do you need me to do?"

"Just your job. We'll send a photographer to the cutting room, snap a few pictures of you holding up film footage or behind the Moviola or what have you. Then we'll put a little write-up in the paper. Now, what do you say?"

Thankfully the phone rang and Clara didn't have to answer right away. He held a finger in the air and picked up. "Yes. Put him through." He swiveled his chair away from her. "Detective." Clara's ears pricked up and she held her breath, intent on eavesdropping.

Mr. Pearce listened for a few moments.

Clara scanned the collection of framed photographs. Aside from his children enjoying upper-class pursuits there was one of an older couple in their sixties—his parents, presumably—in evening dress. They were impeccably dressed and looked the part, probably because he'd found them at central casting, just like his secretaries. Her gaze landed on the pile of screenplays and she remembered the phone number on Connie's script and how she should have asked Mrs. Milligan about it.

"What did you say?" Pearce snapped at the detective and Clara tuned back into the conversation wishing she could hear both sides. "They couldn't have come through the mailroom," he went on. "We screen all the fan letters." Silence from Mr. Pearce as he listened. Eventually he swiveled his chair back around. "We'll up her security on set and outside her dressing room. Thanks, Detective." Clara didn't need to hear both sides to know who they were discussing: Babe Bannon, of course.

After Mr. Pearce had hung up the phone, he stared at it for a beat, frustrated. Then he resumed his professional guise. "What do you say, Miss Berg?" He was back to business. "Women behind the scenes. Are you game?"

## Chapter Twenty-Three

# Max

AFTER CLARA LEFT MR. Pearce's office, on a whim she took the elevator all the way down to the basement level. It would only take a minute, and she wanted to ask Max about Fräulein Riefenstahl. The projection booth was empty. Clara surveyed Max's world like she would a still life: his spare glasses, yesterday's crusted coffee cup, a well-thumbed extension list taped to the wall, annotated with his scratchy handwriting. The *LA Times* lay open at an article on the Nuremberg trials—the prosecution of Nazi war criminals was on everyone's mind in their refugee world. She looked at the clock; it was already noon. Max was probably at lunch. She could try and chase him down at the commissary—but she'd rather talk to him alone. Perhaps she should drop by Mrs. Milligan's instead, and ask about the phone number on Connie's script. Even though the police investigation was intensifying on Babe Bannon, Clara couldn't let the Connie angle go.

*"Klara."* She jumped at her own name and turned to see Max with a box of cleaning supplies.

Clara followed Max upstairs to the lobby, where they stood in front of the awards cabinet. Once a week it was his task to dust the Oscars in the display case. (Apparently Mr. Pearce didn't trust the cleaners to do it.) Max unlocked the cabinet and opened the glass door wide. He picked up the first statue, and Clara handed him the duster, like a nurse handing an instrument to a surgeon. She watched as he swept the duster tenderly over the golden man. Her eyes grew wide and covetous, and she couldn't resist. "Can I hold it?"

Max raised an eyebrow. "Sure, just for a moment." Clara held out her hands to accept the award as though her name had just been announced at the Biltmore ballroom. She couldn't suppress a smile. The statue had that effect. She held it tightly; it was weighty and cool. *A Call to Arms* had won the Best Picture award during the war.

"I spoke to your mother last night," said Max. "She called to see if I wanted the set of standing lamps in your living room." He continued to dust the other statues. "She's worried about you." He gave Clara a meaningful look over the rim of his glasses.

Clara sighed, annoyed. "She worries about everything."

"She blames me, you know—for getting you the job at the studio—encouraging you with this film editing nonsense."

"You think it's nonsense?"

He gave her a knowing smile and shook his head.

"Max, it wouldn't hurt for you to take my side," said Clara. "You could talk to them."

Max reclaimed the Oscar and returned it to its position on the prop film canister—then gave it a last wipe to remove their fingerprints. "She doesn't want to lose you, Klara," he said soberly.

"I can't live with them forever." Clara pushed aside her feelings of guilt and frustration. Right now she had to focus on getting information from Max. Leni Riefenstahl's visit to Los Angeles was eating away at her. She watched him wipe the duster over a statue won in the early days.

"You worked at the studio in the thirties, right?"

He nodded. "I've been here since 1932," he said proudly. "Manny Silver brought over a lot of European talent in those days." She had heard the story of Max's glory days as a silent-film director many times. When he'd made a costly three-hour biblical epic that Mr. Silver and all the critics had hated, he'd fallen out of favor as a director. "What do you want to know?"

Clara ran her fingers over the red velvet cloth in the display case. "Leni Riefenstahl visited Los Angeles in '38. Do you remember?"

Max frowned. "She came to sell her movie of the Olympics—her timing couldn't have been worse. Days after Kristallnacht, and she refused to believe it. 'Germany would never do such a thing,' she said. She was what you call 'a piece of work.' Is that the expression?" He gave a long shake of the head. "No one wanted her around. The Hollywood Anti-Nazi League made it impossible for her. 'No room in Hollywood for Leni Riefenstahl.' That's what our flyers said, and full-page ads in *Variety*. And that funny man on the radio Mr. Winchell said, 'Leni is as pretty as a swastika.'" He chuckled and repeated it to himself.

"No one would meet her?"

Max reflected. "Mr. Disney was a fan—he gave her a tour of his studio. He wanted to screen her Olympic movie, but he panicked—worried the projectionists would go on strike. Our campaign worked." He gave a decisive nod. "In the end he chickened out."

"Did Riefenstahl visit Silver Pacific?" asked Clara.

"No." Max shook his head, but something shifted in his demeanor.

"You never met her, then?" asked Clara.

Max chucked the duster into his bucket. She could see a flash of something behind his eyes. His face tightened. "It was a long time ago."

Somewhere down a corridor a door slammed. His gaze was far away, a distant look, as though recollecting something from the past, then closing a door on it.

"Max?"

"Klara, I really don't remember." He closed the awards cabinet and turned the key to lock it.

He leaned close to her, his expression serious, unblinking. "Be careful, Klara. Don't go poking around in things that don't concern you. The past is the past." He glanced at the clock in the lobby. "Sam will be looking for you." His tone had shifted gears back to normal. "I'll talk to your mother, but I can't promise it will help." He gave her a fatherly smile, picked up his bucket of cleaning supplies, and walked away, leaving her in front of the gleaming army of gold statues.

Her eyes followed him as he crossed the lobby and disappeared downstairs.

## Chapter Twenty-Four

# The Girl

CLARA UNPACKED THE GROCERIES and handed them to Mrs. Milligan to put away. With each item the woman thanked her profusely. "You have to let me give you something for this—I insist."

Clara handed her a bunch of grapes and a tin of coffee. "No need, Mrs. Milligan. Really, it's no trouble."

It was well after one p.m., and she had already been away from the office too long. Still she accepted the offer of a glass of lemonade. Mae was at a neighbor's, and Mrs. Milligan seemed glad of adult company. The two women sat at the small kitchen table. Laundry hung on the pulley overhead, the pipes gurgled from the apartment upstairs, and a breeze wafted in through the open window now and again.

Clara felt the tightness in her chest that precedes asking an impertinent question, but she sensed that with Connie's mother a direct approach was best. "Mrs. Milligan, I wanted to ask you."

Clara pulled the script cover page from her purse and unfolded it. "Is this Connie's handwriting?" She handed over the piece of paper.

The woman took it and studied it. "I think so. The ink's blurred, but I would say yes. Why?"

"Do you recognize the phone number? It might be SPRING three-one-nine-one. Perhaps you overheard Connie asking the operator. Does it sound familiar?"

Mrs. Milligan glanced at it again, her forehead wrinkled in thought. "I can't say that it does. Did the police give you this?"

Clara shook her head. "No, I just came across it and I wondered. I can pass it along to them. It's probably nothing." *Dammit,* she thought; another dead end with this number. Clara sipped her lemonade and tried to think of her other unanswered questions. "You mentioned that Connie had a brush with Hollywood years ago and she was bitten by the film bug. When was that?"

Mrs. Milligan topped up their lemonade from the jug. "Oh, it was nothing really. She spent a few months in Palm Springs working as a secretary. Let's see . . . she met Jim in the summer of '39. Palm Springs would have been the fall of 1938 through the New Year."

"Did she work for someone famous? You mentioned Hollywood," said Clara, trying to tease out the information.

"Dear me, no. It was just temp jobs, filling in for a secretary out sick or on vacation. She was seventeen, just out of typing school and she was trying to gain experience. The town itself attracts Hollywood types. But no, Connie's jobs weren't glamorous. I think she worked at a Realtor's office, and a car company, I believe."

"It was just for a few months?"

Mrs. Milligan nodded. "Connie wanted the excitement of living somewhere else, but she couldn't justify staying because she was barely making enough to live. It's an expensive place. I missed her something awful when she was away." She caught herself on the words, maybe realizing that now she would be missing her daughter always. Clara looked down at her glass, annoyed at herself for pushing all these questions.

But Mrs. Milligan continued. "She didn't even come back for Christmas. I mean, she was supposed to, she'd booked her bus ticket, but the day before she was supposed to leave, she called me all in a lather. She'd been offered another temp job. Some rich fellow needed 'a girl' to help with housekeeping and correspondence over the holidays. She didn't want to disappoint me—it was Christmas, after all—but this job would pay her time and a half, it being over the holidays."

Clara's ears pricked up. "Sounds generous." Who could she have worked for?

"Of course I wondered if it was respectable—working out of someone's home—but Connie had spoken with the housekeeper, and she wouldn't be working there alone. I felt reassured hearing that."

"Was it anyone famous? Do you remember the man's name?"

"Oh, now you're testing me. No idea. I don't think so. I'd never heard of him, anyway." Mrs. Milligan smiled faintly. "Connie was nothing short of ecstatic—apparently the house had its own swimming pool." She shook her head at the memory. "Connie assumed it would be some kind of fairy-tale mansion, but she sent me a postcard of it—one of those modern 'architectural' houses, all rectangles and glass walls." Mrs. Milligan gave a chuckle. "She said it was plain ugly."

Clara arrived back at the studio late from her lunch break. Her mind was turning over everything Mrs. Milligan had said. The Palm Springs connection felt very distant and unlikely. It was a long time ago.

Sam pointed at the clock when Clara walked into the cutting room: 1:55 p.m. "I was going to send out a search party," he said. "Where were you?"

Clara put her purse in the drawer and shrugged off her jacket. "Sorry, Sam. I was visiting Connie Milligan's mother." She assumed the name would immediately fend off any further questions, but Sam was still looking at her, unamused.

"Clara, I understand the past couple of weeks have been very disruptive, given everything that's happened." He avoided saying the words "murder" or "Connie." "But that isn't your business. It's up to the police to do their job. You're forever running off and not being where I need you." He was working himself up a little. "And do you really think you should be pestering this poor woman?"

Clara blinked quickly; she couldn't meet his eye. Sam had never lost his temper with her before.

"The answer is no." She heard the thunk of the splicer as Sam got back to work. "Let's focus on our own jobs, all right?" His tone had thawed slightly. "Your head hasn't been at work since this happened. If you want less responsibility, I'm sure Miss Simkin would take you back in the archive as a runner."

*No, he wouldn't.* Clara's cheeks colored at the prospect of such humiliation. She slumped down at her desk, the idea of a demotion knocking the wind out of her. "Look, Sam." She turned to him. "I'll work late tonight—I'll make up the time. It won't happen again."

## Chapter Twenty-Five

# Griffith Observatory

AS PROMISED CLARA PUT in an extra hour at the end of the day. Gil picked her up after seven, and they drove east through Hollywood toward Los Feliz, in the direction of Griffith Park. The evening air was cool and sweet. After the heat of the day it felt like the city was able to breathe again.

Gil was quiet. The traffic was bad and he was concentrating on the road. Clara squirmed in her seat, itching with questions. After a few blocks, she blurted out, "So? What did you want to say? Is it about the murder?"

He flicked a glance in the side mirror, then changed lanes to avoid a stalled bus. "Two things," he said. "First thing, I ran into the studio fixer."

"The fixer?"

"Works under the auspices of security. Deals with the messy affairs of contract stars. He keeps scandals out of the press, facilitates a quick divorce or pays off a disgruntled ex—that kinda thing." A cab cut in front of them. Gil leaned on the horn. "The studio has a file on stalkers and nuisance fans, as well as the rundown on any inconvenient dalliances or ex-spouses." They slowed for a traffic light while the cab in front ran the red.

"I didn't know any of that." Clara wondered for a moment if Gil's name was in a file somewhere on the lot.

"Well, I ran into the guy—he's ex-army—at the studio barber. We were both having a shave. He tells me someone has been sending things to Babe Bannon—'little love notes,' he called them."

"Fan mail?" asked Clara.

Gil shook his head. "Anonymous threats—several of them over the last few weeks. Not mailed. But dropped off by hand—on set, in her dressing room, even in her car." The engine rumbled as they waited for the light at Western to change.

Clara's mind raced back to that morning in Pearce's office. "I overheard Mr. Pearce on the phone with one of the detectives. He mentioned something about the mailroom and fan letters—and about upping Bannon's security in the same conversation."

"I guess they're not taking any chances," Gil said grimly.

The light turned green, he stepped on the gas, and the car roared to life. They turned left up Vermont and passed huge homes hidden behind lush magnolias and thick walls of cypress. In Griffith Park the road kept climbing and twisting toward the observatory. Nature was always close by in Los Angeles. It threatened to take over: bougainvillea rambling over buildings, warping fence posts; ficus roots cracking asphalt; avocado trees littering sidewalks with overripe fruit. The perfect weather—it emboldened nature, made it reckless, disrespectful of the man-made world.

The sunset was already fading as they pulled into the parking lot. They got out of the car and saw a cluster of people at the main entrance. Clara knew that Gil wouldn't want to go inside when it was busy. Instead they veered right, to the west terrace, and looked at the view: Griffith Park, a surprising wilderness, a sleeping giant in the middle of the city—an escape from the concrete, the automobiles, the noise, the striving.

"Wait, what's the second thing—you mentioned two things," said Clara.

Gil shrugged. "It's probably nothing. You first—any breaks in the case with Connie?"

Clara shook her head. "What case? I have nothing but questions—some observations and discrepancies. It's like trying to cut together footage from two different movies. Nothing adds up."

They followed the walkway that skirted the outside of the planetarium and stopped to lean on the white parapet. It was still warm. Dusk had settled over the park.

"What have you got?" said Gil. "Just tell me one thing—one movie."

Clara thought about it for a while. "Okay. With everyone I've talked to there's a consensus that something was off with Connie in the weeks before her death, but everyone has a different take on it."

"What are they saying?"

Clara described the different reactions from Lloyd, Bannon, Mrs. Milligan, and even Rosa the hairdresser.

"You have to remember," said Gil, "when other people talk about Connie, they're telling you about themselves."

"What do you mean?"

"I learned this in screenwriting. It's not what people say that's important. It's what they're telling you, the subtext. For example, the hairdresser assumes Connie doesn't like the new hair color, because that's the hairdresser's job, to make the customer happy. And if the customer's not happy, then the hairdresser assumes it's her fault."

"What about Connie's mother?"

"That's easy. She assumes Connie is missing her husband because family is important to *her*. She's worried about her daughter, adrift in a new city."

Clara nodded. "I guess Lloyd was feeling left behind because Connie had moved on, and maybe she'd just used him to get onto the lot. He blames the movie she's working on, when the truth is, maybe she just never liked him that much."

"And the movie star doesn't think too much about anyone except herself," said Gil. "My point is, only Connie knew what she was feeling; everyone else is projecting their own ideas."

A sightseeing couple got into their space, so they moved on

to the east terrace, where it was darker, where night had taken hold of the city. A crescent moon pierced through the shaggy fringes of eucalyptus. And in the distance, far below, a string of taillights lined Vermont Avenue.

"Wait, you're wrong about one thing," said Clara. "About Bannon. She was friends with Connie, I'm pretty sure. There's plenty of photos of them palling around on set, and the two of them went out dancing, according to Mrs. Milligan. But Bannon claims she hardly knew Connie."

"Why would she say that?" said Gil.

"Exactly. I don't know. Is she really just an uncaring diva?"

Gil shrugged and let her question hang in the air.

"What if the Connie motive is all wrong and we're asking questions about the wrong person? You talked to the fixer today—those anonymous threats. The cops seem convinced. What if Bannon *was* the intended victim?"

Gil turned sharply. "You *really* believe that?" he said. "That the killer got Connie by mistake?"

"No, I don't," said Clara firmly.

"Neither do I." He leaned against the parapet. "You know why I don't believe it? Because Connie is dead, not Barbara Bannon." He didn't often say her full name, Clara noticed. "I don't buy the look-alike theory for a second—it's all smoke and mirrors."

As he spoke an idea came to Clara like a key gliding smoothly into a lock. She clutched his arm in excitement. "Babe Bannon is a distraction—a deliberate distraction—like Sam's trick for cutting with a mismatch."

"What?" said Gil, not following.

Suddenly aware that she had grabbed him, Clara released his arm. She explained the editing trick that Sam had shown her earlier in the day. "Everyone's eyes are on Bannon. It's a cheat, a trick, and it has worked beautifully. Everyone has fallen for it: the cops, the press, the studio, even Babe herself—she acts tough but she's on edge. Everyone is missing the glaring truth in front of their eyes. Connie Milligan is dead. She was strangled in cold blood—*she* was the intended victim."

Gil nodded soberly. "But we still don't know why."

By now the crowd had dwindled. They strolled around to the front of the observatory and stopped at the statue of the astronomers. Copernicus stared down at them. He had the same bob haircut as Miss Simkin.

"It still bothers me," said Clara. "How did Connie get to be Bannon's stand-in? I think she needed help. She needed to know someone who could pull strings. Her mother said something"— Clara cast her mind back to that afternoon in Mrs. Milligan's kitchen—"about Connie having a brush with Hollywood years earlier."

"The paper said she grew up in San Bernardino?" said Gil, sounding skeptical. "Not very glamorous."

"No, in Palm Springs."

"What was she doing in Palm Springs—vacation?"

Clara shook her head. "No. Secretarial work, before the war." She pondered for a minute, trying to remember what Mrs. Milligan had said exactly. "The ugly house." And in answer to Gil's confused look, she elaborated. "Mrs. Milligan said Connie's employer's house was modern—all glass and steel, and Connie thought it was ugly."

"What guy's house?" said Gil.

"The rich guy she worked for—over Christmas, before the war," said Clara. "I wonder if we could figure out who he was. What if he had ties to Hollywood? What if—" She batted her hand in the air, dismissing the idea. "It's a stretch. Forget it." Clara shook her head. "That was years ago. We'd have to go there to find the house, track down the owner."

"Road trip to Palm Springs?" said Gil.

She looked at him, a smile tugging at the corner of her mouth. "You'd do that?"

He shrugged. "I've got no plans this weekend."

They walked back to the parking lot. Headlights washed over them as they got into the car.

"Hey, what was the other thing you wanted to tell me?" asked Clara. "You said there were two things."

Gil drove off, nice and slow, his eyes fixed to the rearview mirror. "There's a black Chrysler been following us ever since we left the studio. I noticed him last night as well, out front of my apartment building—I think it was the same car."

Clara glanced at the wing mirror. "It's a common enough car," she said, shifting uneasily in her seat. The detectives drove a Chrysler—was this a cop car?

"This one has a wonky left headlight—it's at an angle," said

Gil. Clara looked again and saw, right enough, that the car's lights cast an uneven light, one headlight aimed a little higher than the other.

"Could be a coincidence?" said Clara.

"It's possible." He didn't sound convinced.

They took the winding road through the park smoothly. When they reached the houses on Vermont Avenue, Gil abruptly pulled into a driveway. He switched off the headlamps and placed a hand on Clara's arm, a signal for her to keep still. His eyes were fixed on the rearview mirror. Warm light spilled from windows of the mock Tudor home; it caught the side of Gil's face, and he was cast in bronze, like a mask. Clara held her breath. In the side mirror, a flash of headlights and the Chrysler flew past them. She felt Gil's hand relax, but he kept it resting on her arm. They waited a minute or two, then he backed out of the driveway and they joined the line of taillights on Vermont Avenue.

## Chapter Twenty-Six

# No Room in Hollywood

THAT NIGHT, HER MIND buzzing with the murder case and unable to sleep, Clara picked up Connie's *Saturday Evening Post* and opened it to page 11. She had been so preoccupied with her own memories of meeting Leni Riefenstahl that she hadn't actually read the whole article. "Nazi Pin-Up Girl" was written by a Hollywood screenwriter and novelist—Budd Schulberg— who had worked with the US military in Germany after the war. Their mission had been to find motion pictures to use as evidence against Nazi war criminals at Nuremberg. Leni Riefenstahl's documentaries were at the top of their list. It was fitting because, as it turned out, Schulberg had helped organize the Hollywood boycott against Leni back in 1938.

As with most feature articles, the story began on the opening pages, but the later sections were printed in the back of the magazine. When Clara turned to page 36 to read the rest of the article, she noticed short, blond hairs caught in the fold. A shiver ran down her back. The next section was on page 39, and the article concluded on page 41. Again more blond hairs in the fold. *Connie was reading this article.* Clara was certain of it.

Carefully she checked other pages at random—the article on vets learning to walk, a short story, a PanAm advertisement—no blond hairs. She flipped back to the article. She could picture it like close-ups projected on a movie screen: Rosa's scissors trimming the ends of Connie's hair, Connie buried in the magazine, riveted by "Nazi Pin-Up Girl." The fine hairs falling onto the magazine. Connie had probably brushed them aside, but some had been left behind. Clara had assumed that coming across the article about Leni had been random, a ricochet from her own past, nothing to do with Connie, but now the magazine was saturated with meaning. Clara could feel a flutter in her chest as she put the pieces together. It was no coincidence—Connie had taken the magazine for a *reason.*

Clara reread the article from beginning to end, trying to make a connection. Why would Connie Milligan have been drawn to reading about the Nazi film queen? Had her husband served with Budd Schulberg's unit in Germany, looking for Nazi propaganda? No, Jim had died in France in '44 during the D-Day invasion. Perhaps Connie knew Schulberg, the writer? Was there even a connection to find? Or had Connie simply been diverted by a news article and taken the magazine with her to read on the streetcar?

It was late. Clara's parents were asleep. She tiptoed down the hall to her father's study and rifled through his box of old newspapers to read more about Leni Riefenstahl's visit to California. She placed his desk lamp on the hall floor and spread all the newspapers along the hallway. Anything that mentioned Leni Riefenstahl, she cut out.

Widening her search from Leni's arrival on the *Europa* in November to January 1939, Clara discovered that the film director's two-month visit had generated a huge amount of column inches and gossip—from the political to the salacious, as well as the fawning and trivial. LENI SAYS CLIMATE IS FANTASTIC and GERMAN ACTRESS HERE ON VACATION, NOT LOCATION.

> "Since many years I have wanted to visit in California," she said in explaining her presence here. "This is a beautiful place and I'm taking what you call a holiday, yes?" Following the premieres of her Olympic film in European capitals, the German actress came to America—not, as she explained, in the interest of the picture or of her career. And so, the red-haired woman with the exotic charm and expressive hands is resting in Beverly Hills after a tour of premieres of her picture, in which she was presented to rulers and the world's great. Her picture, "It has broken records everywhere. I hope Americans can see the film."

In the papers Leni denied her trip to Hollywood was connected to her career, and yet that is precisely what Max had told Clara—she was trying to sell *Olympia*. Max was right about her visit being controversial, coming right on the heels of Kristallnacht—the Night of Broken Glass, when across Germany the windows of Jewish-owned businesses were smashed; buildings and synagogues destroyed; thousands of Jews arrested and scores killed. News of the riots sent shock waves around the world.

It was no wonder then, that Riefenstahl had been shunned and denied access to the studios. There was a vigorous campaign against her thanks to the Hollywood Anti-Nazi League. The LA *Times* noted the league's full-page ads in *Variety* magazine: *No room in Hollywood for Leni Riefenstahl.* Even gossip columnist Hedda Hopper got drawn into the slugging match, but she was on the other side of the fence. *Leni's only here to sell her picture,* Hopper wrote, which confirmed what Max had said. And a few weeks later, *I met her the other day and she's perfectly charming.*

Clara surveyed all the newspapers scattered across the floor and remembered some throwaway comment Detective Ireland had made in the screening room—about Connie going to the library on the weekends. He'd been skeptical, but what if she'd been doing exactly what Clara was doing at this very moment: reading up on Riefenstahl, trying to see the whole picture.

It was after midnight now, and Clara's eyes were twitching from the fine print. She was skimming another article and fighting a yawn, when suddenly the words jolted her awake. After being railroaded out of Hollywood by the Anti-Nazi League,

Leni had spent time traveling in California. LENI RIEFENSTAHL SAYS GOODBYE. *"Now I go soon to Europe,"* she declared, *"after having visited San Francisco, Yosemite, and Palm Springs."*

Palm Springs. The name leapt off the page. Quickly Clara calculated the timeline. There had been an official farewell reception for Leni in Los Angeles, given by the German consul, Dr. Georg Gyssling, on January 6. That meant Riefenstahl's trip to Palm Springs would have been before that—sometime in December 1938, with her leaving in the first few days of January at the latest. Connie Milligan had spent Christmas in Palm Springs working over the holiday—*the two women had been there at the same time.* The link between Leni Riefenstahl and Connie Milligan was nearly invisible, as fine as gossamer—a few strands of pale blond hair in the folds of a magazine—but Clara had found the connection.

## Chapter Twenty-Seven

# Palm Springs

THE DRIVE TO PALM Springs was hot and dusty. Despite there being a foot-long rip in the convertible's soft top, Gil had put it up, and once on the highway the shreds of fabric were buffeted by the wind, flapping like the sails of a boat. Clara looked across at him, his hands loosely on the wheel, his left arm resting on the rolled-down window, and she felt that queasy surging sensation, like she was on a boat lurching through chop—equal parts nerves and excitement. As they picked up speed, the rip in the roof would whistle like the wind before a storm hits.

"Run it by me again," said Gil. He rolled up his window to cut the noise.

"Connie did some secretarial work in Palm Springs for a few months in winter 1938—different temp jobs, a realtor's office, and a car company," said Clara. "She was fresh out of typing school."

"And the Nazi filmmaker was in Palm Springs as well?" said Gil.

"I think so." Clara nodded.

"Even if they were there at the same time, would they have crossed paths? Would Connie even know who the German woman was?"

"I don't know, but she read that article 'Nazi Pin-Up Girl' a couple of weeks before the murder," said Clara.

"Could it be a coincidence?"

"Maybe. But Connie took the magazine from the salon; she hung on to it."

"Anything else?" asked Gil.

"At the studio Max, the projectionist, acted cagey when I brought up Riefenstahl's name. It could be nothing. I mean, this whole trip could be a wild goose chase. But still, I want to find out who Connie worked for—maybe there's something in it."

Gil tapped the odometer. "That's a lot of mileage for a hunch, Miss Berg."

"I'll give you gas money," she said, laughing.

He smiled. "I'll settle for lunch."

This reminded Clara of the lie she had told her parents on the way out the door that morning, that she was having a cookout on the beach with the girls from accounting. The ribbon of asphalt stretched out ahead of them, the landscape becoming drier and scrubbier the farther east they drove. The road ahead felt like a dare, some kind of gamble where Clara didn't know the odds.

\* \* \*

They stopped for gas a few miles outside Palm Springs, and Clara went to the ladies' to freshen up. When she returned to the car, Gil had cleaned the windshield and taken the top down. He wore sunglasses, and in the bright sun the crisp white of his short-sleeved shirt made his arms look even more tan. After Clara got into the car, she pulled a pair of shades from her purse and tied a scarf around her hair. Gil started the engine. "Ready?" he asked. Clara nodded, feeling the tug of desire and danger, her senses on fire. As they pulled out of the gas station, it struck her that they were both in disguise and that it felt vaguely criminal—something out of Bonnie and Clyde, a pair of bank robbers about to stage a heist.

About an hour later, Clara and Gil were side by side at a long wooden table in the reading room of the Palm Springs library, an array of newspapers and magazines spread out before them. The warm light, the cool tile underfoot, the musty comforting smell of books, and the companionable silence—it was a balm compared to the dusty highway. The only sounds were the occasional footsteps of the diligent librarian who was helping them; the shuffling of papers; and the persistent coughs from other patrons, mostly old folks in armchairs. So much for Bonnie and Clyde.

Clara was leafing through a magazine on modern architecture. Gil was elbow deep in the Palm Springs social calendar of 1938. Winter was high season, when the Hollywood elite would descend, escaping the LA winter (such as it was) for the warmth of the desert.

"You find anything?" asked Clara.

"Tennis matches and rounds of golf, ribbon cuttings, and tiki parties," said Gil. "The hot place in town is the Racquet Club— where the rich and famous play in the desert."

"No sign of Fräulein Riefenstahl, I guess?" asked Clara.

"Not yet. Maybe she wanted to keep a low profile after being run out of LA."

A click of heels, and the librarian returned with a book for Clara. "There are a couple of examples of modern architecture in this book," she said, opening it to the index. "Both built before 1938." She thumbed through the pages until she landed on a photograph of a modest glass-and-steel-frame construction. "The Miller House by Richard Neutra. It's in town, in the flats. And over the page here"—she flipped the page—"Desert House, up in the foothills, built in 1937. It's larger but still in the International style."

Clara took the book and studied both pictures. "Who's Mr. Miller?"

"That would be Grace Miller," said the librarian.

That ruled out the Miller House. Clara turned the page. "And the owner of the Desert House?" she asked.

The librarian skimmed a finger over the article. "The architect built it for himself." She shook her head. "But this book is out of date. I heard that the chap got into money problems—a rich businessman bought it. A car man—Western Auto, I believe."

Gil nudged Clara. "Connie's mom said she had temped for a car company, right?"

Clara nodded. "I think this is the one we're looking for."

"Here's the address," said the librarian. "On Los Robles Drive, in the foothills, off Rose." She jotted the address on a piece of scrap paper.

"Thanks for your help," said Clara. The librarian nodded and left them to it.

Gil stretched. "Let's take a break. I'm starving."

After a lunch of roast chicken and lukewarm vegetables, they bought a map of Palm Springs and picked up a brochure for an architecture tour in town. Clara studied the pamphlet as they drove away from the main drag and up to Los Robles Drive.

The Desert House was low and unassuming, nestled in the foothills, with the mountains towering in the distance. A few palm trees stretched overhead like sentinels, and a neat lawn in front looked artificial and too lush for the climate.

They got out of the car. "Doesn't look like anyone is home," said Gil as they approached the front gate. There wasn't a car in the driveway, but there was a double garage. "What do you have planned—a bit of breaking and entering?"

"Just a bit of acting." She smiled at him.

They walked up the smooth drive to the front door, and Clara rang the bell.

As they waited, Gil surveyed the house. "I wonder how much dough it costs, a pad like this?"

"Hello?" It was a woman's voice. She opened the door, and a small dog came running up to them, fluffy and yapping. "Snowball, that's enough."

"Oh, good afternoon. Sorry to bother you," said Clara. "We were hoping to look at the house." She fanned herself with the architectural pamphlet. "We're on a tour of modern architecture."

Gil bent down and petted the dog. "We just saw the Miller House," he lied.

"And your front gate was open," Clara chimed in. "It's a little cheeky." She gave the woman her best wholesome smile.

"Is this your house, ma'am?" asked Gil. "A wonderful example of the International style." Clara caught his eye, and he smirked at her.

The woman laughed, genuinely tickled at the thought. "No, silly—I'm the housekeeper, Mrs. Irvine. Come in, come in," she said. "Have a peek." Thoroughly taken with them, Mrs. Irvine ushered them into the house. The little dog circled them, excited by the company.

Inside, it was vast and cool. They stood in the massive open living room. All the furniture was teak wood and cream upholstery. A spacious dining area connected to an airy kitchen—everything was open. The far wall was all glass, revealing a large swimming pool outside. It was very modern and smooth and flowing, to Clara's eye, who was used to the heavy European furniture and the cramped space of her parents' Spanish-style bungalow.

"Don't get many visitors this time of year—too hot," said Mrs. Irvine.

"How often is the owner here?" asked Clara.

"Hardly ever these days. The old man has become frail. Before the war the house was always busy. We've had politicians, a former president, and business folk—even Henry Ford once. Mr. Pearce was in the car business."

*"Pearce?"* said Clara sharply. She shot a glance at Gil.

The housekeeper nodded emphatically. "Kenneth Pearce, CEO of Western Auto."

Clara's heart rate recovered and Mrs. Irvine beckoned them to the back patio. "Come and have a look at the pool," she said, sliding open the glass doors. The little dog raced ahead. They stepped outside and into a blast of heat like a hair dryer in the face. "It's a scorcher today, isn't it?" The sun reflected off the turquoise pool, and it was almost too bright to look at.

Clara took in the setting. The desert was impressive and yet foreboding—there was something prehistoric about the landscape, as if humans and their modern architecture shouldn't be trespassing.

"Spectacular," said Gil, squinting in the sunlight. "Don't you think, honey?" He was overdoing the acting, but his charm was working on the housekeeper.

"You seem like a sweet couple," said Mrs. Irvine. "Where are you from?"

Gil gave her a broad smile. "San Bernardino," he said without missing a beat. "Say, Western Auto have an office in town? A pal of mine, his sister worked for Mr. Pearce before the war.

She was a secretary, a temp over the holidays. I swear it was Palm Springs."

"That would be for the younger Mr. Pearce—their son, Conrad. He runs a movie studio, and if he stayed out here for a bit, he'd hire a local girl to type up his correspondence, that sort of thing—easier than bringing someone out from LA. Cheaper too, no doubt." Mrs. Irvine shaded her face from the sun. "The Pearce family aren't silly with money. That's why they have it, I suppose."

"Conrad Pearce?" said Clara, a little dazed. "Of Silver Pacific?"

"That's right." The dog had found something to bark at over by the fence, behind a bird of paradise. Mrs. Irvine craned her neck. "Stop that, Snowball. That's enough. Leave it!"

Clara grabbed Gil's arm and mouthed *Conrad Pearce.*

"Some office," said Gil, keeping his cool. "It's a cracking view." He gestured to the surroundings.

Suddenly the heat was getting to Clara. Her breath quickened and she began to feel light-headed—*the head of the studio.* The sunlight pricked her eyes, and she blinked quickly, squinting at the starbursts.

"You okay?" asked Gil.

Clara shook her head.

"Yes, let's go in. It's too hot," said Mrs. Irvine. She called the dog. "Snowball, come."

Indoors they were cloaked in cool air. Clara sat at the long teak dining table gripping a glass of water, her heart pounding. She breathed in through her nose and out through her mouth as if she were swimming, and the dizzy feeling began to subside.

Gil and Mrs. Irvine were in the kitchen, where the housekeeper was prattling on. "Before the war we had movie people around all the time—film directors Huston and Capra, writers and actors. That lovely actress, what's her name again, the one who played Scarlett, or was it Melanie, in *Gone with the Wind*?"

Mrs. Irvine was like a wind-up toy once you got her going; she didn't stop talking. It gave Clara the chance to look around. There were a collection of trophies and a couple of framed photographs on the sideboard—she pushed back her chair and went over. A silver cup was engraved *Kenneth and Dolly Pearce, Mixed Doubles Champions. Palm Springs, 1936.* Next to it there was a framed photograph of the couple sporting golf outfits. Their teeth shone very white; they were tan, grinning . . . and familiar. It was on the periphery of her memory. Just out of reach. An upscale setting, an introduction, she was watching through the eyes of a child.

Clara could hear Gil. "I don't suppose you'd remember her, my friend's sister?" he asked. "Around Christmas in 1938. A blonde, pretty."

"Christmas 1938," Mrs. Irvine mused. "Oh goodness, we had so many guests that year. Mr. Conrad invited a bunch of Hollywood folk. I was run off my feet . . ."

Clara stopped listening to Mrs. Irvine. She was suddenly

back on the *Europa—that* was where she had seen them before. The toothy Americans, Kenneth and Dolly Pearce. They were shaking hands with Leni Riefenstahl.

Clara spun around to signal Gil. But Mrs. Irvine was still chattering nonstop. Clara watched the housekeeper's mouth move, but everything was out of sync. Instead Clara was hearing Mr. and Mrs. Pearce in the Winter Garden. She was imagining what they must have said to Leni Riefenstahl: *You must meet our son, Conrad. He's in movies. He runs his own studio.*

"Sweet thing," said Mrs. Irvine. "But I'm terrible with names."

Clara tuned back into the conversation and joined them in the kitchen. "And the guests that winter," she said, too forcefully. "Do you remember the German actress? You must remember Miss Riefenstahl?"

It was as though a bell had rung to signal the end of their conversation. Mrs. Irvine stiffened suddenly, and her eyes flitted between them. "No," she said primly. "I don't remember, I'm afraid. There were a lot of people coming and going." The warmth had left her voice. "I should be getting on. Let you get back to your tour. Frank Sinatra is building a house down the street." She moved to the door, not making eye contact. "I'll see you both out."

The leather seats of Gil's car were burning hot even though they had been gone barely thirty minutes. "Boy, did you see that reaction?" Gil turned the key in the ignition. "Talk about a conversation stopper."

"Leni Riefenstahl *must* have stayed here," said Clara. "Why else would the housekeeper freeze up like that?"

"She was probably told never to mention it to anyone," said Gil. "And we rang the alarm bells."

He executed a swift U-turn. The breeze of the convertible was welcome on Clara's face. "Why did Connie not tell her mother who she had worked for? Wouldn't she have bragged about it?"

Gil put on his shades. "Conrad Pearce is fond of confidentiality agreements. She probably had to sign something to get the job."

Clara shook her head. "I can't believe it, Connie and Leni Riefenstahl here at the same time under Conrad Pearce's roof."

A half hour later Gil and Clara were sitting by the pool of the Palm Springs Racquet Club, shaded by a blue-and-white umbrella. It was members only, but Gil had managed to drop the Silver Pacific studios name, and open sesame, they were shown to a table outside. Gil finished his iced tea, leaned back, and closed his eyes, enjoying the sun, unruffled. It was low season, and the club wasn't crowded.

Clara took a sip of her soda and watched a couple splashing in the pool—engaged in flirting more than serious aquatics. She imagined for a moment it was her and Gil. Then she decided she preferred things as they were, unraveling a mystery—figuring out the clues together. Given the popularity of the club, they were hoping to find more information. Clara had filled him in on where she had seen Kenneth and Dolly Pearce—the American couple on the *Europa*—recalling how she had noticed their photo on Pearce's desk. She had thought they'd appeared perfectly cast—a quintessential older couple. But perhaps that feeling of familiarity was because she had met them before. If she had looked closer, would she have recognized them? Everything was happening so fast, all the dots joining up. The weight of what they had discovered felt oppressive, like the desert afternoon sun.

Although smooth, Gil hadn't been able to talk his way into a look at the Racquet Club's guest register from years past. His request had been met with a pleasant but firm no. "For the privacy of our members," the young chap at the front desk had said. "If you're interested in the club's history, you're welcome to take a look at our hall of fame in the Bamboo Room."

While Gil dozed in the sun, Clara checked her watch for the third time in as many minutes. The Bamboo Room was the club bar, which opened at five. Apparently it contained an array of photos and memorabilia from the club's history. Clara was desperate to find something concrete connecting Leni Riefenstahl's visit to Conrad Pearce. The stilted reaction of a housekeeper wasn't the kind of solid proof they needed.

At five minutes after five Gil stood at the bar and ordered two gin and tonics. The bar had a Hawaiian theme: bamboo cane furniture and bold floral prints. Drinks in hand, they moved to a table near the wall of photos and casually sipped, trying not to look too obvious about sizing up the people in the pictures. Eventually, Gil returned for a refill ("bartenders know everything"), and Clara perused the hall of fame. There were endless shots of tennis tournaments and girls posing on diving boards or playing peekaboo with life preservers. There were a myriad of famous faces in tennis whites: Ralph Bellamy, Clark Gable, and Carole Lombard. Her eyes flickered over the smiling tanned faces.

Gil returned from the bar with a triumphant expression. "Racquet Club New Year's party 1939," he said, laying a photograph album on the table.

"What did the bartender say?" said Clara, opening the album.

"The 'German film star,' as he called her, was here around the holidays before the war—a guest of Mr. Conrad Pearce. They were usually playing tennis or drinking with a crowd of Hollywood people. Remembers her as athletic—played tennis to win; didn't just lie around like a pool decoration."

Clara pored over the snapshots. Tables littered with streamers and champagne glasses; bleary-eyed glamorous people; a 1939 banner and silly hats. She flipped a page.

"There's Pearce," said Gil, pointing to a group shot on the right-hand page. She could hear the excitement in his voice.

Pearce was in a tux at a long table with other revelers. And next to him, a glass of champagne in hand, wearing a coy smile, was Leni Riefenstahl. Clara stared at the photo as if she could enter the frame. "It's her."

" 'Should auld acquaintance be forgot,' " said Gil.

They were both quiet for a moment, contemplating the picture. Some tables in the bar were filling up. They heard a toast and the clink of glasses, a splash in the pool outside.

Clara pried her eyes from the photograph album. "Have you ever seen her films?" she asked.

"Sure," said Gil, swirling the ice cubes around in his glass. "I saw her famous propaganda flick *Triumph of the Will*. It was during the war, before I shipped out. The Writers Guild had a screening so we could see what we were up against." He shook his head and looked into the bottom of his gin and tonic. "I remember stumbling out of that screening, all that precision goose-stepping and the cacophony of *'Sieg heil!'* ringing in my ears." He looked at Clara. "And I thought: 'We're beat.' "


They drove up into the foothills, to see the house once more before they left town. It was dark by now, and the moon had risen. Clara told Gil everything she had found out about Leni's visit to LA, from Kristallnacht to the boycott, and Leni's trying to sell *Olympia* but telling the press she was just on vacation.

They parked just before the house. Bleak and barren at first glance, the desert by night was like a snowscape, beautiful and expansive—otherworldly. The moon was so bright that Clara could see the chrome on the Plymouth glinting as though it were daytime. The shadows of palm trees striped the lawn; a waft of fragrance hit her, subtle and too soft to name. All was quiet and still in the desert compared to the traffic and energy of LA. She had told her parents not to wait up, that she would be late. No one knew where she really was—alone in the desert with Gil. An irrational note of fear struck her, then faded, absurd.

"So what now?" Clara looked across at Gil.

He shook his head. "We found a connection, but I don't like where it's leading."

"I know," she sighed. The idea that the head of the studio could somehow be connected to a murder on his own lot was uncomfortable—it was crazy, when she stopped to think about it.

Gil started the car. "We should get on the road. It's going to take us a few hours to get to LA."

The night air was clean and cool like a drink of water. When they picked up speed on the highway, the soft top whistled Pearce's name. *The head of the studio* was all Clara could think. They didn't talk; the noise of the road and the revelations in Palm Springs were too loud.

After Riverside, Clara was beginning to doze off when a truck veered into their lane and Gil was forced to swerve suddenly. Clara felt a flood of adrenaline—a futile reaction to the danger; their tiny convertible would be no match for a truck that size. After the scare passed, she considered the discoveries they had made in Palm Springs. If they went after Conrad Pearce and if they were wrong, how swiftly their lives and careers could be undone—and worse, what if they were right?

Clara must have dropped off again. When she woke, they were cresting a hill and the lights of Los Angeles were laid out for them. "Gets me every time," said Gil. "This city." She didn't know whether he meant this was good or bad.

Once in LA, they stopped at a red light on Virgil.

"Feel like a nightcap?" said Gil, raking a hand through his hair.

Clara thought of various excuses for why she should get home, but they dissolved on her tongue. "Sure," she said.

He took a long look at her. "Okay. My place."

When the light turned green, Gil turned left instead of right on Santa Monica, toward Hollywood and his apartment.

## Chapter Twenty-Eight

# Franklin Avenue

GIL SNAPPED ON THE kitchen light. "Not exactly the Beverly Hills Hotel," he said as he tossed his keys onto the table, a dinged-up dinette. Off the kitchen, through an archway, was the living room. Clara's eyes followed him as he turned on a couple of lamps and swept a newspaper off the couch. "Make yourself at home," he said, returning to the kitchen.

Clara wandered into the living room. The place was spartan and needed a new coat of paint. There were stacks of books on the floor and a couple of pictures waiting to be hung. Judging by the coating of dust, they had been waiting awhile. A gramophone sat on an end table, and she glanced at the record inside. Jazz.

"Drink?" Gil called out. She heard him flipping open kitchen cupboards. "Brandy? It's French."

"Sure," said Clara.

"Put on some music," said Gil from the kitchen.

Clara turned on the gramophone and put the needle on the record. Being in Gil's apartment for the first time was strange, too intimate and all at once. She didn't sit down. She felt nervy, unable to keep still, like a horse before a race.

Gil walked toward her holding a pony glass in each hand. "Calvados. Got it from a local when I was over there. He'd been saving it until the Krauts left—" He stopped short. "Sorry. I keep forgetting."

Clara smiled and took the glass. "Skip it." She nodded to the picture frames on the floor. "When did you move in?"

"Six months ago." He let out a laugh. "Been meaning to get around to that." They were both awkward. Eventually Gil nodded to the couch. "Have a seat." His smile made her forget what she'd been about to say.

The couch was a dark brown velvet, worn in places but comfortable.

Gil clinked his glass to hers. "To hunches."

Clara took a great gulp of brandy. It tasted of candied apples and set her throat alight. She swallowed a cough. "Strong."

"Easy. It's the good stuff." Gil swirled the amber liquid around in his glass.

Clara watched him. "Who gave you the calvados?" From his face, she saw she'd hit a raw nerve.

Gil took his time. He inhaled a long breath, working up to the memory. "We were in Normandy just after the invasion. Chaos. Some locals were caught up in the skirmish. There was a couple; the wife fell and hurt her ankle. She couldn't walk. Me and a buddy of mine, we got her to safety, but my friend got hit." He was making an effort to keep it simple, but Clara could read the pain on his face.

"What happened to him, your friend?" she said softly.

Gil let out a tight breath. He shook his head. "He didn't make it." He stared through the coffee table and into the past. "We saved the guy's wife. Something good came out of it." He raised his glass a hint. "And he gave me the brandy." He smiled, but his eyes were empty. They sat in silence for a bit.

Clara thought about the invasion. The Krauts, the enemy. She recalled Matthias in his Hitler Youth uniform. He was forever fourteen in her memories, preserved in amber, the fading summer light, Freya's backyard. But he would have been twenty in 1944. Same age as Gil.

"Okay, Detective," he said, shaking off the past. "What's our theory? Lay it out."

Clara set her drink down on the coffee table, took a breath, and began. "1938, Kenneth and Dolly Pearce meet Leni Riefenstahl on board the *Europa*. The American couple is charmed by the Führer's favorite film director. They say, 'You must meet our son Conrad. He runs a movie studio.'"

Gil jumped in: "When everyone else in Hollywood is giving Leni the cold shoulder, Conrad sees an opportunity."

"He wants to purchase the US rights to her award-winning Olympics film," said Clara. The brandy had already warmed her up and evened out her nerves. Her awkwardness at being in his apartment had evaporated. They were back to their companionable rhythm.

Gil nodded. "Leni's timing is crummy—Kristallnacht and all. But Pearce figures the politics will settle down. He's not thinking that war is going to break out—not with the US, at any rate. He whisks her away to Palm Springs—away from the glare of the press and the Hollywood Anti-Nazi League."

"Was it more than a business arrangement?" said Clara.

"Leni and Pearce?" Gil thought for a moment.

"Yes, did they have an affair?"

Gil shrugged. "It's possible. Either way, it doesn't look good now." He drummed his fingers on the table. "Okay, where were we: Christmas in Palm Springs."

Clara nodded. "Right. Pearce needs a secretary to help him with all the demands of his day-to-day running of the studio while he's out of town. Typing memos, placing calls, whatever."

"He hires a temp, a young kid from San Bernardino," said Gil, taking a sip of his brandy.

"What information could Connie have had that would be so dangerous against Pearce years later, after the war?" asked Clara.

"Whatever happened in Palm Springs must have significance now," said Gil. "Nuremberg is all over the press, war crimes, Nazi-loving chickens coming home to roost. Hitler's filmmaker is surely getting convicted of something. Connie sees a little leverage. What if it came out about Pearce's closeness to Hitler's honey?"

"Blackmail," said Clara under her breath. "Connie wanted her shot at Hollywood—wanted to make up for lost time. Unless Pearce gave her a leg up, she was going to spill his past with Leni Riefenstahl—whatever happened in '38 in Palm Springs. And like you said, the timing couldn't have been worse, with Nuremberg in the background."

It was late. They were punch-drunk but too excited to call it a night. Gil stood up and began to pace. "She approaches him—on the set where she's an extra," he said, picking up the story. "She puts the screws on him. He throws her a bone and gives her a stand-in gig—good union hours, her own dressing room. On the set of a big movie, with a huge star. Not bad for a no-name girl from San Bernardino."

"But she wanted more," said Clara.

Gil nodded. "Right, that's when Connie became a problem for Pearce."

They were in sync like a screenwriting duo. "The police see a victim with no power, no influence, few friends, a dull life—save her job at the movie studio," said Clara, summing up the detectives' case.

Gil nodded. "No boyfriend, not many friends. They can't find a motive for her death. They're brushing her off."

Clara was perched on the edge of the couch, eager to chime in. "But her bedroom reveals her longing, her Hollywood dreams—the dreams of a teenager. All the magazines and movie posters, makeup and clothes. Her reality was so far from that fantasy. She was a young widow in a dank apartment with a kid to support. And that distance between desire and reality created something acute in Connie—*desperation.*" Clara was getting breathless. "Desperation acted upon can only lead to disaster—to murder." She swallowed hard. Her heart was hammering.

Gil stopped pacing. "Exactly."

"What do we do now—go to the cops?" asked Clara.

He made a face. "We don't have enough. We need the full picture. Solid proof. Maybe the US contract for *Olympia.* Something concrete that ties Pearce to Leni."

"But *Olympia* was never released in the US." Clara mulled it over. "Maybe that wasn't it at all."

Gil thought for a moment. "What if Pearce wanted to kiss up to the German film industry and keep that lucrative European market open for Silver Pacific films? By '38 Warner Bros. wasn't doing business in Berlin anymore. To keep selling in the German market you had to make concessions, recut films to please the Nazi regime. One by one the other studios were forced out or chose to shut down their German offices. Maybe Pearce used his connection with Leni to stay open for business in Nazi Germany?"

"What about the love angle?" said Clara. "The threat of a scandal, a love affair between Pearce and Hitler's honey? Would that be enough of a motive to make Pearce want to silence Connie?"

"Whatever went on in Palm Springs," said Gil, "Connie would

know. Remember the house, the glass walls, open concept—
nothing would be private."

"All we have is that New Year's picture," Clara pointed out.
"And we don't even *have it* have it. It's at the Racquet Club."

Gil sat down again; they were running out of steam. "Right,
we can't prove Connie was blackmailing him. And we can't go
to the police until we're certain. It's half-baked. Besides, a mogul
like Pearce can buy politicians, ensure favorable treatment from
cops, or worse, have them look the other way. We should keep it
to ourselves until we figure out how we're going to play it."

"Does it scare you? If we're right, it could be dangerous."

"I've faced worse than Pearce," said Gil.

Clara's eyes flicked to the glass of brandy, thinking of how
he'd come by it. "But if we're wrong," said Clara, "and we take on
the head of the studio, we wouldn't just lose our jobs. We'd be
blacklisted by every studio in town."

"That should bother me, I guess." He shrugged. "But since
the war, the things I cared about—a Hollywood career, getting
ahead—most of it doesn't matter." Clara couldn't help but wonder if Ruby Kaminsky fell into that category of things Gil used
to care about. "If the movies are done with me, I'll go back to
newspapers."

Clara thought it over. She wasn't so cavalier. She didn't want
to risk her career. Her only other option was to return to Germany with her parents. "We have to tread carefully," said Clara.

Gil put on a new record and the sound of bluesy jazz filled

the small apartment. He returned to the couch and sat down, closer to Clara than before. There was a lull as they listened to the sad trumpet and the lazy swish of brushes on a snare drum. Clara felt the intimacy of his apartment—the dim lighting, the warmth of the brandy.

Gil must have had the same thought, because he gently took her glass, and set it down on the coffee table. He looked at her, and her heart beat double-time. "Thanks for listening before." He placed his hand on her cheek. His eyes ran over her face. Then he leaned close; she could feel his breath. The case, the clues, all of that noise receded. His lips brushed hers, and Clara melted into his kiss.

All of a sudden there was a banging noise, and Clara's first thought was: *Earthquake.* They pulled apart. After the fright, she decoded the noise. Someone was knocking on the door. Gil stood up. Another thumping knock.

"Who is it—at this time of night?" Clara whispered.

Gil raked a hand through his hair. "I don't know." He strode through the living room, across the kitchen. "Okay, okay, I'm coming," he shouted.

She heard the door open. Moments later Detectives Ireland and Rivetti walked into the apartment as though they owned the place.

Clara sprang off the couch. She knew how it looked—the jazz, the brandy glasses, the low lighting.

"Sorry we're interrupting." Rivetti leered at her, and his cheap aftershave hit her from the kitchen.

"Working late?" said Gil. Clara could hear the unease in his voice.

"A murder case keeps us busy," said Rivetti, smoothing his tie. It was an ugly thing, too bright and busy for a detective.

Ireland nodded at Gil. "You're a hard man to keep up with— took a little day trip, huh?" There was a hardness in Ireland's voice that she didn't recognize. There was none of the courtesy he'd used when talking to Clara before.

She watched as the cops seemed to circle Gil in the cramped kitchen. The air was thick with the kind of tension and antici- pation before someone throws a punch—there wasn't enough room in Gil's apartment for all the weight being thrown around. Clara moved closer and hovered in the archway. The cops stood at either end of the kitchen, Gil between them.

"What's so urgent?" asked Gil.

Ireland thumbed through his notebook.

"A few follow-up questions." He was terse. Clara felt a cold weight press on her chest, making it harder to breathe—they were treating him like a suspect.

Gil lit a cigarette and leaned on the edge of the kitchen table. He did an approximation of looking relaxed, but Clara knew he'd needed something to occupy his hands. The cops had posi- tioned themselves so that Gil couldn't focus on both of them at once, his head turning back and forth like a tennis umpire.

Rivetti tried to make himself look taller. "Let's go back to the night of the murder. You told us you were in your office that evening?"

The cops knew he had lied. Of course this would come back to bite him. Clara stared hard at Gil, willing him to tell the truth.

He nodded. "Yeah, I was at my desk, working on rewrites. Why?"

"Can anyone vouch for you? Your writing partner?" Ireland squinted at his notebook. "Mr. Roger Brackett."

Gil shook his head. "He leaves early. He has a busy social calendar."

"No one else?" Rivetti threw a glance at Clara, daring her to speak up. She checked to make sure there wasn't a button undone on her blouse. He had that kind of stare.

Gil blew a cone of smoke. "I was alone."

In the living room Clara could hear that the needle was stuck at the end of the record.

"And did you leave your office between the hours of seven and nine-thirty p.m. for any reason?"

Gil shook his head again. "No."

Ireland continued. "Guy named Hank Trimble—remember him?" Gil's eyes narrowed. Ireland went on. "He was in an acting class with you way back when. He gave us an account of your relationship with Babe Bannon—sorry—Ruby Kaminsky. Says you two were a hot item until she dumped you for a Hollywood career and a leading man." Ireland locked his eyes on Gil. "You were real cut up, according to Mr. Trimble."

Gil glowered at Ireland, not hiding his disgust.

"It slip your mind," said Rivetti, "your love affair with a movie star?"

"You never asked. And I wouldn't pay too much attention to Trimble. He likes to gossip." Gil tapped his cigarette on the edge of the ashtray with too much force, scattering flecks of ash onto the Formica table.

"What's your relationship with Miss Bannon now?"

Clara held her breath, anxious to know the answer to the question she hadn't dared ask.

Gil shrugged. "Professional. We don't have much to do with each other."

"That right?" said Rivetti, a gleam in his eye.

"No hard feelings, huh?" chimed in Ireland. "Where Babe Bannon's concerned, you wish her nothing but the best?"

"Come on, Gilbert. You were obsessed with her." Rivetti took a step toward him, like he wanted to start a fight. "Bannon becomes a star, Hollywood royalty." He shook his head and couldn't resist a smirk. "Must have burned you up. You couldn't escape her name up in lights, her face on every magazine. Years of wanting her. But every time her name's mentioned, it's in the same breath as Gregory Quinn—the guy she dumped you for." A beat while he let that blow land. Clara felt the sting of it. Rivetti was describing everything she had imagined herself. The doubt crept in. How could Gil not have feelings for Bannon? How could she not still affect him?

"And then the war's over," Rivetti continued. "You return home unscathed. Get this, you get hired on *her* movie—must have felt like fate, am I right? Or maybe that's how you planned it. Maybe now that the competition—rest in peace—is out of the way, you think you have a shot." His smirk had turned to a snarl. "No dice. She doesn't give you the time of day, and that made you sore."

"Is that what she says? Or have you concocted this yourselves? I've got no beef with Barbara Bannon—ask her."

Clara felt suddenly claustrophobic in the tiny apartment. A waft of warm exhaust and the smell of garbage drifted through the open window. She looked at the apartment with new eyes. It went from neat and spartan to small and dingy. She remembered Bannon's home—the tile, the exotic prints, the views from the pool, all of Hollywood laid out before her. Gil's apartment faced the alley.

"And late one night you see her alone on the lot. You call her name. She doesn't even turn around. You lose your temper, grab her from behind. You start squeezing. All that pain, it goes away."

Clara felt her ears buzzing, that queasy roiling motion in her guts. She gripped the molding of the archway.

Ireland finally stepped in. "Crime of passion." His voice was low and confessional. "Only, it was the wrong girl." He gave an apologetic shrug. Good cop. "Maybe you realized it wasn't Bannon right after, but it was too late. Maybe only the next day, when she scared the bejesus out of the crew, walking onto the set."

Clara's mind returned to the stage that day. How had Gil reacted? Shocked like everyone else. She'd been preoccupied with her own emotions; she hadn't had time to register his.

Gil let out a bark of laughter. "You guys are wasted at the police department. They're hiring screenwriters at Silver Pacific. But let me give you some feedback." His voice hardened. "I don't buy it for a second. How'd she end up in the vault?"

"Maybe you had an accomplice?" Rivetti shot a glance at Clara. "Someone to unlock the vault and conveniently implicate the vault boy."

"What?" said Clara, not believing her ears.

Gil shook his head slowly. "If I was truly obsessed with Babe Bannon—as you insist—I'd never mistake some two-bit stand-in for the real deal."

This cut Clara—worse than the cops' theory. It was as good as a confession that he still had feelings for Bannon. The cops noticed it too.

"It was dark," said Rivetti, flicking a glance at the bottle of brandy. "Maybe you'd had a few drinks. You writers drink Scotch like tea."

"I thought that was detectives," said Gil evenly. "I don't drink at work."

Clara could sense that he was trying to rein in his temper. Part of her wanted to reach out and touch him. Another part of her recoiled, like she was watching an animal caught in a trap.

"Bottom line, I didn't do it and you've got no proof," said Gil. He took a long drag of his smoke. "If I had wanted to kill Bannon, I wouldn't have done in the wrong girl."

Detective Rivetti weighed that for a moment, then turned to Clara. "You knew about his past with Bannon?"

Clara nodded slowly. "It wasn't a secret."

Gil's eyes flitted between Clara and the cops.

"Didn't bother you, Miss Berg? Playing second fiddle to a movie star?"

Gil smashed his cigarette in the ashtray and stood up straight. He was taller than Rivetti and better built. "Unless you're planning to arrest me, I think it's time you leave." He glared at the detective, daring him to put his money where his mouth was.

The cops exchanged a look with each other. "All right, Mr. Gilbert," said Ireland. "We'll let you get back to your evening." He touched his hat to Clara.

"We'll be in touch," Rivetti snarled. He turned to Clara. "Watch yourself, sweetheart. When it comes to love, three's a crowd."

They strutted out of the kitchen. "No more gallivanting out of town," said Ireland over his shoulder. "We need to know where to find you."

The door slammed. After they'd gone, their threats and Rivetti's aftershave still hung in the air.

## Chapter Twenty-Nine

# Home

THE NEXT MORNING, CLARA woke with a sense of dread—it took a moment for her mind to catch up. It was Sunday, and yesterday she'd been in Palm Springs with Gil. All the facts they had discovered about Connie working for Pearce in 1938, they all came flooding back in a rush—a reel of film at double speed—all the way until Gil's apartment, their kiss, and the visit from the cops.

Clara sank back into her pillow. The evening had fallen apart as soon as the detectives had left. Gil had shrugged off the accusations, but he'd been rattled. They didn't finish their drinks or return to the couch. The warmth and intimacy of his apartment had evaporated. Clara reassured him that the cops' theory was nonsense, but still, it kept playing over in her mind, a grim shadow play she couldn't un-see. They were both suddenly shattered. Gil called her a cab and paid the driver.

Alone in the back of the taxi, she felt chilled. The brandy

had worn off. Their escapade to Palm Springs seemed very far away. The investigation was no longer a game, it was no longer a dare—drinks at the Racquet Club, fibbing to Pearce's housekeeper, and nosing around his desert house. The stakes had changed. Finding out the truth about Connie's murder was dangerous, and if they weren't careful, it could pull both of them under.

Clara got up and got dressed. It was just past seven. She could smell coffee. In the dining room the table and chairs were gone. Her parents must have found a buyer. Every day it seemed like a piece of their American lives had disappeared, and she was running out of time to get herself situated and find a place to live before her parents left for Europe.

In the kitchen her father was boiling eggs and making coffee. The morning light was soft and golden, and seeing her father bathed in it, and knowing that her parents would be gone in a month, made her feel tenderly toward him. She came up behind him and gave him a hug.

"Klara," said her father. "I feel as though I haven't see you in days."

"I've been busy at work." Clara poured herself a coffee and sat at the kitchen table. "How's *Mutti*?"

"She has a lot on her plate right now, with planning the move—both of us have our own apprehensions about going back to Germany."

"Is she still angry with me?" asked Clara.

"Well, she's taking it hard, yes, but she thinks you'll come around." He turned off the burner and spooned the eggs into a bowl of cold water. "Just try to be gentle with her. It's hurtful to her, the idea of our family splitting apart."

"But I'm eighteen now," said Clara, thumping down her cup.

"I know." He leaned against the counter and smiled the sad smile she knew so well. "I knew that this day would come, when you would leave home, make your way in the world." He sighed. "The thing is, she wasn't prepared to lose you so soon."

His words made her feel wretched. She hadn't considered how her parents felt about leaving her behind; Clara had been so focused on getting what she wanted. It was ironic that they were set against her staying in Los Angeles. The Bergs' arrival in America had been preceded by another argument. She could remember it vividly. It was the outburst that had sent her running to the upper decks and led to her invasion of first class. They'd been in their cramped second-class cabin on the *Europa*. Her mother had been perched on the edge of the lower bunk, her father pacing (barely three steps back and forth).

"You lied—you both lied to me." Eleven-year-old Klara stood, slack-jawed and disbelieving.

"It was a risk, Klara—to tell you what we were planning." Her father stopped pacing and looked at her directly. "Had anyone found out we weren't planning on coming back, they would have stopped us. I could have been arrested."

"We didn't want to put that burden on you," said her mother

with a more pleading tone. "Lying to friends and teachers, keeping such a secret." She was swiveling her wedding band around her ring finger, the way she always did when she was anxious.

Klara couldn't decide which was worse—not returning to Berlin (impossible to imagine) or her parents' duplicity. Couldn't they have trusted her? Her goodbye with Freya had been too casual. In a parting that was forever, she would have embraced her best friend with a whispered pledge of undying friendship. Precious tokens would have been exchanged.

"I won't stay in America. I want to go home! I don't care what you say about Hitler, and the Nazis, and Papa being on a list—*I'm* not on a list."

Her mother shot a worried glance at the door. "Klara, keep your voice down."

"Klara, listen—" her father began.

"No! I won't listen to another word." She stormed out of the cabin, forgetting to take her coat.

She felt ashamed even now—not just about the hurtful words she'd said, but that her parents hadn't trusted her. That they'd known she might betray them.

After breakfast her father was at the sink doing dishes. Clara watched him for a few moments, thinking about what lay ahead the next day. Could she and Gil really take on the head of the studio? Could they find proof to show that he had murdered Connie Milligan? Was Clara brave enough to try? While knowing that in the background the cops were building a case against Gil? The odds were against them.

Clara grabbed a dishtowel and began to dry the dishes. "Papa, when did you know that you had to speak out against the Nazis? How did you know it was the right thing to do?"

He reflected for a moment. "It started with just a small thing—I defended a Jewish colleague who had been forced out. But it was like removing a blindfold. I couldn't un-see the truth. I kept speaking out. It wasn't a choice. It was an obligation— even if I was scared."

"And the university fired you?" said Clara.

He nodded. "Yes. And then I was put on a list, and you know the rest."

"Did you regret it?"

"Not for a moment. We got out, of course. I don't know how I would have felt had it gone badly, if we hadn't been as lucky. I hope I still would have done the right thing."

Could she be as brave as her father? The thing she most wanted—her film career—would be snatched away. She thought back to the day when she got the yes from Thaler. It felt like a lifetime ago.

Her father turned off the tap. "Klara, I wondered," he said, making an effort to sound casual. "Do you want me to call Dr. Gröning?"

Clara stopped drying the plate in her hands and stared at her father. "No." How could he bring that up? "I'm fine."

"He was so helpful last summer. It might be nice to talk to someone. You've had quite a shock—the murder at the studio." He shook his head like it pained him to say it.

Clara put the dry plate on the counter and took another one from the rack. "I don't need to speak to anyone."

She recalled Dr. Gröning's sunny office, the bland artwork and his collection of desert succulents. Clara had insisted they speak English. She would stare at the otherworldly plants—reminiscent of coral or sea creatures—during the sessions. It was easier to describe her feelings when she fixed her gaze on something other than Dr. Gröning's penetrating blue stare. He was German of course, but an earlier émigré. He'd arrived in Los Angeles in '33, which elevated him in her parents' circle. There was a hierarchy in the refugee community—the earlier you fled Germany, the more highly you were regarded. People usually paid a lot of money to talk to Dr. Gröning, and Clara was supposed to feel grateful that he'd agreed to see her as a favor to her parents.

"If you change your mind . . . ," her father persisted. "I'd be happy to call him."

Clara put away the plates in the cupboard with a deliberate clatter. "No, Papa." It was an unspoken agreement. They didn't talk about last summer. It had been just after V-E Day and high school graduation. Clara had been very low. She'd let friendships slide away. She'd stopped going out or answering phone calls. She would spend hours alone at the cinema, at sparsely attended matinees and reruns. In the end it was Max's idea to get her a job at the studio. It wasn't the sort of thing her parents would normally approve of, but they'd been desperate to pull

Clara out of her slump (as they'd called it) and back into the real world. Last summer was in the past, in a box, locked and stored away. It wasn't to be brought out and aired in passing, like a harmless anecdote.

Her father wiped down the faucet and dried his hands. "All right, I'll leave you to get on. Buyers for the couch are coming this afternoon."

Clara nodded mechanically. Out of the corner of her eye she saw him pause to look at her before leaving the kitchen. She pretended not to see.

## Chapter Thirty

# Bungalow Eight

THE BIGGEST CONTRACT STARS each had their own bungalow at the studio. More than a dressing room, it was a refuge, a home away from home, a place to decompress and be alone, to take a nap at lunch, or have a few drinks with co-stars after a long shooting day. Bungalow number eight—Barbara Bannon's dressing room—was located off the main thoroughfares and was a decent drive in a golf cart from the executive building. In fact, it was closer to the postproduction building than Clara had realized.

Crew call time was nine a.m. Bannon's call time was at seven a.m., to allow for hair, makeup, and wardrobe. Clara calculated that she would have time to catch Bannon (alone, hopefully) between eight-forty-five and nine-thirty, after the actress was prepped but before they needed her on set. Miss Bannon was still doing her own stand-in work.

Clara's heart was tap-dancing in her chest as she rapped

on the door of bungalow eight. She couldn't pay attention to her fears. She had to confront Bannon for Gil's sake. If the cops thought the Ruby motive was strong enough to sink Gil, the movie star could at least come to his defense. Clara could hear music coming from inside. She knocked again. "Miss Bannon," she said, raising her voice. There was a dusty honeysuckle clinging to a trellis, and gingham curtains in the window. In a different context Clara could have been on a residential street in Glendale and not in the middle of a studio lot. After a couple of minutes and no answer, Clara held her breath, opened the door, and stepped inside.

Barbara Bannon was standing—in full costume and makeup—on a stepladder, wielding a hammer. She barely glanced at Clara. "Is this thing straight?" She was talking about the picture frame she was in the process of hanging. "I moved it from the other wall. It looks better here, don't you think?"

They sat in Bannon's dressing area, Clara on a patterned couch and Bannon in a swivel chair, her back to the three-way mirror ringed with lights. On the far wall there was a movable rack of her costumes for the movie, as well as a closet for her own clothes. Next to Clara at the end of the couch was a brass drinks caddy. The room was neat and feminine, and Clara felt like they were little girls playing house.

"What about Connie?" said Bannon. She was camera ready and totally intimidating. Clara thought she might melt under the actress's direct gaze.

Clara took a deep breath and threw herself in at the deep end. "I think you lied about Connie. You said you weren't close, gave the impression you didn't care that much. But I believe you were friends."

Bannon simply stared at her. "And? You want a medal or something?" She lit a cigarette and held it carefully, away from her costume.

Clara stood her ground and waited for Bannon to explain herself.

"I'm an actress, and I'm pretty decent at it." If she'd had a tail, she would have been flicking it about now. "You're smarter than those detectives." Clara noticed that Bannon didn't deny it.

"How did Connie get the gig as your stand-in?" Clara studied her closely, the perfect symmetry of her face, nothing out of place, just one eyebrow arched higher than the other. And that small difference made her beautiful rather than pretty.

"I got her the job." She pointed her cigarette in the direction of the stages. "She was working as an extra on the lot, and I was here for a meeting with Pearce, where he told me about the role in *Argentan*. I was in the ladies' bathroom afterward, feeling in rough shape. She passed me a compact. We got to chatting. She cheered me up; she liked to laugh. And side by side in the mirror, we looked similar—same height, shape, and coloring. I liked her enough that I offered her the job, right there in the john." She let out a laugh.

"No one objected?"

"I had to be tricky. I gave her headshot to the AD—someone I trust. He promised to steer Howard to my pick. So that was that. Connie was a lifesaver—you know what they put me through on this movie. We became friends. With Connie, I had an ally, someone to talk to."

She stubbed out the barely smoked cigarette, dispensing with the delay tactic.

"Who made her lighten her hair?" asked Clara.

Bannon looked confused. "She wanted to try a lighter shade. It was no big deal. I called Rosa." Clara felt stupid. She had been so focused on the idea that someone had been molding Connie to look like Bannon. Clara hadn't considered that the stand-in changing her hair would be something so innocent. The article on Leni Riefenstahl was what had made Connie react strangely that day. It had had nothing to do with her hair.

"Do you have any idea who might have wanted to hurt her?" said Clara.

"Look, we were friends, but I have no idea who killed her or why." Bannon turned back to the dressing table and peered at her reflection in the mirror.

Clara got up and stood behind her, refusing to end the conversation. "I think Connie's murder has something to do with the studio, all the way to the top, and so do you. That's why you've been cagey about your friendship. You know something. Admit it."

Babe's face was perfectly lit by the ring lights. "She's dead.

What can I do about that now? Even if I had an idea who killed her, it won't bring her back."

"Whoever did this is going to get away with it," Clara continued. "You can't let Connie's death go unpunished, or worse, let an innocent person take the fall."

"Who?" Babe swiveled around to face Clara.

"The cops are trying to pin it on Gil, because of your history together."

"What!" She got up and began to pace. "They showed up at my house yesterday, firing questions at me. They were trying to pin Randall's stupid letters on Gil."

"Wait—what letters?" said Clara.

Bannon shook her head. "Just one of Randall's little pranks to put me off-kilter—anonymous threats," she spat. "It was childish. He probably panicked after the murder."

So that would explain what Hawks had said at Bannon's house that night, reassuring a paranoid Randall Ford that no one would find out about his prank—that he hadn't caused any harm: *She's alive and well.*

"What did you tell the cops about Gil?" asked Clara.

"That they were barking up the wrong tree and they must be pretty stupid if this is all they can come up with. I tore a strip off them and sent them packing."

"Tell me the rest of Connie's story," said Clara, returning to her seat on the couch. "Please."

Bannon flicked her hair. She ran her eyes over Clara, maybe

wondering if she should trust her. She made a performance of sitting down again. Then she leaned back and struck a pose.

Clara was on the edge of her seat. She didn't blink.

"It wasn't long after the shoot had started, on the anniversary of V-E Day. Connie and I were both down in the dumps. We went out, got a little tipsy. Over drinks she told me she had a plan to engineer her own lucky break. She was going to get acting work, a contract at the studio, and a hefty payday."

Clara's heart leapt to her throat. "How? Did she say?"

Bannon shrugged. "She had leverage; that's how she phrased it. She was fired up, cocky."

Clara was hanging on her every word. "Did she mention any names? Anyone at the studio?"

The actress shook her head. "She wouldn't say. But she promised that when she had all her ducks in a row, she would tell me the whole thing." She raised an eyebrow. "Mentioned she could even help me get out of my contract."

"Did you buy it?"

"Connie wasn't a liar. But I took it with a grain of salt. I figured she was sweet on a director or a producer who was promising her the world." Her voice grew softer. "She had plans. She wanted to buy a little house with a yard for Mae. Enough space for her mother to have her own suite. It was that simple." The sunny words soured in Bannon's mouth. "The night she was killed"—Bannon grew somber—"Connie was here in my dressing room, right there where you are on the couch. She

263

told me she was going on an important date. I knew it had to be this scheme of hers, because she wouldn't tell me who she was meeting or why. It was all hush-hush."

"Did you catch a glimpse of him? Did she meet him on the lot?"

Bannon shook her head. "I left before she went to meet him. I stayed for a bit as she was getting ready, and did the only thing I could do—I did her makeup and told her to borrow an outfit from the costume rail. We were the same size."

Clara looked at the rail of expensive tailored clothes. She could imagine Connie not being able to refuse the offer. During the whole shoot, while Bannon had worn made-to-measure evening gowns, fur, jewels, and sheer silk, Connie had been given something cheap and functional, as long as the color was right, the cut approximate. "And she chose the black cocktail dress," said Clara, looking at an identical copy on a hanger.

Bannon nodded. "The wardrobe department has multiples of all my costumes. I told her to keep it. She had never worn decent clothes before." Babe got up and began to pace again. "I armed her by making her look good. I warned her to be careful, whatever it was she was doing." She stopped pacing, and her gaze drifted into the past. "The next day, Connie was dead and I was terrified. I replayed our conversations, and I realized she must have been playing with fire. She hadn't just been flirting with a producer for a role; she'd been blackmailing someone. Someone powerful." *Pearce,* Clara thought. "I was tight-lipped, acted the diva like we weren't close, like I didn't care a whole lot, because I didn't want anyone to think I knew something about Connie's blackmail scheme." She looked down. "I was scared."

"But why didn't you say something? Why didn't you tell the cops?" said Clara desperately.

Bannon let out a clap of laughter. "The cops in this town are bought and paid for. You think if the investigation points to someone with clout that they'll lock him up? Of course not. They'll find a patsy, a fall guy."

A sharp knock, and they both jumped. A voice said, "Ready for you on set, Miss Bannon."

"Gimme a minute," she called back.

Bannon moved to the window and beckoned Clara over. They peered through the gingham curtains. Clara followed Bannon's gaze. Along the asphalt road, past a rank of parked golf carts, Clara could see the familiar edge of the concrete bunker. The film vaults were a stone's throw from Bannon's dressing room.

## Chapter Thirty-One

# Paper Trail

CLARA HAD TOLD SAM she was going to accounting when she went to Bannon's bungalow. He had raised an eyebrow. "Don't dillydally, Clara." Now she had to hustle in that direction.

On her brisk walk over, she kept seeing flashes of different scenes—1938 and 1946—refracted and moving like a kaleidoscope. Clara could now assume, after hearing Bannon's story, that Connie must have been meeting Pearce the night she was killed. But she didn't have any concrete proof Connie had been blackmailing the studio head. Still, Clara knew she was getting close.

Time cards had been due on Friday afternoon, but Clara had been distracted, to say the least. So she was filling out last week's time card now.

"Mark the production number you're working on," Doris reminded her.

"Oh, right. I'm not used to that," said Clara. This was her first union time card. "Do you know the number? It's *Letter from Argentan.*"

"SP 4025," Marianne called out from across the office.

Clara dutifully filled it out, then stopped, staring at the numbers as if they had unlocked a secret combination. What if the number on Connie's script wasn't a phone number? What if it was a production number: *SP* for "Silver Pacific," not *SP* for "SPRING," the telephone exchange?

Slowly she handed the time card back to Doris and racked her brains for an excuse to ask about it. "While I'm here, one of the editors was trying to find some stock footage—we haven't been able to track it down. Maybe it's been archived in the wrong place. If I give you the production number, can you help me out?" She tried to sound casual, as though this were an afterthought.

"I'm surprised Miss Simkin would misplace anything," said Doris.

"That's just it," said Clara in a conspiratorial tone. "No one wants to call her out."

"Sure thing," said Doris with a knowing smile. She went to a filing cabinet. "What's the production number?"

Clara's heart leapt as she said the numbers aloud: "SP three-one-nine-one." Hopefully talk of stock footage wouldn't arouse interest, let alone suspicion.

Clara craned her neck to watch Doris with her coral nails

flip rapidly through the file folders. She stopped on a file and skimmed its contents. "Here it is." She pulled it out of the filing cabinet and closed the drawer. "Movie called *Amazon Queen.* Looks like they had a script, did some prep work, a day of camera tests—is that what you're looking for?"

"Camera tests?" said Clara, her mind whirring. "Yes, sure. That must be why we couldn't find it with stock footage."

Doris nodded. "I've got a few purchase orders for film stock and camera rentals. The test was in December '38, a small crew on location. Looks like they had a script and found a director. But the production never got off the ground. The film was scrapped."

Clara racked her brains. *Amazon Queen.* She'd never heard of it. "Who was the director?" she asked, offhand, as though barely interested.

Doris squinted at the page, ran her finger across a line of type. "Director by the last name of Richard." She squinted at it. "No, that's not it." She put the file down on the counter in front of Clara and went to another cabinet. "Hang on. Let me check something."

Clara gazed at the manila folder as if she could see through it. She was about to sneak a glimpse at it when Rita glided over on her rolling chair. She picked up a stapler from Doris's desk and snapped its mouth around a sheaf of papers. "I heard you're dating the screenwriter," she said, her eyes bright. "He's handsome." She smirked. "A bit morose for my taste."

"We're . . . friends," said Clara haltingly. But were they more than that? The kiss in his apartment. Then the cops pounding on the door.

"Leave her alone," said Doris, returning with a folder. She laid it on the counter and took out a piece of paper. "Found the director's contract." She waved it triumphantly. "Producers love to misplace things—we make copies of everything. So the name's not 'Richard.' It's 'Richter.' Never heard of him." She tilted her head. "Does that help?"

Clara's throat was suddenly tight. "Can I look at that?" She gave Doris a hopeful smile.

Doris shrugged. "Don't see why not—it was years ago."

Clara took the paper and tried to still her trembling fingers. Her breathing was shallow, and a prickle of sweat threatened to dampen her blouse. A contract in black and white: a three-picture deal between Silver Pacific and L. Richter. First picture titled *Amazon Queen*. Clara was back in the first-class Winter Garden with the glamorous Fräulein Richter, hearing her traveling companion. *Nom de voyage. Even the ship's cat must know you're on board.*

Clara's eyes greedily scanned the fine print. Richter would write the screenplay and direct. It was signed by Conrad Pearce and L. Richter in Palm Springs on December 15, 1938. Witness: C. Milligan.

"You okay?" asked Doris.

Clara used all her willpower to contain the gasp and to

maintain the appearance of nonchalance. But reading that signature, the hairs on her arms stood up. "Yes." She pasted on a smile. "Thanks for checking." Clara went to hand it back but then stopped. "Doris, you mind if I hang on to this? Simkin is such a stickler. She'll want me to produce evidence."

Doris rolled her eyes theatrically. "I know the type. Sure, just bring it back later."

"Thanks," said Clara. "I really appreciate it." And she meant it. Maybe the accounting girls weren't so bad after all.

Her performance over, Clara stepped out of the accounting office as though in a dream, her limbs thick and heavy as if she had forgotten how to walk. But her mind was racing.


Back in editorial, Clara ran into Sam in the corridor. He was heading off to a meeting with the composer and music editor. "Clara, we need to talk," he said.

She nodded, gripping the piece of paper from accounting. Clara knew she was on thin ice with her job, but Leni's contract and where it fit into the puzzle was all she could think about.

"At the end of the day," said Sam soberly. "After the *Argentan* screening."

As soon as Clara shut the cutting room door, she opened her file drawer. She had all the Leni clippings from the LA *Times* in a manila folder. She flicked through the articles. *Amazon Queen.*

That title sounded familiar, or something like it. She skimmed through the articles until she found what she was looking for. She put the clipping in her purse next to the contract Doris had given her. Then she picked up the phone and dialed the switchboard. "Writers' building. Mr. Gilbert, please."

## Chapter Thirty-Two

# Sunset

CLARA ARRANGED TO MEET Gil for an early lunch at a diner on Sunset. It was only eleven-thirty a.m. But the walls had ears at the studio, and she needed to tell him what she had discovered in accounting, without the possibility of anyone overhearing. When she arrived, he was already studying the menu in a booth by the window. She felt a surge of excitement, walking toward his table. Was it the paper in her purse, or seeing him for the first time since the night in his apartment? She couldn't distinguish between the two. She squeaked along the red vinyl opposite him. "Hi," she said, a little breathless.

"Do I need a code word or something?" he said. "What's so hush-hush?"

"I figured something out, something big."

The waitress passed their table. "Be with you in a minute, folks."

He handed her the menu. "Figure this out first. I'm ordering lunch."

"Gil, this is important."

"I can't take two lunch breaks, so I'm ordering something. This better be good, whatever it is—dragging me up to Sunset." He threw her a small smile to show he was kidding.

Clara looked at the menu, not reading the words. The familiarity of their teasing banter reassured her. She hadn't known what to expect. Saturday night at his place—French brandy, the kiss, Ireland and Rivetti barging in and throwing accusations around—it all felt like a surreal dream.

After they ordered, Clara laid out everything she had been waiting to spill from her chat with Bannon. Bannon and Connie *had been* friends; Bannon had gotten Connie the job as her stand-in; and the juiciest part was that Connie had known some secret to use as leverage against the studio, which *had* to have been something to do with Leni. And then Clara shared her discovery in accounting—that the phone number on Connie's script was actually a production number, and how everything had all unraveled from there until she'd had her hands on the contract.

Gil shook his head, incredulous. "Wait, Pearce signed her for a three-picture deal?" He lowered his voice. "Leni Riefenstahl— are you sure?" He blinked at her, dumbfounded.

Clara felt a rush as she opened her purse and retrieved the contract Doris had given her. She handed it to Gil carefully, as though it were coated in gold leaf. "It's signed L. Richter—which was her pseudonym on the *Europa*."

The waitress interrupted with their coffees. "Here you go,

folks." She saved her best smile for Gil. She was pretty—they all were in Hollywood. She sashayed away, giving him a nice view, but Gil's eyes were glued to the contract.

Clara continued: "Hollywood moguls had made a habit of signing European talent—Louis B. Mayer with Marlene Dietrich and Hedy Lamarr. Of course, the difference was that Marlene and Hedy were *fleeing* Nazi Europe. They weren't wearing the crown of Führer's Favorite Fräulein."

"That's some gall on Pearce's part," said Gil. "What was this *Amazon Queen* project? I never heard of it."

"It was Leni's next project, her *dream* project: *Penthesilea.* It's based on the Greek myth about the queen of the Amazons and her tragic love story with Achilles."

"*Pensa*-what?" Gil smirked. "No wonder they changed the name."

Clara took the LA *Times* clipping from her purse.

Gil peered at her purse. "You got a filing cabinet in there?"

She smiled for a second, but then was back to business. "Leni mentioned the film project in interviews when she was over here." She ran her finger down the article. "Here it is. 'Her career? Hollywood? She has plans that will keep her engrossed elsewhere for the next ten years. Her next picture will be filmed in Germany, Tripoli, and Greece in the spring. It will be titled *Penthesilea*—a Greek saga, and in it she will play the title role, a leader of the Amazons.' *Amazon Queen.* It sounded familiar, so I checked back through all the clippings I'd read, and there it was."

"Good job, Clara." Gil nodded as the picture formed in his mind. "Like any savvy director, she was talking up her *next* project, to attract interest, drum up funding."

"And someone was paying attention," said Clara.

"Pearce's parents meet Leni on the *Europa*, talk up their son Conrad, who's in movies," said Gil, recapping their theory. "Pearce meets Leni, invites her to Palm Springs to get away from the bad publicity. But his plan isn't simply to buy US rights to *Olympia*. It's far more ambitious. It's her *next* picture he wants, and her Hollywood career."

"There's something else," said Clara. "Doris in accounting mentioned that there was a camera test for *Amazon Queen*— back in December 1938. She had some purchase orders, a one-day shoot, a small crew."

"Huh." Gil took a long slurp of coffee and thought for a minute. "Pearce is really wooing Leni. He wants to flatter her, show off. Before she even signs her fake name on the dotted line, he arranges a screen test, perhaps." He was enjoying this. "The shoot wasn't that big—a few trusted crew. Maybe in Palm Springs, away from scrutiny and the gossip of Hollywood."

"No one with links to the Hollywood Anti-Nazi League," said Clara. "It's possible the crew wouldn't even know who she was if they weren't following the boycott."

Gil nodded. "Right, she's a decent-looking broad with a foreign accent."

"Also the desert in Palm Springs could fill in for Tripoli or

Greece or wherever Leni had originally planned to shoot on location," said Clara, putting it together in that moment.

"'Forget filming in Europe or North Africa. Look what we can do for you here in California—desert, oceans, mountains, perfect weather,'" Gil said, imagining Pearce's pitch. "Leni Riefenstahl's Hollywood debut." He let out a low whistle. "What do you know? The real 'Silver Blonde' is a redhead, Pearce's titian-haired Nazi film queen."

Clara leaned forward. "Hushing up a camera test is one thing. What *I* want to know is, how could Pearce take the gamble of signing her? How could he even consider it?" She flashed a glance around the restaurant, then lowered her voice. "The other studios boycotted Riefenstahl when she was just here on vacation. Surely her new film would be box office poison."

Gil leaned back in the booth and thought about that for a beat. "Sure, in that moment it doesn't look smart. But Pearce takes the long view. Think of it *without* the benefit of hindsight. Early 1939, and many American business leaders think Mr. Hitler's on the level. Henry Ford, Walt Disney, Charles Lindbergh—all big fans. The America First Committee and Lindbergh's nonintervention gang are gaining popularity in Washington. Their goal was to keep America out of the war. And at this point it looks like they're succeeding—there's no way the US will get mixed up in another European conflict. Pearce assumes the political flap over Kristallnacht will blow over. Maybe his interest in Leni goes beyond her creative talents."

"What do you mean?" said Clara. "The love angle?"

Gil shook his head. "No. Ideology. There are those who'd prefer that our movie industry weren't quite so 'European'—code for 'Jewish.' Leni would be the kind of European they could get behind—auburn-haired and Aryan. I'd say signing Leni wasn't just a creative choice. It was an ideological one as well—the kind of decision Kenneth Pearce and others might have encouraged. I found out that Pops Pearce met Mr. Hitler in '36 at the Olympics, and he was quite a fan of Nazi ideas."

Clara shook her head. "Because of the war, I always thought of America as the good guys. I can't believe there would be Americans who would support Hitler."

Gil shrugged. "You don't need to love Hitler to be anti-Semitic. Take Roger Brackett. He thinks I'm French-Canadian—my last name is *'Gilbert.'*" Gil said it the French way, "Jeel-berr."

"I grew up on the border of New York State and Quebec," Gil continued. "And sure, my dad is French-Canadian, but my mother's Jewish—which Brackett doesn't know. My first week on the job, he said something like 'The Jews have all the jobs in Hollywood.' Just a throwaway line. Another time, we're out for lunch and he talks about me being stingy on a tip: 'Don't be such a Jew about the tip, Gil.' Whatever. It's just an expression, right?" Gil raised an eyebrow like he didn't buy it for a second. "You see, Roger's a perfect example of the thoughtless garden-variety anti-Semitism in this town. I don't think Brackett's some Nazi-loving fascist. I doubt he was a member of the German-American

Bund or the Silver Shirts. It's run-of-the-mill bigotry that comes as naturally to him as breathing."

The waitress arrived with their lunch, and their theories took a break while they ate. Clara mulled the whole thing over.

"Where's Connie in all of this?" asked Gil, offering Clara some fries.

Clara pointed to the bottom of the contract. "Look at the witness."

Gil took the contract and squinted at the signature. "C. Milligan. And it's signed in Palm Springs." His eyes met Clara's.

"Connie probably typed up the contract."

Gil laid down the paper lightly as if it would disintegrate.

After they had polished off lunch and the waitress had cleared their plates, they picked up the story again. "After Pearce signs Leni," said Gil, "she returns to Europe in January 1939, maybe to work on the script or whatever. A production like that would take months to prep. But then in 1939, Germany invades Poland, and Britain declares war on Germany."

"With Europe at war," said Clara, "the project is probably put off or on hold. Maybe Pearce is starting to get cold feet; his prediction that the politics surrounding Leni will blow over is way off course."

Gil nodded. "By the time Pearl Harbor strikes, it's 'sayonara' to Leni's Hollywood career—finished before it even began." He shrugged. "Pearce moves on—win some, lose some. During the war he looks like a patriot—the studio churns out uplifting movies, his contract stars entertain the troops. It was one business idea that didn't pan out."

"Not to mention that his father must have made a packet out of the war—auto parts for the US army," added Clara.

Gil leaned back in the booth with his coffee. "His Nazi flag-waving was an inconvenient blip and Pearce's collaboration with Leni was never made public."

"Until," said Clara, "Connie showed up in LA."

"What I don't get is the timing." Gil shook his head slightly. "Why did Connie wait until now to blackmail Pearce? She'd known about this whole thing since '38. Why not recall all this during the war? Why did it take this article in the *Evening Post*? Couldn't Connie have put two and two together sooner?"

"I don't think she had the full picture in '38," said Clara. "She wouldn't have known who Leni was, and didn't care about European politics. They were glamorous Hollywood folk, and she was probably thinking she was lucky to have a job right out of school. After Palm Springs, she probably forgets about the 'German actress.'"

Gil chewed it over. "Yeah, I buy that."

Clara leaned forward in the flow of her theory. "Reading the article in the *Evening Post* gave her the context—that Leni wasn't just a foreign actress, that she was close to Hitler, that she had directed *Triumph of the Will*. Connie was hit with this right around the anniversary of V-E Day—that timing is significant."

Gil nodded. "She felt raw; she was missing Jim."

"Exactly," said Clara.

"Sure. I mean, it sticks in my craw, to be honest—rich powerful Americans, playing for the wrong side, hobnobbing with Hitler and his favorite Fräulein. The world's rich and privileged scratching each other's backs. Chumps like me fighting on the beach for their freedom, and those fellows making out like bandits because of the war."

The waitress refilled Gil's coffee.

"All right," he said. "We have the thing that Connie had over Pearce. If it came out about Pearce's signing Leni, it would be disastrous for the studio. It's the missing piece—a strong motive for blackmail. What's our next move?"

"Proof," Clara replied. "Can you check the story department? See if there's anything on *Penthesilea* or *Amazon Queen*?"

Gil nodded. "What else do we have—the contract?"

"But it's not in Leni's name." Clara shook her head. "It's her pseudonym: Richter."

Gil sighed. "Right, it doesn't prove much on its own."

Clara pushed away her coffee. It tasted bitter. "Wait." She looked up. "The camera test for *Amazon Queen*. What if Connie was looking for it? That's why she was in the vaults."

"I thought she had a date. That's why she got dolled up and Bannon gave her an outfit."

"That's what Connie told Bannon, so she could use Bannon's dressing room—the vaults are within spitting distance." Clara's brain began to connect the dots. "The date thing was just an excuse. Bannon's dressing room has a clear view of the road. Connie could have waited until security did their rounds, and moments later she was inside. Her plan that night was to get inside the vaults, to find *Amazon Queen*. What if she was already in the vaults looking for the reel when the killer surprised her?"

"Anything else, folks?" The waitress startled them.

"Just the check, thanks," said Gil. The waitress left it on the table, and they sat in silence. Chatter and clinking cutlery filled the benign surroundings of the diner; outside, the cars and trolleys rolled by on Sunset; pedestrians squinted on the sunny side of the street—the humble procession of everyday life.

Gil's eyes met Clara's, and she knew they were thinking the same thing. "We need the film," he said. "We need to find the test of *Amazon Queen*."

## Chapter Thirty-Three

# Silver

CLARA STOLE INTO THE film archive like a thief under cover of darkness. Only, it wasn't nighttime. It was an ordinary Monday lunch hour, when Lloyd, Walter, and Miss Simkin would conveniently be at the commissary, tucking into meat loaf or pot roast. To find *Amazon Queen,* Clara needed information from the archive—a vault number, a reel number—*something* to point her in the right direction. Chancing upon a decade-old reel of test footage in the vast collection of films stored in the vault would be like finding a needle in a haystack.

The familiar office felt dangerous. A charge of electricity prickled the air as she moved swiftly to Lloyd's desk. Next to his collection of used coffee cups and scribbled notes sat a hefty ledger—the master archive list, which was searchable by film title, production number, or reel number. She opened the ledger and skimmed the title names. *Amazon Queen* was never released—or even produced, so she didn't hold out much hope that it would be listed. And she was right. No mention. She flipped to the section listed by production number, her stomach clenched in a tight fist. A test reel was shot after all, it had to be accounted for *somewhere*. Her fingers sparked static as she turned the pages to the entries before the war, specifically the production numbers that started with '31'. Holding her breath, she ran her finger down the list of numbers: 3187, 3188, 3189, 3190. She stopped abruptly—3190 jumped to 3192. There was no entry for 3191. "Dammit," she breathed. How could it not exist?

But then she noticed that the nearby entries were stored in vault five. Maybe that was why Connie had gone there. She could imagine Connie popping by the office to see Lloyd and flirting a little, pretending to be interested in his work in order to get a look at the archive ledger. Maybe she only got a quick glance or she just assumed 3191 would be stored in the same vault as the numbers next to it. Lloyd's jacket hung on the back of his chair. She rifled through the pockets, and sure enough, she found Lloyd's cheat sheet. Connie could easily have helped herself to the vault combinations.

She closed the ledger and stood at Lloyd's desk, contemplating the archive like it was a stage set, as though every commonplace item were a prop, carefully selected and brimming with significance.

Eventually her eyes landed on Simkin's office door. Armed with the film's title, there was one other place that Clara could check: the card catalogue in Simkin's office. It had a record of every film, organized alphabetically by title, with more background information on the production than in the master archive list. She marched toward Miss Simkin's closed door. To cross the threshold of her office felt like a serious breach, but there was no choice if she was serious about finding the film.

With her heartbeat dancing to an uneven rhythm, Clara tried the door, half expecting it to be locked, but the handle turned smoothly, and at once she was inside Simkin's domain. Clara's eyes darted around. Everything was bright and sharp and calling to her. She had to slow down and concentrate.

Simkin's office had little in the way of personality. A desk with a large typewriter, filing cabinets, and her Moviola to check prints. Clara paused at the desk. There were no picture frames or knickknacks, not a plant, a vase, or a china coffee mug. Over twenty years at the studio, since the early days and Manny Silver's reign, and not a shred of herself—purely professional.

Clara noticed one exception to the professional decor: pinned to the wall near the window was a calendar illustrated with birds of California. It made sense that Simkin liked birds. She had the same penetrating gaze, and she was rarely still. Alert to any infraction, she would swivel around in her chair, blinking like an owl—food brought in from the commissary, Lloyd napping at his desk, Clara's incorrect choice of footwear, the wireless turned up too loud.

When Clara had first started at the archive, Max confided that Simkin had been an editor, back in the 1920s before the advent of sound, in the days when movies were still a curiosity, when knitting together the film footage was seen as women's work. After the film industry began to boom, once there was money and prestige, there was a surge of male editors. Some women made the leap to cutting sync sound, but others—like Miss Simkin—were pushed out.

Clara looked at the calendar. It was still on the month of April, where a red-tailed hawk stared at her, witness to her trespassing. She turned the page to May, where an industrious woodpecker, his head crested with a shock of red feathers, tapped at a tree trunk. Instinctively Clara's eyes were drawn to May 16, the day of the murder, and it dawned on her that this was the first time she had been in Simkin's office since that night. She recalled herself that evening, sitting at the Moviola, its lamp bright against the dark windowpane. There was the mirror image of the office in the glass, her own reflection—Clara's double—staring at her as she held the phone to her ear, waiting for Gil's voice, and getting instead the switchboard's perfunctory "No answer, miss." She chewed her lip as she remembered his changing story—he had been working in Roger's office and hadn't heard the phone; he'd found himself on the *Argentan* battle set lost in memories of war. Clara stared through the window and into that moment. Did she have any doubts about Gil? No, she shook off that question immediately; she felt disloyal even thinking it. He was the detectives' fall guy and that was all a fiction, whereas she was uncovering the truth.

Before opening the wooden drawers of the card catalogue,

Clara went to the supply closet. (Simkin liked to have it close so she could keep tabs on who took what.) She flung open the metal doors and opened a random box—cotton gloves, the ones editors used to avoid getting smudges on the film. She took out a couple of pairs and left the closet doors wide open. If anyone came back early from lunch, it would look as though she had stopped into the office to get supplies for Sam. Her cover taken care of, Clara moved to the card catalogue, all the time keeping alert to the sound of a footstep or the hinge of the door.

Rows of narrow wooden drawers housed the index cards of alphabetized film titles, every project shot at the studio since the early days. Simkin favored the purity of numbers—a production's title could be changed several times before a film's release. Therefore, the alphabetized titles weren't updated as often. Perhaps there was a chance that the *Amazon Queen* record was still here. The long narrow drawer with *A* to *C* was smooth to open. The wood was warm and soft. It looked like oak. She flicked through the five-by-seven index cards of *A* titles: *About Time, All for One, Amazing Grace*—that last card gave her a false surge of hope. She flipped to the next card and felt a jolt of electricity zing through her body from scalp to toe. *Amazon Queen* (3191). But the exhilaration soon faded: a neat pencil line ran through the title. Clara squinted at the other notes on the card. *Camera test, Exteriors, Technicolor.* There was a vault number that had been scratched out, and next to it in Simkin's neat cursive: *SR* underlined and the date 1941. What did it mean, *SR*? Clara turned the card over.

It was blank on the back. She held it up to the light, to see if she could make out the old vault number, but to no avail. That familiar futile feeling washed over her. Another dead end.

"It's freezing in here," said a voice. Miss Simkin marched back into her office rubbing her hands together. Clara's thoughts scattered.

"The editors must be at the thermostat again," Simkin continued, setting her purse on the desk and grabbing her jacket from the back of the chair.

Clara slotted the card back into its place and closed the drawer. She reached for her cotton gloves in the supply closet, faltering with her delayed pantomime.

"I've ordered more of those," said Miss Simkin, nodding to the gloves. "Someone must be eating them, we go through so many." Then she glanced at the card catalogue drawers. "You need help finding something?" Simkin missed nothing.

Clara closed the supply closet and grasped for a lie—she could randomly pluck one of the film titles from *A* to *C* and claim she'd been checking something. She quickly assessed her options. If there was a last chance of finding *Amazon Queen,* she would need Miss Simkin's encyclopedic brain. Her heart thumped. "In the card catalogue," Clara said. "What does it mean when a title is crossed out?"

Miss Simkin tucked her purse into the desk drawer. "The film is no longer in the vault," she said in a brisk tone. "It was either damaged or unusable—most likely destroyed."

"Oh." Clara's heart sank. "Why destroyed?"

Simkin fastened her eyes on Clara like April's hawk. "Why, what are you looking for?"

Clara shrugged. "Nothing," she lied. "I haven't seen a title crossed out before. The note says 'SR 1941.' I was just curious what it meant."

"Show me," said Simkin. Clara swallowed hard, put down her prop gloves, and went to the card catalogue. She slid out the *A* to *C* drawer and flicked through the *A*s, hoping she wasn't making a mistake by confiding in Miss Simkin. The film librarian peered over Clara's shoulder. Clara, breath held, plucked out the card, imagining it was radiating something powerful and dangerous.

*"Amazon Queen,"* Clara said. "Production number three-one-nine-one. Why is it crossed out?"

Miss Simkin always had an answer for everything; she had a "right" way of doing things; she would over-instruct and nitpick; her knowledge of every reel in the vaults was legendary. But in response to Clara's question she said nothing. The moment stretched as Simkin stared at the title, a curious look on her face, her gaze drifting through the card to somewhere else.

"Miss Simkin?" Clara prompted, and the film librarian blinked quickly, remembering herself. Her eyes returned to the index card.

"It was scrapped. Silver recovery—melted down for parts essentially." Simkin pointed to the date. "Back in 1941."

"Destroyed?" said Clara, watching her former boss carefully, and she caught a flicker of something behind Miss Simkin's eyes.

"Many of our silent-era films were sacrificed for their silver, especially during the war." Her tone was back to being business-like as she returned to her desk and began to shuffle through paperwork. "The silver on the emulsion was deemed more valuable than the picture on it. Shortsighted, of course." She gave a small shrug, her shoulders already up to her ears. "We have a limit on how many films we can store in the vaults—with the leap to sound and then to color pictures, many of the old black-and-white films got scrapped." She picked up a wad of papers and moved to the filing cabinet. "Why were you looking for it?" Simkin asked. Her tone was casual, but Clara saw the whites of her eyes as she cast a glance at the door. She must be checking that no one was around to overhear their conversation.

Clara toyed with the cotton gloves. "No reason," she said, watching Miss Simkin flit around the office like one of the birds on her calendar, unable to keep still. "I came across the title," said Clara innocently, "and I'd never heard of it."

"No one asked you for it?" Again, the question was light—a casual inquiry—but there was a tightness to her voice.

"No," said Clara.

"Well," said Simkin, relaxing her shoulders. "You'd best get back to Sam." Their conversation was over; the subject was closed. Clara couldn't push it without revealing more.

She left the film archive, her mind reeling. As she climbed

the stairs to editorial, she thought it through—silver recovery. In her first days at the archive she had studied the postproduction manual, cover to cover, and she had read about this process of melting down old silent-era films. The footage was destroyed when the silver and celluloid were recovered. It sounded plausible. But there was something that didn't add up: Miss Simkin had referred to *Amazon Queen* as an old black-and-white silent film. The test reel for 3191 had been shot in color—it was marked on the index card in Simkin's own hand. *Technicolor.* The librarian would never make a mistake like that. It could only mean one thing: Miss Simkin was lying.

## Chapter Thirty-Four

# Gold

CLARA LEANED AGAINST THE carpeted wall outside the screening room, waiting for a film to finish. Waiting to see Max. As the minutes ticked by, her mind drifted back to the archive and replayed Simkin's reaction to *Amazon Queen*. Why had she lied? It gave Clara the same feeling as when she'd asked Max about Leni's visit to the studio, how he'd gotten strange and warned her off. What were they trying to hide?

It was late afternoon, and Clara couldn't hang around much longer or Sam would miss her. The comedy—she assumed from the volley of high-pitched dialogue and slapstick sound effects—was in its third act. The muffled audio track vibrated through the screening room wall and down the back of her neck. She moved away from the wall and began to pace. Both Simkin and Max had been in HANL, the Hollywood Anti-Nazi League, in the lead-up to the war—Max was vocal about it, Simkin less so, but she had overheard her mention it once to a veteran sound editor. Why would either of them protect Pearce? Max of all people had no love for the studio head's politics. Max's own family was from Vienna, and not all of them had made it out. Auschwitz, he had told her once. The Jews from Vienna had ended up at Auschwitz. Max's complicity in the Leni cover-up—if that's what it was—didn't make sense. She had to talk to him again.

Eventually Clara recognized the crescendo of dialogue, and the last zinger was delivered. After the jaunty music rose to a fanfare, the door opened and a posse of executives filed out, all of them stone-faced. Clara waited for the last straggler—a stenographer shuffling notes—before slipping into the screening room. She turned immediately to her right and walked up the few steps and into the projection booth.

*"Meine kleine Klara,"* said Max. He was unloading the reel from the projector.

"Hi, Max," said Clara, smiling at the familiar refrain. She wasn't his "little Klara." She was at least two inches taller than him. "How was the comedy?"

Max raised his bushy eyebrows. *"Schrecklich,"* he said.

"That bad?"

"Nobody laughed for an hour and forty-five minutes."

It was their usual back-and-forth, where Clara resisted speaking German and eventually Max would lapse back into English. She drew up her perch, an apple box pilfered from the grip department, and sat down near the projector. She clasped her hands on her lap. "Max, I need your help."

He stopped what he was doing and looked at her, brows knit together, then went back to his task, loading the reel into its canister. "Help with what? I already spoke with your mother. She wasn't impressed."

"No, it's not about that." Clara took a deep breath of resolve, her eyes pinned to him. "In 1938, Leni Riefenstahl visited the studio. After being chased out of town by the Hollywood Anti-Nazi League, she traveled to Palm Springs, where she was a guest of Conrad Pearce at his desert compound." Max put down the reel and turned to face her, a hint of suspicion on his usually kind face.

"I'm assuming you knew all that?" said Clara.

He shrugged. "Why are you focused on dragging up the past?" he said, his voice clipped.

"Because it's not the past, Max. Leni's visit to California might be connected to the murder at the studio."

"The Milligan girl?" he said, surprised. "How?"

"Connie Milligan worked as a secretary for Conrad Pearce in Palm Springs around the time Leni visited." That got Max's attention. "If you think back, can you tell me everything you remember about Leni's visit?"

Max exhaled a long sigh. "*Ja*, it's true, Riefenstahl came to the studio. She had also been to see Mr. Disney. She had been all over town trying to sell her Olympic picture to the US market. Most studios turned her away. HANL even had private detectives trailing her—they knew all the moves she made in town. *No room in Hollywood for Leni Riefenstahl.*"

Clara nodded impatiently; he'd told her all this before.

"After a tour of Silver Pacific," said Max, "Mr. Pearce decided it would be safer to show Leni's film at his house in Palm Springs, away from all the bad publicity. He took me aside and asked me to drive out to his desert house and handle the screening." Max's expression soured. "He said he trusted me to be discreet."

"You screened *Olympia*?" asked Clara.

Max nodded and sat down heavily on his beaten-up stool. "All four hours of it." He shook his head. "There must have been sixteen, seventeen reels of the damn thing." He gazed through the projector window at the blank screen, remembering. "I should have refused, but I was afraid to say no—to say no to Mr. Pearce. I knew exactly what she was—a Nazi. 'It's just a movie, Max. It's the Olympics, not politics. Don't be so serious.' That was Pearce's take on it." He frowned. "And yet in '38—even after Kristallnacht—I agreed to Mr. Pearce's request." He smoothed down his tie. "I'm not proud of it, okay?"

Clara understood that he felt ashamed, but she couldn't spare him. She had to find out more. "What do you know about *Amazon Queen*?"

"*Ach so.*" A sharp look in his eye. "You've been busy, clever girl." He shook his head. "I haven't heard of that film in a long time." He shrugged. "It was just a camera test out in the desert, a small crew. I didn't know about it at the time. Mr. Pearce kept it a secret."

"I asked Miss Simkin about it," said Clara. "She claimed the reel was melted down for silver—destroyed. I think she's lying. She pretended it was an old black-and-white picture. But the camera test was shot in color."

Max nodded. "You're right, it was a beautiful color nitrate. They spared no expense."

Clara's mouth fell open. "You've seen it?"

Max removed his glasses and blinked a few times. "The first I heard of it was in December '41—I remember because it was after the attack on Pearl Harbor. Such a strange time. The US was now at war." He shook his head, remembering. "It was right before the holidays when Miss Simkin came to me." He held his glasses up to the light, then cleaned them methodically with the fat of his tie.

Clara leaned forward. "Go on," she said, eyes wide.

"The studio was quiet. Most people had left on vacation. Miss Simkin showed up in the projection room. I remember so clearly because normally she never brought the dailies over herself. But she stood there in the doorway." He gestured to the door behind Clara. "She was clutching a reel. She told me that Mr. Pearce had asked her to destroy it. She handed it to me and said something like 'The past shouldn't be swept under the rug.' She said I would understand as soon as I saw the footage. If I agreed with her, I was to hang on to it." He put his glasses back on. "I don't think Mr. Pearce would ever guess that someone like Miss Simkin would disobey an order. 'Film widow.' That's what they call someone like her, a mature woman who works all her life for the studio—no husband, no children. A stupid expression. But she was someone Pearce trusted."

"And—what did you do?" asked Clara, unable to keep the eager note out of her voice.

"After I watched it, I felt sick to my stomach." His lips curled. "Leni Riefenstahl, as pretty as a swastika—and in that beautiful color nitrate." He shook his head.

"She was in the film?"

Max nodded. "Oh, yes. Starring role: queen of the Amazons. The whole town was turning her away, and our studio boss was planning Leni Riefenstahl's Hollywood career. That's some chutzpah." He laughed without smiling. "By now it was 1941 and America was at war with Germany. If word of the film got out, it would look very bad for Mr. Pearce."

"Wait—why did Simkin bring it to you? Why didn't she just shelve it somewhere? It would be easy for her to hide it in the vaults," said Clara.

Max shook his head. "She didn't want it in her archive. She never wanted to know where it was. She could tell Pearce, without lying, that the reel was no longer in the vault. You see, her loyalty to the studio, to Pearce, had been tested." He sighed. "Everyone knew the Pearce family politics, but we ignored it for the most part. Until Riefenstahl's visit, it didn't spill over into the running of the studio. I found out later that Simkin's nephew was killed at Pearl Harbor. I believe that for her to follow orders and destroy that film would have made her feel complicit. She couldn't do it."

Clara thought back to Simkin's stiff reaction to the missing film. It made sense now. She hadn't been covering for Pearce, she had disobeyed him. The mention of the film must have brought back memories of her nephew. "Where is it now? Do you still have the reel? It's solid proof, Pearce's motive for murdering the stand-in Connie Milligan."

"Mr. Pearce?" Max folded his arms. "I don't admire everything about the man—his politics, for starters—but that's a big accusation, *murder.*" The word settled around them, a sour note in the air. "Klara?" He peered at her over his glasses.

"Why not? You don't think Pearce would do anything he could to stop a scandal involving *Amazon Queen*? Connie knew all about it. She witnessed them sign the contract. Her death can't be a coincidence," said Clara. "I know that somehow Leni's visit in 1938 is connected to Connie's murder. If I could just find the reel of film . . ."

Max remained silent.

"Max, you've got to believe me." Clara kept pushing. "You said you wish you'd stood up to Pearce when he made you screen *Olympia*. Now's your chance to do the right thing. Tell me, where is it? Where did you put the reel?"

Max didn't have a chance to respond. The screening room door banged open; the projection booth shuddered. Breathless, Walter, the new boy, stepped into the booth laden with reels.

"Howdy, Max. Oh, hey, Clara," he said, too upbeat. "Sam was looking for you. Said something about a photographer taking your picture?"

Clara's shoulders sank. The "Spotlight" column. Some poster girl for editorial, when she was never at her desk. Could she level with Sam and explain what she was up to—what was at stake?

Walter held up three canisters. "Here's the cut footage for the *Argentan* screening."

Max roused himself and put the reels onto his workbench. It felt cramped with the three of them clustered between projectors. Walter grinned, and Clara glared at him, wishing he would leave. She was finally getting somewhere with the search for the missing film, and here was Walter, muscling his way in where he didn't belong.

Max squinted at the first canister Walter had brought. "Film trivia for you kids." He turned to them. "Best Picture 1943?" he asked randomly.

"What?" said Clara. Where had this non sequitur come from? "What are you talking about?"

"Best Picture 1943—for the movies released in '42. You don't know the answer?" he said with mock outrage.

"*Casablanca,*" said Walter, proud of himself.

Max tutted playfully. "It finally got the statue in '44. Actually, they submitted it in '43 as well, but that's another story."

He turned to Clara. She answered automatically. "Best Picture 1943: *A Call to Arms.* A Silver Pacific film." Max nodded and smiled knowingly. He turned and plucked a small key off a hook on the wall. "This is your prize, Klara," he said, handing it to her. He retrieved a duster from the bucket of cleaning supplies under the bench. "The Oscars look dusty. Would you mind cleaning them?" He handed her the cloth.

Clara bristled. "You want me to clean?" She wrinkled her forehead.

"Yes, go on." He nodded to the reels of *Argentan.* "I've got my hands full here." She stood there dumbfounded. Walter smirked, enjoying her irritation.

"Go on," Max whispered, giving her a pointed look.

Clara stared at the key, a vague idea blooming at the back of her mind. She went to leave. At the door of the projection booth, she paused and looked back at them. Walter had taken her place on the apple box and was stretching out his legs, settling in for a chat. And Max—she was struck with a sudden wave of pity, watching him thread the film, his knobby fingers, thickly veined; glasses perched on the end of his nose; posture hunched, so old suddenly.

The lobby of the executive building was calm. Clara found herself in front of the Oscar display case—an army of gleaming statues, the crushed-red-velvet backdrop—key in one hand, duster in the other. She glanced about her, a knot of nerves in her chest, but then she supposed there was nothing as innocuous as a woman cleaning something.

Gingerly she unlocked the cabinet and surveyed the awards. The statues shone like liquid; they didn't need cleaning. She stuffed the duster into the waistband of her skirt and reached for the Best Picture Oscar from 1943, *A Call to Arms*. It was cool and smooth. She replayed the conversation with Max; the stoic gold man in her hands gave nothing away. Her eyes drifted to the velvet display. Then it hit her in a flash—of course! The Oscars were placed on prop film canisters. She felt a surge of adrenaline, and in a deft move, she had traded the Oscar for its film canister pedestal. As soon as she held it, she could feel the weight—it was no prop. There was film inside. The statues appeared pretty much as they always had, one a hint less elevated. She swiftly locked the cabinet and turned to cross the lobby, the stolen reel glowing hot in her hands. She hesitated for a second—where to watch the film? She couldn't go back to Max. He was preparing for a screening with Mr. Pearce, no less. Editorial. Sam needed her back anyway, and she could watch it on his Moviola once he left for the screening.

Her heart beating like a drum, Clara strode out of the executive building as if she'd just robbed a bank. Scanning her surroundings, alert to danger, she reminded herself that nothing appeared out of the ordinary—she was a vault girl carrying a film canister. No one could guess its significance. The flood of knowledge made her swell. Her strides were long and purposeful—the thrill of the chase, uncovering the truth. Oscar gold was what Pearce would have wanted for Leni. And an army of statuettes had guarded his secret all these years. Until a no-name stand-in had come along. It was the reel Connie had been searching for in the vaults, and Clara had found it. *Amazon Queen.* It was proof in her grasp, the reason to silence Connie Milligan, the motive for murder.

Thirty feet from the Writers' Block, she saw a black Chrysler pulling away. Despite the warm afternoon light, she was filled with dread. As the car sailed past, she saw Detective Ireland at the wheel, and in the backseat sat Gil, flanked by Detective Rivetti. They weren't smiling. A chill like an encroaching shadow spread down the length of her spine.

## Chapter Thirty-Five

# Hollywood Precinct

WHAT HAPPENED NEXT PASSED in a kind of blur. Driven by habit, Clara found herself back at editorial. Thankfully, Sam wasn't in the cutting room. Perhaps he was next door with the assistant editors. She put the reel of *Amazon Queen* in her desk drawer, then grabbed her jacket and purse. Minutes later Clara found herself outside the studio gates on Melrose, hailing a cab. "Hollywood precinct," she told the driver.

It was late afternoon when the taxi dropped Clara at the white art deco building. The only other time she had been in a police station was when she was thirteen, after her mother's purse had been snatched. Just sitting in the waiting area under the eyes of so many cops had made her feel small and guilty of something.

Today was different. She informed the bespectacled desk sergeant that she needed to speak with Detective Ireland right away, and a uniformed officer took her upstairs. She met every pair of eyes, feeling like Rosalind Russell in *His Girl Friday* about to break a scoop and save the day.

When she entered Ireland's office, he was on the phone. It was cradled under his chin, and he was flicking through paperwork with one hand, ashing his cigarette with the other. He didn't appear overly surprised to see her. He gestured with the hand holding the cigarette for her to take a seat.

She perched on the hard chair, palms clasping her knees, desperate to know what they'd done with Gil. Overhead a ceiling fan sliced through the cigarette smoke and spread it across the already yellowed ceiling. The detective grunted into the receiver every so often. The wait was excruciating. Clara could barely sit still, brimming with her secret knowledge as the ash grew on the detective's cigarette and the fan lazily spun in circles.

Ireland nodded. "I'll call you after it shakes out. . . . Sure. Thank you, sir." As he hung up the phone, Clara sprang to her feet.

"Where's Gil? Did you arrest him?"

Ireland smashed his cigarette into the ashtray. "Good afternoon, Miss Berg. Why don't you sit down." When Clara remained standing, feet planted, he sighed wearily. "Your friend's next door in an interview room. We haven't charged him with anything—yet."

Clara clenched her fists. "You've got it all wrong."

"We have a witness, puts a man of his description in the vicinity of the vaults around the time of the murder. He's going to have to do a lineup." Ireland gestured to the chair again.

"A witness?" Clara sank down onto the chair, the recollection of his changing story nagging her—*No answer, miss.* "What happens after the lineup?"

The detective leaned back in his chair like a king on his throne. "If we get a positive ID, we'll see if he wants to cooperate."

"Confess, you mean," she shot back. Clara shook her head. "He didn't do this."

Ireland gave her an incredulous look. "He was on the lot the night of the murder, just his word that he was alone in his office, no one to vouch for him. He has a romantic history with Barbara Bannon—one he neglected to mention when we questioned him." Ireland shuffled some papers on his desk, looking for something.

"That was years ago." Clara sat forward, her eyes boring into Ireland's receding hairline. "Babe Bannon is a distraction. Connie Milligan was the victim—not Miss Bannon."

Ireland reluctantly looked up. "There was no motive to murder Connie—"

"Yes, there was," Clara cut in.

Ireland raised an eyebrow, almost amused. "I'm listening," he said, humoring her.

"Did you know that Connie Milligan worked for Conrad Pearce—years ago, when she was seventeen? She was his secretary for a few weeks, out in Palm Springs."

That got the detective's attention. He straightened, and a small muscle twitched at his eye. "Go on," he said, serious now.

In a rush Clara told him about her theory, about Leni Riefenstahl's visit to California in '38, about the movie contract and *Amazon Queen*, about Connie working for Pearce over the vacation, and how Clara had found the magazine article in Connie's room: "Nazi Pin-Up Girl." When she finally came to a halt, Clara felt exhilarated, out of breath, heart pounding as though she'd run the trail up to Cedar Grove in Griffith Park. She waited for Ireland to catch up.

The room was dead silent, as if both he and Clara were holding their breath. Eventually Ireland relaxed back into his chair. "That's quite a story." He tented his fingers, contemplating her. "You got any proof?"

"The magazine article about Leni in Connie's bedroom. And the test film from 1938—I have it. I think that's what Connie was looking for in the vaults. And Connie told Bannon she had some leverage, something she could use to get ahead at the studio."

Ireland frowned. "Miss Bannon never mentioned that to us. Do you know if there was a blackmail note or any proof of Connie actually meeting with Pearce since she'd started working at Silver Pacific?"

Clara shrugged. "I haven't had a chance to figure it all out yet. There could be a note. Pearce's secretary might know of a meeting."

Ireland pressed on. "Why was Connie blackmailing the studio head? I mean, what did she want out of it?"

"An acting career," said Clara. "Connie also told Miss Bannon that she could get Bannon out of her contract."

"Again, Miss Bannon didn't mention any of this to us." Clara's triumph was fizzling. Ireland thought for a moment. "But for argument's sake, let's take a run at it. Let's say Connie blackmailed Pearce to get a boost for her career or to help Miss Bannon, as you said. So Mr. Pearce has a motive. Does he have means, opportunity?"

"He's the head of the studio," said Clara emphatically. "He could have access to any locked door on the lot—he owns the place."

Ireland gave a small shrug. "Possible. And opportunity? Where was he the night in question?"

Clara flushed. She hadn't even thought of that. She had been so busy with puzzle pieces and the thrill of the chase, she hadn't considered the obvious. "I don't know—I remember when he showed up in his big black car at around ten."

Ireland found his notebook and flipped through it. "About three hundred witnesses saw him in Pasadena at the sneak peak of the romantic comedy *Two to Tango*," he said, reading from his notes. "The director, the producer, the other producer, and the writer were all there sitting on the same row. Mr. Pearce didn't move for a hundred and eighteen minutes, looking sadder than a wet weekend, according to the director. Turns out, a hundred and eighteen minutes is way too long for a romantic comedy."

"He has an alibi?" Clara asked, dismayed.

"It's airtight." He kept his eyes on her. "Unless they're all in on a conspiracy, including the usherettes and the cinema management." Clara stared, unbelieving, at his jowly face, his skin red like meat. "Conrad Pearce didn't leave the theater." Ireland closed his notebook and slapped it onto the table. "He couldn't have done it."

Clara slumped back in her chair as though she were a boxer between rounds, on the losing end of a fight. "Mr. Pearce is a powerful man," she said, refusing to believe that her theory had just collapsed. "What if he hired someone to do it?"

The detective's eyes were sharp and watchful. "You really think he's gonna commit a murder on his own back lot, go to the trouble of making it look like the victim was his contract star?" He shook his head. "Disrupt filming, lose money by putting the crew on hiatus—not to mention it's bad publicity for the studio? The whole thing is overblown—it's *complicated*."

Clara flinched. Maybe he was right. She thought back to stage eleven, when Mr. Pearce, immaculately dressed, had made the announcement that Bannon was alive. He'd been polished and professional. She thought about his pristine office, all that white furniture. If a crime had a personality, this murder wasn't his style. She blinked quickly, trying to think it through. "But the Leni article, the connections between Connie and Mr. Pearce? If he was desperate enough to keep that quiet . . ."

"You found some neat coincidences," Ireland went on, "but let's face it. It's all backstory. Nothing—no hard evidence—points to Pearce." He took a beat. "Seems like you're hung up on the Nazi filmmaker yourself."

Clara's eyes darted to Ireland's. He wasn't trying to be cutting. His expression wasn't unkind. And he was right on the money. Leni Riefenstahl was Clara's mystery, ever since she'd turned up the handkerchief in her box of keepsakes.

"After the lineup, I have to give Mr. Pearce an update on the case. I can ask him about Connie and Palm Springs."

"You won't mention my name," said Clara, quickly.

"Course not," said Ireland. "My guess is he'll have no recollection of the hired help from eight years ago. Look." He let out a sigh. "If she'd worked here at the station, it's possible I wouldn't have recognized her either. She was, what, sixteen, seventeen at the time?"

Clara nodded slowly.

"Let me ask you this," said Ireland in a softer voice. "How well do you know this screenwriter guy?"

"We're friends."

"That all?" He peered at her.

Clara couldn't give a straight answer because truthfully she didn't know where she stood with Gil. Her non-answer hung in the air, a tacit admission.

Ireland reached for a file on his desk. "Just so you know, the stuff with Bannon wasn't ancient history." A queasy feeling rose in Clara's gut. "We have a letter he wrote to Bannon from France. About seeing her in a movie when he was fighting over there." Ireland took a piece of paper from the file. "He said the movie saved his life. Sounds like he was still pretty hung up on her." Ireland handed her the letter. "This was only a couple of years ago." Clara took the pages lightly, as if they were aflame. She swallowed hard. She recognized Gil's handwriting from the scribbled yellow legal pads he used at work.

"Where did you get this?"

"The studio has a file of all this stuff. They keep tabs on fan mail and stalkers, and anything from an ex that could prove inconvenient for publicity." Ireland's gaze was level on her. "I also spoke to his commanding officer. Francis Gilbert was pretty messed up, by the end of the war. He was in a hospital for a while—psychiatric. After he was discharged, there's the arrest record: bar fights, drunk and disorderly, that sort of thing. Eventually he got the gig at Silver Pacific. Maybe that twist of fate—getting hired on *her* movie—well, maybe it pushed him over the edge."

Clara let her eyes fall to the letter. She had barged into Ireland's office, Gil's Girl Friday—Rosalind Russell to his Cary Grant—claiming the detectives had gotten it all wrong and that she had managed to crack the case. But it was Clara who'd gotten it wrong. In her hands was the truth, the real story—Gil and Ruby's—where Clara was a latecomer glimpsing their all-consuming love affair from the cheap seats. The air in the office was stale; she couldn't breathe. "But what if you're wrong? I still can't believe . . ." She trailed off.

"All this isn't easy to swallow," Ireland continued. He gently retrieved the letter. "You have feelings for him, I get it. But right now I need you to think back. Did Gil ever express interest in the vaults? Did you take him there, show him around? Could he have seen the vault combination? That's the one piece we're missing."

Since the murder, Clara had suppressed the memory, but now she held it up to the light. The first time they'd really been alone together. She had been showing off all she knew about the vaults, the fire hazard, all the facts of how nitrate burned and couldn't be extinguished. The excitement of being alone with him. She'd stood right behind him, feeling the heat of him through his shirt. She'd wanted him to turn around and kiss her, right there against the film racks. Her cheeks burned at the memory.

Clara nodded slowly. "I showed him the vaults—a few weeks after we met. And there's one other thing you should know." Ireland's eyes were locked on Clara's. She had to tell the truth. "The night of the murder, I called Gil in his office. He didn't answer; he wasn't there."


Ireland walked her out of the busy precinct. She felt people's eyes on her along the hallway, down the stairs. She was back to being the thirteen-year-old girl.

Instead of taking the streetcar, Clara walked the half hour to the studio. The cars and buildings and people on Melrose faded into a painted backdrop. Her mind was back in Ireland's office, on the letter. Gil had written to Bannon to tell her he'd seen her movie. He had been fighting overseas, surrounded by death and destruction, his life on a knife edge. And seeing her once more, even if it was on a screen, had meant so much to him. He said he felt like it had saved his life. It had given him the strength to keep going.

Clara could picture the French village after D-Day. The locals watching along with the troops: *un film Américain.* The excitement would be palpable. The catcalls and wolf whistles when Babe Bannon came on-screen, her face twenty feet high, luminous, unforgettable—so close but unreachable. The first time Gil had laid eyes on her in two years. It must have seared him to look at her. The sound of her voice so familiar. She would be layers removed from him: as her character and then as the movie star—another fantasy—but the girl he knew couldn't disappear completely. His Ruby—he couldn't turn away. He might have appeared like any other GI, gaze locked on the screen, but she was his girl.

And then the knife twisting in the wound: Gregory Quinn. A two-shot of them together—a lot of double-talk and innuendo. Gil would feel the heat of their chemistry sizzle off the screen. This wasn't acting—it was the real thing. The guys in the audience would feel it too. After their rowdiness and crude comments, they would settle down, mesmerized by the golden couple. Each man would put himself in Quinn's shoes, or his character's—it didn't matter which. They would leave the battle-scarred town in the French countryside behind, and every one of them would drift past the crude canvas screen and into the magic of the movie, each guy channeling Quinn's "man enough yet vulnerable" shtick to capture Bannon's heart. Gil would scan the audience: Every goddam soldier was in love with her. The comfort of seeing her turned to pain. It would constrict his chest and shorten his breath. Her face looming over him, close enough for him to see every detail he knew from memory. She was no longer his. Now she existed only on-screen, and he had no hope of seeing her again.

Until *Letter from Argentan*.

## Chapter Thirty-Six

# Amazon Queen

IT WAS EVENING BY the time Clara returned to the studio. She dragged herself upstairs to editorial. Along the corridor the cacophony of Moviolas had died down for the day.

She found the cutting room deserted, then remembered that Sam would be at the *Argentan* screening with Mr. Pearce. Had Detective Ireland already given the studio head an update on the case? Perhaps he'd mentioned Clara after all—some girl in editorial playing detective—and they'd laughed about her crazy theories. She cringed, recalling the scene at the police station. What future did she have at the studio after she had accused the studio head of murder? Not only that but she had pushed the limits of Sam's patience, pursuing the investigation instead of her editing duties. Jobless and without references, suddenly her prospects in Los Angeles looked bleak.

She had asked Max once about the old days—if he missed directing. After the biblical epic bombed they wouldn't hire him as a director anymore. He'd shrugged and recounted what a producer had told him at the time: "Hollywood wants you or it doesn't, and you don't have a say." He had given her a sad smile. "It's not such a nice business, Klara."

Clara slumped down on her chair and let the quiet settle over her. She hadn't bothered to turn on the lights; the evening gloom suited her mood. She listened to the sound of her breath, grateful she didn't have to relay to Sam where she had been and what had happened at the precinct—that Gil had been arrested, that he would most likely be charged with murder. She still couldn't believe it was true. And yet a question had niggled at her ever since she had found out about his past with Ruby. How had he gotten over losing Barbara Bannon? The answer was simple: he hadn't. She had assumed her uneasiness was jealousy, comparing herself to a movie star. But was it something else? Was that worm of bad feeling a seed of doubt—had she known all along but hadn't seen? She recalled Detective Ireland's words: *How well do you know this screenwriter guy?*

She opened her desk drawer and took out the *Amazon Queen* reel. The canister was cold and hard. She set it on the desk and stared at it. The film existed, and *Clara* had found it. Like Hitchcock's MacGuffin—the papers, the diamonds, the *thing* the characters are after—what she and Gil had been chasing. Her triumph when she'd realized the film was under the Oscars, hidden in plain sight. But what did it matter now? Her theory had fallen apart. It was just a metal canister like any other on Sam's film racks.

All her energy had been focused on this dirty secret, the studio's dalliance with Hitler's filmmaker. And Gil had played along. He'd helped convince her that there was a trail to follow, that they were chasing the truth, uncovering Pearce's Nazi-sympathizing past and connecting it to Connie's murder.

She scraped her chair back and began to pace. Pearce's motive to kill Connie was utterly convincing, it was so tangible. But Conrad Pearce had a rock-solid alibi. Not one person but an audience of three hundred—a row of studio people, a cinema manager, and several usherettes. And the idea that he might have hired someone to do it? She shook her head. When scrutinized under the harsh overheads of Ireland's office, her whole theory had paled. A prickle of embarrassment made her flush even now because, apart from Pearce's alibi, the story was far-fetched. Like Ireland had said, it was complicated. (A look-alike victim, Bannon's name leaked to the press, all for show to distract from the real crime.)

Whereas Gil's history with Bannon, the letter from France, his holding a torch for her, coupled with his trauma from the war, his discharge record—that wasn't far-fetched. The crime of passion had been blunt and obvious—if Gil couldn't have her, no one would. A moment of impulse and a tragic case of mistaken identity. They had a witness. Gil had lied to the cops—and to Clara. He had seen the vault combination. It all stacked up.

In trying to prove the Pearce motive, Clara had been led by her fascination with Riefenstahl, chasing a ghost from her past, when the truth of Connie's death had been right in front of her.

She had been swayed by the attention, by his handsome face. She flushed, replaying scenes from their friendship. Gil was the misdirect, the distraction, and she'd fallen for it. Fallen for him. Was he really capable of murder?

The room was too dark. She moved to the window, yanked at the cord to slice open the venetian blinds. The last scraps of sunlight had vanished. The sky was golden, tinged with flames of tangerine in the west. Clara turned back to the dimness of the cutting room, everything in it remote and inhospitable. The rim of the *Amazon Queen* canister glinted in the dying light. When had it last been watched? By Simkin and Max, back in '41. She let go a breath. She had come this far.

Mechanically Clara turned on the Moviola and loaded the reel, squinting at the brightness of the lamp. She pushed down on the pedal, and the machine clattered to life. As the head leader counted down, Clara felt a tight ball of anticipation in her stomach. The synch-pop was silent (the reel was MOS). Then the slate appeared in frame: *Camera test, prod 3191.*

The slate vanished to reveal a wide exterior of a desert, and the camera assistant pulled focus to a group of horses and riders in the distance. Someone must have called action, because the group began to move in a slow canter toward camera, like cowboys in a Western—a quintessentially American image—save that they were dressed in flowing robes and armor. As they got closer, the main horse—a white Arabian—was out front, and astride it (sitting a rather jerky canter) in golden armor, with auburn hair flying, was Leni Riefenstahl in her Hollywood debut.

It was shocking and oddly mesmerizing. Even on the small screen of the Moviola, the power of the film—it was a gorgeous color nitrate print. Unlike the grainy newspaper pictures or the black-and-white snaps of Leni and Pearce at the Racquet Club, these images—moving and in color—breathed life with every frame. Finally, proof of Leni's designs on Hollywood and the studio's complicity. As though Clara hadn't altogether expected to be right. Leni Riefenstahl in full Technicolor. It brought her back to her eleven-year-old self on board the *Europa*, in awe of the glamorous passenger, wrestling with what she considered her parents' defection—her deeply flawed understanding of the Nazi regime.

Investigating Leni's visit to California had made Clara face not just the past but the conflict inside her. It was an old battle, Clara's eternal battle. There were two selves: German and American. Two neat and distinct compartments in her mind, two different people distinguishable by the spelling of her name: Klara and Clara. One a German child desperate to join Hitler Youth, enthralled with parades, especially with cavalry officers; the other a young American woman in love with movies—a new arrival on the vast continent of adult life. But since the murder, Klara and Clara had bumped into one another. They'd begun to converge. The past wouldn't stay put. That little Aryan *Mädchen* wreaked havoc on the present with her sunny childhood memories. The childhood that Clara had tried to suppress came flooding back: Freya, Matthias . . . Ruth.

Clara advanced the reel. Now there was a series of close-ups of Leni—she preened and posed, regal and warrior-like in her costume. She appeared more comfortable on her own two legs than on four. Another setup flew by, B-roll of the desert, a close-up of horses' hooves galloping past. It was effective. Clara could get a taste for the epic they'd planned to film. The California desert could surely stand in for Greece or Libya, or wherever Leni had originally wanted to shoot. Pearce had been wooing her, seducing her, giving her a taste of what she could expect from a lavish color production, with the Silver Pacific studio machine and expertise behind her. Hollywood: the ultimate prize for any film director.

Toward the end of the reel there was a series of static shots of Leni on horseback. At the end of a take, her horse spooked— a little bunny hop forward—jolting her in the saddle. A male figure entered the frame. He held the reins as Leni dismounted, and then they embraced. Clara leaned forward, a coiled spring on the edge of her chair, focusing all her energy on the square of light. The camera cut. Clara stopped the reel, put it in reverse, and rewound to the head of the take. Her foot hovered over the treadle of the Moviola like it was the gas pedal of a hot car. She watched the take again, holding her breath. The man stead-ied her horse while she dismounted, sliding elegantly off the saddle and into his arms. They kissed, together in frame—an unplanned two-shot. The camera cut, and jumped to the slate of the next take. Clara rewound and watched it a third time, freezing the frame on the two of them: Leni and her California lover—the screenwriter Roger Brackett.

Clara's heart beat in her throat. *Roger and Leni.* He was friends with Pearce; he'd been at the studio since the early days. She recalled him at Bannon's party: *The Racquet Club staff couldn't tell off Clark Gable.* The Racquet Club in *Palm Springs.* Roger the socialite in his heyday, Oscar winner, in demand, holding court. His comments to Gil assuming he wasn't Jewish. A love affair: Roger and Leni. She sat paralyzed. All the pieces fell into place. Connie must have known about them. She'd been there in December 1938, privy to all of it. And then a few weeks ago, around the anniversary of V-E Day, Connie stumbled on the "Nazi Pin-Up Girl" article. She was already feeling bent out of shape, missing Jim. In the background the ongoing coverage of the Nuremberg trials, bringing Nazis to justice. How bad would it look for Roger if his dalliance with Leni got out? Connie blackmailed *Roger.* Clara had the right motive all along, but the wrong murderer. Gil was innocent, of course he was. A wave of relief swept over her.

But what to do about it? She reached for the phone—then stopped short. Who could she call? Gil was locked up, and the detectives wouldn't entertain more outlandish theories—she had already worn out her welcome with Ireland. Her mind leapfrogged to the next thought: she needed evidence—from the present day, not a story from the past. To convince the detectives, she needed to find *something* linking Roger to the murder, to Connie Milligan. She glanced at the clock. Roger was in the *Argentan* screening with Sam and Pearce. His office would be empty.

Clara turned off the Moviola and dashed out of the cutting room, quick footsteps along the hallway. *Roger Brackett.* The name reverberated off the corridor walls. Her footsteps drummed down the stairs, the synapses in her brain firing. The misdirect with Bannon. MOVIE STAR MURDERED. All the petty Hollywood grudges picked over by the papers, distracting the cops—what a production. It had a screenwriter's touch. She streaked across the empty studio lot. The scent of jasmine was as pungent as on the night Connie was murdered.

## Chapter Thirty-Seven

# First Draft

THE SCREENWRITERS' OFFICE WAS unlocked. Clara knocked for show as she peered around the door. "Hello! Mr. Brackett?" she called out to the empty office. She slipped through the anteroom past Gil's desk, walking lightly, as if the vinyl floor were thin ice. She had to be quick. She didn't know how long Roger would be occupied at the *Argentan* screening.

Clara had never been in Brackett's office before. It was spacious, and he'd had it painted—not the standard-issue white but a warm buttery cream. Against the wall under the double windows there was a low patterned couch, a decent rug, and a coffee table strewn with newspapers and magazines; at the far end of the room sat a large desk in blond wood and a matching bookcase. Clara began her search on the bookcase. The top two shelves were cluttered with trinkets—an old camera, a houseplant, miscellaneous awards—and the lower shelves were lined with leather-bound copies of his scripts. She could imagine Gil rolling his eyes at Brackett's "literary cannon"—the man's ego was bigger than his office.

On the wall next to the bookshelf were framed photographs. Clara peered at one: 1937, the year he won the Oscar. Roger was seated at a table with Pearce and Carole Lombard, his Oscar gleaming against the white tablecloth. He looked dashing in his tux—and younger, his hair darker, his mustache the same. His expression was cocky, almost confrontational; he stared down the camera like a challenge. It was a more potent, dangerous Brackett than the gossipy dandy she had encountered at the studio. Clara shuddered and moved to the desk.

An ashtray sat on top of a pile of script pages. There was a tablet of yellow paper covered in notes, and a dark red agenda. Clara pounced on it—Roger's diary. She flicked through it, turning to the night of the murder, and then carefully back through the previous weeks to the start of filming. It was his social calendar: dinner dates, rounds of golf, a lunch for the board of a museum, a dentist appointment. Nothing significant. She scanned the phone numbers on the back pages, imagining that the vault combination might jump out at her, but as far as she could tell, it was just studio contacts and restaurants he frequented.

She opened the top drawer of the desk and rummaged through the contents: a brand-new shirt still in its box, a spare tie (silk), a map of Los Angeles, a hand mirror, a toothbrush, and dental paste. She closed it and tried the bottom drawer—it was locked. She rattled it. What could be inside? Blackmail letters? A weapon? But then she felt a wave of futility. Why would he hang on to anything damning, anything to connect him to the murder? Clara could hear the soft tick of a wall clock. *Think, think.* She bit her lip as she inspected the items on the desk again, moving the ashtray and fanning out the script pages. *Argentan* revisions, typed up by Gil. If only she could find *something,* she could help him. From somewhere across Hollywood a distant siren wailed. It had the effect of an alarm. She should leave.

As she swept the script pages back into a neat pile—she stopped. Script pages. Leni's German screenplay of *Penthesilea* would have needed to be translated, rewritten for Hollywood. Her eyes darted to the bookshelf with its rows of leather-bound screenplays. A magnetic force pulled her toward it. All of Brackett's scripts organized in chronological order. Her pulse ticked up as she scanned the volumes, eyes flitting across the titles— *The Paris Bride; A Weekend Affair;* a couple of Westerns; and the Oscar winner from '37, the musical *My Genevieve.* She ran her finger across the leather spines and landed on *Blind Summit,* a crime drama from the forties that had tanked—she skipped back. A jolt as the gold letters flashed at her: *Amazon Queen.* Clara let out a small gasp—Roger hadn't even attempted to disguise it. Her fingertips tingled as she reached for it. It was tightly packed on the shelf, reluctant to budge. Her nails scraped the leather spine.

A noise from outside, and Clara froze.

She held her breath. Seconds ticked by, which she measured

by the beat of her heart—*one-two, two-two, three-two, four-two.*
The stillness held. The sound must have come from another office. The walls were paper thin. She tugged at the script until it slid out. Her heart was now hammering along on a double-time jazz beat. She opened the screenplay. On the title page, there was an inscription:

> *Mein lieber Roger,*
> *To our collaboration—on and off the page.*
> *All my love,*
> *Leni*

(And then some joke in German about beating him at tennis.)

Of course, he must have helped Leni with the English version of *Amazon Queen*—her English wasn't good enough to write a script on her own. Connie would have been hired to type up the pages because Roger hated to type. In the rush of adrenaline Clara could barely focus on the sea of words. She flicked through the pages: battle scenes, love scenes, dramatic monologues—all the ingredients of an epic. *Amazon Queen* had been sitting here all this time, just steps away from Gil. She could have burst out laughing, but she noticed that the paper in her hands was trembling. Before she could turn to the last page, the script fell open at a bookmark. No—a photograph. Recognizing the faces, a nauseous wave swept over her. Leni Riefenstahl and Roger Brackett stood on a lawn, smiling broadly. They flanked a sober-looking man in a dark suit—his infamous mustache . . . the Führer himself. Leni, Brackett, and Adolf Hitler. The excitement of Clara's discovery curdled to revulsion. The photo quivered in her hand, and she turned it over. *Berlin. Spring, 1939.*

"Hello there," said an affable voice.

Clara's head snapped up to find Roger Brackett in the doorway.

"What are you reading?" He tossed his hat onto a chair and ambled toward her.

Clara was frozen to the spot, watching him approach, unable to speak. The voice in her head shrieked. He still wore the mask of charming-man-about-town—he didn't know what she was holding. Clara slotted the photograph between the pages and tried to shove the script back onto the shelf, but her hands were thick and clumsy. She fumbled, and the smooth leather-bound volume slipped from her fingers and thudded onto the carpet—the photograph slid out.

Brackett bent down and picked up the script. He squinted at the title. There was a beat before he spoke. *"Amazon Queen."* He tucked the photograph into his jacket pocket. "Not one of my best," he said. "Only a first draft. And you know what Hemingway says about first drafts."

Clara's mouth was dry. "Have you met him, Hemingway?" It was a silly question, but she was forcing herself to appear normal and light. She wished she could pretend—just for a moment—that he had nothing to do with Connie's murder. She wanted to conjure the other Mr. Brackett: the witty gossip, the dandy, impeccably dressed and as lazy as a cat. But their eyes met, and Clara saw behind his mask.

"I stayed at his place in Key West." He was incapable of resisting the chance to name-drop. "Hem taught me how to make caipirinhas—you need a boatload of limes." A wry smile. "The man can drink."

His dialogue was classic Brackett, but there was a tightness to his voice, a stiffness in his manner. As he returned the script to its correct place on the shelf, Clara had a crazy notion that she could spin a yarn, pretend she'd been looking for something else. She could play dumb. Maybe he didn't know why she'd been looking for it. But her mind came up empty. Besides, Gil was in a cell—it was too late for games.

She squeezed her hands into tight fists. "I know." She held his gaze. "I know about you and Leni, the contract for *Amazon Queen*. All of it." Her words tumbled out in a rush; her breath was fast and raspy.

In the silence that followed she felt her courage draining, replaced by fear.

Brackett considered her for a long beat, a coldness behind his eyes. "Take a seat." He gestured to the couch. It was an order, not an invitation. He remained standing, blocking her path to the door—she couldn't make a run for it without tackling him.

She sank onto the couch. Faces grinned at her from the magazines on the coffee table. There was a pretty teacup, and a plate with crumbs. The soft furnishings, the cozy setting, were at odds with the threat of the man in front of her. Would he do the same to her as he'd done to Connie? A renewed jolt of fear surged across her body. She could feel a pulse throbbing at her neck. Did he notice the twitching vein?

*Keep him talking.* It was Gil's voice she imagined.

"Queen of the Amazons—it was a role she was born to play," said Clara. Her voice sounded young and soft.

"She couldn't ride a horse, you know." He shook his head. "For all that athleticism." He drew a chair over and sat down between Clara and the door, like a guard. "She took lessons when she returned to Germany." He smiled faintly at the memory. "Got herself her own mare, Märchen—means 'fairy tale.'" Clara had never noticed how smooth and rich his voice was. He could have been an actor, one of those irrepressible supporting roles. When it came to actors, everyone thought it was about appearance—the face—but Sam had told her that the essential thing was the voice, that the audience responded more to sound than to picture.

"She was like that, determined," he went on, "when she got the bit between her teeth—pardon the pun." It was absurd. They were chatting like old pals, but underneath, a silent alarm kept her senses heightened. Gil's voice again: *Don't fall for the smooth charm—he's dangerous. Figure out how you can get away.* To her left was the door, the path to it blocked by Roger; to the right was his desk. Clara flicked a glance at the telephone. She would barely be able to pick up the receiver, much less get two words out, before he'd stop her. Behind her the blinds were drawn on the second-floor window. But as long as he was talking, she was safe. She could stall for time. Someone might come by the office—a custodian or another writer.

"Why Leni Riefenstahl?" said Clara. "Why sign such a risky prospect?"

"She was talented," he said simply.

"And the Hollywood boycott?"

Brackett waved his hand in the air, dismissing it. "The boycott was for show, to sell papers. Hollywood likes to play politics. I mean, Kristallnacht was hardly Leni's fault." He let out a laugh. "She was in New York when it happened." He shrugged. "I believed she should get another shot—once the fuss had died down. I mean, Kristallnacht didn't stop the moguls from selling their movies in Germany. It was a huge market." He was still bitter about it. "Hollywood doesn't have principles if there's a profit to be made." He'd had time to justify his actions over the years, file off the unattractive edges, smooth over his inconvenient choices.

"What about *her* politics?" said Clara, thinking back to those images in *Triumph of the Will*, of the Führer coming down from the sky like a god, and the goose-stepping parades and the saluting and the screaming euphoria of it all. And Leni on a cherry picker up a flag pole to get the perfect crane shot.

"She was ambitious." A flare of anger riled him. "You do what you need to—to get ahead."

"*Triumph of the Will* sold Hitler to all of Germany as someone to admire, to unite behind," said Clara, finding her courage. "It convinced the rest of the world that he was someone to fear." She remembered Gil's reaction to seeing *Triumph of the Will* at the start of the war and thinking "We're beat." That fatalistic feeling had echoed the world over because of Leni and her powers of film persuasion. *Just politics.*

"She wasn't in the Nazi Party," Roger went on.

"Even better—she had the Führer's ear," said Clara with a surge of defiance. She recalled the photo of Brackett and Leni with Hitler. "Why did you go to Berlin?"

He considered her through narrowed eyes. "Pearce sent me, it was business." Prompted by Clara's confused expression, he elaborated. "Hitler had promised Leni that he would finance *Penthesilea*—from his own personal funds. He was going to build her a huge film studio near Berlin. But it wouldn't be ready for over a year. He didn't know she had signed a contract with Silver Pacific. That worried her. And Goebbels—who ran the film industry—wasn't always on Leni's side. I went over to Berlin to pitch the idea of a co-production. Shoot here in California. Make the movie in English. Instead of an expensive domestic German picture with little return on investment, share the production costs and make it an international hit: big box office, global recognition. Goebbels had plans for expanding the German film industry. With a thousand-year Reich the Jewish moguls wouldn't be running the show forever." He smirked. "But prizing Leni from Hitler's control was tricky. With some convincing from Goebbels and yours truly, he signed off on it and would still back the picture."

Clara let out a gasp. "*Hitler* was going to bankroll *Amazon Queen?*" The scandal went much deeper than she or Gil could have imagined. If any of this got out now, the studio would be done for.

"We finished the script that spring of '39. Plans were moving forward. We'd shoot in the fall. Pearce and I assumed that by then, the HANL crowd would have calmed down—a year later and Kristallnacht would be a distant memory. Public feeling was on our side. A lot of people didn't want to get involved in Europe's problems. Lindbergh was popular: America First. But then we hit a snag." He shook his head. "September 1, 1939."

"Hitler invaded Poland," said Clara.

"Exactly. And shortly after, Britain declared war on Germany. Pearce got cold feet, axed the project." He gave a small shake of his head. "That was the end of *Amazon Queen*." He let out a long sigh. "Leni's Hollywood career could have been incredible," he marveled. He said it like that was the most regrettable fallout—the war had gotten in the way of his lover's career. "What's prompting your curiosity anyway? That business with Leni, it's all in the past."

She felt like he was testing her, daring her to bring up Connie's name—the person they'd been dancing around. She dug her nails into the patterned couch. "Connie Milligan. She know all this?"

Brackett flinched at her name.

"On the *Argentan* set—did you remember her from Palm Springs?" Clara kept pushing.

He let out a laugh. "Do you know how many blondes you come across in the film industry?"

"But she remembered *you*."

"She might have mentioned something the first day on set— 'I worked with you before'—but I assumed it was on a movie. She never mentioned Palm Springs or Leni . . . at first."

Until she read the article that jogged her memory. Clara's knee was trembling; she steadied it with her hand.

"What did she want?"

"To give me a piece of her mind, blow off some steam. She'd read some article about Leni in the *Evening Post*. She was mad at me—at herself. She had admired Leni in '38. 'The foreign actress.' Said she had felt giddy just to be around us. Back then she hadn't known about the controversy, about the boycott or even who Leni was. Back then Connie Milligan was a small-town secretary with stars in her eyes."

"Did Connie try to blackmail you?" asked Clara. She could feel her pulse galloping along, out of control.

"At the beginning she wanted small stuff—a walk-on part, a speaking role, a screen test, a meeting with a director at any of the studios." He batted his hand like it was nothing. "I could give her all that and more."

"And later?" Clara said.

He gave a laugh. "She got greedy. A Hollywood career wasn't enough." With a gust of irritation, his voice rose. "She wanted to punish the studio for being on the wrong side of history." He rolled his eyes. "She wanted to go after Pearce. She wanted justice."

"Go after him how?" asked Clara.

"What do you think?" he snapped. "She would go to the press, go public."

"What did you do?" She tried to sound neutral.

He threw his hands up in mock surrender. "I convinced her I was on her side. I tried to buy some time."

"Was Pearce involved? Did he know what Connie planned to do?"

Roger sneered. "Pearce doesn't get his hands dirty. That's what money can buy you. I talked to him over a round of golf— not about Connie specifically, but I took his temperature on a potential scandal if news of the Leni contract got out."

Clara listened as Roger barreled on unprompted; he was getting riled up.

"Pearce shrugged off the past. For him it was simple. He'd met Leni before the war. The project hadn't moved forward. When war broke out, the studio made good on army films for Uncle Sam and sent its best contract stars to entertain the troops. Silver Pacific did its bit; his conscience was clear. He told me: 'We have a new enemy, and it's called Communism.' But I knew, if anything was made public about Leni, *I* would take the hit, *I* would be sacrificed. Salacious articles about my affair with her. Photographs would surface. Most of the studios are still run by Jews. I would be blacklisted, my career over. And Pearce would let me rot to save himself, his studio." He had a wild look in his eye. Connie had put his livelihood in peril, his legacy. She had threatened his best work of fiction—himself. He was nothing without that. He had been desperate.

"Pearce never made the connection that Connie Milligan, the stand-in, had been his secretary years before?"

"He runs a studio. He didn't remember a temp's name from eight years ago," he snapped. "I was alone against a woman on a crusade with nothing to lose." There was a sheen of sweat on his face. "I had a few days to come up with a plan."

The day of the murder. Clara didn't blink. She remembered she had left the *Amazon Queen* reel cued up on the Moviola. Would anyone find it? Would anyone put it together if something happened to her?

"I overheard Connie ask Bannon if she could use her dressing room that night. I waited and watched outside the bungalow. Bannon took her sweet time to leave."

"And then?"

"As I was about to go inside, Connie left in a hurry, caught me off guard."

Clara nodded. Connie had been heading straight to the vaults.

"You followed her?"

He nodded. "Couldn't figure out what she was up to at first. But then the penny dropped. *Amazon Queen*, the test reel. I knew it had been destroyed. Pearce had told me. But I was furious that she would go that far, to try to find that film." Clara noticed his mid-Atlantic affectation drift in and out as he got riled up. "Connie Milligan, a secretary, *a stand-in*," he sneered in disgust. "A few weeks on the lot."

He talked as though Connie's low rank in the Hollywood hierarchy justified his actions. His need to defend himself was palpable—and Clara was right there, a willing audience. "Your back was against a wall. You had to do something," she said. She was baiting him to tell her more.

"Connie Milligan was a no one. Another hopeful. Another blonde. This town gobbles them up. No one cares—it's true. Admit it. After the public found out it wasn't Babe Bannon in the vault, they didn't care. Some lives are worth less than others."

An invisible young woman like Connie, no one would miss her. She'd been disposable. And by this logic so was Clara. Her stomach seized up at the thought of how this would play out. What was he going to do to her? Danger thrummed down her spine, and she gripped the edge of the couch as though it were a precipice and all Roger had to do was push her off.

"The vault wasn't part of the plan, but perfection is the enemy of good. I saw her standing there, looking like Bannon's twin—in her costume, her makeup done. It wasn't as tidy a location as the dressing room, but it still played."

When the phone rang, they both jumped. Brackett looked at it like he'd never seen the contraption before and didn't know how to stop the intermittent noise. He let it ring; it lasted an eternity. Clara flicked a glance at the door. Finally Roger darted toward his desk. Clara made a run for it, but tripped on the edge of the coffee table and stumbled. She heard a drawer open. As quick as a cat, Roger was in front of the door. He had a neat revolver pointed at her chest. Roger was done talking.

## Chapter Thirty-Eight

# The Vault

MAGIC HOUR HAD FADED by the time Roger marched Clara across the lot, his silk-lined blazer draped over his arm, concealing the gun. She moved forward like an automaton, her feet betraying her with every step. But she had no choice, with a gun at her back—he'd killed before. The studio lot was on the cusp of night. The sky had drained to a washed-out shade of cotton candy, and the last few cars were lined up at the gate to join the procession of lights on Melrose. Clara's mind spun. Where was he taking her? How could she get away? Her eyes scanned rapidly for a means of escape, a way of attracting attention or distracting Roger. Where were the extra security guards and the police cruiser that had been stationed on the lot since the murder? Clara's chest caved in. With Gil in custody—the perfect fall guy—as far as the cops were concerned the killer had been caught. She began to feel frantic, her fists clenching and unclenching, all while she walked calmly as instructed.

To any onlooker they would have appeared innocuous. Roger might even have seemed courteous, his left hand touching her back, guiding her in the right direction. He navigated them carefully to avoid anyone at close range—not a difficult task at this hour. As a precaution he avoided the wide walkways. Instead he had them zigzag between the vast soundstages. The buildings loomed over her. If only she could be transported to one of the fictional worlds on the movie sets and out of this one. The loquacious Roger from moments earlier—spilling details of how he'd planned a murder—had been replaced by a more sinister silent version. She couldn't predict what he would do next. But there was no doubt that she was in danger.

When they rounded the corner of stage eleven, they almost collided with two custodians and a cart of cleaning supplies. Clara gasped, but before she could utter a word, she felt the barrel of the gun poking into her right kidney—a reminder to keep quiet, to not try anything. All it would take was a squeeze of the trigger. She heard Roger apologize, and all too quickly the men continued on in the opposite direction, their voices and the squeaking cart fading to nothing.

They passed the actors' bungalows. She had a flash of Connie in Bannon's dressing room on the night of the murder: Bannon doing her stand-in's makeup, the mirror ringed with lights, Connie trying on the actress's costume and swiveling around in front of the full-length mirror. The borrowed heels clicking on the asphalt as she strutted toward the vaults feeling armed and powerful, poised to find dirt on the studio—to blackmail her way into a career or to burn the whole place to the ground. Either way it must have felt intoxicating.

They were approaching Gower on the west side of the studio, where there was a pedestrian gate. She wondered if Roger was planning on leaving the lot. But instead of turning to the exit, he nudged her on, and Clara realized with a sense of dread that, of course, he was taking her to the film vaults. A chill in the air made her shiver. She slowed her pace, but Roger prodded her. "Keep moving." As they reached the concrete building, Roger looked over his shoulder—there was no one around.

"Are you going to strangle me too?" She gave this line a kind of impertinent edge as though she were channeling an indignant Katharine Hepburn.

"Nonsense." He sounded offended. "Vault five, come on." He ushered Clara to the end of the corridor. "Open it." It had been two weeks since the night of the murder—was history repeating itself?

It was dim in the corridor; Roger hadn't turned on the lights. She flubbed the combination and had to start over, her fingers trembling.

"Come on, Girl Friday," said Roger.

*Girl Friday.* She remembered him sticking up for her when Thaler had reluctantly given her the apprentice editor job. She had been duped into believing that he was decent, that he cared about giving a young woman a shot, that he was on her side.

She got the right combination and opened the outer door. Roger waved the gun toward the vault. He jerked his head. "Go on."

With trepidation Clara pushed open the inner door and stepped inside. Roger hit the light switch on the corridor wall and the vault came to life. The floor was spotless—someone had attacked it with bleach—the murder of two weeks prior wiped clean away. She blinked at the reels, neat and gleaming in their metal canisters, towering toward the ceiling on either side. She could imagine Connie searching in vain for the reel that was supposed to be in vault five, not knowing it wasn't there, that it was supposed to have been destroyed, that Max was hiding it under the Oscars.

Roger followed her inside and pulled the inner door closed. Clara backed away from him. The tight space was claustrophobic. She glanced behind her, but there was nowhere to go, just a cobwebbed airshaft. He put the gun down, slowly, on top of a canister, giving her a warning look not to try anything. Clara could feel her chest rise and fall rapidly. He put his blazer back on, shrugging the shoulders into place, fixing his cuffs. Clara's eyes darted past him to the door. She could make a run for it, but she'd need the strength to overpower him—and in the narrow space that would be impossible. The proximity of real danger was screaming at her; she *had* to get out of that vault.

Roger removed his belt and came at her. Clara took the chance and charged him. She pushed him hard with her shoulder as though ramming a door, and tried to scrabble past. But as she lunged to open the inner door, he grabbed her, and she felt a sharp crack on the side of her head. She was stunned and swayed to one side, cradling her head, cowering against another blow. He was holding the revolver, butt facing out—he must have clocked her with it.

"You done?" he barked.

Brackett stuffed the gun into his pocket and picked up the belt, which he'd dropped in the struggle. He dragged her to the back of the vault, shoved her against the film racks, pulled her arms behind her back, and began to tie her wrists to the metal upright of the shelves.

Momentary relief—the belt was to tie her up, not to strangle her. The terror ebbed, but she was still rigid, heart thumping. "Is this really necessary?" Again Katharine Hepburn piped up—as though his actions were an inconvenience to her dinner plans. "I won't be able to unlock the door from the inside." But underneath she was a swirl of panic, claustrophobic at the idea of being trapped in the vault.

"Stop talking," he said. His voice was as cold as slate. As he wrestled to secure her wrists, she could hear his labored breathing in her ear.

The belt was tight, and the metal upright dug into the heels of her hands. Her head throbbed. She tried to breathe through the pain, in and out, in and out. She thought of the night of the murder; her parents' party and Otto's sonata came swimming back to her. She tried to focus, convincing herself to remain calm until he left. He wasn't going to shoot her or strangle her. He must have wanted her out of the way, presumably so he could make a getaway. A security guard might check on the vaults; they'd upped their rounds since the murder. At worst, Lloyd or the new kid would find her by morning. She licked her lips. Her mouth was dry. *Take it easy, Clara. Have a Coke.* Her head was foggy. She was drifting somewhere. *Focus,* her rational voice said again. She had to stay alert. She coached herself to go over what would happen: in the morning Lloyd would find her, he would let her out, she would call the detectives, Gil would be released. Her eyes drooped. She felt woozy again. She blinked quickly. She had to talk, stay awake. It could be dangerous to succumb to this drowsy feeling.

"Did you plan to frame Gil all along?" she asked.

Roger finished tying her up. He checked that her constraints were tight enough and stepped back. His face was empty of any emotion—that scared her more than the gun in his pocket.

"Gil was my wild card," he said. "I knew there was tension between him and Bannon from day one at the read-through. Couldn't figure it out. Until later." He smiled. "I suppose he must have been very much in love with her." A wicked gleam in his eye. "I had him stay late that night, alone in the office. Another suspect for the cops to eliminate, and someone to muddy the waters, someone with a link to Bannon. But Gil proved more than useful: he became *the* suspect. I ran with it, I improvised. I made sure the police thought he was still in love with her."

Clara was queasy. "The letter from France, was that you?"

He gave a little bow and took off an imaginary hat. "A decent forgery, I thought." He smirked. She felt dizzy, and for a moment there were two Rogers bowing in the vault. She blinked through her double vision. She could feel a trickle of blood run down her temple, into her hair.

Through the pulsing pain she watched with confusion as Roger removed a canister of film from the racks. He opened it and unspooled the footage across the floor. Then he took another and did the same. A third and fourth he removed from their canisters; he placed them—still tightly wound—on top of the loose footage.

"What are you doing?" Clara stared at him, bewildered.

"No loose ends, my dear. American audiences, they like their films tied neatly in a bow. No ambiguities, no guesswork—we're not European."

Roger stepped out into the corridor. She waited for him to lock the door as she stared at the mess of film footage snaking over the floor. Then she heard a match strike and she could smell tobacco. It sharpened her senses and jolted her out of her stupor. Roger hovered in the doorway and took a long inhale on the cigarette.

"Roger, put that out!" It was suicide.

He raised an eyebrow and gestured to the NO SMOKING sign

on the wall. "You're right. The whole place could go up." He smirked and stepped into the vault.

"Roger, don't. Put it out. This is crazy," said Clara, terror shooting up her back. She was aware of the towering racks of flammable film all around her.

Roger held the cigarette in one hand and a book of matches in the other. "It's a filthy habit," he said, and tutted. He wedged the butt of the cigarette inside the book of matches, the burning end sticking out a couple of inches. "I imagine Conrad has insurance, and it's, what—an accident, or maybe suicide, with your boyfriend arrested for murder?" With absolute horror Clara realized how it would play out. The cigarette would take a few minutes to burn down and would ignite the book of matches, which would set the film alight, and then—whoosh. The loose footage, like dry tinder, would burst into flames and light the compact reels. The whole vault would be ablaze. Roger would have time to escape the vaults, and maybe even the studio lot, before the fire trucks came screaming.

"No, Roger. No!" She was begging him. "Please—don't."

Carefully he placed the improvised incendiary near the unspooled film. He had the concentration of a props man positioning an object before the camera rolls. Focused, efficient, cool under pressure. He nudged the matchbook closer to the loose film and then, as if the AD had just called "Action!" he ducked away, swiftly closing the doors. She heard the combination lock spin. The light went out.

Clara began to thrash against her constraints. There was a faint bar of ambient light from the corridor. The only other source of light was the ominous ember of the cigarette, a tiny glowing coal about to ignite an inferno.

In the darkness the sheer terror of her situation took hold. Clara screamed until she was hoarse. She started to cry. No one had heard Connie the night of the murder—they wouldn't hear Clara either. She was trapped in a concrete bunker, the doors locked tight, insulated by hundreds of reels of film—reels of fuel. Nitrate film contained the same chemicals as explosives. And the whole place was about to blow sky high.

Quickly Clara slipped her heel out of her shoe. She lifted her foot, curled her toes to keep the shoe from falling off, aimed in the darkness, and then pitched it toward the cigarette. It went long—she heard it land on the concrete. One more try. She wished she were wearing the sturdy rubber-soled lace-ups instead of the flimsy heels. She flung the other pump off her foot toward the faintly glowing target. A rustle as it landed on the film stock—but the cigarette remained smoldering. She cast a wild gaze about her: blackness. She was surrounded by film reels—her passion, and now the fuel to a fire that would kill her. Her pulse raced, she couldn't breathe—she was completely trapped. She watched the cigarette burn. How many times had she witnessed such an innocuous thing, a burning cigarette? She could see it now, Gil's hand on the wheel of the convertible, cigarette between his fingers, the way he would ash it over the side of the car at a stoplight.

This ploy of Roger's was theatrical, absurd, terrifying. But then she thought of the charade with Bannon and what Roger had done to Connie, and for what—to save his reputation, to prevent a scandal, to protect his image, his fading career. And with Gil found guilty and Clara out of the way—no one would ever know the truth.

Clara fought for her life. She struggled hard, but the racks laden with reels were immovable. She tried to wriggle her wrists free, but Roger had wrapped the belt so tightly, all she got was raw chafed skin. She tried to rub the belt against the metal rack to wear it down, but the leather was tough. It would take forever. All she had was seconds. Her head throbbed.

She reached her stockinged feet toward the loose film, to pull it, tease it away from the cigarette. She could barely reach it—her toe grazed the edge of a loop of film, but she had hardly any purchase. Then she heard something shift like a log displaced on a fireplace, and she worried she was accelerating the process. The cherry on the cigarette was smoldering millimeters from the edge of the matchbook now. It wouldn't be long. She had a flash of Miss Simkin describing how old films were destroyed. *Melted down for silver.*

She tensed, waiting for the inevitable. Her palms were sweating; she was shaking. Her stockinged feet were cold on the concrete floor. Now the burning cigarette end had reached the book of matches—it caught in a flash. The brightness burned her eyes, and there was a reek of sulfur in her nose. She watched with horror as the gold crest of the Biltmore hotel was swallowed by flames, she imagined it devouring the futile warning: *Close cover before striking match.* The flames licked the edge of the film stock. She turned her head away and squeezed her eyes shut. Any second now the film would catch. Clara braced herself for the inevitable, the tornado of flames, the blinding heat. The link between her and Connie forged in death, to share the same fate—murdered in the film vaults. One strangled, the other burned alive in a nitrate fire.

## Chapter Thirty-Nine

# Blonde

A NITRATE FIRE TAKES hold with such speed and intensity that it will continue to burn even when doused with water. Nitrate creates oxygen, its own fuel, as it burns. It sounds like a tornado, like an airplane engine down a runway—it roars. All the facts that Clara had learned about nitrate since she'd started at Silver Pacific studios, all the anecdotes of accidental fires and tragedies, unspooled through her mind in a blink: film collections lost forever, cinemas burned to the ground, a matinee filled with children. The power of film: to bewitch and to destroy.

As Clara cowered in the vault with her eyes closed, her body rigid, waiting for the inevitable, she was transported to their kitchen in Berlin, the red-and-yellow oilcloth, the smell of pickled herring. The memory was so vivid that she could feel the vinegar prickle her nose, and her taste buds smarted— miraculous what trickery the mind performs.

But no—Clara really could smell vinegar. It was overpowering. She opened her eyes. Incredibly, the film hadn't caught. She squinted hard at Roger's little time bomb. The matchbook flare was small and sputtering, and the frames of unspooled film appeared to have collapsed and melted. Then it hit her. Acetate film smelled like vinegar, and unlike nitrate, it wasn't flammable. The small rolls of film that Roger had randomly pulled off the shelf and unspooled were 16 mm—an acetate base. Her relief was short-lived. She couldn't know if all the reels he had pulled were acetate. There was still a risk. The change in temperature, the heat from the matchbook that was still smoldering, something could still spark and catch. Not to mention that if there were old or damaged reels of nitrate decomposing, they gave off a flammable gas. The wait, the not knowing, was excruciating.

Time passed. The matchbook was out. Her wrists were throbbing and her head felt foggy. She could hear girls' voices in German as she drifted in and out of consciousness. They were calling her name. She was running toward them. Early-morning light, and they were walking to school. A threesome of linked arms, in step—Klara, Freya, and Ruth. Two blond heads and Ruth's dark brown waves. Ruth Hoffman.

In a rush Clara was transported to Freya's garden at the end of summer 1938. The three girls were sprawled on the lawn, banished from Freya's house while Frau Thome bustled through housework and a batch of baking. Freya lay on her side, absently ripping at blades of grass, her blond hair fanned over her shoulders. Klara and Ruth were bickering. "Klara, it's not broken. I can fix it." But Klara snatched the flower crown from Ruth and tossed it toward Frau Thome's rosebushes, where it hung snagged on a thorn.

Groups of three are tricky. As Freya's neighbor, Ruth was by rights a closer friend—Klara had only been around since elementary school. But recently the dynamic had changed. Freya's father was an official in the Nazi Party. And Ruth's family were Jewish. A rift had grown between the neighbors, which Klara secretly welcomed.

The bickering stopped with the unexpected return of Freya's brother, Matthias. Eclipsing the sun, he stood over them, his huge backpack weighed down by a tent. Freya and Klara leapt up.

"Matti!" Freya squealed. She tackled him with a hug. Klara beamed at him. He was taller and broader than the last time she'd seen him.

Ruth became quiet.

He shrugged off his pack, which landed with a thud and a clank; then he opened his water canteen and took a swig. Klara watched as a rivulet of water escaped his mouth and splashed onto the collar of his uniform. At fourteen, Matthias existed in the heady stratosphere of teenage adventure, having spent a month with his Hitler Youth troop in Austria.

Matthias's eyes flickered over Ruth. "What are you doing here?" He spat on the ground next to her.

"Don't be mean, Matti," Freya said weakly.

Ruth flushed a deep crimson.

They all sat down again. Matthias moved deliberately away

from Ruth and stretched out on the grass next to Klara, who smirked without thinking, eager for the older boy's attention.

Three blond heads against one dark one.

When Klara finally met her friend's gaze, it was betrayal that registered on Ruth's face. Her trusting eyes, her steady friendship stamped on, tossed aside for one moment of approval from Matthias, pumped up and peacocking in his uniform.

Freya's mother called out to them. She was crossing the lawn carrying a tray.

"I should go home," said Ruth.


Clara heard voices again. She was still in Freya's yard and the voices were calling out to her in German, but they were muffled, or under water. A door banged. It jolted her awake. As she came to, she realized she was still in the vault.

*"Klara, Klara?"* Finally she recognized Max's voice in the corridor.

She responded—a hoarse, unintelligible cry. But would he hear her through the doors? "Max! I'm in here. Vault five." But he didn't have the combination. She started to rattle it off. "Fifty-five, twelve, five, fourteen." Or was it five, fifteen? The numbers swam before her eyes.

Suddenly the vault door burst open. There was Max and Miss Simkin. "Clara!" Their shocked faces reflected the state she was in, tied up, tear-stained, and bloody. In the distance the whine of sirens grew louder.

350

                                    *       *       *

That night, after Clara's head wound had been patched up by
the studio doctor, after the police had gone over her story, after
she'd been driven home in a police car with Max as chaperone—
Clara lay in bed, groggy and aching, unable to close her eyes.

Around ten p.m. the doorbell rang. Clara could hear agi-
tated voices. Moments later her mother showed Gil into her
bedroom. Her face was severe and disapproving. "He wouldn't
leave until he saw you," she said in German. Then she turned to
Gil and switched to English, "Five minutes."

Clara assumed she was dreaming when she saw him standing there in her room, incongruous against the flower wallpaper,
as if he were on the process stage and the wrong background
was being projected.

He came over and knelt down by her bedside, took her
hand, and placed it against his cheek. "Clara—I can't believe—"
He squeezed his eyes shut.

"You're cold," said Clara.

He gave a soft laugh. "After the cops let me go, I drove like a
bat out of hell across town. I had to see you."

Gil told her Brackett had been apprehended. The detectives
figured a more seasoned criminal wouldn't have hung around,
but Roger's vanity—his Achilles' heel—had kept him tethered.
His white Packard was spotted outside a dry cleaner's on Vine
just before closing. Apparently he'd needed newly laundered
suits for his getaway. Not one for brave acts or daring, he had

given himself up almost immediately when the police had surrounded the building—some kind of Western shoot-out wasn't his style.

Gil leaned close. "I'm glad you're okay, Clara." He kissed her softly. In the background Clara's mother hovered at the bedroom door, arms folded. Gil took the hint and was unceremoniously ushered away. Clara could hear her mother in clipped English telling him that her daughter needed rest, not updates on the case.

Later that night as Clara skirted the edge of sleep, thoughts of the past—things forgotten, long since put away—drifted into close-up: images, moments, like frames of film retrieved from a dusty vault and held up to the light. Her collection of Russian dolls on the mantelpiece of her bedroom in Berlin; the pattern of cracks on the pavement outside their apartment; the smell of lilacs, thick with blossoms, nodding to her by Freya's front gate. Inevitably she returned to that day in September '38 in Freya's backyard.

After Ruth left, the others devoured Frau Thome's baking. Matthias's reservations about civilian life were forgotten as he helped himself to a slice of his mother's *Baumkuchen.* The girls constructed new flower crowns as Matthias regaled them with tales of camping in forests and hiking over streams. Captivated, Klara listened to him talk passionately about *Heimat und Volk*— Austria and Germany coming together into one big *Vaterland.* As he described his Alpine adventures, she let herself imagine.

Next year it would be *her* turn.

Klara's parents hadn't permitted her to join Hitler Youth, the *Bund Deutscher Mädel,* or BDM for short. *You're too young, end of discussion.* Her parents' reaction had seemed irrational. Who could object to fresh air and rambling, outdoor sports and sing-alongs? Klara wouldn't connect the dots until later. Until the crossing to America.

Freya's mother, on the other hand, had signed her daughter up the day she'd turned ten—a source of bitter envy on Klara's part. Klara would linger by the noticeboards at school, staring at the poster of a smiling girl with braids: *Auch du gehörst dem Führer.* "You, too, belong to the Führer." And another one: *Girl, come. You, too, are part of us.* How often she had gazed at these idols, these BDM girls, and thought, *One day.* After many arguments and bouts of sulking, her parents had finally relented and a compromise had been reached. The following year she would be allowed to join the BDM. Of course it was a false promise on her parents' part—the Bergs would leave Germany at the end of October '38—never to return. But this was only September, and Klara was unaware of what was to come.

Freya upended a bag of tent pegs.

"Leave that," said Matthias. "It took me ages to pack everything properly."

Klara prodded the canvas tent. "Let's put it up."

Matthias closed his eyes and groaned theatrically. Enthusiasm spent, he was now lying on the grass, his head propped up against his kit bag. "Now? I just got back."

His show of reluctance didn't last long, and for the rest of the afternoon, under the shade of the copper beech, the Thomes' lawn became an outpost for *Hitlerjugend* troop 173.

The unraveled canvas smelled of sweaty gym class and grass clippings. Klara got a burn on the palm of her right hand pulling the guy rope taut. She didn't care. Watching Matthias strike the wooden stakes sent a thrill through her with each blow. His arms and neck were bronzed a shade darker than the tan of his uniform, his flaxen hair almost white in the sunlight. He seemed older. When he caught her staring at him, she volunteered a question about knot-tying—her blush disguised by the hard work of setting up camp.

They lounged inside the tent, which was stuffy and dim, with just a chink of sunlight slicing through the tent flap. They drank tart lemonade topped with raspberries, which exploded on Klara's tongue. She could taste the following year—1939—picturing Freya and herself side by side in the regulation white blouses, blue skirts, and neckerchiefs. Like sisters, arm in arm.

With the cake finished, Freya headed for the kitchen in search of second helpings. It was hot in the tent, but Matthias and Klara didn't decamp. Flashes of sunlight glanced off Matthias's hair. He tugged at the leather toggle to loosen his neckerchief. Lying on his side, head propped up on a hand, he looked directly at Klara as though seeing her for the first time—not as Freya's friend and a fixture around their house but as a girl. She held his gaze, the air thick and still between them. His Hitler Youth pin glinted in a sunbeam, a small black swastika on a red diamond—as bright and benign as a ladybird. He removed her flower crown and set it down. "You don't need this." He caressed her blond hair lightly. "This is your crown." Without warning he leaned forward and kissed her. Swift, firm, deliberate. There was a formal quality to the kiss, as though it were a handshake or a wave—a social obligation. When he drew back, Klara stared at him, unable to find anything appropriate to say—this had never happened to her before. But beneath her shock was delight. She bit the inside of her cheek to keep a grin from escaping. Freya returned with a plate of cookies. The tent was abandoned; they spread out on the lawn.

In years to come the distinctive smell of canvas and trapped summer would transport her back to this afternoon. Every summer would be daisy-chained to this one. In 1943 a camping trip with high school friends to Santa Barbara would catapult her back to the Thomes' backyard and to Matthias, his image (to her eleven-year-old eyes) the epitome of male beauty. Over time she recut the memory, and the episode with Ruth was left on the cutting room floor of her mind. Eventually Ruth's presence that day faded completely; it was just her and Freya bickering, the looming cloud of going back to school the source of their irritation. She recalled Matthias's return and the tent and of course the kiss. Walking home in the fading light, the feeling of fulfillment, on the cusp of arrival. Was this what growing up felt like? In less than two months the Bergs would leave Germany for good.

Once, they had been three. A friendship drama for the playground, the inevitable follies of immaturity and jealousy, ended up playing out along Nazi Party lines.

Klara would never see Ruth again. When school started up, Ruth wasn't there. Her family had moved without saying good-bye. It wasn't until years later that Clara found out the truth.

News began to trickle out after the Allied invasion, and in March 1945 a letter from Berlin arrived. It was from their old neighbor, Frau Krupke, the woman who had packed up their apartment—it was an account, the dreadful tally, of what had become of friends and neighbors. She revealed on page three that the Hoffmans had been taken to Auschwitz and all of them had perished.

It was late, after midnight, and Clara lay in bed, exhausted, but her mind wouldn't stop churning. Hours earlier she had stood in the dark waiting to die. Thoughts and images had surfaced, imagining Ruth in a concentration camp, standing in the dark waiting for the gas, and all the horrors that Clara had heard of, the crematoriums, the smoke stacks, the burning bodies; stories of scavenging for gold and silver fillings from the ashes. Silver recovery.

Finally Clara began to drift off to sleep. She could feel the pitch and lurch of a ship beneath her—and yet she wasn't on a ship, she was in her bedroom in Berlin, she could see her set of

Russian dolls on the mantelpiece. She opened the dolls, one by one. Each wooden nesting doll appeared to be a different version of herself. When she reached the smallest one—the tiny doll that didn't open—she discovered it was painted in shiny red and black, emblazoned with the crooked cross of the swastika. Her own dark little Nazi heart.

The dream skipped ahead. Freya, Ruth, and Klara walking to school arm in arm. She could hear a phrase repeated, over and over, as though she were pressing the foot treadle on a Moviola—rewind and play, rewind and play—to find the edit point. It was Detective Rivetti leering at her. *Three's a crowd, three's a crowd.*

## Chapter Forty

# The Pool

DETECTIVE IRELAND CAME TO the cutting room, unannounced, a few weeks after Roger's arrest. It was June and the days were getting hotter, the evenings longer. Just shy of six p.m. and Clara still had the blinds down to cut the glare.

"Mrs. Milligan wanted you to have this." Ireland put a package in brown paper on her desk. "She's packing up to go back to San Bernardino with the little one."

Clara took it. "What is it, a book or something?"

He gave a small shrug. "You'll see." The detective looked out of place standing in the cutting room, hat in hand. "How's that head?" he said. "You took quite a knock. Right as rain now?"

Clara smiled. "Yes, right as rain."

The detective edged toward the door. "I won't keep you. Movie magic is busy work."

In truth, she wasn't busy, now that the shoot was done and Sam's assembly of the footage was almost finished. He had already left for the day, and Clara was done typing up the list of additional dialogue to be recorded for the final sound mix. Sam had given her a second chance, and she wasn't going to mess up again.

Ireland paused at the door. "You were right on the money, Clara. Good copper instinct."

"Thanks, Detective," she called after him, but he was already gone.

Clara unwrapped the brown paper to reveal a notebook with a green speckled cover and gold print numbers on the front: 1938. Seeing that date sent a jolt of electricity through her.

Connie had started off strong in January of that year, diligently recording everyday life—a shorthand test, a new skirt, a date at the soda fountain. By the end of February the entries had petered out, only to start up again in December, when she got hired to work for Mr. Pearce in Palm Springs. What girl wouldn't want to document every moment—being away from home for the first time, in a winter resort town for Hollywood stars? She had turned seventeen in the fall—the date in late September was circled. In rummaging through her bedroom for clues, the police would have dismissed an out-of-date diary. A teenage girl's ramblings could have no significance—boys and bobby sox. But in these pages, in round blue handwriting, the truth was written.

> *Mr. Brackett and the German lady spent the afternoon pretending to write their script. She prefers doing laps in the pool.*

Clara imagined Connie watching them greedily through those huge glass windows, concealed by the bright reflection of the pool.

*Mrs. Irvine says the German lady is Hitler's girlfriend. Nonsense—I think she's been at the sherry. What woman would take a second look at that ugly severe-looking fellow. He's always shouting. The German lady only has eyes for the screenwriter.*

Connie had helped Mrs. Irvine prepare for a party in honor of the "German actress." Connie was asked to serve drinks. Her eyes nearly fell out of her head when Mrs. Irvine told her how much a case of champagne cost. There was a different receptacle for each kind of food and drink. She didn't envy Mrs. Irvine cleaning up after—all those dishes. Connie was soaking up every detail, storing it, hoarding it. Nothing would go unnoticed because she coveted this glamorous world. It was what Clara had done at the studio; nothing was casual or ignored.

That same evening of the party, in one of the guest bedrooms, piles of fur coats lay across the bed. When no one was watching, she stole to the room and lay down on the sea of fur, soft against her cheek, the hint of perfume on a sleeve. Outside, a bright moon cast shadows of palm trees across the surface of the swimming pool, it lay as still as a photograph.

As Clara turned the pages of the diary, a couple of photographs slid out. The first snapshot must have been taken at the

Palm Springs Racquet Club. Clara recognized the blue and white umbrellas. Seventeen-year-old Connie Milligan was sitting on the diving board posing like a starlet, in a two-piece bathing suit. The bottoms had a little skirt that flared out. The other picture—a desert shot—made Clara's heart stop for a beat. Connie, her eyes caught in a blink, was holding a slate up to the camera. 'Camera test: SP3191.' *She must have visited the shoot,* Clara thought to herself. *That's* how she had found the production number—she had it all this time. Perhaps after reading the Nazi Pin-up article she turned to her diary of that winter in Palm Springs. She found the snapshot and scrawled the number on the cover of her script.

The diary for 1938 included the first week of January '39. Wednesday the fourth was her last day working for Mr. Pearce. He had taken off that morning to go back to Los Angeles. Connie was to type up the last correspondence, which Mrs. Irvine would post. Mr. Brackett and the "German actress" planned to have a last game of tennis at the Racquet Club—they would drive back to Los Angeles from the club. In the background Mrs. Irvine was cleaning the rooms noisily—according to the housekeeper, Mr. Brackett was always the last to leave, the kind of guest who just wouldn't take a hint. *Leaving after Mr. Pearce, the impertinence.*

As she read the pages of the diary, Clara could feel every moment as though she had lived it, as though she herself had sat by the glass walls of Pearce's desert house, licking stamps and gazing out at that perfect turquoise pool. . . .

Connie finished typing the last letter; then her eyes drifted automatically to the window. She had been tempted by that pool since her first day at the house. For her last day, she wore her bathing suit under her dress, and the skirt kept bunching up in an uncomfortable way when she sat down. When should she ask for permission? She couldn't find quite the right moment. The rush of Mr. Pearce's departure, Mr. Brackett lollygagging, Mrs. Irvine in a tizzy about some new curtains she had to order.

And like that, the morning slipped away. The correspondence was finished and Mrs. Irvine was getting ready to run to town. As she collected her things, Connie realized with a sharp pang that she had never so much as dipped a toe in the water. Her chest caved in with disappointment—it was too late.

"I'll be off to the post office, and then I have to see about new curtains for the guest bedrooms," said Mrs. Irvine. "Mr. Pearce prefers to choose the material himself. I've been given orders to send swatches to him in Los Angeles—waste of postage, if you ask me. What man wants to pick curtains? But he's particular, I suppose."

Connie was only half listening as she gazed at the slab of water glistening in the sun.

Mrs. Irvine took the letters, and they went out the front door together and stood on the driveway to say goodbye. Connie recalled her first day at the house. The concrete driveway had looked as though it had been poured that day—Connie had feared she'd leave a footprint. And now it was her last day and there would be no trace of her in that beautiful ugly house.

"Sure you don't want a lift, dear?" Mrs. Irvine opened the car door.

Connie shook her head. "I'd prefer to walk. It's such a nice day, and my bus home isn't until the afternoon." She already had a plan forming as the words tumbled out.

"Goodbye, dear. You've been a great help."

After a brisk hug, Connie set off down the driveway and onto the thick ribbon of asphalt—no sidewalks, just the desert scrub on one side and the mountains rising above her on the other. The lots were huge in that part of town—nearly a block to the next property. She waved when Mrs. Irvine drove by in her Ford station wagon, and Connie watched her car sail past the next huge home—a Spanish affair—and turn down the hill toward town. Connie slowed her walk and counted to ten before she turned around. As she hurried back toward the house, she worried that Mrs. Irvine might suddenly return. What if she had forgotten her purse or her shopping list? Connie cast a glance over her shoulder. The road remained deserted. All was still. The swimming pool was waiting for her.

She let herself in by the side gate. She didn't need to access the house to get to the pool. There was the bench with clean towels, rolled up like pigs in a blanket. She grabbed one, kicked off her shoes, and slipped out of her dress.

Her delight at that first swim. The warm sun, the cool water—not having to share any of it. It was one of those moments when being alone felt euphoric. She splashed around like a kid, gleeful. She closed her eyes, and the sun turned to starbursts on the ends of her lashes. She imagined the house was all hers, no one to bother her or ask her to do something, type something, or fetch something. She didn't have to do anything for anyone.

She dried herself off and put a fresh towel on the sun lounger. The grounds were immaculate. She closed her eyes. She could hear the thrum of a hummingbird, then a lazy bee. Heaven. This must have been what the German actress had felt like when she'd lounged by the pool.

Connie had been dazzled by that woman—by her glamor, by the exotic accent, the very force of her. When are passions born? Connie and movies, a flame burning in the dark. Something sparked in her when she was gazing at the actress doing laps in the pool, something covetous.

The slam of a car door woke her. Connie started. The dream of her private swimming pool evaporated. Her heart began to pound. She heard voices. Footsteps. The jangle of keys in the front door. She grabbed her clothes, purse, and shoes. Where could she go? The side gate was on the other side of the pool. She'd have to run past the glass walls—they'd see her from inside. She'd have to hide.

She ducked behind a bird of paradise near the fence. Her suit was still clammy. Was it Mr. Pearce? He was supposed to be halfway to Los Angeles by now. Suddenly she was a trespasser. Her heart was a fist punching its way out of her rib cage. Voices floated outside; someone had opened the patio door. With horror she noticed that she had dropped a shoe on the path. And the lounger was moved. There was an imprint on the cushion and puddles of water by the pool's edge. Would they notice? Would they find her? Her mind whirred with excuses. She could pretend she'd forgotten something—at the bottom of the pool? She cringed. *Great thinking, Connie.*

She heard the patio door slide open wider, and the voices came outside. They were clearer now. She recognized them—it was Mr. Brackett and the German actress. Connie crouched deeper into her hiding spot behind the bright green fronds of the bird of paradise, a sharp beak of a flower poking at her. She dared to peek between leaves and she watched them set up two loungers side by side in the sun. They grabbed fresh towels and ignored the ones she had used.

Connie stared at her shoe. Would it give her away? Her heart felt like a trapped bird, wings beating against her rib cage. Her throat was dry, and her eyes still stung from the chlorine in the pool. Minutes went by. Finally Mr. Brackett and the German woman relaxed onto their sun loungers, facing away from the house. Connie took her chance. She ducked down, grabbed her shoe, and darted in the open patio doors and through the house to the front door. As she slipped past Mr. Brackett's car in the driveway, she heard a splash. Their pool now.

She yanked her dress over her head and carried her shoes, her feet filthy from hiding in the bushes. The road was as deserted, as dead, as a Sunday morning. She walked briskly but not in a panic. Once she reached the next house, she risked a look back. Mr. Pearce's house sat as it always had, boxy and lined with glass that reflected the desert. There was no one in the drive shaking a fist at her; there was no one chasing her down the street. She exhaled a laugh. It was a lucky escape.

Clara had closed the diary and sat for a time. Her mind's eye a film camera, this was the infinite image of Connie that she would replay: the seventeen-year-old girl in bare feet and wet hair, walking along a desert road swinging her shoes, the sky a brilliant shade of blue.

# Late Show
## OCTOBER 1946

THE VISTA MOVIE THEATER was quiet. It was midweek, and the rain had started that afternoon and hadn't let up. Gil and Clara arrived under the marquee, shaking off the downpour, laughing and out of breath. At the kiosk they bought tickets for the late show and entered the lobby; a comforting fug of cigarette smoke, wet umbrellas, and popcorn enveloped them as the rain continued to lash down outside.

Clara had the letter from Bonn in her purse. She had read it over twice on her lunch break. Her parents were bracing for their first German winter. Her mother was writing to ask if she wanted anything special sent to Los Angeles for Christmas, and what about Max, didn't he love those ginger cookies from the Christmas markets? Clara shook her head. It was only October. She had struck a deal with her parents. If she lived in the same apartment building as Max, she could stay in LA—apparently he would keep an eye on her. It was a third-floor bachelor in the Los Feliz Manor right on the boulevard, and they rode the streetcar to work together.

At the concessions stand Clara got popcorn and Gil picked up the latest issue of *Variety*. BARBARA BANNON SIGNS WITH WARNER BROS. He nodded to the front cover.

"No surprise," said Clara. The fallout from the murder had given her the leverage she needed. Pearce hadn't put up a fight. Connie had helped her after all, Clara thought sadly. "Is the review in yet?"

Gil flicked through the pages until he found it.

*Letter from Argentan, a psychological thriller starring Barbara Bannon and Randall Ford, is the latest release from Silver Pacific. The publicity campaign appears to be making the most of Bannon's return to the big screen, her image transformed from Gregory Quinn's lover (on- and off-screen) to a first-rate actress in her own right. A compelling performance and tight direction from Howard Hawks proves Bannon can carry a picture without a leading man on the marquee. The film should appeal to the femme trade, as it relies heavily on the woman's picture but with a good dose of suspense. No wonder that Silver Pacific's publicity campaign is exploiting the drama of "The Silver Blonde" murder, which took place on the lot during filming.*

Gil let out a harsh laugh. " 'The Silver Blonde.' They can't help themselves. No mention of Brackett—I guess they removed his name from the credits."

"Why should he get a credit?" She offered him popcorn, and he tossed a few buds into his mouth. "Come on, it was your rewrites and Sam's cutting that saved the picture." Clara nudged him. "Everyone knows it."

He shook his head a little. "There'd be no picture, really, without you," he added. His gaze lingered on her, and she smiled.

They headed for the theater and showed their tickets to the usherette. As they took their seats, the previews were playing. A few more patrons trickled in, and Clara observed the usherette in the dim light and imagined Connie when she'd first came to LA—all her dreams and plans for the future when she'd passed through the gates of Silver Pacific studios.

Eventually the portrait lights of the Vista theater dimmed. The usherette turned off her flashlight and leaned against the wall, gazing up at the screen. Clara wondered how many times she had seen the picture: Hitchcock's *Notorious*, starring Cary Grant and Ingrid Bergman.

The trumpeting of the RKO logo, and Clara's attention was pulled to the screen and she let Connie go. She felt that familiar thrill, those electric seconds of anticipation before a movie begins. She reached for Gil's hand; just the right amount of strength in his grip, a perfect fit around hers. The credits played over a swelling score. As Clara watched the opening scene, she had a flash of what it would have looked like on the shoot day: Ingrid Bergman leaving a courtroom, hounded by reporters. Watching actors perform in person can be underwhelming and repetitive, nothing like the end result on-screen. Film has an almost magic capacity to transform. There is a weight and dazzle to it; something to do with the chemical layers, the silver halide crystals add a physical element, a glitter that augments real life into something else, something wonderful. The spell of cinema. The grandeur and scope of a wide shot; or the breath and intimacy of the close-up. You watch the actors as you would your own reflection. The film is happening to you, not just the character. You are not a bystander simply watching. You feel: you are.

For a couple of hours Clara and Gil lost themselves in the movie, inhabiting the cares of Ingrid Bergman and Cary Grant, and forgot—they let go of the past and the present and even themselves. From that infinite darkness, the silver screen was all that existed.

# AUTHOR'S NOTE

When this novel existed as no more than a spark of an idea, I set out to write a mystery inspired by film noir. The style of film-making prevalent in the 1940s and 1950s, characterized by its striking black-and-white photography, pessimistic antiheroes, jaded detectives, and femmes fatales. As a teenager, I devoured these films—they felt adult and dangerous. In these stories the women were powerful and cunning, the men simmered with barely contained emotion, and the final scene usually brought destruction, not a happy ending.

Once I delved into research for the book, the shadow of World War II loomed over sunny Los Angeles. Film noir wouldn't exist without that conflict. Indeed, many noir directors, like Billy Wilder and Otto Preminger, were Jewish immigrants from Europe who had arrived in the United States after fleeing Nazism in the 1930s. The idea of a young German American protagonist in a postwar setting intrigued me, and I realized that recurring noir themes—alienation, guilt, and deceit—were a perfect fit for such a character. Someone torn between her past and her present. The murder in my novel takes place in 1946, but I knew that the key to the mystery had to be buried in the past.

*The Silver Blonde* is a work of fiction; however, Hitler's filmmaker Leni Riefenstahl did indeed come to Hollywood before the war. Given that my mystery hinges on her time in California, I'd like to separate fact from fiction and give readers some context for her visit and what happened after.

As in the novel, Riefenstahl sailed to New York on the *Europa*, arriving in November 1938, just as news of Kristallnacht broke. Her visit created a great deal of publicity, and she was touted as the Nazi film queen and Hitler's girlfriend. All the newspaper quotes in the novel—from Hedda Hopper in the *Los Angeles Times* to excerpts from the *Saturday Evening Post*—are faithful. The boycott organized by the Hollywood Anti-Nazi League worked, for the most part: Leni failed to sell US rights to *Olympia*; she was denied entry to the studios (with the exception of a visit to Disney); and she was publicly given the cold shoulder by the film community. She fared slightly better with her Olympic connections, who organized a screening of her movie and a reception in her honor. But ultimately, she was run out of town. She made several trips to Palm Springs, California, where, according to Steven Bach's excellent biography *Leni: The Life and Work of Leni Riefenstahl*, "She had taken a new lover of unknown identity."

As a writer, my "what if?" reflex kicked in. What if one of the studios had been receptive to her? What if, in the historical climate of 1938, with the United States trying to stay out of Europe's conflicts, someone took a gamble on Fräulein Riefenstahl?

At the time, public opinion favored nonintervention in global conflict. Charles Lindbergh, America's favorite aviator, was a noted white supremacist and became the spokesman of the America First Committee, a political group pushing for American isolationism. This movement would gain popularity until the attack on Pearl Harbor. And just like Lindbergh, many prominent Americans were fans of Adolf Hitler, including Henry Ford, whom Leni visited in Detroit before she went to California. Silver Pacific studios is fictional, but I imagine the Pearces as old-money types, a family in which the patriarch would have been a supporter of Lindbergh and his ilk.

The other key to imagining a Hollywood career for Riefenstahl was the woman herself. She was talented and "ferociously ambitious." She had Hitler—if not her lover, certainly her career champion—wrapped around her finger. Before her arrival in the United States, *Olympia* had just won the Mussolini Cup at the Venice Film Festival, beating Disney's *Snow White*. Leni had been fêted across continental Europe with lavish premieres attended by royalty including the kings of Denmark, Sweden, Norway, and Belgium. With Europe at her feet, it seems inevitable that Leni's gaze would turn to Hollywood. And with her considerable ego, ruthlessness, and drive, why wouldn't she expect the red-carpet treatment?

The Hollywood Anti-Nazi League were vocal in their campaign against Leni, but in general, the studios at that time were careful not to offend the Nazi regime. Remember: At this point, war with Germany was years away. Hollywood studios had to tread carefully. Alienating the lucrative German market was risky, and for the most part (with the exception of Warner Bros., who closed their Berlin office in 1934), the studios tried to stay out of politics—there is rarely a mention of Nazis in Hollywood films until the 1940s. Of course, by the time the United States entered the war, the studios had rallied and were making their own propaganda films, like *Mrs. Miniver* and *Casablanca* (see the filmography on page 383).

The best historical fiction has a connection to the present. It allows us to examine our world through the lens of the past. As my story took shape, events that should have been relegated to the history books came roaring onto the front page: the rise of far-right groups in Europe and the United States; Nazis marching on American streets; the rise of the America First movement, along with the darkest elements of populism—xenophobia, racism, nativism. Propaganda and conspiracy theories spread on social media, and narratives were shaped and skewed on cable news. Suddenly my story took on a greater relevance as I found myself seeing the worst elements of our world through the lens of 1930s Germany. Had history been forgotten?

At this time I attended a screening of *Triumph of the Will* and a panel discussion hosted by the USC Shoah Foundation. It is remarkable that Riefenstahl's film endures to this day. Its imagery has influenced many contemporary classics—including Star Wars and Lord of the Rings. Watching the opening scenes, it was the wall of sound that hit me first—a deafening cacophony of *Sieg Heil*s and a sustained euphoria of screaming crowds at Hitler's arrival in the town of Nuremberg. It was truly chilling.

From that opening shot of his airplane in the clouds, Hitler was portrayed as a god descending to the mortal world. I was watching this infamous propaganda film with the benefit of hindsight, but I couldn't help imagining what it must have been like for a German audience in the 1930s. How could they *not* be mesmerized by these images and the rabid cheering of fellow Germans? In that darkened screening room, I felt as though I had time-traveled. Just watching, I felt complicit. I drove home in lashing rain—a very noir type of night—and I thought about my novel. I had set out to write a love letter to classic Hollywood and it had led me to explore film's darkest corners. Watching *Triumph of the Will* on the eve of the 2017 US inauguration made me realize that the tools of propaganda and manipulation will always be used by those in power and by those who crave it, and that every generation has to fight for democracy, decency, and truth.

When we consider the horrors of the Nazi regime, it is hard to imagine how a whole country could be complicit, could turn a blind eye and participate in cruelty, in mass murder. In my research I came across Melita Maschmann, a high-ranking official in the Hitler Youth movement. Years after the war, she reckoned with her Nazi past in a frank and detailed memoir, *Account Rendered: A Dossier on My Former Self.* In it, she remarked, "The ghastly thing was just the fact that it was not gangsters and roughnecks, but decent, intelligent and moral people who allowed themselves to be induced to acquiesce [to] something deeply evil and to serve it. . . . What I learned about myself and what we all should learn, even those of us who are not forced to such self discovery, is that the frontier between good and evil can run straight through the middle of us without our being aware of this."

What happened to Leni Riefenstahl? Did she ever make her precious *Pensethilea*? Even though Hitler (according to Goebbels's diary) had agreed to personally finance her film about the Queen of the Amazons, it was never made. And the massive film studio designed by Nazi architect Albert Speer for her personal use was never constructed. Leni's career goals were thwarted by geopolitical events. In 1939 Hitler invaded Poland, which precipitated France and Britain declaring war on Germany and the beginning of World War II.

Leni did make one more film during the war. It wasn't an expensive color epic, but a return to the sentimental mountain fairy tale she'd found fame with earlier in her career. *Tiefland* (meaning "homeland") was about a beautiful gypsy woman caught in a struggle between an aristocrat and a farmer. Leni wrote the script and directed and starred in the film, which required scores of Sinti and Roma extras. The Sinti and Roma were considered undesirables by the Nazi regime. Leni found her extras (68 adults and children) at the Marzahn internment camp near Berlin. They were not paid; instead, their fee was given to the camp authorities. After filming, they were returned to the camp—and to their fate. In 1943 they were deported to Auschwitz, where many of them perished.

Leni Riefenstahl was never convicted of war crimes, but

she was let off with the designation of "fellow traveler," or Nazi sympathizer. She would fervently deny all knowledge of the horrors of the Nazi regime for the rest of her life—no remorse or self-reproach, just protestations of innocence and a mountain of lies. Leni would claim that she had only ever been "an artist," existing above the political fray. Unlike Melita Maschmann, there would be no reckoning with her former self. She died in 2003 at the age of 101.

# GLOSSARY

Silver Pacific studios is fictional. I was lucky to have the help of film experts and former editing colleagues during my research, and I drew on my own experiences as an apprentice editor and assistant editor. Any small liberties taken with the depiction of post-production in the studio system are to benefit the story.

**apprentice editor:** An entry-level union position in the editing department. The apprentice works under the assistant editor and picture editor.

**archive:** The film library on a studio lot.

**assistant director:** The 1st AD plans the shooting schedule and runs the set, relaying the director's instructions to the crew.

**assistant editor:** Works under the picture editor, organizes dailies, keeps track of footage and paperwork, sometimes assists with cutting scenes.

**backdrop:** A painted background on a film set, usually on canvas or flats.

**call sheet:** A document providing information for the day's shoot, e.g., scenes to shoot, location, crew call times, special equipment.

**call time:** The time when the crew is to report to set.

**cinematographer:** Head of the camera department, also known as the director of photography (DP).

**clapper loader:** A member of the camera department, also known as second camera assistant (2nd AC). Loads film reels, operates the slate, handles paperwork.

**continuity:** Maintenance of seamless action and consistent details between different shots. On set, this is the job of the script supervisor, or "continuity girl"; in post-production, it's the job of the editor.

**crane shot:** A shot from a camera mounted on a crane, usually for a high, wide-angle view.

**cutting room:** The editing suite.

**dailies:** The unedited footage from a day's film shoot. Also, the viewing of that footage in a screening room, usually from the previous day's shoot. (See also "rushes")

**dolly shot:** A shot from a camera mounted on a wheeled cart (dolly) that can move forward, backward, or beside the subject of the shot. Usually the dolly is mounted on tracks for smooth movement.

**head leader:** A length of film at the beginning of a reel, often with a countdown and a synch pop.

**lost film:** Many silent films were destroyed, either by accident in vault fires or deliberately. Studios had a storage problem, and these films were deemed worthless, especially after the arrival of talkies. The films were sold for scrap and effectively recycled, melted down to recover the silver content and celluloid.

**martini shot:** The last shot of the day.

**matte painting:** A painting on glass to create the illusion of a background environment. The term is still used today for digitally painted backgrounds in VFX and animation.

**mismatch:** When the transitions between shots or scenes, otherwise known as continuity, don't match in the cut footage.

**MOS:** No sound recorded. The term could have been coined as an abbreviation for "motor-only shot" or "motor-only synch," referring to the way synch sound was originally recorded. Another theory is that a director with a thick German accent would ask for a scene to be shot "mit out sound" (*mit* is German for "with").

**Moviola:** Early editing equipment that allowed the editor to view footage while editing.

**NG:** Film jargon for "no good," used by the script supervisor to mark an unusable take.

**nitrate:** A type of film stock, used before 1950, with a highly flammable nitrocellulose base (the same chemicals as explosives).

**pick-up shots:** Additional photography needed to complete assembly of a movie.

**process photography:** Another term for rear projection.

**rear projection:** A shot in which actors are filmed in front of a projected background.

**rushes:** Another term for dailies.

**setup:** One camera angle usually comprised of several takes.

**sides:** Scenes from a script to be shot on a particular day, usually printed smaller than regular script pages.

**slate:** Identifies the scene, setup, and take number when the camera begins to roll. Provides a synch point for sound and image when the sticks are clapped together.

**splicer:** A tool used to cut spools of film.

**stand-in:** A person who takes the place of a principal actor during the technical setup before filming (e.g., when the DP lights the set, the camera sets focus, and the director rehearses blocking). While not a double, the stand-in is the same height and build, with the same coloring, as the actor. They don't appear on film.

**stock footage:** Generic footage that can be used by different films: e.g., an establishing shot of a city skyline.

**synch:** When sound and image play in time.

**synch pop:** The short pop of sound on the countdown leader. Allows the projectionist or editor to check the synch. Today, referred to as the "two-pop."

**tail leader:** The length of blank film at the end of a reel.

**tracking shot:** When the camera moves with the actor.

**trim bin:** Editing equipment that holds strips of selected film. In nitrate days, the metal lid was kept closed when unattended because of the risk of fire.

# FILMOGRAPHY

When I was growing up in Scotland, I would watch classic Hollywood movies with my father. It was our shared passion, and it became a tradition: we would rewatch our favorites year in, year out, and they became as familiar as old friends. Much later, this love of cinema led me to a career in film editing in Los Angeles.

During the research for this book, I was lucky enough to attend some nitrate screenings at UCLA's Billy Wilder Theater and the American Cinematheque's film festival Noir City at the Egyptian Theater in Hollywood. It's a rare thing now, as very few theaters are equipped to handle flammable film stock. Watching a film in its original form as it was intended to be seen, up on the big screen—there's nothing quite like it. To share my passion for classic Hollywood, I wanted to highlight the films mentioned in the novel, as well as those which inspired the fictional Silver Pacific movies, *Letter from Argentan* and *A Call to Arms*.

***Casablanca*** (1942), directed by Michael Curtiz
The ultimate wartime romance, this is the movie playing during the prologue. Starring Humphrey Bogart and Ingrid Bergman and featuring a slew of notable supporting roles, including Dooley Wilson, who sings the famous theme song, "As Time Goes By." This film still transports audiences—a true classic. *Casablanca* won the Academy Award for Best Picture in 1944.

***Double Indemnity*** (1944), directed by Billy Wilder
The definitive film noir based on James M. Cain's hardboiled novel. Stars Fred MacMurray as a flirtatious insurance salesman and

Barbara Stanwyck as the manipulative Mrs. Dietrichson, who wants
to bump off her husband for the insurance money. There's definitely a
dose of the steely Barbara Stanwyck in Babe Bannon's character.

*Gilda* (1946), directed by Charles Vidor
A noir gem starring Rita Hayworth in her iconic femme fatale role.
The visual style, especially the way Hayworth is lit in certain scenes,
influenced my descriptions of the cinematography in *Argentan*. But
the kind of sizzling performance Rita Hayworth gives as Gilda is more
reminiscent of how I imagined Babe Bannon's earlier roles with Quinn.

*His Girl Friday* (1940), directed by Howard Hawks
The reference in the opening chapter is to Rosalind Russell's whip-
smart reporter character, who spars with her editor and ex-husband,
played by Cary Grant, as she tries to land a scoop for the paper. This
screwball comedy is known for its rapid-fire, overlapping dialogue.
"Hawksian" women are often tough and intelligent, not meek or
overly feminine.

*Laura* (1944), directed by Otto Preminger
Based on the novel by Vera Caspary. A young woman is murdered,
and the detective investigating the case becomes enamored of her
portrait. Laura herself shows up halfway through the movie very
much alive. This plot twist inspired Bannon's entrance on Stage 11
at the end of the first act. Indeed, this especially noir theme of
doubles is very present in the novel; many characters have not only a
doppelgänger—most obviously Connie Milligan and Babe Bannon—
but also two versions of the same person: Ruby Kaminsky and Babe
Bannon; eleven-year-old Klara and eighteen-year-old Clara.

*Mrs. Miniver* (1942), directed by William Wyler
*A Call to Arms*, my Silver Pacific Oscar winner, is a nod to this American film set in an English village during World War II. It won the Academy Award for Best Picture in 1943 and is credited with consolidating American support for the war. Director William Wyler told reporter Hedda Hopper upon its release: "We're in an all-out war—a people's war—it's the time to face it. Let's make propaganda pictures, but make them good." Indeed Nazi propaganda minster Joseph Goebbels feared the power of this film. "There is not a single angry word spoken against Germany; nevertheless the anti-German tendency is perfectly accomplished."

*Notorious* (1946), directed by Alfred Hitchcock
A stylish romantic suspense film, and my all-time favorite Hitchcock. With her German father convicted of treason against the United States, Ingrid Bergman is recruited by Cary Grant's handsome CIA agent to help ferret out her dad's Nazi friends in South America. Famous for its long kissing scene, which managed to get around the censor's three-second rule, Hitchcock proved he was more than just the master of suspense. Bergman and Grant are sublime, and Claude Rains is almost sympathetic as the Nazi villain head over heels for Bergman.

*The Philadelphia Story* (1940), directed by George Cukor
A frothy romantic comedy, based on the successful stage play, starring Katharine Hepburn, Cary Grant, and James Stewart. Hepburn also starred in several films directed by Howard Hawks and embodies that strong, no-nonsense, determined kind of woman Clara tries to channel when her life is in danger during the novel's climax.

*Rebecca* (1940), directed by Alfred Hitchcock

A gothic suspense movie. Joan Fontaine and Laurence Olivier star in Hitchcock's adaptation of Daphne du Maurier's famous novel. *Letter from Argentan* incorporates elements from *Rebecca* as well as other melodramas and suspense films, such as *Suspicion, Gaslight,* and *Mildred Pierce.* Melodrama was referred to as the "woman's picture."

*To Have and Have Not* (1944) and *The Big Sleep* (1946), both directed by Howard Hawks

These films starred real-life lovers Humphrey Bogart and Lauren Bacall. The first is an adventure romance based on an Ernest Hemingway novel, and the second is the seminal film noir based on Raymond Chandler's detective novel of the same name. The Bogart/Bacall relationship was, of course, the touchstone for the romance I imagined between Babe Bannon and Gregory Quinn. Bacall was only nineteen when she starred in *To Have and Have Not.* As the actress later described it: "No one has ever written a romance better than we lived it."

# ACKNOWLEDGMENTS

Many people supported me on the journey of writing this book. I'm incredibly thankful for:

My fabulous agent Brenda Bowen and the Book Group; at Delacorte, editing dream team Krista Marino and Monica Jean, with assistance from Lydia Gregovic; publisher Beverly Horowitz; cover designer Neil Swaab; text designer Cathy Bobak; copyeditor Bara MacNeill; and the RHCB Marketing and Publicity teams.

The Banff Centre for Arts and Creativity, Canada; writing residency mentors Cecilia Ekback, Peter Behrens, Anne Fleming, and Pasha Malla; the camaraderie of fellow writers and the beauty of the mountains.

The Motion Picture Editors Guild and Sharon Smith Holley; film editor Lisa Zeno Churgin, for securing access to the old nitrate vaults at Paramount Studios. Chuck Woodfill, at the Paramount Archives. Dirk Westervelt, editor, mentor, and friend— grateful for all the years in the cutting room, not to mention the vault tour of the Fox lot. Ed Marsh, for his limitless film knowledge. Antoine Saito, for research help and for giving me my first editing job. Jonas Thaler, for being nothing like Thaler in the book.

Beth Ann Bauman, for her brilliant mind and sharp feedback on early and later drafts. Laura Nicol, writing sister and dear friend—I couldn't have made it through this without you. For all the inspiring conversations and BC escapes, my adored cousin Eilidh McAllister. Cinephile Jason White for the nitrate screenings. Hilary Hattenbach and Jared Mazzaschi for the Silverlake retreats. Sabine Heller and Kirsten Westervelt Foster for the German translation.

For their friendship: Lisa Marra, Jen Underdahl, Katy Wood, Andrew Pask, Annette Wu, Terence Heuston, Tinh Luong, Liz Bolton, Cindy Lin, Kristen Lamberston, Fia Cooper, Nutan Khanna, Alain Demaine, Elza Kephart, Maria-Elena Martoglio, Elizabeth Lawrence, Brent Lambert, Chris Russell, Lauren Feige, Lucy Proctor, Rebecca Blackwood, and my siblings, Fiona Ross and Ewan Ross.

My husband's family, for cheerleading and childcare: Nadine Watson, Amy Glading, Michael Muench, Barry Glading, and Rosemary Kelly.

I am, as always, grateful to my parents, Elsa and Hamish Ross: thank you for your unwavering support and for sharing your love of cinema. Lastly, I am most indebted to my own little family, Shane, Callum, and Ozzie the dog.

## ABOUT THE AUTHOR

ELIZABETH ROSS is the author of *Belle Epoque,* a finalist for both the William C. Morris Award and the California Book Award. Her career working as a film editor in Los Angeles inspired her second novel, *The Silver Blonde.* Originally from Scotland, she lives with her family on the coast of British Columbia, Canada.

elizabethross.com
 @RossElizabeth
 @elizarosswrites